## ACKNOWLEDGEMENTS

We would like to say thank you to our publisher Darren Laws at Caffeine Nights Publishing and Literary Agent Brie Burkeman at Brie Burkeman & Serefina Clarke Literary Agency, for their continued hard work, support, dedication and tireless enthusiasm. Mark (Wills) Williams, once again for the excellent art work for the 'Reprobates' cover and Gemma Beckwith for her up-to-date police knowledge.

We couldn't do it without you!

Caffeine Nights Publishing

# REPROBATES

# RC Bridgestock

Fiction aimed at the heart
and the head..

Published by Caffeine Nights Publishing 2014

CONDITIONS OF SALE

Published in Great Britain by Caffeine Nights Publishing

www. caffeine-nights com


British Library Cataloguing in Publication Data.
A CIP catalogue record for this book is available from the British Library

ISBN: 978-1-907565-72-4

Cover design by
Mark (Wills) Williams

Everything else by
Default, Luck and Accident

# DEDICATION

To all our family for their continued love and support, and to the The Forget Me Not Hospice Charity, Huddersfield that supports children with life threatening/limiting conditions and their families in West Yorkshire.

# REPROBATES

# Chapter One

'Spring forward, Fall back,' the rhyme floated through Dylan's mind. He was glad when this time of year came. The longer daylight hours meant criminals didn't have the comfort of that extra cloak of darkness. However, today it meant an hour less in bed.

On the horizon he watched the light of the impending dawn peep over the distant hills. The rays of the morning sun waved and flickered, bending and shooting upwards and outwards. He saw the light spread in between the earthy mounds into a kind of pearly haze, stretching its arms and scattering the darkness as it reached out towards him. He travelled the main road into Harrowfield as the sun slowly rose to its feet, up and over the dull green backdrop of the Sibden Valley and beyond the hill into Southowram. Nearing St Peters Park the first rays of sunlight penetrated the forest and he began to see the grey green trunks of oak trees and the brown remains of last year's bracken. Jack yawned and wound down his window slightly, stopping for a moment at a red traffic light. He heard the birds whistle and call. A draught upon his neck caused a shiver down his spine.

The warmth of the bed he had just left, with Jen in it, beckoned his return. Maisy had been in a peaceful slumber, 'bottom up' in her cot when he'd looked in on their daughter.

'Cutting teeth's no fun, is it sweetie?' he'd said softly as he winced at her flaming red cheek. Maisy had flicked her ear irritably and her eyes twitched which Dylan took as his cue to leave quickly before she sensed his presence and woke – Jen would never have forgiven him.

Max hadn't stirred, other than to roll the whites of his eyes, when Dylan stepped over him at the foot of the stairs. It wasn't his usual greeting of excited hairy limbs and drool. 'Maisy kept you awake too mate?' There was no other response than one weak flap of a tail.

Being a police officer wasn't easy – least of all for the Sunday early turn. Dylan's work was as much a choice of lifestyle as a job, that was challenging and unpredictable at the least for both him and his family. It was a vocation that never stopped asking questions of his ability. The long, changeable shifts and the crisis-driven nature of the work often turned life on the home front into an emotional roller coaster. But then nothing worth doing was easy and that saying applied to his wife too, for loving a cop.

Dylan drove his car slowly through the opened hefty, metal gates into the secure backyard at Harrowfield Police Station. Its emptiness spoke volumes about the lack of staff working at that particular hour. Jack Dylan was today what the police term the 'on call shift' senior detective for the area. He would spend his working hours on site and be readily available to immediately respond to any reports of serious crime. The generally quiet, Sunday early turn duty was as a rule a good opportunity to get stuck into the copious amount of paperwork, that seemed to grow like a fungus, in his in tray. Quicker than the plant on my office windowsill, he thought. Chuckling to himself he recalled the uniformed officer playing a prank on a lady in the admin department where Jen worked. The fragrant green leafed gift she had lovingly tended from a sapling turned out to be a cannabis plant he'd retrieved from a crime scene. Once their bumptious Chief Superintendent Hugo-Watkins got wind of it, it backfired dramatically on the PC who ended up doing a six week stint of nights. Common sense didn't always accompany the title of a police officer.

Dylan opened the Incident Room door and stood for a moment, rarely had he seen it looking so desolate. The telephones were silent. There was no constant hum of conversation or the tak tak tak sound of the typists at work. A sound to him that was like a thousand crickets, on a warm evening, chirping on the keyboards.

Dylan walked past the rows of haphazardly abandoned office chairs. A clear-desk policy in force meant the computer terminals were the only thing thereon, other than the odd telephone dotted about here and there. He walked directly to his office at the head of the Criminal Investigation Department, turned at his door and scanned the CID office. The place looked frozen in time. He shivered, unlocked his office door and turned on the lights. The fluorescent bulbs flickered and then juddered into action. He heard a door slam loudly in the outer office and he knew only too well that the silence would be short lived, as he slid into his cold but comfy big old leather chair and switched on his computer terminal. His finger hovered over the keys. At the command, he input his password. His telephone rang. He reached out and took a deep breath of air into his lungs in anticipation.

'Dylan,' he said brusquely. He proceeded to clear his throat.

'Good morning, sir,' said an overly jovial voice. 'Force Control.'

'The room that never sleeps...'

'Absolutely!' Richard Pauley said. 'We've just received a call from the Mortuary. Someone's broken in and stolen a body.'

'Or maybe someone's broke out?' Dylan interjected, his lips pursed, his eyebrows raised. His pen lingered over his notepad.

'Well you never know sir, stranger things have happened. After thirty years in this job nothing surprises me any more,' said the civilian employee nonchalantly. 'Uniform are at the scene and are requesting CID supervision.'

'Any more info?'

'The mortuary attendant arrived at work to find the fridge alarm activated, a fridge open and one of the bodies, that of a female is missing.'

'Do we have a name?'

'Of the corpse?'

'Yes.'

'No, sir. Can I show you attending? Uniform are already there.'

'Guess so,' Dylan said, fingering the papers in his over-spilling in tray. He wrinkled his nose, hung up the phone, grabbed his coat and was on his way out of the door when he caught sight of Detective Constable Vicky Hardacre getting out of her car.

'Put a spring in it, we're off to the mortuary,' he called.

Vicky moaned. 'Oh no,' she said, her lips hardly moved.

'A missing body,' Dylan said, as she approached.

'I wish my head was bloody missing,' she said. 'That's all I chuffin' need.'

'It's the last thing anybody needs,' he said patting her heartily on the back. 'But look on the positive, we'll be walking out,' he said, smiling at her as he opened his passenger car door for her to get in.

'I guess... Well at least it's not a post-mortem,' she said, as he sat down in the driver's seat, next to her. Her head tilted to one side as if she was weighing up the odds. She belched loudly.

Dylan frowned and pursed his lips as he looked in his rear view mirror and proceeded to negotiate his way out of the car park.

'Too many lagers and a bad curry,' Vicky said shaking herself. 'Gotta mint?'

Dylan reached in his pocket and without looking at her he threw a packet into her lap.

'Bodies don't just get up and walk out of a mortuary,' she said, pulling a face. 'Unless... Hey, suppose we have a vampire at large in Harrowfield?' For the briefest of moments her voice took on one of an excited child then her eyes became large round animated balls. She held her stomach and groaned.

'It's frightening to think how your bloody mind works,' Dylan said glancing across at her disbelievingly.

She shrugged her shoulders and grimaced. 'Whatever.'

'Whatever what?'

'Whatever, sir,' she said.

# Chapter Two

It was a short drive to Harrowfield Mortuary and the roads were void of the usual rush hour traffic, which made the journey appear all the more eerie. Vicky was unusually quiet on the approach to the town.

'Better keep your eyes peeled for anyone who looks like a zombie then,' whispered Dylan not taking his eyes off the road.

Vicky slowly brought her hand up to her mouth and burped. Dylan could hear her stomach churning.

'Funny ha ha!' she said turning towards him and slowly rolling her hooded eyes. 'Although, come to think of it there were a lot of people coming out of that night club this morning looking very much like... Got a drink?' she said as she involuntary heaved. Dylan saw a flicker of panic in her eyes.

'Don't you dare...'

She hunched her shoulders and shook her head in short jerky movements, clenched her teeth and swallowed hard.

He glanced across at her grey, waxy complexion as she gasped and leaned her head heavily on the headrest. Her eyes opened slightly. She looked sideways at him and moaned. Dylan stopped the car. Vicky opened the door. 'I'm going to be sick ...' she said, before promptly throwing up in the gutter. Dylan sat in silence staring ahead. He could hear Vicky taking deep quick breaths, fighting the nausea. It was Dylan's turn to roll his eyes. He tapped her on her hand. She opened her eyes and he offered her his handkerchief. Gratefully she took it. 'I knew I shouldn't 'ave...'

'Whatever,' he said. 'The water is in the glove compartment.'

She nodded her head.

'You take more looking after than our Maisy,' he said, starting the car engine. Vicky closed her door. Dylan steered the car out of the kerb to continue their journey.

She gave him an eyes half-closed sideways glance, threw him a smile that was more of a thank-you and unscrewed the top off the bottle. 'And you'd know that because you're always at home to look after her,' she said putting the bottle to her lips.

'You're treading on thin ice,' Dylan growled.

'True though, isn't it?' she said, brusquely taking another sip of water. She turned to him, drew a hand across her mouth and smacked her pale, thin lips together.

***

Dylan stopped the car outside the mortuary alongside a marked police car. He slowly turned to his Detective Constable with a raised eyebrow and steely glare that she knew meant she'd overstepped the mark. He remained silent. She was right and he knew it.

The old, grey stone structure of the mortuary was hardly a welcoming sight, with rotten wooden window frames that still held single pane glass. A rusty, metal fire escape clung haphazardly to one wall but it looked so frail and inadequate and Dylan doubted it would hold the weight of a squirrel, never mind a human being. In its day the edifice had probably been formidable, but it had been sadly neglected, like the cobbled street access with its crater sized potholes. Drab and dreary was an apt description.

The rusty hinges of the heavy oak door creaked as Vicky pushed it open. She held her stomach. The smell of formaldehyde was overpowering. Instantly, with lips clamped together Vicky put her hand over her mouth, turned and hurriedly retraced her steps. A uniformed officer approached Dylan.

'She okay?' she said, indicating over her shoulder the fleeing Vicky.

'She will be,' he said gruffly.

Police Constable Fearne Robinson read to Dylan from her pocketbook, the details she had obtained. 'The missing body is that of a Kirsty Gallagher, thirty years of age,' she said, pushing a rogue ringlet of copper hair back under her black velvet hat. 'She was brought into the mortuary on Friday morning, according to Mr Harper, the mortuary attendant over there, who will explain the circumstances to you himself in a minute, no doubt.' PC Robinson cocked her eyebrow in an unsmiling expression.

Derek Harper dressed in a dark green, button through overall was making his way towards the pair, but before he reached them the door opened and slammed a few seconds later as Vicky marched in. Dylan acknowledged her with a stern nod and Fearne introduced them both to Mr Harper. The CID officers flashed their warrant cards in his direction. Dylan hadn't come across

Derek Harper before. He was like a muffled presence in the room. A gaunt looking chap, about six feet and one inch tall and around sixty years of age Dylan guessed. The man was exceptionally thin, almost skeletal. He had no colour to his complexion and his shirt collar appeared to be too large for his scrawny neck. His face looked hot and polished like his balding head. Derek spoke quietly but quickly, 'I'm covering the early turn shift and the last thing I expected was this. Is nothing safe any more?' As he spoke he gently stroked the head of a naked corpse on a nearby trolley. He held out his hands. 'I'm still shaking. It's really upsetting. How could anyone…? That window's been forced,' he said, turning to point to the window near the entrance. 'At least the alarm worked. It's still ringing in my ears.'

'Someone set off the security alarm?' asked Dylan.

'No, the fridge alarm,' said Harper. 'They all work independently. When the temperature goes below two or above four degrees centigrade that signal alerts us to a fault. I thought that's all it was at first but no, the door to number twelve was wide open and a body was there on the floor.' All heads turned to look in the direction he pointed. 'I put him back inside obviously,' he said.

'But, I thought you said a body was missing?' asked Vicky with a furrowed brow.

Harper looked at the Detective.

'It is,' he said, looking confused.

'But if the body was on the floor?' asked Vicky.

PC Robinson shook her head in Vicky's direction and put her pen to her lips.

'How long have you worked at the mortuary, Mr Harper?' asked Dylan.

'A few months.'

'And before?'

'I used to prepare the ground for their internment.'

'That's no doubt a very lonely occupation?' asked Dylan.

'It's a necessary job that someone has to do. I don't mind my own company and the peace and quiet,' Harper stared defiantly at Dylan.

PC Robinson's eyes moved in DC Vicky Hardacre's direction, but her head remained still.

'The rheumatoid arthritis means grave digging's too physical,' he said quietly and proceeded to mouth the last two words when barely a sound came from his lips.

Vicky looked bemused. Her malady somewhat forgotten.

Dylan scanned his surroundings. Vicky sat with Mr Harper. Dylan invited PC Robinson to give him a tour of the crime scene, a few yards away.

'The mortuary has the capacity for twenty-four bodies in the refrigerated units, sir,' she said. 'There are six rows of four. Which means that fridge number twelve is at the bottom of the third, at the far end,' she said.

'Remind me, when was the lady brought into the mortuary?'

'Ms Gallagher? Friday morning, sir.'

'I finished Friday lunchtime,' said Derek Harper. 'It was my turn to work today. She was due for the knife tomorrow,' he said tossing his head in the direction of the fridges. 'Tomorrow was supposed to be her post-mortem to ascertain the cause of death. There'll be hell to pay over this,' he said. 'I've telephoned Mr Fisher.'

'Mr Fisher?' asked Vicky.

'His boss,' said Fearne Robinson.

'Shocked he was,' said Derek Harper. 'He should have been in my shoes.'

'So let me get this right. This other person, he was in the same fridge as Ms Gallagher?' asked Dylan.

Harper nodded.

'Is that normal?' asked Vicky.

'God no! But it was Old Alfie, died of heart failure on Thursday.' Mr Harper's mouth seemed to boggle the words. 'Fridge number thirteen broke down... Number thirteen might be unlucky for some, but not for him,' he said. 'I had to put him on top of her.' Derek Harper bowed his head and lifted his eyes to the ceiling smiling uneasily at Dylan. 'Be assured, I knew Old Alfie. He wouldn't have minded.'

Vicky shivered.

'So "doubling up" I guess isn't an approved practice?' asked Dylan.

'I used my initiative,' he said tapping his head. 'She was a bit of alright was Kirsty Gallagher. Didn't have a mark on her.' As he spoke he put on a green plastic apron and plucked two disposable gloves from a box, 'Sorry, I hope you don't mind if I continue.' He didn't wait for an answer but continued with one hand resting on the corpse's thigh. 'I must get this one back in the fridge.'

Dylan looked across at Vicky. 'How did you manage to move Alfie with your rheumatoid... condition?' Vicky asked.

'Ah,' he said. 'I used the hydraulic trolley. I couldn't do this job if it wasn't for that.'

Dylan turned to PC Robinson. 'Take a detailed statement from Mr Harper will you and I mean everything he can tell you. Don't touch anything until SOCO, CSI, whatever they're calling themselves these days, arrives and have done their bit. When Mr Fisher has a minute get him to call me will you. I want a word.'

'Will do, sir.'

'We'll need both of their prints and DNA for elimination purposes.'

'Understood,' she said, turning to Derek Harper as she flipped her pocketbook open and poised her pen over a clean page.

Dylan guided Vicky away by her elbow. 'Look at the mortuary register. Take down the details of when and where Ms Gallagher was brought in from and by whom, next of kin, etcetera. I want as much detail as there is.'

'He looks like an undertaker, speaks quietly like one but some of his comments bother me,' she said, pulling a face at Dylan.

'I'll be having a word with his boss. For now, we need to make sure Kirsty Gallagher is nowhere in this building. All the fridges will need checking and I want to know what's exactly wrong with fridge number thirteen. I also want to know what the normal practice is if the fridges are full and should he have recorded any decisions he made whilst he was in charge?'

'Would all the bodies in the fridges be naked and frozen?' Vicky said. Aware once again of the smell of formaldehyde she held her stomach as it did a somersault.

Dylan nodded.

Tilting her head back Vicky fanned herself with her pocketbook. 'Any chance of lifting any marks or fibres from Old Alfie's body? Because whoever took Kirsty Gallagher would have had to lift the guy off her, wouldn't they?'

'A possibility.' Dylan said. He scratched his chin. 'Anything's worth a try. No doubt we will find Derek Harper's dabs there.'

'Mortuary attendants don't always wear gloves. Or at least this one doesn't. You'd think they would, wouldn't you?' she said, as Dylan moved towards a dissecting table.

'Had you noticed these marks that could be associated with something being dragged?' Dylan pointed to the floor.

Vicky shook her head. 'How could I? I was watching him,' she said. Her eyes went back to Derek Harper who was looking in their direction.

'I'll get CSI to check it out.'

'Crime Scene Investigators. It's a lot easier to call them SOCO.'

'Well that's TV for you. Let's find out as much as we can about Ms Gallagher. We will need to do an in-depth intelligence check on Harper as well. CSI should be here any time. Then we can get things moving in respect of the search. Make sure they check the point of entry and exit to confirm a break-in and see if there is anything else there that suggests the body was removed via the window.'

'Don't you think it would take more than one person to get her out of that window?'

'I'd think so. Or someone strong.'

'You'd have thought whoever planned to take her would have considered that, wouldn't you? I'm guessing she didn't weigh that much. That poor woman, she's just died, she's stripped by him presumably, then no sooner as she is she left in the fridge some frozen, naked old man is put on top of her. That's fucking sick by anyone's standards.'

'He's definitely not reminiscent of the genuine, sincere person that we usually meet at mortuaries, is he?' asked Dylan. Control Room called Dylan on his personal radio. Dylan turned and walked a few steps to answer.

'Just to inform you that Sergeant Megnicks is at Fishpond Lock on the canal banking, first left turn after the Harrowfield Building Society building on Watergate Road. A full set of men's clothing has been found abandoned on the towpath. Underwater search team has been requested. She says she will liaise with you there.'

'Noted, keep me updated.'

'Will do, sir.'

***

Karen Ebdon the Crime Scene Supervisor arrived with their equipment; Louisa Edwards in tow. She examined the open window.

'It's been forced from the outside,' she said in a quiet voice as they watched some minute fibres being lifted expeditiously from the windowsill by Louisa. She found fresh glove marks on the glass pane.

The fridges were checked for the missing body but without gain.

'All the fridges are in use. Kirsty Gallagher was brought to the mortuary by ambulance after being found dead at her home address,' PC Robinson said. 'No obvious visual injuries but thirty-year-olds don't suddenly drop dead, do they?'

'Who dealt with the initial incident?' Dylan asked.

'I don't know, sir.'

'Was it a uniform job?'

'I don't have that information to hand, sir.'

Dylan was thoughtful. He hadn't heard that CID had been involved, so that in itself was suspicious, yet there didn't appear to be an obvious cause of death. Had someone in his office attended and not informed him? He could feel the adrenalin pumping through his veins.

'Who was night detective Thursday night into Friday morning, Vicky?' Dylan called.

'Ned,' she shouted back.

'That'd be Detective Constable Duncan Granger to you, PC Robinson,' he said.

'The address we have for Kirsty Gallagher is 14, Bankfield Terrace, Harrowfield, sir,' she said.

Dylan knew the Boothtown area well. The houses were back-to-back, one bedroom, terrace properties.

'Did she live alone?'

'That, I don't know, sir.'

'Who called the ambulance, do we know?'

PC Robinson shook her head. 'Vicky? Come on we've another job to go to,' Dylan said, scribbling a note in his pocket book. 'Control Room,' he said over the airways. 'I want a thorough search of the immediate vicinity of the mortuary and the seizure of any CCTV in the area.'

19

PC Robinson excused herself to speak to the CSI Supervisor. Vicky joined Dylan.

'Well I've dealt with funeral directors selling family flowers on market stalls, even crematorium attendants removing the brass handles from coffins and re-selling them, but this beats the lot...'

'I once charged someone with necrophilia,' said Dylan.

'Did you?' Vicky asked. PC Robinson looked across at her in a peculiar manner. 'Is nothing sacred?' Vicky said in a much quieter voice.

'It would appear not,' said Dylan casting a glance across at Derek Harper's sorry looking face. 'Why do you think people choose cremation rather than burial these days?' he asked.

'Well, personally I'm claustrophobic and hate rodents so I can't stand the thought of being put in a box and buried six foot under for little animals to nibble away at me.'

'Mmm... me neither,' he said barely moving his lips. 'Come on, we've got enquiries to make and I need some coffee,' he said steering her out of the door.

'By Christ, get your priorities right, why don't you?'

'I intend to,' he said giving her a lopsided grin. 'Where the hell is Kirsty Gallagher and who would take her body from a bloody mortuary?' he asked looking puzzled.

'More's the question, who would want to and why?' asked Vicky curling her upper lip.

'Operational Support Unit will do a thorough search for us here. We'll call at the cafe on the way to the canal.'

Vicky's brows furrowed. 'The canal?'

'Clothing's been found on the banking and the underwater search team are probably in the water, about now,' he said looking at his watch, 'checking for a body.'

'Lovely,' Vicky said flatly.

'Come on. What other job would give you as much excitement as this on a Sunday morning?' Dylan asked deeply breathing in a lungful of fresh air as they departed the mortuary.

'Or, I could still be snuggled up in my nice warm pit,' she said nuzzling into her sheepskin jacket collar.

'A day away from work is a day wasted!' Dylan said.

'Is that what you tell Jen?'

'I don't know what you mean. Jen wants to go back to work and I'm supporting her,' he said.

'So, when's her first day back then?'

'Tomorrow. You know what she's like. She's got me all organised. I'm to take Maisy to the childminder's.'

Vicky raised her eyebrows at him.

'Well unless this is a runner…' He stopped and looked at her hesitantly. 'That might be a problem. But it'll work out,' he said, shrugging his shoulders. 'She'll have a back-up plan for if I'm not there.'

'Let's hope so,' Vicky said, with a look of apprehension.

# Chapter Three

'Wherever Kirsty Gallagher's body is, unless she's refrigerated, it's going to be decomposing and might hamper the interpretation of the post-mortem findings,' Dylan said pensively as they waited for their coffee.

'But it won't change the value of the PM will it? A lot of countries embalm bodies as a matter of course before disposal, don't they, making refrigeration unnecessary?'

'Yes, but they're usually buried within three days anyway, mainly because of the heat.'

'The main purpose of embalming is sanitisation, presentation and preservation. Stems back to the ancient Egyptians' beliefs that mummy's empowered the soul after death which they believed would return to the preserved corpse,' she said unwrapping a knife and fork from a cheap white serviette.

'Hey, I'm impressed,' said Dylan.

'Don't be, it's a morbid fascination of mine,' said Vicky indifferently as she picked up the salt and pepper pot and re-homed them on the table next to her side plate.

'Reactions to death. That is something you need to be aware of when dealing with families of the bereaved.'

'Well, if I was hoping for an uplifting sort of day – I guess I'm not going to get one,' she said. With eyes raising up to the ceiling she breathed in deeply through her flared nostrils. 'You superstitious?' she asked, stifling a yawn.

'No, not really. Why?'

'They say everything comes in threes' Vicky said, with menace.

'And I think I'd rather have you hungover than thinking too deeply,' he said.

\*\*\*

The cafe was quiet. Hot fat could be heard spitting from a large, cast iron frying pan that sat upon the old, black gas range in the corner. A yellow, gooey residue mixed with crusty baked bean sauce resided on an abandoned plate at the table next to them. Bacon and egg sandwiches, dipped in tomato juice and mugs of coffee was on their order, and they waited patiently. The break allowed them to gather their thoughts. The middle-aged man who sat at a neighbouring table wiped his plate with a wedge of fried bread that resembled a sponge. When he placed it in his mouth he put his forearms on the table, either side of his plate and sighed with deep satisfaction. He belched loudly after draining his pint pot. Vicky looked at him with distaste. 'Dirty bastard,' she said, turning as she did so towards the table covered in a red gingham vinyl tablecloth in the far corner.

'Kettle calling pot comes to mind,' said Dylan.

'Touché,' she said. Dylan's eyes followed her gaze but the occupant of the table had her head bent and her face was obscured.

'Don't look now but I think that's Jen's friend Penny,' she said. 'Looks like she might be waiting for someone. She keeps looking at her watch.'

'Good, in that case she won't come over,' Dylan said, leaning towards Vicky. The plates of food were put before them.

'Brown or red?' asked the waitress.

'Both,' said Vicky.

'Enjoy,' said the young waitress with a smiley, sing-song voice as she put the bottles of sauce on their table.

'No worries there,' he said to the young girl, nodding in Vicky's direction as she tucked in.

'What? I need something to line my stomach don't I?' she said.

***

Not half an hour later with their stomachs full and strong coffee starting to kick in, Dylan turned off the car engine in the lay-by at Fishpond Lock.

'The woman in the cafe?' she said as they alighted.

'Penny Sanderson?'

'Maybe she was waiting for that guy who passed us just now, running across the car park, towards the cafe, with the flowers. I thought I recognised him.'

'An ex of yours maybe?' Dylan said.

'He would have been history right sharp, if he had asked to meet me in a transport cafe and brought flowers from the garage.'

'How do you know the flowers were from the garage?'

'It's the nearest place. You don't need to be Einstein to work that one out.'

'What do I always tell you? Never assume, Vicky, never assume.'

'Hello,' the uniformed sergeant called as Dylan and Vicky approached her. 'It may be something, then again may be nothing sir, but we've a full set of abandoned men's clothing here. Thought I'd better let you know about it, with you being on-call. The search team divers say it's about ten foot deep here.'

'No ID I suppose?'

'No such luck. The men's clothing rules out the body from the mortuary, I guess?' she said with a lopsided grin.

'So, we're looking for a streaker?' Vicky said, apathetically scanning the canal path in both directions.

Sergeant Megnicks studied Vicky with a poker face.

'I don't think so.'

'Vicky,' Dylan growled, pausing to stare in her direction before addressing the pile of clothes at his feet. Bending down he could all but see his reflection in the handmade, size ten leather brogues. 'Suggests to me maturity and wealth. What does it suggest to you, Vicky? ' he asked, looking up with a raised quizzical brow.

'Suicide, sir?' she said.

Dylan tutted and shook his head. 'What's the golden rule?'

'Never assume,' she said, thrusting her hands into her coat pockets.

'Come on, think. Why would anyone take their clothes off and fold them so neatly if they intended to kill themselves?' he asked, questioning himself as well as his detective. He stood very still and instinctively surveyed the surroundings with his experienced eye.

Derelict factory buildings with broken windows and crumbling concrete bordered the opposite banking of the water, where he could indeed see a marker board indicating the ten foot depth. What would the dark waters and the Underwater Search Unit personnel tell him? They were already in their drysuits routinely searching.

'You're assuming he's old and worth a bob or two because of his clothes,' said Vicky.

'Where is he?' Dylan said studiously looking down in the water from the water's edge.

'There's no sign of a struggle, so he's one of two things. He's either down there, or running around starkers. I've heard reports of that sort of thing in this area,' she said.

'Rather him than me,' PS Megnicks grimaced. 'Have you seen the colour of the water?'

Suddenly there was a splash nearby. Vicky took one step closer to Dylan. The water separated, a diver's head appeared, which initially looked like that of a seal. Instantly PS Megnicks was off in the direction of the commotion. She spoke with the diver and all went quiet as the diver went back underwater. The rest looked on. A million scenarios came into Dylan's head as he waited in silence.

'Penny for them?' asked Vicky, noticing how quiet he had become. 'What a horrible job it must be to be a diver, unable to see anything and having to rely on a fumble around. I certainly wouldn't want to swap my uniform for a wetsuit.'

'What uniform?' Dylan said looking her up and down.

'Drysuit.' Sergeant Megnicks said.

Vicky looked at her with a scowl as she walked towards her.

Dylan observed the divers, attached to their attendants on the banking – their communications lifeline. They continued to search quietly and methodically in a mesmerising arc formation.

'I used to call them wetsuits too until I joined the unit. But I soon learned that a dry suit provides thermal insulation or a passive thermal protection to the wearer immersed in water,' said Carey Megnicks.

Vicky cocked her head to one side. 'Interesting.'

'The drysuit protects the whole human body except for the hands and feet. The main difference between wet and dry suits is that drysuits are made to stop water entering. This generally allows better insulation. Drysuits are more suitable for use in cold water. However, saying that they can be awfully uncomfortable in hot weather.'

'I bet.'

Before PS Megnicks had time to continue in her instruction, a diver, hand in the air, confirmed a find and they moved into the next phase of their well-practiced operation, to remove the body from the water to the canal side. A white waxy arm broke through the dark water and within minutes a naked corpse lay upon a sterile body sheet, on the canal banking in front of Dylan and Vicky.

Dylan closely scanned the marble-looking deceased, his mind noting all that he surveyed. A hairless body with something attached to the nipples?

'Well, he certainly had no intentions of coming back up,' Vicky said pointing to the rope that was wrapped around the dead man's ankles, tied to a concrete block. His hand clutched a swatch of grass that they could also see growing at the water's edge.

'Looks like rigor mortis developed immediately after he died,' said Dylan.

'Why the fuck would anyone shave off their body hair and put paperclips on their nipples?' asked Vicky.

'The saving grace is that the press aren't here,' Dylan said doing a 360 degree scan. He could see crime scene tape had been placed across the footpath ensuring no one stumbled across the incident. In the quietness it could be heard flapping in the breeze. He was happy the scene was sufficiently sterile.

'An ambulance has been requested and en route,' said PS Megnicks.

'What a waste of time. He's dead,' said Vicky. Dylan shook his head. 'Well, anyone can see he's bloody dead,' she said.

'And we all know the format, Vicky, the paramedics will have to certify him dead.'

'Isn't it sad that anyone would want to end it here, of all places?' asked Vicky.

Dylan tutted, 'How many times do I have to tell you, never assume. Like I said before, would you fold your clothes so neatly if you were going to commit suicide?'

Vicky shrugged her shoulders and pouted. 'I don't fold mine now.'

'Typical!' he said. 'The guy can't have been in the water long. Bloating is minimal and the clothes he appears to have abandoned on the banking aren't wet.'

The paramedics walked casually down the banking to confirm to the officers what they already knew, life extinct.

The divers in the water were gathered at the water's edge in deep conversation with PS Megnicks who was leaning towards them on her haunches, on the towpath.

'Sarge, continue searching around the immediate area where you found him will you? I want to know if there is anything else of interest down there,' called Dylan.

'Will do,' she shouted.

Vicky bent down to the body. 'Where did he buy those horrible luminous green paperclips from? Pound shop do you think? Take it from me it's not a good look, mate,' she said, speaking to the corpse.

Dylan knew Vicky well enough to know the humour she displayed at times like this was her defence mechanism. It stopped her being drawn into the sadness. In his experience every police officer coped differently with the horrific sights they saw.

Dylan gave her a weak smile as he turned and walked a few yards towards the divers, making the call to HQ control for necessary arrangements to be made for the body to be taken to the mortuary. As he watched he saw divers bringing to the surface large stones, lumps of concrete, handfuls of clamps and placing them one by one and side by side on the banking. All of the weights had one thing in common, they all had pieces of rope fastened to them.

'Paperclips, clamps, clothes pegs, elastic bands,' a diver was saying to Dylan as Vicky walked up behind him.

'This gets weirder by the minute. There must have been more than one of them at it,' she said. Vicky counted, 'One, two, three, four, five, six, seven, eight, nine, ten, eleven!'

'A meeting spot?' asked Dylan.

'You think?' asked the diver.

Dylan shrugged his shoulders. 'Who knows.'

Yet another slab of concrete was brought to the surface carried by two of the team. A few minutes passed. There was lots of activity then a diver held up his arm once more signifying a find but this time he had something shiny in his gloved hand.

'What is it, a knife?' asked Vicky squinting her eyes up to see.

Dylan dropped to his haunches. He put his hand to his temple to shade his eyes from the ray of sunshine that appeared at that moment from beneath a cloud.

Slowly the diver swam towards them. He had found a pair of new, shiny, scissors.

'Well, we can rule out Harry Houdini then,' said Vicky.

'Why, don't you think a would-be escapologist would be naked?' Dylan asked.

'Could be I suppose, if he didn't want to get his clothes wet?'

'Where's his towel? Come on, I thought you were worldly wise?' he asked. 'The scissors are your clue to unlocking this puzzle.'

'Eh?' She frowned. 'Go on then, instead of looking smug, spill the beans.'

'Sex.'

'Sex? Not now boss,' Vicky said her mouth forming a perfect 'O'.

'Look here, he's tied a stone to his ankles and then gone in the water, with his scissors in his hand. He's masturbated. Which gives us the reason why the deceased was in profound lactic acidosis at the time of his death as a result of a sudden, frenzied struggle and went into rigor mortis immediately. Most likely he's done this lots of times before. Except this time, he's got over excited and dropped the scissors before he could cut the rope to free himself. It's simple, he's drowned. It's what they call auto erotic asphyxiation. They say you get the same sensation when they put a noose around your neck and "hang yourself,"' he said raising his hands to draw invisible quote marks in the air. 'Only recently, I went to a suspicious death where a man had a noose around his neck. There was a stool on its side nearby but not quite near enough for him to reach. It turned out he'd jumped off the stool to get the erotic sensation and in doing so he'd accidentally kicked it over, so he couldn't save himself. This guy's trousers and underpants were round his ankles, which in that case was our clue. He had an awful case of Tardieu spots on his lower legs when we got to the scene. Brings a whole new meaning to the term swingers, doesn't it?'

'Bloody hell, how could that excite anyone?'

'That's one question I can't answer.' Dylan laughed half-heartedly. 'Just never be shocked, never wear blinkers. You'll find out people go to bizarre extremes for sexual gratification that would turn most people's stomachs. And unfortunately sometimes, like in this instance, they end up dead.'

'Why no identification? Do you think there was more than one of them at it on this occasion? Maybe the others found him, panicked and took his ID with them so that he couldn't be linked to them through association?' asked Vicky.

'Possibly. What puzzles me is how did he intend to get dry without a towel? Or did someone take that as well? I want nearby roads checked for abandoned vehicles, CCTV etcetera. Some knocking on doors wouldn't go amiss. If there are any around here to knock on,' he said, looking around the secluded location.

'Mmm... might be a haven for the birds and the bees but nothing else to bear witness to the act I suspect,' said Vicky. 'Well this is the last thing I expected from a call out to a body in a canal.'

'What do I constantly remind you about? Never assume.'

'If I hadn't seen this with my own eyes, it's not something I could've imagined, let alone assumed.'

'Sometimes when there isn't an obvious answer to a death it may be down to some sexual perversion that we could never begin to understand. Always keep your mind open. You'll see a lot worse, Vicky, this is at the lower end of the scale for this sort of sordid activity, believe me.'

'I hate to think what's at the top end.'

'You'll realise very quickly that even you're normal,' he chuckled. Vicky punched him on his arm.

'Come on, let's get some enquiries done to see if we can find out who he is,' he said nodding in the direction of the dead body.

'Let's hope somebody reports him missing soon.'

'I fear because he is an adult, it's unlikely to be soon.'

'But if he's married, with kids?'

'You didn't notice the wedding ring?'

'Give me a break.'

'Detail is an important distinguishing characteristic for a good detective. I thought you'd have learned that at training school. But you'll always remember to check for rings on fingers from now on.'

'All the training in the world can't begin to teach you... Oh my God, what are you gonna tell his wife,' she said.

'Not me, WE are going to tell her it, as it is. A detective, for your information, never stops learning – that's part of why I love the job. Don't you think it's interesting searching for the unknown, pushing the boundaries?' he asked.

'Not the morning after the night before,' she said grimacing.

'Yeah, well that's something else you'll learn – the night before isn't worth it. Look sharp. We have a body to find and another to ID as soon as,' Dylan said striding out ahead. He raised his hand to the officers searching further down the canal banking. 'Thank you. Give me a shout with any update, will you?'

PS Megnicks raised her hand in acknowledgement. 'Will do, sir.'

***

At the station, enquiries had already started into Kirsty Gallagher's background, whilst at the same time police officers were searching anywhere she might be.

'What about the media?' asked Dylan. They would be chasing a headline for the evening news and tomorrow's newspapers.

'What shall I say? What can I say?' asked Vicky.

'We won't make reference to the body found in the canal today. We'll make an appeal in respect of the missing body from the mortuary. I think that takes priority. This way, in my experience the two jobs wouldn't be competing with each other for headline news. I'll draft a press release.'

'Thanks,' said Vicky.

Dylan penned immediately.

*'In the early hours of Sunday morning, person or persons unknown, forced an entry via a window into the Mill Street Mortuary, Harrowfield. Having done so they removed a corpse, details of which cannot be released at this time or until relatives have been notified. This is a particularly rare and disturbing incident for everyone concerned. Harrowfield Police appeal to anyone with the slightest information about this matter to contact them direct or via Crimestoppers.'*

Time as usual had passed without realisation.

'Jen,' he said to his wife when she picked up the phone. He could hear her laughing. 'I did mean to call earlier, but they've kept me on my toes. We've got a missing body from the mortuary, of all places, and a naked man dead in the canal.'

'Oh, my God. No fiction writer could begin to spin the strange tales of a real-life detective,' she said.

His smile was one that reached his eyes. He loved to hear Jen laugh. 'What's so funny anyway?'

'Maisy. I was putting her tights back on and she just said, "socks" to which I replied, "Well done Maisy they're big socks." She attempted to copy me as she does, and it sounded like big cocks.'

Jen's laugh was infectious and he could hear Maisy demanding her attention in the background.

'She's obviously feeling a lot better?'

'Yes, the tooth is through.'

'Good. How you feeling about tomorrow, nervous?'

'A bit, but I'm looking forward to doing the personnel role. By the way Max is off his food.'

'That's not like him.'

'He's pale.'

'How can a dog be pale?' he chortled.

'You'll see. He just is. Anyway, we'll soon see how serious it is. I'm serving up roast lamb for dinner. Will you be home on time?'

'Should be. Once I've got the wheels in motion here, there's nothing much else I can do. Unless we suddenly find the missing woman or find out who our body in the canal is. Let's aim for about half-five shall we?'

He put down the phone, a smile still on his face. Vicky walked into his office.

'This is what we know,' she said, handing him some paperwork.

Dylan took it from her, unfolded the sheets of foolscap and began reading. Kirsty Gallagher was single. She was thirty years of age and lived alone. Concerns were raised on the evening of Thursday 27th March by neighbours when her curtains had remained closed throughout the day. Police forced entry to 14, Bankfield Terrace and found her slumped in an armchair, in the lounge. Paramedics attended and pronounced life extinct. The report completed by the officer on the case suggested that nothing in the house appeared disturbed and there were no visible injuries or marks to her body other than her tattoos. The house had been secured and keys found within, which had been retained by police. Utilities had been turned off. Kirsty Gallagher had not been suffering from any recent illness according to her GP. At present the incident was being treated as an unexplained sudden death until the outcome of a post-mortem, which was scheduled for Monday 31st March. Detective Constable Duncan Granger had attended, but due to the unexplained circumstances of her death he had made the decision to ensure the scene was secure and that it remained so, until a cause had been established.

'Sadly, it appears she has no known relatives,' said Vicky.

He let the papers fall onto the desk and looked up at Vicky questioningly. He spoke softly. 'Ned's got enough wool on his back to know I'd want to know about this,' he said. His eyes crinkled at the corners. 'I'm surprised he didn't send me a one-liner. I'll speak to him tomorrow. We've got to ask ourselves why would someone steal a body, Kirsty's body? Is the person responsible frightened what the pathologist might find at the post-mortem do you think?' he asked. 'What could they be trying to hide?' he wondered. 'We need to get back into her house and get it examined by Crime Scene Investigators, gather phone data, and utility bills; seize any correspondence we can find. Can you sort that for tomorrow when the team's back in? I want to know what's been happening in her life recently and with whom.'

'Just looking at who's on duty tomorrow boss. We've no Sergeants,' Vicky said running her long, newly manicured fingernail down the duty roster.

'Oh yeah,' he said distractedly. 'That little problem should be sorted soon.'

'How come?' she asked, not taking her eyes off the computer screen.

'I've asked personnel if I can act someone up for CID experience and they've agreed.'

'You have?' she asked. 'They have?' Vicky turned her head to look at him. Her long blonde fringe flopped in front of her eyes. She brushed it to the side. 'Who?'

Dylan looked at her intently. 'That's for me to know and you to find out,' he said. His widening smile softened his face.

Vicky opened her mouth and closed it again without a peep.

'Well, that's a first.' He grinned. 'My Sunday dinner is going to be on the table,' he said looking at his watch as he rose from his chair. 'So I'll be away from here because I'm on-call tonight as well.' Dylan put his arm into the sleeve of his coat. 'Get done what you can and we'll continue our enquiries first thing tomorrow, unless something happens before then, and if so I want to know. Okay?'

32

'Okay,' she said. 'Will we know tomorrow who's *acting up*?

'No, it'll be Tuesday at the earliest, Vicky.'

\*\*\*

Jen was pleased to see Dylan. It made such a difference to be able to get dinner out of the way and Maisy in the bath at a reasonable hour, especially since tomorrow was a big day for them all.

'Clothes in the wash bin please before you pick Maisy up,' she said. Dylan bent down to kiss his daughter in her playpen. 'Your mummy always knows when I've been to the mortuary.'

'More's the pity,' she said with a puckered brow. 'That smell, it's vile.'

Max didn't jump up and greet him with a wagging tail but his golden retriever tail swished slowly on the wall in the hallway at the foot of the stairs. He lifted his head momentarily but as if it was too much effort he lay back down and grunted. 'Has he moved today?'

'Not much. Don't you think he looks pale?' asked Jen.

'No.'

'Well he's definitely not himself,' said Jen as she followed Jack upstairs with a pot of tea in her hand and pile of ironing over her arm.

\*\*\*

With Maisy in bed, her nursery bag packed, a duty roster on the door for Dylan's benefit and sandwiches made in the fridge, Jen flopped down on the sofa.

Dylan was falling asleep in the armchair. Max leaned heavily against his leg and turned to lay his head on Dylan's lap. 'What's up, mate? Not feeling good?' Dylan asked, gently stroking the dog's head.

Jen looked at her husband. A worried look upon her face. 'He looks bloated,' she said, leaning forward to feel his enlarged stomach. 'If he's no better tomorrow I'm calling the vet.' Max's eyes were weak and watery. He rose onto all fours, wobbled and flopped down a few feet away. Moaning loudly he shut his eyes.

'Is Penny coming to walk him?'

'Yes, and she knows him well enough. She'll keep me posted.'

Jen looked as if a light had just sparked behind her eyes. 'Oh, forgot to tell you.'

'What?'

'Penny has only landed that part-time cleaning job going at the nick.'

'She has?'

'Yes.'

'Good for her,' said Dylan.

'Now Carly and Troy have grown up a bit she was looking for more work and the job was advertised so she applied and got it. It's only part-time but hey, it gets her foot in the door until something more suitable comes up,' she put her hand to her mouth and yawned.

Tomorrow would be the start of another era with Maisy going to nursery and Jen back in the saddle in the admin department at Harrowfield Police Station. 'Early night?'

'Have you ever known me say no?' Dylan said with a cheeky smile.

# Chapter Four

Dylan and Jen were woken by the sound of Max retching. Jen telephoned the vet for some reassurance.

'The amount that a dog is sick can make the problem look incredibly more acute than it actually is, Mrs Dylan,' said the vet. 'He has probably been eating something he shouldn't or gobbled down his food. I am on site from half past seven.' The vet sighed heavily. Jen imagined him looking at his clock in his nice comfy bed as she'd often seen Dylan do when they were woken in the middle of the night. 'See how he is in an hour or two, shall we?'

Jen felt confused from waking suddenly. Her heart beat rapidly. 'But there's blood...' she said, aghast at the sight.

'Can you bring him in?' he asked with a sudden note of urgency. 'One of my colleagues will be there to meet you.'

'Can you not come out?'

'I can, but it'll cost you around six hundred pounds, if I do.'

\*\*\*

Jen could see Dylan quietly and industriously collecting cleaning materials from under the kitchen sink. It was almost as if his mind went into work mode at times like this, and he proceeded with the job-in-hand without fuss or complaint. She looked at Max with an expression of helplessness and sitting on the stairs she pulled on her boots. Max was still but his breathing was heavy. Her movements were cautious as she knelt down at his side. Dylan came and stood next to her and looked at her questioningly.

Jen spoke to Dylan in a whisper. As if Max would understand what she said. 'The vet wants me to take Max to the surgery straight away. You'll have to get Maisy to nursery. And tell Avril I may be a bit late will you?' she asked, gathering her thoughts and the collar and lead from the hook behind the door. She accepted the towel and plastic bags Dylan handed to her. 'Come on fella, let's go,' she said soothingly.

Dylan nodded his head. He looked past her at the clock in the living room, a roll of kitchen paper and more bags in his hand. 'It's only half past five, you'll probably be back long before you have to go into work,' he said.

'It's my own fault. I knew I should've rung yesterday,' she said crossly. Jen encouraged Max to move with a gentle tug of his lead.

'The vet might be just erring on the side of caution because of his history,' Dylan said, trying to calm his wife.

Maisy started whimpering. Jen raised her eyes up the stairs.

'I'll go see to her, and deal with this mess,' he said. 'You get off.'

*** 

It was cold. Jen found herself in the driveway with Max, helping him get into the footwell of her car, which in the state he was in, was no easy task. Once achieved, she hurried around to the driver's side and got in. Her hands were shaking. A sudden slip of the foot on the clutch made the car jerk and it rolled forward, almost hitting the garage door. But this small incident recovered her emotional poise.

Jen drove carefully, it was still pitch black and the quickest route had no street lighting. She noticed she was holding herself rigid and felt every twist, turn and bump in the road for Max. As she reached the top of Sibden Hall Road she saw in the distance a cloud of far-off lights spangling over Harrowfield Town below. She felt a moment of relief.

The vets' practice on Pellan Lane appeared to be deserted when Jen arrived. Negotiating the narrow gated entrance and the gravel pathway she eventually parked as near to the door as possible. She turned off the engine. Max looked up at her with big, brown, sad eyes and tears sprung into hers. On alighting she saw the dark outline of a figure, through the window, heading towards the door of the building. Jen eased Max carefully from the car. The lights in the foyer sprang to life and a vet Jen hadn't seen before stood in the doorway. 'Mrs Dylan?'

'Yes. '

'Come on in. I'm Sam, Sam Gouldthorp,' she said. Jen looked at the stone steps before her and the longer route of the wheelchair access and debated for a moment the easiest way forward. With pure willpower and the desire to please, Max made one last big effort to climb over the threshold of the veterinary entrance and then, as if it had taken his final ounce of strength, he collapsed on the floor. A sob caught in Jen's throat as she saw Max splayed, on the tiles. Instinctively the vet bent down to him and as Jen soothed him Sam left, returning just a few minutes later with a large canvas sheet. 'We'll use this to carry him in,' she said. They swapped glances of concern.

The smell of the vets' surgery, reminded Jen of the one Dylan carried on his clothes, from the mortuary. Her stomach tightened. Sam Gouldthorp's eyes looked vaguely puzzled behind her professional looking glasses. She rubbed her hands together rapidly. 'Sorry, they're cold, fella,' she said before proceeding to examine Max. Her open mouth showed a set of brilliant white teeth – without a smile. 'He's been sick. There was blood. Did you bring me a sample?'

'No, I didn't... The man on the phone didn't ask...' Jen shook her head. Her face looked drained.

'Didn't he?' She gave Jen little blinking glances and made a movement with one hand above the dog, as though stroking the air before reaching for a tissue. 'His nose is bleeding,' she said wiping a droplet from the dog's engorged nostril. 'Has he knocked it?'

Jen shook her head, 'Not that I know.'

'He has no energy, he's obviously unstable and his attention to what's going on around him is minimal, wouldn't you say?'

Jen nodded her head and stroked Max's paw lovingly.

The sheet that they had used as a hammock to carry Max into the examination room table now lay beneath him in a crumpled bloody state.

Sam appeared thoughtful. She took off her gloves and ran her hand through her hair. 'Max appears to have some bruising and haematomas under the skin. Have you noticed blood in the stools or bleeding from his rectum at all?'

Jen shrugged her shoulders. 'No. But I haven't been looking.'

'I need to keep him in and get him on a drip to keep him hydrated. I want to run some tests,' she said touching the soft, golden fur on his ear.

'Any ideas what might have caused it?' asked Jen.

'I think he's been poisoned.'

'Poisoned?' Jen asked, raising her voice.

'You haven't put any rodent poison down recently have you?'

Jen shook her head and felt herself sway.

'Are you okay?' the vet asked, looking at Jen with trepidation.

Jen nodded and swallowed hard. 'I'm fine.'

'I'm not sure if he's actually eaten the poison. Has he been engaging himself in chasing rodents lately?'

'No, not that I know of... He is going to be alright isn't he?' Jen's heartbeat quickened.

The vet remained silent and thoughtful. Apprehensively she looked at Jen over her glasses. 'You sure you're okay?'

'Tell me. Will he be okay?'

'We need to take this one step at a time, Mrs Dylan, but I can assure you he's in good hands.' Sam smiled kindly. 'The blood tests will hopefully tell us what we are dealing with quite quickly and we can start treating the cause when we know for sure.'

'You'll ring me? ' Jen said, her eyes brimming with tears as she watched Max's eyes close. The room spun and she grabbed hold of the table.

'If you're going to faint...'

'No, no, I'm fine.'

'Don't worry about Max, that's just the drugs taking effect,' she said quietly.

'I'll be back soon, baby,' Jen said, bending over his face. She put her hand on the top of his warm, furry body and planted a kiss on his head. Jen inhaled deeply. She needed to get out of the room before she threw up. She wasn't about to force Sam Gouldthorp to administer first aid on her too.

\*\*\*

The house was unoccupied when she arrived home. Jen wandered around willing herself to accept its emptiness. Toys littered the floor. Their home appeared to reflect her dishevelled self. She glimpsed herself in the hallway mirror and pressed her lips tight together as she caught sight of Jack's familiar scrawl upon the yellow Post-it note. Tears tumbled down her face and she brushed them away with the sweep of her hand.

*'Hope everything is okay,'* the note read. *'Love you! ☺ J X'*

\*\*\*

Lisa was heading into Dylan's office to pick up his ringing telephone when she caught sight of him arriving. 'Ah, he's just here, Sergeant Megnicks,' she said cheerily. 'I'll hand you over to him,' she said passing Dylan the phone.

Dylan smiled but it didn't reach his eyes. He took the phone from her outstretched hand across his desk.

'Hello, sir. Just a little bit of info for you regarding our man from the canal.'

'Yes?' Dylan asked, shrugging out of his coat.

'The search of the immediate area has revealed a large bath towel that's in relatively new condition, stuffed in the middle of bushes on Watergate Road. We think there may be a connection.'

'Sounds positive,' said Dylan, dubiously.

'That's not all. Further along the road there is what appears to be an attempt to conceal a mountain bike in the same type of hedging.'

'So, we're thinking he might have cycled to the canal?'

'Possibly, sir.'

'That doesn't really fit with the clothing left on the banking though does it? Wouldn't you expect him to be wearing training shoes if he was riding a bike?'

'There is that but... but I've saved the best till last. We've found a post code stamped on the underside of the bicycle frame which relates to an area about three miles up the canal towards Tandam Bridge. And before you ask, we are looking into that enquiry as a priority.'

'The body that's missing from the mortuary is going to take precedence this morning. But good work. Keep me posted.'

***

Dylan sat quietly reading over what information they had in relation to Kirsty Gallagher, which wasn't as much as he would have liked at this stage. What had caused her death? Avril Summerfield-Preston appeared before him. So quietly had she arrived at his desk that it was as if she had passed through the wall. Her manner was quite the opposite. 'Jen was supposed to be here,' she said abruptly.

'She had to take Max to the vet. I'm sure she will be in as soon as she can.'

'Better be before nine forty-five,' she said nodding at the clock, 'otherwise she will be out of her core time and might as well go home until lunchtime,' she said raising her eyebrows. 'On her first day back too, tut tut.'

'Oh, you're all heart, Avril... Is that it?'

'I don't make the rules, Dylan. But I abide by them and will not lose sleep over enforcing them. I'm running a busy office and if Jen can't hack it then maybe she shouldn't be coming back to work at all,' she said stiffly before turning on her oversized heels. Wobbling she fell into Lisa who was carrying a cup of coffee into the office for Dylan. Vicky followed Lisa in and the coffee splashed over the carpet and all over the papers that Vicky had in her hand. Avril steadied herself by way of grabbing hold of the filing cabinet and without looking back walked out of the door.

'Knob,' Vicky said. 'Sorry would've been nice.'

'She been drinking, do you think?' asked Lisa. 'I'm sure I got a whiff of something.'

'What you doing rattling her cage?' Vicky asked, watching Dylan's dark facial expression with interest.

'I didn't. She wanted to know where Jen was,' he said flatly. 'And don't you two go starting any rumours.'

'I just bumped into Jen clocking in. She said Beaky would be on the warpath. Don't worry, she made it, albeit by the skin of her teeth. Bless her, she was as white as a sheet,' said Lisa.

'I'm sure that Avril is a bloody witch. A drunken one at that. Her friends ought to tell her that putrid perfume she wears doesn't hide the smell of last night's booze,' Vicky said throwing her blonde mane in the direction Avril had walked. 'Oh, yes, I forgot she doesn't have any friends, does she Lisa?'

'She's a proverbial thorn in my bloody side, I know that,' said Dylan.

'Then you should be thankful to her,' said Lisa.

Vicky gave a short laugh that sounded like a pig grunting. 'How do you work that one out?'

'A thorn in your side will drive you to find someone or thing to remove it. Without her, you wouldn't have travelled as far in your life to find peace and happiness. It's a quote from someone. I can't remember who,' she said with a smile as she placed the cup of coffee in front of Dylan and walked out.

'Yeah, whatever,' said Vicky as she sat down and mopped up the liquid that had spilt on her paperwork with a tissue from her pocket. 'You watch, what goes around comes around.'

'Well it can't come soon enough for me. If it wasn't for the fact that she knew so much... well, let's just say I'd have her guts for garters,' Dylan spat.

Vicky raised her eyebrows. 'And what's that, pray?'

'It's private. Nothing for you to worry yourself about,' he said.

\*\*\*

40

DI Dylan's thoughts were interrupted by Lisa's voice from where she had retreated to her desk outside his office. 'Sergeant Megnicks on the phone for you again, sir!'

'Dylan,' he snapped as he picked up the phone.

'Just had it confirmed that the bike was stolen from outside number 27, Maple Crescent, Tandam Bridge. The house is literally on the canal bank towpath. The trusting owner had placed it outside his front gate with no lock to secure it, in fact nothing more than a "For Sale" sign.'

'Damn,' said Dylan. 'So the bike might not be connected?'

'The "For Sale" sign has been recovered by the officer attending and it's awaiting fingerprint examination so we'll have to see if we have any marks of significance.'

'Update me as and when.'

'Will do, sir.'

\*\*\*

Lunchtime and the identity of the man found in the canal still remained a mystery.

Dylan picked up his phone and dialled the press office. 'Debbie Canavan?' asked Dylan.

'Yes.'

'Dylan.'

'Thanks for ringing,' she said.

'I've got that update you were requesting on the dead man we recovered from the canal yesterday,' he said.

'A brief description of the clothing would be great to give out to the press. It might jog someone's memory, and in turn assist in his identification for you maybe?'

'I'll get it faxed over,' he said checking his watch. 'Crikey, I'm due at the mortuary at ten thirty for the post-mortem.'

\*\*\*

Jen sat at her desk. Her mind in a turmoil. 'Jennifer,' shouted Avril Summerfield-Preston, from the bowels of her office. She appeared at her door and headed in Jen's direction. 'I need to do a back-to-work interview with you, but first I want you to go to pick up some papers from court and get my dry cleaning,' she said. Retrieving a dry cleaning docket from her purse she thrust it into Jen's hand.

'Can I just ring and see how Max is, Avril...'

41

'Now would not be a good time,' she said, screwing up her nose. She folded her arms, turned and smiled sweetly at Jen.

Suddenly Jen felt angry, an anger that only Avril Summerfield-Preston it appeared could conjure up in her. Jen was thankful for the support of her work colleagues who were all perplexed by Avril's persona or had been at the end of her scornful conduct at one time or another.

*** 

Dylan crossed the tarmac in the police station's yard to his car, he turned. Where was Detective Constable Vicky Hardacre? Was it too much to expect her to be following him as requested? Detective Sergeant Paul Robinson appeared as if from nowhere.

'Great timing. You, my friend need a real job to get you back into the routine of proper police work. You've been languishing on that development course at training school for far too long. In fact is that a spare tyre I see round your midriff?'

'Three cooked meals a day, with pudding,' Paul said patting his stomach. 'The wife's not impressed.'

'Wait till you see your sister Fearne. She'll have something to say about those added pounds.'

'What Fitness Fearne? She already has. She also said she'd been working with you.'

'Yeah, she did a good job for us. I was impressed. That reminds me I need to update you regarding the missing corpse and the man pulled from the canal. Oh, and by the way Vicky's going to be "acting up". Keep it under your hat she doesn't know yet.'

'She is?' he said. He gave Dylan one of his big broad toothy smiles.

'She's the only one in the office qualified, and she's more than capable.'

'The supervisory experience will do her the power of good. Hey, glad it's you rather than me going to the mortuary.'

'Aye well, someone has to do it.'

'It feels good to be back. The duration of that bloody course was way over the top.'

'Aren't they all?' Dylan said raising his eyes to the sky. 'Another tick in a box for you, though. Bloody hell...' he said looking at his watch, 'talking of mortuaries we should be there now. V I C K Y, it's time to go,' he shouted across the yard.

'Glad to know nothing's changed,' Paul laughed, nodding towards Vicky who was dodging around parked cars, papers under her arm, texting with one hand, one arm in her grey bubble coat and a half eaten slice of toast hanging from her mouth.

***

The pair were met at the mortuary by Professor Stow's theatrical wave from his chubby pink hand. 'Tea for me, strong and sweet, preferably with a shot of brandy,' he said to his assistant with a wobble of his big, fat, red chin. There was unusually no belly laugh associated with the larger-than-life character.

'You okay? You don't seem yourself,' said Dylan.

'I have to be on my best behaviour,' he said. His top lip curled back exposing his teeth, as he grabbed Dylan's arm to steady himself. He stepped into his coveralls. 'And, between you and me I absolutely hate being watched,' he added in a whisper.

'Watched, who's being watched?' asked Vicky. Her voice was without enthusiasm at what lay ahead.

'I've got an eminent surgeon with me today. They're assessing us again.' Head down, Professor Stow looked over his half-rimmed glasses and smiled, as he acknowledged the smartly dressed man who had just walked into the room. He was wearing a three piece suit, his outer coat had a velvet collar.

'Eugene Regis,' he said holding out his hand to Dylan. He nodded in Vicky and Professor Stow's direction. Dylan noticed the strength in his grip.

'A man of few words unfortunately for me,' Stow whispered out of the corner of his mouth to Vicky as Eugene turned his back on them to find a place for his shiny black briefcase. 'Truth be known, I can't figure out what he's thinking about my old fashioned ways. We're dinosaurs to these youngsters, you know,' he said.

Vicky raised an eyebrow at Dylan and smiled before moving quickly to help the doctor. 'Let me help you, Doctor Regis.'

'Mister,' he said to her in a cold but polite manner.

Without looking at Vicky, Eugene Regis felt inside the inner breast pocket of his suit jacket and extracted a key. He opened the locker. Vicky shrugged her shoulders at Dylan who shook his head.

'You wouldn't want to cross him, would you, boss?' asked Vicky sidling up to Dylan.

'He's known as the good doctor,' Stow said to Dylan. He couldn't tell if he was being sarcastic or not.

Mr Eugene Regis took off his coat and hung it very precisely so it didn't crease. He turned, extracted a pen and paper from his briefcase and secured it on a clipboard before standing upright with his paperwork neatly tucked under his folded arms.

'He doesn't give a lot away does he?' asked Vicky.

'What do you want to know?' asked Dylan.

Vicky giggled. 'Hey, I'm a detective aren't I, and he's one hell of a good looking guy.'

\*\*\*

Dylan relayed the circumstances of how the naked body of the unidentified deceased was discovered and what had been found at the time in the canal. Professor Stow listened intently. This information was paramount for the pathologist to give the officers the best chance at time of death. The more well-known post-mortem changes, such as rigor mortis, livor mortis and algor mortis progress on a relatively set schedule; however, many external and intrinsic factors may affect their development.

The team were gowned, suited and booted and the face masks, that hung around their necks, were the only items that needing pulling into place.

The light from the fluorescent tubes bounced off the tiles that covered the floor and the walls of the examination room, where the temperature wasn't much above fifty degrees.

Three steps into the room and a man-shaped lump was in full view, upon the stainless steel examination table at the centre. Vicky stopped in her tracks and Dylan urged her forward. The gentleman's distorted, bloated head was cocked back, open mouthed, his tongue black. The officers, Sarah Jarvis for Crime Scene Investigation and the exhibit officer Detective Constable Andy Wormald stood at the side of the dissection table. Professor Stow put on a pair of blue latex gloves as did Sarah and Andy. Professor Stow pointed to the green discolouration starting to appear on the man's bloated abdomen. There were folds of greasy looking skin around the deceased's yellowing hips, however, otherwise it was a body of an average-looking middle-aged man. He looked more like a wax sculpture or mannequin than an actual person to Vicky.

The naked body was laid on his back. Arms by his side, the green grass still grasped tightly in his clenched fist. The ankles where a ligature had dug deep into the flesh were relatively clean as the water had washed the ante-mortem soft-tissue haemorrhaging, causing the injury to resemble an artefact. The carcass had the remnants of more canal debris upon it. The hair looked greasy and matted.

'It's the stillness, isn't it?' Eugene murmured unexpectedly to Vicky who was stood closest to him.

'And the bloody smell,' she said, not taking her eyes off the deceased's face.

'A little better than the one we had earlier though; a man had died in the woods and he'd had his face eaten off by bees,' said Eugene Regis. She smiled. It wasn't always easy to judge what someone was thinking behind the mask but the skin at the side of Eugene Regis's big brown eyes crinkled.

'Usual samples, Dylan, I presume?' Professor Stow said. He appeared a little more at ease as he began to cut and pull samples of hair from the corpse, with the expertise of someone who had done the procedure a million times before.

Vicky flinched as he yanked at the pubic hair and she saw Eugene Regis do the same, she smiled at him. 'I guess that's one foolproof way to tell if a person is dead,' she said.

'I bet having that stud put in hurt more,' Stow said, pointing to the man's piercing. 'I suppose you'll want it removing from his penis?' he asked, looking up from his work at Dylan, who nodded in the affirmative. He handed the item to the exhibits officer who was holding a container out at arm's length in anticipation. The noise the metal made dropping into the empty container echoed around the room.

'External evidence secured. Let's get him swilled down,' said Stow, holding his arms up as he stood back from the table.

Without undue ceremony the mortuary assistant hosed down the body with a hand-held sprinkler that was attached to the autopsy table. The water formed small rapids that ran quickly down a well at the perimeter.

'We'll take the blood samples before beginning a closer inspection, shall we?'

Mr Regis nodded his head and appeared to tick a box on the paper attached to his clipboard.

Professor Stow took a deep breath as he untied and removed the rope around the dead man's ankles. 'Tut tut, if only he'd been a scout he'd have learned how to do a slip knot,' he said with indifference.

Eugene Regis's brows knitted together in a frown.

'Okay, let's start. Feet first. We can see the rope he used has left bruising and cut into the skin, no doubt due to the weight of the boulder. If we look closely,' he said bending down to scrutinise the ankles, 'we can see similar scars on both feet. This indicates to me that he is by no means a stranger to having his ankles tied to a heavy weight, in this particular way. Here, I can see at least a dozen old abrasions which are similar to those that I have seen on bodies who have self-abused.'

Carefully, he removed the paperclips from his nipples. 'Again, if we look closely we can see marks where he has previously used similar objects to do the same.'

'That makes sense as similar objects, clamps, clothes pegs and the like were found at the scene,' said Dylan.

Professor Stow nodded. 'In my opinion the deceased enjoyed the intensity of the pain and the sense of drowning to satisfy himself. This is called erotic asphyxiation or in simple terms it is when the brain is deprived of oxygen and induces a lucid semi-hallucinogenic state. The accumulation of carbon dioxide increases giddiness, light headedness and pleasure, all of which they say heightens the masturbation sensation.'

'How gross,' Vicky said.

Eugene Regis gave her a blinking sideways glance.

'These,' Professor Stow said, indicating points at each side of the deceased's neck, 'are the carotid arteries which carry oxygen rich blood from the heart to the brain. When compressed in such circumstances as hanging, or strangulation there is a sudden loss of oxygen. We can also see a little interest from the canal life who have been at his lips, eyelids and ears.' He continued the external examination in silence. 'Okay,' he said pushing his glasses further up the bridge of his nose. 'Let's open him up.'

The group took a step forward and then leaned back at the smell from the gases that emerged when the incision was made and the gastric emptying began. Professor Stow weighed the organs.

'His heart shows signs of cadaveric spasm which isn't surprising since we can already see his fist tightly clutching the grasses that surrounded him underwater, in a desperate attempt no doubt to free himself of his snare. In my opinion the decedent, or deceased person if you prefer, was in a state of profound lactic acidosis at the time of death and this was a consequence of the violent struggle, and went into rigor mortis immediately.'

Vicky looked across at Dylan and gave him a knowing nod. He had suggested the same to her at the scene.

Professor Stow continued to visually examine each internal organ and after checking the precise weight of each he instructed the mortuary assistant to put them back inside the chest cavity and sew him up. The stitches were large as if his trunk was a mail bag and Vicky flinched at every one. Much to the amusement it seemed of Eugene Regis.

'Not particularly neat, but sufficient to stop things falling back out,' said Stow with a little cough. 'Autoerotic is a collective term for this type of sexual fetish. People say the rush is very powerful and as addictive as cocaine. I am satisfied that he was alive when he entered the water.'

'How do we know that?' asked Vicky bending closer to the dead body.

'Froth in the mouth is a clue. But if we look at what they call diatoms under the microscope, it shows they've travelled to the liver, brain, kidneys etcetera in the blood stream. If he were dead when entering the water these minute little blighters get no further than the lungs. Nothing for you to worry your pretty little head about. We see it regularly, don't we?' Stow asked with a glance at Mr Regis who nodded, just the once. 'My findings agree with you, Dylan. The man in my opinion stripped off, tied his feet to the stones to weigh himself down and either jumped or lowered himself into the water. He then masturbated and when he'd ejaculated, he intended to free himself by cutting the rope. But in his excitement he dropped the goddamned scissors. They were his escape mechanism, you see and that part of his plan failed. So he drowned.'

'Men are so weird!' Vicky said seriously. Five sets of eyes looked at her.

'Present company excepted, of course,' she said quickly.

'I'm sure as you progress in your service, dear, you will see that although the majority of cases such as these are men, be assured there are a lot of women out there who involve themselves in strange eroticism in some shape or form. "Nowt as queer as folk," as they say in Yorkshire and this one falls into that weird category of those who have accidently killed themselves practicing bondage, whipping, hanging, even having sex with animals. The male's erection can remain afterwards because of cadaveric spasm but that's the undertakers' problem not mine, thank the Lord,' he said. His eyes went up to the ceiling. 'Now, we must fly, mustn't we Mr Regis? We've a busy day ahead. I'll do my report for the Coroner in due course.'

The group left the examination room and headed towards the office.

'I'll flower this one up and use it at one of my after dinner speeches. Brings a whole new meaning to enjoying Britain's waterways,' Professor Stow whispered to Dylan with a subdued belly laugh, as they walked together down the corridor.

Eugene and Vicky walked behind.

'You're not from around here are you?' asked Vicky.

'No, York.'

'You staying over?'

'Yes.'

'Near here?'

'The Waterfront Lodge in Brighouse.'

'Oh, the food in their restaurant is amazing,' Vicky said. 'And I happen to know Prego is Dylan and his wife's favourite spot too. I might see you in there for a drink one night?'

'You two not an item then?'

'Me and Dylan?' Vicky chuckled. 'No, he's my boss.'

'Well, maybe you'd like to join me for dinner one night?'

'Dinner as in dinnertime or dinner as in Dinner?' she said with a furrowed brow.

'Evening meal,' he said. 'Here's my card. Ring me,' he said.

'I will,' she said holding his gaze a little longer. 'Old Stow, how's he doing?' she said.

'He's good. You can't beat experience and it shows in there, doesn't it?' Mr Regis smiled. 'But don't tell him I said that. I like to keep them on their toes.' His eyes appeared to dance mischievously and he looked even more handsome to Vicky when she could see his face.

\*\*\*

Vicky was grinning from ear to ear. 'What you got to smile about?' Dylan asked.

'Just got myself a date.'

'A date? Who with Regis?'

Vicky nodded.

'I can't leave you alone for two minutes can I?'

'Well, you've either got it or you haven't.'

'Well, don't go upsetting him. I want to keep my job,' said Professor Stow seriously.

'I don't think there is any fear of that,' she whispered.

\*\*\*

Dylan was sitting in his office chair talking on the telephone to Sergeant Megnicks. He was updating her with the post-mortem results. 'It'll be a straight forward report for the Coroner now,' he concluded.

Vicky put a warm drink on his desk. 'Multicoloured paperclips? Now, what does that tell you?' she asked Lisa as she fingered the items in Dylan's desk tidy.

'What was wrong with the old silver ones?' he asked as he put the phone down on its cradle.

'Not my idea, sir,' Lisa grinned as she eyed Vicky who sat innocently nibbling a biscuit.

'I'm not "into" pain, and if you were that observant then you would see there are no luminous green ones,' he said. 'Now, let's find out who our John Doe is. Goodness knows what else we're going to uncover with this investigation.'

'I feel sorry for the family. How the hell do we, you, tell them that their nearest and dearest has died in a filthy canal... and like that?'

'We'll cross that bridge when we find out who he is and if he has any family. He could be divorced, live alone, not have any kids,' said Dylan slurping the skin off the top of his hot milky coffee. 'Nice, thanks,' he said, raising his mug in the air. 'If he does they'll have to be told how he died. Otherwise it is going to be an even bigger shock to them at the Inquest.'

'I hate to think what the headline will be in the local rag.'

'Well you can be sure they won't pull any punches and dependant on who he is and what his profession was. That could also fuel the storyline and its place in the newspaper. But bear in mind what Professor Stow told you, no matter how unpleasant it is to hear, you will go to some hangings that to all intent and purpose look like a suicide. There will be no evidence at all suggesting why the person killed themselves in that particular way. I've been to some where I know the immediate family have sanitised the scene, removing all evidence of paraphilic activities to save embarrassment, before they called the emergency services. But they will never admit it.'

'Really? They would rather their death be classed as suicide instead of misadventure? You'd think they'd be too shocked to act so quickly, wouldn't you?'

'In some cases I'm sure they know about the fetish but choose not to face up to the consequences. Come on we've got work to do, can't be hanging around drinking coffee. Places to go. People to see,' he said standing up he drained his cup.

'Ha, ha, funny... or not. I used to think my ex was weird when I copped his private collection of porn movies but with hindsight I guess he was quite normal.'

'They all start somewhere,' said Dylan. Vicky opened Dylan's office door to leave.

'Sir,' Lisa shouted from her work station. 'Paul Robinson is at Kirsty Gallagher's house and is asking if you could join him?'

'Tell him I'm on my way,' he said plucking his jacket from the back of his chair.

*** 

Dylan's first impressions on entering 14, Bankfield Terrace was that it was a very neat little house. Nothing seemed out of the ordinary, or appeared to have been disturbed.

'I thought you might want to come and see what we've found,' Paul said as he met him at the bottom of the steps. Paul like Dylan was wearing protective clothing. He followed him back up the stairs. 'I've called CSI out.'

The pair entered the bathroom. 'First. There are two toothbrushes. Which suggests to me that she had someone staying. If that's so we should get DNA, right?'

Dylan nodded.

'Next, the bedroom.'

Dylan followed close behind.

'Two things here.' Paul pulled back the old, worn and slightly frayed around the edges duvet. 'Here we have a brand new bottom sheet. Can you see all the creases in it where it's been folded around the cardboard packaging?'

Dylan was about to speak but Paul held up his hand. 'I know what you're going to say, "so she doesn't iron the bottom sheet, so what." But there is no sign of a dirty sheet in the wash bin, or washing machine and no cardboard in the bin.'

'Dustbin?' asked Dylan.

'Checked. All the bins inside are completely empty and recently cleaned out with some sort of disinfectant, which is mighty strange, don't you think? Also, here, there's an empty bedside drawer at the far side of the bed,' he said. 'Something just doesn't feel right.'

'Anything else?'

'Not at the moment, but I'm hoping the neighbours might be able to answer some of our questions when we speak to them.'

Paul followed Dylan down the steps to the small lounge area where Kirsty had been found. Dylan stood with his back to the chimney breast.

He looked around. Soaking up the atmosphere in the room. To his right was a single armchair and a television on a glass stand. The floor was highly polished.

'I want to see the photograph of her, taken in situ, before she was taken to the mortuary. She was found in the chair. The question is did she die there, or was she placed there afterwards? It's nice, this beech flooring,' Dylan said, stooping down to touch it. His eyes were immediately drawn to the gas fire.

'Paul, we may have an answer, look,' he said pointing to the pipe. 'It's not capped properly. Either that or it's been tampered with. We're lucky there hasn't been a gas explosion. Has the gas and electric been turned off?'

Paul was down on his haunches beside him. 'Yes, it was turned off as a matter of course before the house was secured.' His eyes followed the wall of the chimney stack. 'There are traces of soot and a definite discolouration on the wall above.'

'Could she have died from carbon monoxide poisoning do you think?'

'And was it an accident, or not?' asked Paul.

There was a noise in the street outside and both men looked up at the window, then back at each other.

'The window. It's been taped up,' said Dylan rising from his haunches. 'Possible chance for prints on the tape.'

'Do you think someone was trying to get rid of her body so that it couldn't be proved that her death was murder?' asked Paul.

'In an attempt to do the perfect murder?' asked Dylan.

'Do you think there is such a thing?'

'No, some just take longer to detect than others,' Dylan said. 'We'll discuss it with the Crime Scene Investigators when they arrive. We might need Forensic here sooner rather than later. I want house-to-house enquiries and let's get some urgency into the actions of her telephone usage.'

'That's another thing. We haven't quite turned the house upside down yet, but there's no obvious sign yet of a mobile phone. You'd think she'd have one, wouldn't you? Doesn't everyone these days?'

'Find out from the uniform that attended the scene if they can help and have a word with Ned when he comes on duty. He was the night detective. See if there is anything else they can tell us. We need to find the significant other in her life and dig deep into her background, then we might find a motive,' said Dylan.

'It would help if we knew where her body was,' said Paul.

'Too true it would. It's looking like someone has attempted to remove all the clues that will lead us to finding out how she died, but don't worry they will have made a mistake, they always do. It's up to us to find it. Don't forget we'll need her DNA. Easiest place is probably from her hairbrush, the toothbrush or anything else we can find that you think will give us a profile. So that if, when, she turns up we have something to identify her with. Looks like your first day back is straight into a murder enquiry m'old son.'

'Aye and an unusual one at that.'

'Yeah it is. Now let's get it sorted. Bloody hell,' he said looking at his mobile phone. 'Two calls from Jen and no bloody signal!'

'Maybe that's why she didn't have a mobile phone then, boss if there isn't a good signal in the area?'

'I think we should keep looking.'

# Chapter Five

It felt good to be back at work for Jen, even work that included Avril. Jen walked in to the front office of Harrowfield Police Station for the second time that morning. The duty Police Sergeant Malcolm Bean stood at the desk attending to paperwork. He offered her a little flaccid smile.

A muscular man in builder's boots and a cut away T-shirt leaned heavily against the counter. Jen pressed the bell and stood patiently at the internal door. Penny stood beyond the glass screen with her face pressed to the window. 'Coming,' she mouthed. Jen saw her friend scurry to the door. 'You free for lunch?' she said, as she opened it, duster in hand. 'They've changed the code,' she said apologetically.

'Must have been whilst I've been out on Avril's errands.'

Penny smiled coyly over Jen's shoulder. Jen turned to see the man at the counter wink at her.

'Who's that?' she said.

'I'll tell you later,' Penny said. Her face was flushed. 'It'll be lunchtime shortly, can we catch up about twelve thirty before I take Max for his constitutional?' she said, gushing with excitement.

'You won't need to walk him today. I had to take him to the vets this morning and they've kept him in.'

'Oh God. Is he okay?' Penny said, her eyes grew wide and her mouth hung open.

'Truth is I don't know yet. The vet thinks he might have been poisoned. He hasn't been chasing rodents when he's been out with you has he?'

Penny shook her head. 'No. You okay, you're shaking?'

'I'm anxious. What with Max and now I'm back to clocking in and out every time I go in and out of the building. It just doesn't help having Avril on my case again.'

'She'll understand surely?'

Jen pulled a face.

'Oh yes, it's Godzilla we're talking about isn't it?'

'Exactly.'

'Try not to worry. I'm sure Max will be okay,' she said, patting her friend's arm reassuringly.

A brief smile lit up Jen's face. 'Yeah, hopefully. At least I'm only working part-time,' she said.

'It's alright for some.'

'Two and a half days a week. I can cope with that.'

'I wish I only had to work two and a half days a week. But walking Max for you isn't really like a job, is it?' Penny's eyes danced with excitement. 'I've got a new fella,' she said, nodding towards the counter.

'What?'

'It's early days,' she said lowering her voice. 'We've only managed to meet up a few times, what with the kids always being around. He buys me flowers,' she said. A dreamy look passed over her face. 'You could say I'm officially in love. Well, tell me what woman of a certain age wouldn't say no to a toy boy?' she grinned with a nod in the direction of the reception area.

'No! You're a quick worker I'll give you that. But if he makes you this happy then that's good enough for me,' Jen said taking a sharp intake of breath.

'What's up?' asked Penny.

'Don't know. Call it a gut feeling but I'm having my back-to-work interview with Avril today and I never know what she is going to spring on me. I must go.'

'Pessimist,' said Penny.

'You forget I know her of old.'

'Ah, yes,' Penny said.

'Avril's dry cleaning.'

'What did her last slave die of? You're too bloody soft by half.'

'Yeah, well, that's me. I guess I'm not going to change now, am I? See you at lunchtime. And Penny,' she said as she was leaving. 'Be nice to Malcolm. He's a lovely genuine guy. Treat him gentle,' she said.

'Of course,' said Penny with a puzzled look on her face. 'Malcolm?' Penny thought as she saw her friend run towards the steps.

Familiar faces nodded 'hello' to Jen as she walked on the top corridor towards the admin office.

'When you bringing Maisy in to see us?' asked Margaret the disbursements clerk, sweetly when Jen reached the office. 'Ah, it's so lovely to have you back.' Margaret reached out and gave

Jen a motherly hug. 'It must have been hard for you leaving the little one with the childminder this morning.'

'Jack's doing that bit. It's only three mornings a week, so it's not too bad. I'm working two full days and Wednesday morning.'

'You are?' Margaret asked, quizzically.

'Yes, that's what I agreed with Avril, why?'

'Huh, another one with a kid who won't be here in the school holidays,' mumbled Donna from her desk in the corner. Rita who was filing some paperwork made a face at her behind her back. Jen tittered despite her anxiety.

'Jennifer!' screeched Avril Summerfield-Preston from within the neighbouring office.

Jen half-smiled. 'Well she's consistent, I'll give her that. Nothing's changed?' she asked. Margaret shook her head. Jen's stomach sank.

'You'd better believe it,' Rita said as she passed Jen. 'Welcome back to bloody Auschwitz kid.' Rita had her hands full of evidence bags that were all shapes and sizes. Jen opened the heavy fire door for her. 'I'll be in the property store if you want me,' she said.

Jen stood at Avril Summerfield-Preston's office door, but before going in she stopped, lifted her head and took a deep breath. Having put a fake smile upon her face she knocked three times and entered. The room was warm, quiet and still. Avril's fingers tapped gently on her desk as if transmitting a code in blunt, brief sentences. Her forehead showed its usual frown. There would be no allowances made for her staff with children, she'd agreed with Donna. A mother's place in her opinion was in the home.

'You've been a long time, Jennifer,' she said. 'Sit down.'

Jen was prepared but she dithered. 'The court was busy and the queue at the dry cleaners...' she gabbled on mindlessly as she sat down in the chair opposite Avril. Avril's face was turned towards the computer and for what seemed like an eternity she didn't speak. Jen sat quietly with her hands clasped tightly on her lap. Her face was tense. She sensed no warmth in Avril's greeting. Eventually Avril gave Jen a strange, dark glance as if she was peering from behind a curtain.

Jen moved her lips, but no noise came out of her mouth. How did this woman have the ability to render her mute? 'I guess I'm going to be a bit rusty,' she said eventually, giving the woman a nervous smile.

'You'll soon get up to speed, when you've been on the courses I've booked you on at Headquarters,' she said.

Jen squirmed inwardly.

'Well, I guess I should welcome you back,' she said mirroring Jen's false smile. 'I trust you won't be making a habit of pushing the core time to the minute, like you did this morning?' Avril's eyes flickered.

Jen shook her head.

'However, since you appear to find getting to work on time a bit of a bind, I may just have the solution.'

'Oh no... It's not a problem. It was Max. I had to take him to the vets. I assure you I did clock in on time.'

'I know,' Avril said as she fanned her face with Jen's clocking in card. The card made a flapping sound. 'I checked.'

There was a knock at the door. 'Excuse me, drinks?' Margaret asked, carrying two mugs into the office at arm's length. Jen threw her a grateful look. Avril didn't look up at Margaret but moved her arm to the side so Margaret could place the mug on her desk in front of her.

'Normally it will be fine,' Jen said. 'Thank you Margaret,' she said softly.

Jen watched Avril slowly take some papers out of a large brown envelope. 'These are for you to sign,' she said stroking her long, beak like nose with her finger that Jen noticed had an ink stain on it. She handed them over in a very stilted, deliberate fashion. A strong smell of her heavy, pungent perfume came Jen's way and made her eyes water. It smelt like a concoction somewhere between potpourri and church incense. 'We've, that's Chief Superintendent Hugo-Watkins and myself, have decided it would be best all round if you worked every afternoon, Jennifer. That's over five days and not necessarily always weekdays either in the future,' Avril smiled, a real smile and when she did Jen noticed the angles of her mouth lifted in an odd way, almost as though she was unaccustomed to smiling.

Jen winced. 'Ah, that might be a problem...'

Avril's eyes seemed to narrow. 'Then find a solution,' she said, with a slight turn of her head and a lift of an eyebrow. Jen felt as if she had been slapped in the face. 'Lesley, our new lady who will be working the other side of your post will be doing mornings. You can pick up the work that she is not familiar with, at least until she is fully up to speed.'

'But, personnel is a new role for me, too. We agreed two and a half days a week, Avril. I've arranged it with the childminder and Jack...'

Avril's stare was deliberate. She was obviously enjoying the altercation and her command of it, which made Jen feel all the more uncomfortable.

'Oh, I'm sure Dylan will be fine with it once you explain. Sign here,' she said leaning over her desk to point on the dotted line.

Jen's heart was racing but she didn't pick up the pen. 'No, actually, this is nothing like we agreed,' she said. Jen became conscious of the stopping of the tapping on Donna's typewriter keys in the adjoining admin office. Avril seemed to grow ten foot tall in front of her eyes. Dylan had warned Jen that she should be under no illusions of thinking that Avril would have mellowed after the experience at Maisy's birth. Jen threw a whimsical smile of sadness in her direction.

'I'm not signing anything. This feels like the start of constructive dismissal to me.' Jen stood.

'Well, I don't see an alternative.'

Jen walked out of Avril's office without looking back. Tears of rage filled her eyes and she wiped them from her cheek. Donna looked on. Damn, why did she always cry when she was angry?

***

Jen had never seen Penny so effervescent. So much so that she allowed her skinny latte to go cold and the cheese that dripped from her Toastie congeal on her plate as she talked and talked about her new-found happiness. 'It might just be a cleaning job to you, Jen but it's opened up a whole new world for me. You never told me working at the nick was so exciting? There is never a dull moment.'

Jen couldn't help but smile at her friend's eager face. 'You'll change your tune when the novelty wears off.'

'Well it beats stacking shelves at Tesco any day,' she said smiling broadly. 'Cleaning will do until I get a job in admin like you. Malcolm is very kindly showing me around all the computer systems. He says the more I know about how to use them and what they are used for, the better for me when it comes to the application and interviews. He's going to help me with my application too when a job comes up. Maybe Dylan could put in a good word?'

'I don't know if he can if I'm honest, but you can ask him.'

'How's Max?'

'I'm just on my way to the vet now. Penny could I ask you a favour?'

Penny nodded as she gulped down the last of her cold coffee. She grimaced and put the cup down hurriedly.

'Look, I haven't thought this through yet, truth be known she's just sprung it on me, but the bitch...'

'Beaky?'

'Yes, Beaky. In her infinite wisdom she wants to change my hours. I've told her I can't, but in my experience if she wants something she usually manufactures a way of getting it. Do think you might be able to walk Max more for us if we need you?' she asked hesitantly.

'Oh, gosh. I don't know. What with me working, the kids and my new fella...' she said.

'It's a hell of an ask, I know. Don't worry, I was just sounding you out.'

'I will if I can.'

'Look, don't worry. It's not your problem. Dylan and I will work something out.'

***

Jen's face was glum when Jack Dylan walked through the door that night. She was sitting on the sofa.

'Not a good day?' he asked.

'We need to talk,' said Jen. 'Over dinner?'

'Ouch, that bad?'

Jen gave him a weak smile.

Dylan kissed the top of her head. He felt the slight twitch of her shoulder. She rose, stretched and yawned.

'I'll plate up shall I?' she said.

'How's Max doing?' Dylan called as he climbed the stairs.

'He's doing okay, but they're keeping him in until they have got his bloods back from the lab,' she said following him into the hallway and heading towards the kitchen.

'I'll go shower and get these clothes bagged up for the cleaners,' Dylan said offering her his jacket over the handrail.

'Urgh, yes please,' she said wrinkling up her nose.

There was a warm, comforting, cooking smell radiating from the kitchen. Dylan looked in on Maisy who was sleeping soundly in the nursery. She had recently assumed a new sleeping position. He stroked her back. Her bottom stuck further in the air. 'That can't be comfy little one,' he whispered touching her chubby cheek. She stirred but only to snuggle further into the cot sheet. Her cherub-like lips were pursed. She looked angelic. He tiptoed out of her room and walked slowly and quietly down the stairs through the hallway and into the kitchen.

Dylan stuffed his shirt and towel in the washing machine in the utility room and sat down next to Jen at the kitchen table. A long low moan came from the baby monitor and they shared a look of pride. 'I still have to pinch myself to believe she's ours,' he said.

Jen's tired eyes wrinkled at the corners. 'Me too.'

'See nothing can be that bad when we have each other,' he said cupping her chin in his hand and leaning forward to plant a kiss on her lips. 'Maisy snores like you,' Dylan said, distracted as he salted his dinner before putting a fork full of food into his mouth.

'She does not,' she said looking at him aghast. 'Tell me, how you do that?' She screwed up her face.

'What?' he asked baffled.

'Eat liver and onions when you've seen... well what you have today?' she said pulling a face.

'What at the mortuary?'

'Yes.'

'I've told you before, the body on the slab is a vehicle for the soul, a carcass, a shell to me. The person is dead and gone and there is nothing anyone can do about it. So, the only thing I can do for them and their loved ones is to find out how and why they died and put the culprits behind bars. Another glass of wine?' he asked, raising his glass.

Jen shook her head.

Dylan stood and went to the fridge. He poured himself another drink. 'So go on, tell me. I'm sorry. I was so busy today I hardly gave Max a second thought.'

'It's not Max we have to worry about at this particular moment.'

Dylan cast her a questioning look.

'It's whether I'm going to be able to continue working at the nick,' she said.

'Why?' he asked.

'I refused to sign my contract today. Avril says she wants me to work five afternoons a week now instead of the hours we agreed and she says that might be weekend work too.'

'She can't do that.'

'That's not what she says and she also seemed pretty confident that it'd be okay with you.'

'She did, did she?'

\*\*\*

It was five forty-five a.m. and Jen had barely slept. Maisy could be heard chatting away in her cot. Dylan turned to face Jen and lifting himself on one elbow he smiled down at her lovingly. 'It'll be fine. Look, she's actually done us a favour without knowing it. Sign the contract today before she changes her mind. If you work every afternoon then we don't have to pay Penny to walk Max at all. You can walk him before you go to work. The difference in the childminder's fee for Maisy is neither here nor there.'

'I know, and I can take Maisy and pick her up so I'm not relying on you. Maybe we could pay Penny to come and do a couple of hours cleaning for us instead so that she doesn't lose the money I've promised her?'

'I don't know about that... but if I could have a full breakfast before I go to work?'

'Don't push it,' she said.

'But if Penny does come in to clean for us and the childminder feeds Maisy her tea? We'll manage, won't we?' he asked.

Jen withheld judgement. 'You mean I'll manage.'

'Yeah, well. But it's what you do best... manage,' he said with a smile. 'I'm going to get off early. I want to call in at the vet before I go to work. I want to know what the score is with Max.'

'Be a love and get Maisy up whilst I start breakfast will you?' she said, throwing her legs out of bed.

'Do I have to do everything?' he asked, with a grin. Jen put her dressing gown on and walked back towards the bed. She bent down to kiss him. 'Yes.'

\*\*\*

Max was lying still in his cage. 'He's lost weight,' Dylan said to Sam Gouldthorp. 'I thought by now he'd be on his feet wagging his tail?'

'It's a bit too early for that,' she said. 'But we're hopeful you will be soon, aren't we old boy?' Sam opened the cage door and reached in. Max moved his head towards her hand. 'We think he might have ingested an application of coumarins, they're a group of plant-derived polyphenolic compounds which belong to the benzopyrones family. They are commonly found in this country in rodenticide. We are treating him accordingly. You wife says he doesn't chase rodents and doesn't know how he may have ingested rat poison, have you any ideas where he might have come across it?'

Dylan shook his head.

'The other explanation is that he may have taken a pharmaceutical application such as an analgesic. Do either of you take Warfarin?'

Dylan shook his head. 'He is going to be okay, isn't he?'

'It could have easily proved fatal, however, we are very pleased with how he is responding to treatment. He is showing signs of improvement.'

'He is?' Dylan said looking at the dog's hooded eyes.

The vet nodded.

'I'll take your word for it,' Dylan said.

\*\*\*

Dylan's mobile phone rang as he opened the door to leave the surgery. 'Sergeant Megnicks, sir. Just to let you know the bicycle we found on Watergate Road? Fingerprints have been lifted off the "For Sale" notice and we're going out to take elims from the owner today. Whether the job's connected or not is another matter but we may be lucky enough to catch the thief at least.'

'It's highly probable due to the isolated location that the bike was stolen, and that whoever did take it fled on the canal towpath that connects the two incidents though, doesn't it?'

'It does.'

'Thanks, I'm impressed,' said Dylan.

\*\*\*

Kirsty Gallagher's home was under intense scrutiny. Nothing would be left to chance. How many people did Dylan know that would honestly have the balls to break into a mortuary at night and take a body? Not many. This was no ordinary burglary. The jigsaw had to begin with the deceased and her life. The old investigators' saying find out how a dead person lived, and you'll find out why they died, was a good place to start.

The investigative team's first briefing was at ten a.m.

'Paul, leave the officers searching at Kirsty Gallagher's and return for the briefing. I want to ensure all the staff have the up to date information from you,' Dylan said.

*\*\**

Once everyone was assembled, Dylan chaired the briefing and outlined the discovery of Kirsty's body at her home.

'There were no obvious signs of a cause of death, I am told by DC Granger.' Ned Granger nodded his head. 'He attended the scene as the night detective. Her body, as we know, was taken from the mortuary before her post-mortem and at the moment its whereabouts is still unknown.'

'What else can you tell us about the ongoing search of her home, Paul?' Dylan said.

Detective Sergeant Paul Robinson was a little hesitant at the start of his speech but his confidence soon grew. Dylan watched him with pride. He was more than capable of doing his new role and he covered all the salient points. 'Somebody has taken the time to put clean sheets on the bed. There was no dirty washing in the washer or the laundry basket and her bins had been emptied and washed out. In my view, someone didn't want us to know they had been there. We have found no mobile phones at the address and it appears that a gas pipe in her lounge where she was found dead has been interfered with.'

Dylan concluded the briefing. 'I want to know if she has a vehicle and if so where is it? When did she last use her bank card? I, too, think someone out there doesn't want us to know about their relationship with the deceased. My instinct is that she has been murdered and the offender or offenders have cleaned up afterwards. I also think whoever it is has been involved in the removal of her body from the mortuary before the post-mortem to be sure we didn't find out how she died. We are looking for someone who has thought about their actions and carefully planned this act. They think they've got all eventualities covered and now it's up to us to find where they've made a mistake and bring them to justice.'

The team started to disperse. 'Paul, my office, please. I want to go over some details with you.'

The two men sat opposite each other. 'Which enquiries are you marking priority?' Dylan said.

'House-to-house, medical records, financial background, her occupation and workplace. Also, we need to find out who her friends were. We have no information of any immediate family.'

'When was Kirsty Gallagher last seen alive and by whom? Did she have a mobile phone? If so what was her phone number? Who was the service provider? Is it still being used? If so, where is it?' Dylan said without taking a breath. 'They're all urgent enquiries. The sooner we find who did this the more chance we have of recovering her body.' Dylan pushed his chair back and stood up. He paced the office, stopping at the window for a minute to look out into the yard. He saw PC Fearne Robinson in full uniform standing directly outside. Dylan could hear her muffled voice. She appeared to be in deep conversation over the airwaves when he saw a blue-grey pigeon flutter down onto the windowsill between her and the window frame. The officer was so engrossed she wasn't distracted by the bird. Within seconds a marked police car entered the car park, picked her up and exited in haste, with blue flashing light and the sirens sounding. The bird watched all that was happening, waited until they had gone before flying away.

Dylan caught Paul watching him. 'What?' Dylan said.

'You remind me of a caged animal.'

'I think better on my feet.'

Paul Robinson got up to leave. Dylan was still thoughtful. He looked over his shoulder when he heard Paul open the door.

'As you pass ask the girls where my coffee is?' he asked.

'Only you could say that and get away with it. I've seen many others try and get a mouthful of abuse. How'd you do it?'

Dylan winked in his direction.

Dylan was still at the window when Lisa knocked on his door with a cup in her hand. 'Tea money's due,' she said holding out her hand as she put the mug on the desk. Dylan reached into his pocket to extract his wallet and gave her a five pound note.

'You only owe me a quid.'

'The amount I drink?' he asked. 'Anyway I get waitress service, well worth the extra.'

63

'Thanks,' she said, smiling before heading back into the main office. She left the door ajar. 'Nice to be appreciated sir,' she said. Dylan saw Ned Granger flash one finger in the air at her. 'Ned!' growled Dylan.

Tea, coffee, milk, sugar it all had to be bought. There was no police fund for visitors either, hence it all came out of the team's pocket. Dylan knew some people took it for granted; a big mistake in his book. His telephone rang.

'Sergeant Megnicks, sir. We've got a prolific shoplifter called Kyle Russell in the cells and the custody officer tells me he has a wallet in his possession that doesn't belong to him. Of more interest to us is that he says he found it at the side of the canal where it had been left with a pile of clothing. He's also admitting stealing the bike from Tandem Bridge. He's told us he's looking for a way back into prison, so he's quite willingly admitting what he's done.'

'That's refreshing,' said Dylan.

'I'm having his prints checked against the marks lifted from the for sale sign, but it all looks positive. Now, what you want from me is the name and address on the wallet, don't you?'

'I've got a pen and paper right here.'

'Barrington Cook, Flat 17, Midgely Court, Tandem Bridge.'

'The new mill complex overlooking the canal?'

'Yes, I've already done some digging and it appears that he lives there alone, but don't take my word for it. I'm not one hundred per cent sure. There is no info on him to tell us what his occupation is. Do you want your detectives to follow it up?'

'Yeah, I'll get Detective Constables Hardacre and Wormald to liaise with you. Then they'll do the enquiries at the complex. Probably better that they go out of uniform at this moment in time. Thanks again and pass on my regards to your team.'

'Will do, sir, I'll wait to hear from the detectives.'

'I'll make sure you get the necessary feedback,' said Dylan.

Things were looking up. They had some positive leads to follow up. A message on Dylan's computer caught his eye. He lifted his head and saw that DC Vicky Hardacre was just about to leave the Incident Room.

'DC Hardacre,' he shouted. 'My office.'

For once Vicky wasn't sure of his mood by his voice. Was he annoyed? It certainly seemed like he was from the tone, but why?

She turned on her heels and walked into his office fully expecting a dressing down, but for what she wasn't sure.

'Sit down,' he said.

Dylan's eyebrows were lifted and he nibbled at his bottom lip – it was not a good sign.

Vicky had left the door open and he rose from behind his desk and shut it. Dylan sat back down and studied her face. The computer keyboard keys ceased to tap in the outer office. Vicky remained silent, she couldn't read him. What on earth had she done?

# Chapter Six

Penny could tell Jen had been crying.

'Oh, my God!' she said seeing the distraught look on her friend's face. Penny burst into tears. Jen quickly put her arm around her and hugged her tight.

'It's Max, isn't it? I knew it,' she said, sobbing into Jen's shoulder.

'Heavens, no. Max is going to be okay. I'm upset because I have a bit of bad news. We're not going to need you to walk him any more and I feel bad. I know you used the money for Troy's karate lesson.'

Penny's relief was tangible. 'You bloody idiot,' she said laughing through her tears. 'I thought...'

'I'm sorry... I never thought you'd think that.'

'So,' she said more composed. 'You're going to work afternoons? You sure you can manage?'

'Well, I hadn't much choice. I've signed the contract now. Jack and I discussed it last night and like he says, at least I'm not having to rely on him to take Maisy to the childminder's and pick her up, so Beaky's plan could actually work to our advantage. Don't tell her though,' she said. 'I can walk Max myself before I come to work. It would be a real help, seeing as I'll be working everyday though, if you'd do us a spot of cleaning or ironing once or twice a week?'

'Of course. Thanks for thinking of Troy,' Penny said. 'You sure Jack is okay with it?' she asked.

'He's fine. He wouldn't trust anyone with a key to our house but hey, you've had one longer than him,' she laughed.

'When do you want me to start?'

'This week?'

'Any specific days?'

'No, whenever you can fit it in to your busy schedule is fine,' she said.

\*\*\*

Vicky wasn't a stranger to Dylan's wrath. She had seen 'that face' before. He shuffled paperwork about on his desk when he was troubled. She wriggled in her seat.

'Ants in your pants?' he asked, leaning forward with his forearms on the desk.

'Just get it over with,' she said raising her shoulders. She screwed her eyes tight up tight and wrinkled her nose.

'Okay.'

Vicky folded her arms.

'I've been informed by HQ that from today Detective Constable Hardacre is no longer on my team.'

'What?' she squealed. 'What've the twats out there been saying about me? Cos whatever it is I never...'

'I've an email from HQ here that says...'

'Oh right, so whatever they say is gospel now is it? Typical!'

Dylan held up his hand. 'Well actually in this case yes and I'm quite happy about it.'

'You are?'

'You're going to be my Acting Sergeant, Vicky.'

She cocked her head, raised her eyebrows and took a lungful of air. 'You've picked me to act up? Me?' she asked, looking genuinely surprised. 'And the twats at HQ have agreed? Bloody hell boss, thank you. I won't let you down.'

'You better not. Don't forget to let Dorothy in Duties know. Now before you get ahead of yourself, I've got a job for you.'

Vicky moved to the edge of her chair and her mouth remained slightly opened.

'I love it when you're rendered speechless,' Dylan said. 'We believe the man we found in the canal is a Barrington Cook and,' he said handing her a piece of paper, 'we have an address for him. Go and have a look around to see if you can find out when he was last seen. I'm sure they'll have CCTV at the complex.'

'Provided it's in use. Family? Job?'

'According to the checks already made by uniform he lives alone. I don't know any more.'

'I'm on my way,' she said jumping to her feet.

'Have you forgot something?'

'No?'

'More coffee, sir?'

'You'll look like a bleedin' coffee pot!'

Dylan cocked his head and smiled.

'Just this once, but remember now I'm a sergeant.'

'Acting Sergeant.'

'I might not have time to make you coffee.'

'Oh, I'm sure you will always have time, Vicky.'

'Whoopee!' she said bouncing over to the door. The door slammed behind her and he heard her let out a squeal. 'I'm acting up!' she shouted.

***

The canal death enquiry appeared to be moving at a pace and ultimately Dylan knew it wouldn't be long before they had all the relevant information for the Coroner. It was time today for his focus to shift to the mystery surrounding the sudden death and subsequent unusual disappearance of Kirsty Gallagher from within the confines of what should be one of the safest places on earth, a mortuary. Picking up the phone he fingered through the papers on his desk for Mr Fisher's telephone number. Derek Harper's boss needed to be spoken to. To his surprise, the man himself answered the telephone in a fine rolling voice.

'Mortuary, Mr Fisher speaking.'

'Mr Fisher, Detective Inspector Jack Dylan, Harrowfield CID.'

'Hello sir, good news, the freezers are all in working order, the window is repaired and arrangements are in place for security to be revised. I am assuming that's why you rang?'

'No actually, but thank you for the update. I'm actually ringing you in confidence about one of your team, a Mr Harper.'

'Derek. Not the brightest button but a very willing work horse. He's not been inside with us long.'

'My colleague and I, who visited the mortuary on the morning Kirsty Gallagher disappeared were both concerned at some of the comments he made to us at the time.'

'Really?'

'Yes, hence this phone call. Mr Harper also admitted to us placing two corpses in the same fridge.'

'Yes, Inspector, I heard about that and I can assure you we had words. It's a totally inappropriate and unacceptable thing to do. As you can appreciate personnel is difficult to find in this profession. But I will look at his suitability for the post and arrange further training for him. In the meantime I will keep an eye on him.'

Dylan felt reassured Mr Fisher would take the appropriate action. For now he had more pressing matters to deal with.

Detective Sergeant Robinson was waiting at Dylan's door.

'You got a minute, boss?'

'Of course, how's the house search going?'

68

'Slow, if truth be known, but it's thorough and on a positive note we have found her car. It's a black Renault Megane which was parked a few yards up the street from her house. On inspection that also seemed extremely clean inside and out. I'm wondering now if she had some kind of obsessive compulsive disorder.'

'You think?'

'I've just been informed by Ned Granger that he has found a picture under the sun visor on the driver's side, so maybe we have a lead.'

'Male, female?' Dylan said.

'Male. I've been speaking to the CSI Supervisor, Karen Ebdon who has confirmed to me what we already thought boss. Someone definitely cleaned up at the house after the body was removed to the mortuary. Now who would do that and why?'

'Interesting. Who indeed?' Dylan shook his head.

'I have an appointment with her doctor, maybe that will tell us something more about her lifestyle.'

'At the very least it will tell us the last time she visited her GP.'

'Hopefully, I'll have some more for you at the debrief. I've arranged for Sergeant Clegg, team leader at the house-to-house search to be here, so we'll also have his up to date input.'

'Her occupation and place of work?' Dylan asked.

'Well, you'd think that would be easy wouldn't you? But, we haven't found anything significant yet.'

'Family?'

'Again boss, nothing known yet. She appears to have kept herself very much to herself.'

'Oh, for the days of a gossip over the backyard wall, or nipping into the neighbours to borrow a cup of sugar.'

'Sir?'

'Nothing. Let's get the picture that's been found in her car blown up and get some copies made. We might get a quick ident if he's local.'

'See you later,' he said with a raising of his hand as Dylan's mobile phone rang.

'Vicky?' he asked.

The connection was lost. It rang again.

'Boss, I'm in Barrington Cook's flat and you're not gonna believe this.'

# Chapter Seven

'Not another body?'

Vicky was standing in a vestibule with three doors opening from it, one to the left, one to the right and one facing her.

'No boss, but a substantial amount of rope and the same type visually as that that was tied to his ankles.' Vicky bent down to scrutinise it. 'No clues as to where it was purchased though,' she said.

'Never mind. It's a good find. If we can match it to the pieces of rope recovered from the canal, and tied to him it will confirm he took the rope with him.'

\*\*\*

DC Wormald was cautiously peering into the room on Vicky's right. The walls throughout appeared grey from lack of paint. He turned his head and looked at Vicky, the corners of his mouth went down. There was a pine bed within with other bits of furniture to match. On entering he noticed a couple of hair pins that were somewhat out of place on the top of the dressing table next to a hairbrush and a red lipstick. Vicky picked up an old picture with a gloved hand. It was of a woman sitting on a throne who looked as if she could have been in drag.

'He is, was, an accountant,' Vicky said picking up an official looking letter that had already been opened and was lying on the grey worktop in the squalid, dim kitchenette. There were as many as two dozen empty bottles of wine lined up next to the fridge. 'And I thought I had a problem,' she said to Andy.

The flat was cold and Vicky shivered. 'No laptop or mobile phone that I can see, you?' she called.

'No,' said Andy.

The flat was sparsely furnished and the furniture in it was basic. A pair of black leather armchairs, a black wooden wall unit and a couple of pictures amounted to the contents of the lounge area, apart from the mandatory large flat screen TV, a VHS video recorder and a DVD player which stood alongside stacks and stacks of neatly piled videos and DVDs.

Andy Wormald joined Vicky. 'No computer equipment as far as I can see. But then again there is nothing "lying around" is there. Everything is very neat and tidy – they might be hidden away.'

'No up-turned chairs or open drawers,' Vicky said. 'Look at that collection of Adult DVDs and videos. To all intents and purposes these appear to be unused.' She picked up a case from the TV stand. 'I'll bet you a tenner this isn't Mary Poppins,' she said.

'Yeah, and I'm not as green as I'm cabbage looking – I agree.' There was a DVD in the machine and he pressed play. The TV screen displayed child pornography.

'You seen enough?' asked Vicky. 'Better make sure the lot are seized.'

'For sure.'

'We'll call at your lass's on the way back for a quick brew shall we? I hope you're still seeing Marlene at the hairdressers it'd be a shame to lose a tea spot.'

'I am,' Andy said. A slight blush in his cheeks.

She took out her phone and dialled Dylan's mobile and told him about the obscene images.

'Anything else obvious?' he asked.

'At some time he was an accountant or bookkeeper of some sort but really he's nothing more than one strange deviant git if you ask me.'

'Leave it with uniform to deal with. It no longer requires a detective's involvement. That's one problem resolved but we still have a body to find.'

'Such a promising start too... turned out to be a bit of a damp squib didn't it? I had a feeling finding Barrington Cook's body was just the beginning of something big,' said Vicky.

'It's a result. Don't forget from the evidence available we can prove exactly what has taken place, and how he lost his life.'

A message came over the airwaves. Dylan was quiet. Vicky listened intently. 'Kyle Russell's fingerprints are confirmed as those on the bike "For Sale" sign, sir,' she said.

'Nice and neat for the Coroner. Do we have a next of kin for Barrington Cook yet?'

'No.'

'Let uniform do the death notice if you find it. I need you back here.'

'Yeah, they're welcome to that job.'

'Not easy to stomach, but putting it bluntly our man was a self-abuser just like those who use drugs, alcohol, sharp implements... In his case he used sex to get his fix.'

'Our daily dose of the weird and wonderful.'

'That reminds me, I want to talk to you about you and Andy working with Paul and Ned...'

'That's not very nice, sir.'

'Less of the wisecracks. We need all hands on deck to try and find our body snatcher. No tea spots on the way back. I need you back here ASAP, like I said.'

'Tea spots, us? Would we?' she said, crossing her fingers. Andy stifled a laugh.

'I'm sure Dylan's chuffin' psychic,' she said as she put her phone away.

A knock sounded at the door. Andy went to answer it.

'Yes, I'm Detective Constable Wormald,' she heard him say to the uniform officers who entered.

'All up to speed?' asked Vicky. 'Guess we can leave it with you then, kid!'

# Chapter Eight

Dylan sat quietly soaking up the information they had about Kirsty Gallagher at the debrief. His officers had been proactive.

Detective Sergeant Robinson outlined the day's findings to the gathered team members. The group were tired. The Incident Room was crowded. The aroma of perspiration hung in the air like a heavy oppressive cloud.

'We now know that Ms Gallagher had quite a few little jobs. Her main income was one from secretarial work. She temped a lot, working occasionally at Fernlee Middle School, Murfield Post Office, Prestigious Funeral Directors. Neighbours we have spoken to say she was a pleasant individual. Known locally for her tattoos.' Paul showed the picture that had been found behind her car's sun visor. Even with his head down, Dylan could tell by the sound of paper rustling that copies were being handed around.

'Her doctor says he hasn't seen her for six months. Back then she was prescribed a course of diazepam, for short-term relief of anxiety. But she wasn't on any long-term medication. We have gathered a lot of data from the house that needs examining in detail. Her telephone provider has been established and urgent enquiries are being made of them. You all have your own enquiries to be getting on with, but the next action is waiting for you to look at. Isn't that right Lisa?'

Lisa nodded her head at the pile of paperwork with references to enquiries to be made that sat on her desk. Anyone of those actions could be their next big lead.

'Someone has had time to plan and prepare, I feel sure. Did Kirsty put the photograph in her car or did someone else to try to mislead us? Let's keep digging, keep your mind open and remember there isn't such a thing as a perfect murder,' said Dylan.

'What I can't understand is, if someone she knew was intent on getting rid of her, then why didn't he or she remove her body from her home address instead of waiting for it to be taken to the mortuary where they'd have to break in to steal it?' asked Andy.

'Maybe it was their intention but she was discovered by us, before they had time to move her,' said Paul.

'Bet they panicked when they discovered she'd been taken to the mortuary? There was definitely no sign of anyone else at her house when we were there the night her body was discovered,' said Ned.

'We need answers to these questions and more... Tomorrow's another day, as they say. Thank you everyone. Go home and sleep well. See you back here tomorrow morning nice and early,' said Dylan.

The briefing over, Dylan returned to his office and prepared to leave. Briefcase in his hand he had just turned out the light and was about to shut his door. The outer office was empty. His phone rang. For a moment he stood and looked at it. Its persistence however made him go back and pick it up.

'Dylan,' he said brusquely.

'Inspector, Brian Fisher.'

'Mr Fisher, what can I do for you?'

'I've taken the opportunity to speak to Derek Harper further.'

'And?'

'And having done so, I have advised him about his conduct and given him a written warning, which I think will do the trick.'

'I certainly hope so and I also hope you don't have cause to regret your leniency,' said Dylan. 'Thank you for letting me know.'

Dylan made a mental note to tell his officers to be aware of Mr Harper's attitude and to report back any impropriety in the future.

He was out the door before his telephone could ring again.

Max was at the forefront of his mind...

'The news is good. Twenty-four hours and Max can come home all being well,' said Jen.

# Chapter Nine

'Help! Please help me.' Were the first desperate words that Control Room operator Richard Pauley heard from a hysterical female when he answered the 999 call. He was well aware it was pitch black outside. Time was no more than a casual significance to the staff, working in the windowless room.

'Try to stay calm. Could you give me your name, address and postcode? Then, I can get help on its way to you.'

'Jane Simpson, 14, Danone Way. HD5 OER'

'Jane, how old are you?'

'Thirty-eight. Please,' she gasped, 'tell them to be quick. He might be still here,' she whispered.

'Jane, help is already arranged and on it's way, you are not delaying anything by talking to me now. You should hear their sirens very soon. Can you tell me what's happened?'

'I've been attacked... in my house... I'm scared,' she said.

'Where are you at the moment?'

'In my kitchen, on the floor. I daren't move.'

'And who do you think might be there Jane?'

'The old man. He went into the hallway after I stabbed him. He was trying to strangle me. Please hurry.' Jane's voice was trembling uncontrollably.

Richard knew she was in shock. He could hear her teeth chattering.

'Listen to me, concentrate on what I'm saying. The police and ambulance should be with you any minute.'

Her breathing was fast and shallow.

'Jane, take some deep breaths for me. Jane. Keep talking to me...'

'My legs. I can't move.' She whimpered.

The high Georgian window in the kitchen expressed a ray of light, the reflection from the security light.

'I'm going to die.'

'You're not going to die, Jane. Listen to me. Can you see into the hallway?'

'No, it's too dark,' she said.

'Can you hear anything?'

'No!'

'Jane, you're doing really well. Are you hurt?'

'I can taste blood,' she said. She raised her fingers to her mouth and touched her swollen lip. 'I think I cut my hand on the knife. My head hurts. He pulled my hair.'

'Jane, like I said you're doing really, really well. Keep talking. The police and the ambulance crew should be with you imminently. Were you alone in the house?'

'Yes. I don't feel well,' she said. Richard could hear a definite slur in her voice.

'Can you hear the sirens?'

'Yes!' her voiced raised. 'Thank God,' she said. Jane's breathing was laboured and her voice started to ebb away.

Jane was sprawled out on the floor, listening to her heart beating hard and fast.

'Jane! Whatever you do, don't hang up; keep talking to me,' Richard said with a vein of urgency in his voice. 'Without going into the hallway is there an open door or one that needs unlocking to allow us entry?'

'I'll open the back door. I'm shaking so much...' she said. Richard Pauley could hear Jane moving towards the door. 'They're here,' she said. She stood at the open door where she fell into the arms of Police Constable Gavin Druce. He took the telephone from her hand.

The first paramedic on the scene ran in close behind PC Druce and took her limp body from the officer. Jane Simpson allowed herself to be shepherded to a chair.

'Control, PC Druce. We'll take over now. Paramedics are on site. I'll update you once we know what's happened and have searched the house.'

'Thanks for that,' said Richard Pauley.

'Householder is in shock, no life threatening injuries. Search now commenced.'

Gavin Druce and PC Fiaz Hand prepared themselves, batons drawn, they were in control of the situation. No verbal communication was necessary between the pair as with trepidation they walked carefully towards the door to the hallway. The motionless body of a man lay spreadeagled, face down on the hallway floor. PC Druce dropped to his knees at his side and shouted to the paramedics to attend to the man. Standing, he proceeded to open the lounge door, peering around the room for further occupants. PC Hand headed up the open staircase in quick time.

The felled man was wearing a full head mask of an old man with grey wispy hair and a large crooked nose. A mask that the officer knew was readily available at the supermarket. At the left hand side of the body Gavin noticed a large black handled carving knife, which on closer visual examination appeared to be heavily bloodstained. There were two visible stab wounds in the middle of the victim's shoulder blades and his light coloured shirt was saturated in arterial blood.

Checking his pulse the woman paramedic looked up at PC Druce. Her lips were pressed to a pale hardness. Fleetingly she closed her eyes and shook her head.

PC Hand having completed the search on the upper floor was on his way down the stairs. He shook his head at his colleague and PC Druce knew there was no one else present in the house. Consciously they disturbed nothing else at the scene.

The male paramedic was talking calmly and reassuringly to Jane, as the woman paramedic prepared her to be moved to the ambulance. She wrapped a thin blue blanket around Jane and tightened the strap on the wheelchair so she didn't fall. Jane sat very still, staring ahead. The male paramedic noted her tremulous limbs and looked at his colleague. The door to the hallway was open slightly and as the paramedic pushed her past the entrance she saw the body laid out on the floor. She turned her head away and screamed hysterically into her hands. Only when they got outside the door and stopped did she appear conscious of faces looking down at her. The faces of the paramedics who proceeded to try and calm her.

'PC Druce to Control, we have a murder scene. We have a male pronounced dead by the paramedics in the hallway of the house. It appears he has suffered stab wounds. Could you send further assistance to secure and preserve the scene and will you inform on-duty CID?'

He knew that the detectives on arrival would take charge of the crime scene.

Jane Simpson would soon be on her way to Harrowfield Hospital for her injuries to be treated but since she was responsible for a person's death it was only a matter of time before she would have to be arrested. It was decided that PC

Druce would travel with her for continuity. When she rang in on the three nines she had told Richard Pauley that she had stabbed the intruder – he was dead.

'I'll need a duty statement from you,' PC Druce told the paramedics. 'And CID will need to speak to you later. I'll also need Ms Simpson's clothing for exhibit purposes.'

It was essential that they took samples from her with her consent, but before she was cleaned up they needed to secure any contact evidence that there might be. PC Druce turned to her, 'When you rang nine, nine, nine you told them you stabbed the intruder?' He cautioned her.

'Yes,' she said, breathlessly. Her eyes had a vagueness about them. 'I don't understand.' She looked confused and dishevelled.

'The intruder is dead apparently from stab wounds, so therefore I am arresting you on suspicion of murder,' he said to her.

'I'm not a murderer,' she said turning her head quickly from side to side. Her eyes looked wild and full of anger. 'This is a bloody nightmare,' she said, over and over again. 'He was going to kill me... I had to stop him.' There was blood on her lip and a little on her chin.

The male paramedic and PC Druce exchanged glances over the woman's head. She was a rather anaemic woman, the paramedic thought seeing her lying on the bed in the ambulance. PC Gavin Druce sat opposite her on a chair and buckled his seatbelt. The ambulance doors were closed.

Vicky Hardacre was the on-duty CID supervision. Although she had passed her exams for the rank of Sergeant, she had to await the next round of promotion boards before being considered substantive, which meant in the meantime Detective Inspector Jack Dylan could request her to be in his team as an acting Detective Sergeant, and headquarters had approved the request. This incident meant she would now get her first taste of what the additional pressures and stresses were that came with that role. It was her first opportunity to prove to everyone she was competent.

Acting Detective Sergeant Hardacre felt very alone. She arrived at the scene with Detective Constable Wormald. Whilst she had attended murder scenes on numerous occasions, this was different. She was the most senior police officer at this scene and she was aware that others would look to her for direction. She was now the one responsible for making decisions and she had to record why she'd made them. Afterwards people would judge her on how she dealt with the issues that arose here and now and the judgement calls she made on the spur of the moment. That was afterwards, in their nice cosy offices where there was no hurry about their task. Her first job as supervision was a murder. It couldn't get more serious. She was in no doubt that she was under the microscope.

'Guess it's sink or bloody swim, Andy,' she said as they got out of the unmarked vehicle. Her heart was pounding and not used to feeling hurried she felt the immediate rush of adrenalin.

'Sarge,' Andy Wormald said respectfully.

PC Hand updated them both with a sallow and expressionless face. Vicky was aware of his eyes fixed upon her. In her entire career no one had spoken so directly to her, or so it seemed. They'd talked at her, over her, through her, around her but never in a way he did now that she was the most senior rank at the incident. It felt strange.

'PC Druce is on route to the hospital in the ambulance with Jane Simpson, Sarge,' he said. 'Her injuries are minor. What we have been able to establish so far is that she says she disturbed an intruder who attacked her and she was in fear for her life. It appears she pulled a weapon out of the knife block, on the kitchen work surface and stabbed him more than once. There are two stab wounds to his back but we haven't moved him, so I can't tell you if he has any other injuries. He was pronounced dead at the scene by the paramedics who came to attend to Ms Simpson. I've got uniform commencing a log of attendees and taping off the immediate area.'

'Anyone asked for the D.I. to be called out yet?' asked Vicky.

'No, that's your shout Sarge.'

Vicky's lip curled up at the corner.

DC Wormald was busy giving their names and collar numbers to Police Constable Tracy Petterson who was now collating attendees at the scene. A necessary documentation to record persons present at various times at a crime scene.

Blue lights announced the arrival of the on-duty uniform Inspector, Justin Gaskin. He screeched his car to a halt and unfolded his large frame from the vehicle before swaggering over to the pair. 'Sounds like one evil burgling bastard met his match to me,' he said in his bombastic manner. 'Been inside yet? Let's have a little looksy shall we?'

'No, you won't have a looksy. You know the score. Andy and I will be the only people entering the crime scene – this is CID's responsibility and I'm in charge,' said Vicky who stood her ground in front of him.

His bulging green eyes leered at her from under bushy, red eyebrows. She quivered inside. 'Come on, we need to know what we are dealing with, nobody needs to know, kid.' His giant frame over-shadowed her.

'Yes they will, because it will be on record and another thing, I don't think Dylan will take kindly to someone contaminating a crime scene just to be nosey, do you?'

Justin Gaskin was a egoist. Standing six feet and seven inches tall to Vicky's five foot ten he looked down on her and she looked up at him with a steely glare.

'Okay, if that's how you want to play it act...ing Sergeant Hardacre,' he said with a snarl.

'With due respect, sir, it's a murder scene. It's my call as the senior detective and we don't play at it.'

'She needs a strong man like me to control her,' he said to DC Wormald out of the corner of his mouth. Andy looked at him with the contempt his words deserved.

Vicky was right. Gaskin knew it, and although he outranked her, she was the on-duty senior detective in charge. Vicky had the expertise and responsibility for the crime. Without awaiting a response from him she asked control to call out DI Dylan to meet her at the scene and arranged for the crime scene investigator to attend, along with their scene supervisor.

Inspector Gaskin stared at her through his designer glasses, and although his face was the colour of his hair he remained outside the taped area.

Vicky stood with Andy. 'It is rumoured Avril Summerfield-Preston was one of his conquests,' she said out of the corner of her mouth.

'Not so bright then is he?' asked Andy.

'Rumour has it Dick Rogers copped them in a compromising position once.'

'I've heard that rumour too. You'd better watch your back with Gaskin though, he's as vindictive as his hair is red,' he said looking troubled.

'Thanks for the heads up. Come on, we, as the detectives need to get suited and booted and without disturbing anything get a visual overview of the body in situ before Dylan arrives so we can brief first hand.'

# Chapter Ten

Maisy had got into a habit of waking in the early hours, much to Jen's despair. It was one o'clock in the morning and she was trying to soothe her daughter back to sleep. Dylan could hear Jen moving around the nursery, and the broken hum of conversation as she walked to and fro past the nursery door.

Jen crept back next to him in bed twenty minutes later.

'She off?'

'Just.' Jen yawned.

The phone rang. Jen pushed her head further into her pillow and eyes wide she lay motionless looking up at the ceiling. The call was short in duration.

'I'll be with you in thirty minutes,' Dylan said. Jumping out of bed he headed for the bathroom. Jen sat up. 'You stay wrapped up, I'll manage,' he said.

'No, I'm wide awake. I'll go down and make us both a warm drink,' she smiled wanly. As she passed the wardrobe she put her arm inside, reached for a clean suit, shirt, tie and as if in automatic pilot hung them on the back of the bedroom door. With well-practiced swiftness she opened drawers and grabbed Dylan's underwear and a handkerchief and threw them on the bed.

In the kitchen she could hear Dylan moving around overhead. Her waking mood was not a happy one. Five minutes later she appeared in the bedroom with a cup of tea for herself, a coffee and a slice of toast on a tray for Dylan. 'Eat it, you don't know when you might get anything else,' she said, climbing back into bed and pulling the duvet up to her chin. 'I've put some bananas, cereal bars and a bottle of water on top of your briefcase.'

He bent down and kissed her, a slice of toast in one hand and a cup of coffee in the other. Albeit for putting on his jacket he was ready to leave. He smelt of soap and toothpaste and his face was damp to the touch. 'Looks like a woman's disturbed an intruder, he attacked her and now he's dead. It could be a runner. Vicky's on-duty supervision.'

Jen's mouth was a straight line. 'But, if she was attacked surely it'll be self defence?'

'That might be the outcome at the end of the day, but she'll have to go through the system like any other killer.'

'Yeah, well the system stinks.'

'It's overloaded too. 'Now try get back to sleep. You've got to work tomorrow or rather today,' he said looking at the clock.

\*\*\*

As Dylan pulled out of the driveway he saw the bedroom curtain flicker. He waved in case Jen was watching. Looking in his rear-view mirror as he drove away he saw the bedroom light go out.

It was a fine, clear night and he wound down the window to clear the mist that formed quickly on the inside of his windscreen. The cool air helped clear his head. The night was dark but not so much so that he couldn't distinguish landmarks on the roads he knew well. He passed over the Heddle River, drove alongside an avenue of trees and parked next to the compact blackness of the long laurel hedge that separated Jane Simpson's property from the next.

He was conscious that this was Vicky's first dead body as a supervisor and he hoped that she recalled all that she had been taught. As the Senior Investigating Officer he would cut her no slack. This was no exercise. Her actions and decisions could be the difference between the killer not only being caught, but also convicted. He knew how she would be feeling. He felt slightly nervous for her, as a parent does for a child. The aptitude she showed tonight was as much a measure of his own ability and judge of character, as it was of her as a leader.

\*\*\*

Fourteen Danone Way was a detached property set back from the roadway. The nearest neighbours at either side were about thirty to forty yards away he noticed on arrival.

Dylan stopped at the cordon of crime scene tape. He got out of his vehicle carrying his own coverall sealed in a plastic bag. He walked over to give his details to PC Fearne Robinson who had taken over from PC Petterson as the Loggist. He was immediately approached by acting Detective Sergeant Vicky Hardacre and Detective Constable Andy Wormald. So far so good he thought to himself as he scanned the controlled crime scene.

'Good morning, Detective Sergeant, Andy,' he said with a nod of his head.

'Morning, boss,' they said in unison.

'Morning, Dylan,' said Inspector Gaskin.

'Sarah Jarvis, Crime Scene Supervisor, has just arrived,' Vicky said looking towards the marked van. 'And PC Gavin Druce is at the hospital with the householder who he has arrested on suspicion of murder. Jane Simpson states that she stabbed a male intruder who attacked her in the kitchen. PC Druce and PC Hand were first at the scene and PC Petterson and PC Robinson arrived shortly afterwards. The paramedics have pronounced life extinct. DC Wormald, will you update the boss about the body in the hallway?' asked Vicky.

'Male, face down on the hallway floor. There are two visible stab wounds to his back. At his side, on the floor is a knife that appears to be bloodstained. He's wearing a full head mask, which is still in situ. The mask is that of an old man with a large crooked nose. You'll have seen the sort in shops around Halloween. It's got wispy grey hair and a bald head... you know the sort. That's about all I can tell you at this moment in time, sir. Neither the initial police officers attending or ourselves have disturbed anything, although there has been a visual check made of all the rooms to make sure there was no one else present, before we ensured the scene was secured.'

'Thanks, Andy, glad you didn't attempt to remove the mask. Is he wearing gloves?'

'No sir, he isn't.'

'Is he black, white?'

'White, boss.'

'Our householder?'

'Is Jane Simpson,' said Vicky.

'What was she wearing?'

'A light coloured, cotton dressing gown that was heavily bloodstained, I am told by PC Hand. PC Druce has got the retrieval of these as exhibits underway. Apparently she was in shock when they took her to the hospital in an ambulance but has only minor injuries.'

'Do we know roughly how old she is?'

'Late thirties boss, according to Control.'

'Thanks, Andy, who have we got for exhibits, Vicky?'

'I've called DC Granger out, boss.'

'Will you be needing anything further from me, Jack?' asked Inspector Gaskin. 'I've some reviews to do on two in custody for something else that happened this evening.'

'No thank you, not at the moment, thanks,' said Dylan.

The team watched Inspector Gaskin get in his car and drive away. He raised his hand to Dylan. Andy went to speak to the CSI team.

'Boy, am I glad he's gone,' said Vicky to Dylan.

Dylan looked at her questioningly.

'He wanted to go into the scene before you arrived, but I told him it wasn't happening. Don't think he was happy with me. Bloody Wooden Top.'

'Ignore him. Let's face it, if you had let him in the cordon, I'd still be shouting at you both now. That's after I'd had you up for neglect of duty. You did the right thing. Well done, I'm proud of you. It's not easy to say no to people of a higher rank.'

'Andy told me to watch my back with Gaskin.'

'If you want my advice, don't trust anyone but yourself. Believe me, I say that from experience,' he said with a cynical expression upon his face. 'Okay,' he said walking towards the wider audience. 'Once everyone's arrived, we'll get suited and booted into protective clothing. And then you and I, Vicky, will go in with Sarah and PC Hand, seeing as he's already been inside, and we will have a close look at what we've got. So to your first job as a deputy Senior Investigating Officer, Sergeant Hardacre.'

'Acting Sergeant.'

'Not for long if I have my way, Vicky. Not for long.'

Vicky Hardacre had worked on DI Jack Dylan's team for some time and she knew how thorough he was. She was thankful that he had been on-call.

Preparing to go into a crime scene was no easy task. Suited and booted meant all over body protective clothing which included gloves, overshoes and masks before they were as much as allowed to approach the door. Dylan let Crime Scene Investigator Stuart Viney under CSI supervision Sarah Jarvis set up a three hundred and sixty degree angle camera, and put down stepping plates inside the house, thereby making sure evidence on the ground was not lost by the officers trampling over it. There was one chance to protect and secure a crime scene. Which he knew only too well.

The group started to walk in single file on the path created by the metal foot plates. The stepping stones laid the way through the kitchen and into the hallway. Vicky led the way. Dylan stopped her with his hand on her shoulder before they entered the house. The mask muffled his voice. 'I want you to interpret the crime scene,' he said.

Her eyes flashed from him to the doorway.

'Don't look so worried. I'll add anything that I feel you've missed. It will allow you the opportunity to consider what the scene tells you, rather than me taking control that's all.'

'Okay,' she said as she stepped over the threshold and into the kitchen. 'Knife block is upturned on the worktop, but the knives remain in situ. The kitchen window is slightly open. Point of entry maybe? However, the plant that is on the window sill and bottle of hand wash is undisturbed – odd.'

'Good. You'd think anyone attempting to come in that way would have knocked something over, wouldn't you?' asked Dylan.

'There is nothing in here that suggests a struggle has taken place to me. The stools are upright under the breakfast bar. No obvious sign of blood splashing,' she said looking around the room and then her eyes went to the ceiling.

'Agreed. The state of the room hardly confirms a violent attack.'

They moved to the hallway where the body lay.

The necessary photographs were now being taken.

'Remove the mask,' Dylan said to Sarah Jarvis. Sarah carefully pulled back the mask and placed it in a clear plastic evidence bag provided by CSI Stuart Viney.

'Just seeing someone wearing that thing is enough to give you a bloody heart attack,' said Dylan. He dropped to his haunches by the deceased's side.

The deceased's eyes were open. He was a clean shaven male with dark curly hair.

'Can I smell aftershave, boss?'

'Brut,' said Dylan, Ned and Stuart.

'I thought, I could smell aftershave,' said Vicky. 'But it's not one I recognise.'

'We're showing our age fellas,' Dylan said.

Vicky stood quietly looking around.

Dylan scanned the clothing the deceased wore. Light coloured checked shirt, denim jeans and trainers. 'What's missing, Vicky?' he asked. She saw the back of his neck wrinkle as he looked up the stairs.

'A coat?'

'A coat. Yes,' he said standing to face her.

'Let's turn him over and have some photographs of him in situ before we remove him to the mortuary.'

Stuart Viney knelt down and turned the body onto his back with Ned's help. Beneath him was a large pool of thick arterial blood. He had another visible stab wound to his chest.

'Straight through the heart,' said Vicky.

'Possibly. So, she stabbed him at least three times. He's about the same age as her I would hazard a guess. Did she know him?' asked Dylan.

'I wonder,' said Vicky. 'Well, even if she did she's hardly likely to recognise him in that bloody mask is she? I've got a gut feeling something is not quite right about this. But I'm not sure what... Everything seems too neat and simplistic,' Vicky said.

'I have the same feeling,' said Dylan.

'An intruder wearing a mask like that... God, once you started lashing out with a knife, you wouldn't stop would you? I'd have imagined it would have been more a frenzied attack,' said Vicky.

'Okay, let's arrange for him to go to the mortuary. Ned, will you go with him for continuity and to ensure we seize his clothing. Hold on, just check his pockets for any identification.'

Ned stooped down. He fumbled around in his pockets.

'Nope, zilch,' he said.

'Can we have a snap of his face so we can show it, in interview, to Ms Simpson to see if she recognises him,' said Vicky.

Dylan nodded in her direction. He was pleased with her approach and contribution. He turned to Sarah. 'Nothing apparent but I'd be interested to see if you locate any blood splashing on the walls, ceiling etcetera, which may indicate where the attack started if nothing else.'

'No problem,' she said.

'Okay Vicky, let's start upstairs and work downwards and see what else we can find.'

\*\*\*

One bedroom was decorated for a child – although no child appeared to live there. Dylan saw untidy shelves full of bits and pieces arranged in a haphazard fashion. There were boxes both opened and sealed.

'Maybe she hadn't lived here long,' said Vicky as though she was reading his thoughts.

He opened the double doors of the master bedroom, and stood measuring the interior's contents with his professional eye. A king-sized bed all but filled the room. There was a mirror on the ceiling. The duvet cover was neatly spread across the furniture, not a crease visible.

'She was dressed for bed, but she hadn't got into bed,' Vicky said.

There was an en-suite. Dylan pointed to the linen basket.

'Looks pretty full,' said Vicky.

'I want the knife she used. Ensure it's brought along to the mortuary in one of those sealed transparent tubes so that the pathologist can see it, will you?' Dylan asked. Vicky nodded her head.

'No sign of any men's toiletries. One toothbrush. She lives alone? The press are going to be all over this one,' said Vicky.

'Better think what you're going to tell them.'

'Me boss?'

'Yes you, acting Sergeant Hardacre.'

# Chapter Eleven

Vicky and Dylan sat savouring a bacon roll.

'Okay, so you've had time to think, what's your next move?' asked Dylan.

'Well... I'd like to hear what Jane Simpson's got to say but on the face of it, we have a masked intruder who's been stabbed to death by a female householder trying to protect herself.'

'She was in her bloodstained nightwear on the arrival of the police; we'll get an exact time from the control room when she rang three nines. That doesn't suggest she was expecting visitors to me and she hadn't got into the bed because that hadn't been disturbed,' Dylan said thoughtfully. 'Let me see your press release before you email it to HQ press office, will you?'

'FD 52,' came the shout over the airways.

'Go ahead, Control,' answered Vicky to her supervisory call sign.

'Jane Simpson has been discharged from the hospital and is on her way back to Harrowfield Police Station with PC Druce. He'll liaise with you there.'

'Ten four. Thanks for that,' said Vicky before continuing her discussion with Dylan. 'We'll get a fuller picture once we've been able to interview her.'

'Make sure you ask her how and where on his body she thinks she stabbed the intruder. I want the facts recorded.'

'Why? Don't you believe her?'

'We have to prove what happened, for her benefit as much as everyone else's, remember. The evidence will corroborate or refute what she says took place. Just do a short statement for the press, and make sure you interview in Room 1 so that I can downstream; if I can't be in the interview at least I can watch and listen in on the monitor.'

'I noticed the deceased didn't have a wedding ring on, but there appeared to be a mark where one might have been once.'

Dylan smiled. 'You see, I told you you'd never forget to look at the ring finger after the dead body we pulled from the canal. I must confess I didn't notice if he was wearing a ring or not, but I would have looked for it at the post-mortem,' he said sheepishly.

'I've asked Andy, before he leaves the scene, to bring a full set of clothing for Jane Simpson. PC Druce has the clothing she was wearing at the time of the incident bagged and tagged for us, and she can't stay in a paper suit forever.'

'That's thoughtful, Vicky. And Ned is seeing to the immediate exhibits with crime scene investigators before securing the scene and arranging the necessary overnight protection by uniform?'

'That's correct.'

Dylan would, when back at the station with Vicky, arrange the Incident Room and staffing of the murder enquiry to commence at daylight. A fresh search team would be sent to the house and its immediate exterior.

At the police station Jane Simpson would require a solicitor, who would more than likely want her to rest after such a trauma and the lateness of the hour. Dylan and Vicky weren't for arguing. They would relish a few hours sleep themselves before they commenced the enquiries, in earnest, later in the day.

It was decided that Vicky would sit in with Detective Constable Andy Wormald at the first interview with Jane Simpson when they would ask her to take them over what had happened. 'With only a few challenges,' Dylan said firmly.

Vicky handed the press release she had scripted to Dylan for him to read:

*In the early hours of this morning a female caller from the Paddock area of Harrowfield rang on the three nines emergency line asking for help. She had disturbed an intruder at her home. Police on their arrival found the body of a masked man in the hallway, who also appears to have been fatally stabbed. Enquiries are continuing.*

'Good. Email that to HQ Control now under the heading of *Urgent Press Release* and for the attention of the duty press officer. Then we can do no more until we can hear what Jane Simpson has to say.'

The pressure and tension appeared to have abated.

'She must have been bloody petrified. I would've been,' said Vicky.

'Anyone would. Tell Andy I want a softly, softly approach to her in the interview.'

\*\*\*

Home and a hot shower beckoned. Dylan felt weighed down by a sudden wave of fatigue. A million things were going round in his head. He was in charge of a murder investigation and very conscious he had to remain alert and focused.

Jen's patience held by a thread as Maisy toyed with her breakfast. It was six o'clock. Dylan arrived home, washed his hands in the kitchen sink and planted a kiss on Maisy's head whilst he dried them. He took his mobile phone from his jacket pocket and placed it on the table next to her, with his car keys. Jen stood at the sink and he went to stand behind her, circling her waist with his arms. He leaned his head on her shoulder and nuzzled into her neck.

'Sleep well love?' He asked, planting a kiss on her bare shoulder.

'Try not at all,' she said. 'It's not easy when I don't know what you're going to deal with. I worry.'

'Well you shouldn't. I can look after myself.'

A noise from behind them made them both turn quickly. Maisy, Dylan's phone in hand, was dancing to the ring tone she'd induced.

Jen's smile was wide. Dylan yawned but his eyes smiled happily behind hooded eyelids. Maisy grinned at them, showing off her new baby teeth.

Dylan walked into the dining room and sat down in the chair next to the window. Jen watched from the kitchen as his eyes closed and his chin dropped towards his chest. The morning newspaper fell in through the letterbox but the noise didn't wake him.

Jen put her finger to her lips and Maisy copied her.

'Baby,' Maisy said in a hushed tone as she watched her daddy sleeping.

\*\*\*

Two hours later, Dylan bounded into the Incident Room which to his delight was already starting to take shape. There was busy, cheerful chatter and an influx of personnel, some people he knew, others he hadn't worked with before. All were expeditious.

Coffee in hand, feet up, Dylan's eyes were glued to the video screen in his office, which at nine thirty showed nothing more than a dark, interview room. Suddenly he saw with the turn of the handle the heavy grey, fire door swing wide open. One hand of Vicky's remained on the door lever and her shoulder was to the door out to the corridor, as she reached round the door jamb with her other hand to switch on the lights. Instantly the dark, windowless room was illuminated and Dylan had a clear picture on his screen. Jane Simpson and Solicitor Yvonne Best from Perfect & Best Solicitors, who worked out of the old Co-op building in Harrowfield followed her in and DC Andy Wormald was the last to enter. He shut the door behind him. Vicky invited the ladies to sit opposite them at the empty table. She put her paperwork down. Dylan was pleased to see Jane Simpson had used Perfect & Best. He felt sure that the solicitor's being a female would bring her some comfort. Jane Simpson rubbed her arm frantically. She was physically shaking.

'Sorry, it's a bit cold in here, isn't it?' asked Vicky. 'It will soon warm up,' she said smiling at the ladies before commencing the introductions for the purpose of the tape machine. She outlined the reasons for Jane Simpson's arrest. 'Do you feel well enough to do the interview, Jane?'

'Yes,' Jane Simpson said. She was very quietly spoken and Dylan reached forward to turn up the volume on his monitor. He could see tear stains on Jane Simpson's cheeks and her face was red and swollen; her eyelids looked sore. Jane pulled the sleeves of her cardigan down over her hands and wiped under her eyes and her running nose. Yvonne Best reached in her handbag and passed her a pack of tissues.

'You sure you're okay to continue?' Vicky said.

'I want to get it over with.' Jane blew her nose into a tissue.

'In your own time then, will you tell us from the beginning what happened last night?'

Jane Simpson appeared to focus her mind. She sat very still and avoided eye contact with the officers. She spoke in a rhythm, as if reading the words from the wall behind Vicky and Andy. 'I'd had a drink. I'd fallen asleep on the settee. I don't know what time it was. It felt late. I went into the kitchen to get a drink of water to take with me to bed and suddenly I was grabbed by my hair, from behind.' Her fist clenched. 'I was dragged backwards. I opened my mouth to scream but nothing came out and by the time I'd recovered he had stuffed something in my mouth. I think I hit my head. He turned me round and grabbed me by the throat and I couldn't get my breath. I thought I was going to die. I remembered feeling confused because it was an old man who held me but he was very, very strong. There was a struggle. I reached out and I felt the knife block on the worktop with my right hand. God knows how I managed to pull one out, but I did, and I lashed out at him. He managed to grab the knife but I wouldn't let go. I felt it run through my hand. Then his grip loosened. He turned and staggered towards the hallway. I froze. I remember feeling numb. I grabbed the phone from the wall, fell onto the floor and hid behind the breakfast bar. That's all I can remember, until the police and paramedics arrived. They told me he was dead.' Jane Simpson clenched her stomach, breathed in deeply and closed her eyes. 'I'd killed him.'

'We can take a break if you want?' asked Vicky.

'No. I'm fine,' Jane said. Her face and lips had faded to the colour of her platinum hair.

'How many times did you stab him. Do you remember?'

'Two, maybe three? I don't really know. I just kept lashing out until he was gone out of my reach.'

'Do you know how he got into the house?'

'No, I thought about that. A window maybe? I'd burnt some toast earlier in the day and opened the kitchen window slightly.'

'No boyfriend or man on the scene at the moment?' Vicky said.

'Once bitten twice shy,' she said with a faint glimmer of a smile.

'Any ideas who the intruder might be?'

'No.'

'Jane. Did you know the intruder was wearing a mask?' Vicky said.

'Was he?' she said attaching herself to her seat by her hands.

'I have a picture of the man under that mask. Will you look at it please and tell us if you know who it is?' asked DC Andy Wormald.

Jane Simpson leaned away from the table. She turned slowly to look at her solicitor. 'Must I?' she said.

'If you feel up to it, it may help.'

Jane Simpson took a deep breath and nodded her head.

Andy put the photo face down on the table and pushed it across in front of her. He turned it over speaking the fact he was doing so and he read out the exhibit number for the purpose of the interview tape.

Jane Simpson jumped to her feet instantly. 'No, no it can't be Billy! That's my husband, my ex-husband! Oh, God, I think…

I'm going to be sick,' Jane Simpson said. Yvonne Best's eyes flashed in the direction of the two officers and then back to the face of her client. She stood and holding Jane Simpson by the arm helped settle her back down in her seat.

The interview was suspended and Jane Simpson was taken from the room in tears.

Dylan played the tape back over and over again. Was he imagining it? Or did Jane Simpson get to her feet prior to her being able to see the photograph?

At the request of Mrs Best, further interviews were postponed due to her client's physical and mental wellbeing. The officers would resume interviewing later in the day.

The post-mortem of the intruder, now believed to be Billy Simpson was scheduled for the next day. It gave the team an opportunity to recharge their batteries and reassess what intelligence they had so far.

# Chapter Twelve

'I know I was supposed to be picking Max up from the vet today but can you do it?' Dylan asked Jen as he walked out of the kitchen. She heard him running up the stairs.

'Do I have to do everything?' she said through clenched teeth. 'Bloody job!' she said out loud as she finished mopping the kitchen floor after breakfast.

Maisy looked across at her from her high chair, where she had been happily playing with her books and bricks. Jen saw the soft hair of her blonde eyebrows knitted together and her sweet little lips took a dive at the corners. 'Cross?' she said.

'Oh, I'm sorry. Yes, mummy is cross,' she said with a scowl, 'but not with you darling.' Jen wiped her brow with her forearm as she went to her daughter, kissed her on the cheek and lifted her out of the chair. She held her tight.

Dylan's mind was on one thing and one thing only, murder.

'Maisy shall we go and see Max today?'

The little girl nodded enthusiastically.

'Shall we see if he can come home with us?' she said as she walked into the lounge.

Maisy squealed with delight.

'That's a yes then,' Jen said kneeling down on the floor. With Maisy still in her arms she pulled out her changing mat from behind the chair. Laying her daughter on it she gently tapped her nose. 'You are so like your daddy. But don't you ever, ever grow up to be a detective because you'll never be at home.'

'Right that's me off then. See you when I see you,' Dylan said as he popped his head around the door. His jacket over his arm and his briefcase was in his hand. He blew a kiss and vanished out of the door. She heard a purpose in his stride as he walked down the hallway.

'Will you be home for tea do you think?' Jen called after him which was met by the slamming of the front door. 'Love you too,' she said.

Nappy changed, Jen picked Maisy off the floor and carried their daughter to get the coats from behind the front door.

\*\*\*

Dylan had agreed with Vicky that if she and Andy continued with the interview of Jane Simpson he'd accept the short straw and go to the mortuary.

'Where art thou, fair maiden?' Professor Stow asked when they arrived, his fat red cheeks wobbling as he gleefully sought the preferred person usually in tow. 'I have a present for her.'

DC Ned Granger reached out for the box of chocolates. 'For Vicky?'

The professor smiled but hung onto them.

'She's in interview. Anyhow, what's she done to deserve a present?' asked Ned.

'I'm very pleased to say Mr Eugene Regis furnished me with a glowing reference and I have no doubt...' Professor Stow pulled Dylan to one side and said out of the corner of his mouth, 'that she was party to it,' he said.

'I'm pleased,' said Dylan taking the coverall handed to him by the mortuary assistant.

'And I'll make sure she gets the chocs,' said Ned taking the box from Stow.

'Well if you're sure,' Professor Stow said looking over his half-rimmed glasses suspiciously at the detective. 'I thought Eugene Regis might be with us today too but it appears not, he must have seen enough,' he said to Dylan.

Karen Ebdon arrived. 'You know Karen our Scenes of Crime supervisor, Professor?' asked Dylan.

'Oh yes, we've had many a naked body between us, haven't we Kazza?' he asked signalling her to follow him into the examination room.

The pathologist was already suited and booted. 'Ned Granger is our exhibits officer on this one,' Dylan said as they all made their way towards the examination table.

Professor Stow eyed him suspiciously. 'Well don't get those exhibits mixed up with the chocolates, they were rather expensive,' he said.

'You can trust me sir, I'm a police officer,' Ned said with a glint in his eye.

Dylan didn't respond but there was an expressive shake of the head before he went on to outline the attendant circumstances of when, where and how Billy Simpson had been found.

'Well, there is one thing for sure. He won't be terrifying anyone else will he? Well done to Ms Simpson. If she hadn't done what she did perhaps it would have been her stretched out on the slab before us.' Professor Stow sighed. 'I've seen the knife block being involved in so many fatalities these days. They're often left far too accessible in my view. I keep mine in the kitchen cupboard out of sight and suggest you do the same. One never knows does one? Let's get on. I've another post-mortem at Leeds after lunch and then I'm onto Sheffield.'

***

Dylan stood quietly as he watched Stow methodically and thoroughly examine the body and take the relevant samples. Dylan searched in his pocket for his mints. Where were they? Damn, he can't have replaced the packet he had given to Vicky. He would just have to grin and bear this one. He could taste the putrid smell as Stow opened the body. The pathologist's voice was very clear and precise as he spoke for the purpose of recording his findings.

Two hours later he spoke directly to the team present. They sat in the office. It was warmer than the examination room and it felt nice for Dylan to take the weight off his feet. The room where the post-mortems took place had to be kept cool for obvious reasons, but the trademark type of tiled flooring was often unforgiving in being the cause of shooting pains up both Dylan's legs. Professor Stow rubbed the back of his calf muscle vigorously.

'Cramp?' Dylan asked.

'One downside of this flaming job,' he said. 'As you saw I've taken the relevant samples and nail scrapings. The man received three stab wounds. One to the chest, which went straight into his heart. This was the killer strike, as it were. The two others to his back are deep wounds but they missed his vital organs. As you could see there was a lot of blood inside the body cavity. Can I have a look at the knife you've brought in?' he asked, turning to the exhibits officer.

Detective Ned Granger handed him the weapon seized at the scene. It was held in a see-through container. Professor Stow studied it carefully. 'Yes, that may well be the weapon that inflicted the wounds to the back. They were caused by a single-edged blade. But the one that did the real damage was a double-edged knife which is quite clearly defined where it's pierced his

97

clothing, his skin and the wound itself. The particular blade you are looking for I suggest is at least six inches in length and half the width of the knife used on his back. In the examination room you saw I measured the depth prior to opening him up. The tip of that knife entered his heart and it must have been driven with some force for it to go as far as it did into his body. I also think that the two wounds to his back were most likely done when the body was face down on the floor. I base that purely on the angle that the knife has entered the body. This angle represents the position of someone knelt over the body at the point of the stabbing. I can see by your faces you weren't expecting that?'

'I wasn't,' said Dylan. 'So, let's get this straight. In your opinion there were two knives involved in this crime?'

'That's correct. The blade that caused his death was much thinner than this one here. I take it you have only retrieved this knife so far?'

'Yes, and it has been suggested by the accused that only one knife was used,' said Dylan.

'Well, now you know different.'

'Then all is not as it seems,' said Dylan. 'Thank you, Professor Stow.' Dylan turned to Ned. 'We need to have the clothing he was wearing checked over to show the two different cuts made to it by the two different blades.'

'If you do find another knife I could probably tell you from the measurements if it could possibly be the one that was used. Most important to me for this particular wound is the cutting edges. The wounds to his back were created by a knife with one sharp edge, like this one. The killer wound is definitely a double-edged blade.'

\*\*\*

Dylan pulled into the garage on his way back to the police station, picked up some extra strong mints, and popped two directly into his mouth on his way back to the car. Only that way could he get rid of the taste of the mortuary.

'What's the score with Kirsty Gallagher, Paul?' asked Dylan when he arrived at Harrowfield CID office.

Detective Sergeant Paul Robinson got up from his seat and followed DI Dylan down the gangway of the Incident Room to Dylan's office. He closed the door behind him. 'I've got the team delving into her personal background and others checking the items we seized from her home but there's nothing to get excited about yet. We've got no ID of the man in the photo found in her car yet either. It so bloody frustrating. I'm just waiting for that breakthrough but it appears no matter what we do we are coming up against brick walls.'

'Keep going, you'll get there,' Dylan said.

There was a rap at the door and Vicky Hardacre walked in. Paul Robinson nodded to his colleague and walked out.

Vicky called back into the main office. 'Get the coffees in, Andy, it's your shout.'

Dylan looked at her through half-closed eyes. 'You mimicking me, lady?'

'I'm just a chip off the old block, boss.' Vicky chuckled.

'Yeah but Andy did as you told him without a murmur. You always create a fuss.'

'It's called control boss,' she said. Vicky made an upturned fist. 'Control.'

'Whatever. You were missed at the P.M,' said Dylan.

'I was?' she said sheepishly. 'Eugene?'

'No, Professor Stow.'

'Oh,' she said wrinkling her nose.

'He sent you a gift.'

"He did?' she said her eyes opening wide.

'He reckons you played a part in Eugene Regis giving him a good report.'

'You bet. He owes me.' Vicky winked at Dylan.

'If I was to bet on anything. I'd put my money on Ned eating the chocolates he sent you by way of a thank you by now,' he said.

\*\*\*

Vicky looked out of Dylan's door glass and eyeballed Ned who was grinning at her like the proverbial Cheshire cat from where he sat at his desk. She got up quicker than Dylan could say Jack Flash. Bolted through the door and ran down the office only to see him put the last chocolate into his mouth. With his mouth so full he couldn't speak he offered her the empty box.

'You rotten sod,' she said taking the box from him and proceeding to stuff it in the paper bin. 'I hope you're bloody sick.'

Ned swallowed hard. 'Don't get your knickers in a twist. There is always a positive. I did you a favour. You're fat enough,' he said puffing his cheeks out to her disgruntled face.

'That's the last straw. I'll get you back you'll see,' she said. Turning on her heels she winked at Lisa as she passed by her desk.

'Whooh I'm so scared,' he called after her with laughter in his voice.

'You're scared what?' she called back, raising one eyebrow at Dylan as she stood before him as he sat at his desk.

'I'm scared, Sarge!' he yelled. She smiled and sat down.

Andy walked in the office and sat next to her. 'He will be,' she whispered to him.

'Playtime over children?' Dylan asked.

Vicky screwed up her face. 'Oh, he'll be sorry...' she said smiling.

'Right, let's move on. You two have just had another interview with Jane Simpson.'

Vicky and Andy nodded.

'At any time did she mention using more than one weapon in the attack?'

'No,' they said in unison.

'Okay, so tell me, what is she saying?'

Dylan sat back in his chair, and resting his elbow on the arm of the chair he put his finger to his lips and listened intently.

'She seemed a lot calmer than before. We now know the intruder was her ex-husband Billy Simpson. She said she immediately recognised him, from the picture – hence her reaction which she apologised for. But she swears she had no idea it was him at the time of the attack. She still maintains she thought she was fighting for her life with an unknown intruder.'

'Didn't she recognise his voice?'

'She says he didn't speak,' said Andy.

'Andy's right, basically she confirms what she said yesterday, that she'd been watching TV, went into the kitchen to get a drink before bed and was attacked by a masked intruder. She fought for her life and managed to grab a knife which she stabbed him with.'

'Did she not say yesterday that she was in the kitchen when she telephoned on the three nines and suggested he went into the hallway but she didn't follow?'

'That's right boss and she repeated that in this morning's interview,' said Andy.

'So next we need to be asking her how she explains where the knife was she used to stab him, which as you know was in the hallway when we arrived? The post-mortem also showed that the stab wound to the chest went straight into his heart with great force, according to Stow and it was this that caused his death.'

'But you are going to lash out with every bit of strength you have if you're being throttled like she says she was,' Vicky said.

'But could you manage that much brutality with someone's hands around your throat? The pathologist reckons the wounds to his back were done by someone knelt above him when he was lying down. Which would explain why the knife was in the hallway wouldn't it?'

'So, she's not being honest with us then, boss?' Andy asked.

'No, she's not, and that's not the only thing that's she's not been honest about because the post-mortem shows that there were two knives used to stab Billy Simpson. The one we have recovered is likely to be responsible for the wounds to his back but not for the chest, that actually killed him. That knife, Stow tells us, would be doubled-edged and a lot longer and thinner than the one we seized at the scene. So at present we don't have a murder weapon.'

'Why would she lie, boss?' asked Andy.

'That's for you two to find out in the next interview.'

'The bitch! She's a bloody good actress. I was thinking what a bloody heroine she was for how she was coping,' said Vicky.

'Now what we're saying is that she is not simply a killer in self-defence, but a premeditated murderer,' said Andy.

'That's for us to prove. Let's get Ned to take our exhibits to the forensic lab as a priority, what time is your next interview scheduled for?'

'Half two, boss,' Vicky said.

'Okay, we will look at our interview strategy. Let's get her to "tie herself up in knots", before we unleash the post-mortem results on her.'

# Chapter Thirteen

Jen and Maisy walked through the vets' surgery to pick up Max.

'He's made a friend,' said vet, Sam Gouldthorp.

Max stood by the side of a cage his tail swishing from side to side. Behind the wire was a basset hound his big, sad brown eyes looked guilty.

'That's Meatloaf,' she told Maisy. 'He's devoured the contents of his owner's handbag and she's not confident she can remember everything that was in there, so he's in for observation. He's a regular, aren't you, Meaty?' she said.

He didn't bark but made a strange sort of half howling noise that brought a smile to Maisy's face.

'Max has lost a bit of weight but I'm sure it won't take him long to put it back on will it, mate,' she said ruffling his ears. 'And remember no more chasing rodents!'

'Don't worry, he'll be on a lead from now on whenever we take him out,' Jen said.

*\*\**

Jack Dylan was sitting in his office, door closed to avoid interruptions. His eyes were glued to the video monitor covering the interview room where Detective Constable Andy Wormald and acting Detective Sergeant Vicky Hardacre were once again sat opposite Jane Simpson. Lin Perfect was the solicitor from Perfect & Best. Lin was the taller of the two women who ran the lucrative legal practice in Harrowfield. He knew well enough that Yvonne and Lin were no fools and neither did they suffer fools gladly.

Introductions of who was who and the caution was over. Vicky commenced the interview.

'Jane, going back to our last interview. In brief, you told us that you had been drinking whilst watching television, fallen asleep, woken up around about midnight you think, and gone into the kitchen for a drink of water to take to bed, when you were attacked by a masked intruder who grabbed you from behind. In fear of your life, a violent struggle ensued during which you managed to grab a knife from the block on the kitchen worktop and you stabbed him more than once. You saw him stagger into the hallway and that's the last you saw of him until the police arrived. On arrival they found him dead in the hallway. You didn't know who your attacker was because of the mask until we showed you a picture of him in interview. Is that right?'

'Yes. But, now I know the man to be my ex-husband Billy Simpson. I had no idea it was him at the time. I haven't had contact with him for ages.'

'What I'm thinking is that if you haven't had contact with Billy for such a long time why would he break into your house and try and strangle you? I presume he wouldn't have a key?'

Jane Simpson shook her head. 'No.'

'Can you think of anything that has happened recently to make him so mad that he'd want to do this to you?'

'Don't you think I've been asking myself the same question? I can't believe he'd do such a thing.'

'When the intruder, Billy, went into the hallway obviously wounded why didn't you escape and raise the alarm?'

'I don't know... I guess I just froze ... I don't know. I thought he may have left.'

'But wouldn't your front door be locked?'

'Yes, but I guess he would remember I always left the key in the front door so that's why he headed in that direction.'

'Did you hear the door open and close?'

'No... I don't remember,' she said shaking her head in short, sharp, jerky movements.

Andy had remained silent throughout, letting Vicky ask the questions but couldn't restrain himself any longer.

'What I want to know is, why would you lie to us, Jane?'

Jane Simpson sat bolt upright in her chair. Her whole demeanour suddenly changed. 'I most certainly am not lying. How could you think that? You saw him with your own eyes, in that horrible mask.'

'Let us not forget, what we saw at the scene was a dead man, a man that we have established you were responsible for killing,' said Andy.

'But, I didn't mean to kill him. I thought he was going to kill me. Look at the bruising on my neck,' she said. Jane turned her head, revealing clearly the bruising she said he had inflicted on her.

Andy produced the clear plastic tube that contained the knife that had been recovered from the house. For the purpose of the tape he identified the exhibit using it's unique reference number.

'Is this the knife you used to stab Billy Simpson? For your information this was found at the side of his body.'

'It is one of my knives. They were a wedding present.'

Dylan was pleased that Vicky was allowing Andy to continue to question Jane Simpson. She clearly didn't like his questions and he was seeing different reactions from their prisoner.

'And you can confirm to me that that's the only weapon that you used?'

'Lord, I was just lucky it was in arm's reach. I had to stop him somehow...'

'You say you just lashed out at him? You don't really know how many times you stabbed him do you?'

'I just hit out. It was frantic. He was trying to strangle me for god's sake. I didn't count the blows.'

She was becoming agitated and Dylan was waiting for her reaction when they told her about what the pathologist had said.

'Frantic you say? Mmm...'

Jane immediately nodded in response.

'I know you're still lying to us,' said Andy.

Lin Perfect looked puzzled. Her eyes shifted to look up at the camera. She knew Dylan would be observing.

'What would you say if I told you from Billy Simpson's post-mortem examination we know that two knives were used to stab him.'

Jane Simpson's jaw dropped.

'Two different knives. And we only have one weapon. You're not telling us the truth are you, Jane?'

Unblinking her eyes seemed to stare right through the detective and fix on the wall behind him once more.

Vicky took over the interview. 'What went on, Jane? Tell me, what really happened that night? The pathologist tells us that he believes the wounds to Billy's back, because of the angle they were inflicted mean that he was lying face down on the floor when the attack on him took place. Is he right?'

Ms Simpson's eyes rolled to look sideways at her solicitor but her head remained perfectly still.

'I think because of the recent disclosure, I need to consult with my client before we proceed. Therefore could the interview be suspended, please,' said Lin Perfect.

The request was granted and arrangements were made for a further interview in two hours.

Andy rose from his chair, that was bolted to the floor, as was the table, and he reached out to stop the tape.

***

The corridor was empty as Andy and Vicky strolled back to Dylan's office. 'I thought she had had a lucky escape and now it appears she's seen her ex off,' said Andy.

'There is one thing for sure, there's a lot more she can tell us, but the thing is will she?'

'She'll spill the beans,' he said, 'I know it.'

'Assume nothing,' she said to him and smiled as she pushed open the double doors. 'What's funny, Sarge?' asked Andy.

'What's funny? Did I just say never assume?'

'Yes.'

'Seriously. It's official, I'm turning into bloody Dylan!'

# Chapter Fourteen

Both the interior and exterior of the Simpson murder scene was subject to a PolSA search with a qualified police search advisor. The murder weapon was to all intents and purposes remaining elusive to them.

Dylan delivered his orders over the phone. 'Seize any likely knife or knives from the address.' Dylan told the search team headed by Police Sergeant Simon Clegg. 'Can you seize any items of clothing in the laundry basket, or washing machine for examination with regard to us obtaining DNA? With a bit of luck this might provide us with the evidence to put someone else at the house.'

'Send the mask off to Forensic, Ned. It doesn't look new to me. Who knows what we might find from it?'

\*\*\*

Vicky and Andy were sitting opposite the DI in his office. There was a storm brewing outside. The windows rattled with the strength of the wind and in minutes it was as dark as night.

'If only we had the results from Forensic right now at our fingertips,' Dylan said. 'Imagine how that next interview might go?' He sat twirling his pen through his fingers as he deliberated. 'Ah... Efficiency, that's what I like to see,' he said, as Lisa walked in with warm drinks on a tray and biscuits on a plate.

'It's all about being prepared, knowing what your first question would be...' said Vicky. 'Like where's the coffee in Dylan's case,' she chuckled.

'Ever thought about joining up?' Dylan said turning to Lisa.

She shook her head. 'Not on your Nelly,' she said. 'I've got a life.'

'Yeah, there is that,' he said morosely, briefly wondering if Jen had picked Max up from the vet.

Vicky stood. 'Hold on, I just remembered,' she said following Lisa out of the office. 'I packed sandwiches this morning. Sustain me a lot better than a poxy Rich Tea,' she said heading for the door.

Dylan stood and looked out of the window with his cup in his hand. He looked thoughtful. 'Blow, winds, and crack your cheeks! Rage! Blow! This storm has no pity for wise men or fools,' he said. He turned to Andy.

'King Lear,' said Andy.

Dylan nodded. 'Mmm… impressed.'

\*\*\*

A flash of lightning was followed shortly by a crack of thunder, and a hail of frozen rain splattered the windowpane. The second strike of lightning came and the thunder roared causing them both to jump.

'I'll bloody kill him!' Vicky stormed back into the office.

'Who?'

'Ned, he's only gone and eaten my sandwiches, again.'

Dylan shook his head.

'I swear I'll have him,' she said.

'Double, double toil and trouble. Fire burn and cauldron bubble,' Andy said to Dylan.

'What you on about?' asked Vicky.

'Nothing.' Dylan laughed.

Whilst the storm did its damnedest, the three officers sat around Dylan's desk. They discussed the next interview which would prove just as turbulent as the weather and one of Shakespeare's plays, with any luck.

The evidence so far was showing the detectives that all was not as it first seemed, and it was growing more apparent with each interview that Jane Simpson wasn't telling them what really happened that night. But if she had nothing to hide why not?

'Was there someone else at the house that night?' Dylan said.

'Had the ex disturbed them?' asked Vicky.

'Or had she planned it all along?' asked Andy.

'She doesn't look the murdering type,' Vicky said screwing up her nose.

'What type's that, Vicky? What do murderers look like? If only we knew...'

'Point taken,' she sighed. 'When we checked the house we noticed that the toilet seat was up. I think that suggests a man had been there.'

'Her ex maybe?' asked Andy raising his hand to his brow. The thunder clapped ever harder and the forked lightning looked like it had sliced the sky in two.

'Bloody hell,' exclaimed Vicky, covering her ears.

'Better make sure it wasn't one of our lot that used it. When I was a CID aide, I remember going to a domestic murder scene with my boss. The officers who were supposed to be guarding it thought they'd make themselves useful by putting all the furniture back. They had "a bit of a tidy round", and were sitting watching telly with their feet up and having a cuppa when we got there. I can still hear the boss screaming at them.' Dylan chuckled.

'Nah, bloody hell, nothing like that happened here. I'm more than confident none of ours would use the loo at a crime scene,' said Andy. 'Vicky does have a point though.'

'Okay,' said Dylan. 'Put your theory to Jane Simpson in interview and see if we get a reaction. Although, I have a feeling you might get the silent treatment from now on.'

'But we have enough to charge her with, boss, don't we? She might've lied about the circumstances but she's confessed to the stabbing.'

'It'd be nice if she talked. We're going to have to wait for Forensics to confirm our theories but it does appear that Billy Simpson was intentionally stabbed to death. Was it her who did it?' Dylan pondered. 'She was certainly there, and party to what took place. I'll have a word with the Crown Prosecution Service. You never know which way they're going to go... a bit like that weather.'

The sun's rays were now strong and warm on Dylan's back. So she could see Dylan's face across the desk Vicky put her hand up to her brow. 'My feelings are if she doesn't talk we charge her. Sergeant Clegg's team and the house-to-house operation should be well under way now. We'll see if they turn anything up. If not, you're just going to have to go in to interview and do your best with what you've got to throw at her at the moment and see if she'll talk. That's all we can do.'

Dylan's phone rang and he picked it up. 'Sergeant Murphy from Keighley, what can I do for you?' Dylan said, indicating to the pair that they had finished the meeting, Vicky closed the door after her. Andy walked ahead of her to his desk.

'We have the remains of a naked body in the River Worth, Coney Lane near the Worth Valley Railway. Do you know it?' Sergeant Murphy asked.

'Yes, I know the Worth Valley Railway. Go on,' said Dylan biting the end of his pen. He shifted to the edge of his chair and his heart quickened a beat.

'The underwater search unit are on route. Their ETA is thirty minutes. There's no way to get to the body without them unfortunately. Visually the corpse appears very bloated and decomposed.'

'Is it a man or woman?'

'We can't tell but I read a bulletin about your missing corpse, hence the phone call.'

'Any missing persons in your area?'

'The usual Mispers but nothing new on the system. Just thought we aren't that far away from you; about eleven miles as the crow flies. Maybe it's worth a look?'

'If we set off now we should be with you about the same time as the search team.'

'Thank you,' said Sergeant Murphy.

'No, thank you for not hesitating to ring me.'

Dylan sprang to his feet and opened his office door. 'Paul,' he shouted, 'get your coat on we're going for a ride.'

'Will you be back in time for Jane Simpson's next interview, boss,' said Vicky.

'Don't know, they've found a body in the river near the Worth Valley Railway. It is possible it's Kirsty Gallagher.'

Detective Sergeant Paul Robinson was on the phone but Dylan saw him stand, pick up his coat and seek the sleeve of his suit jacket.

*Off to a body in the river at Keighley,* Dylan typed in his text to Jen. *Will be in touch as soon as I know what's what x*

Jen pulled her bleeping mobile out of her bag and read the message from Dylan. She threw it back. Donna scowled at her from across the office. Her phone immediately bleeped again. This time when she looked she saw it was from Penny Sanderson. *What's going down?* read the text.

'Someone's annoyingly popular,' Donna mumbled.

'Ignore her,' said Rita. 'Some of us do have friends Donna.'

*Such as?* Jen texted back.

*Such as, I've just seen Dylan rushing out of the yard.* Jen smiled. Penny it appeared was taking the welfare of her new 'police family' very seriously.

*A body found in a neighbouring Division, nothing for you to worry about.* Jen texted back.

\*\*\*

Once given directions for a crime scene it wasn't hard to pinpoint the exact location. If it wasn't the wail of the emergency vehicles, or the copious amount of crime scene tape it was the flashing blue lights that illuminated the sky that got the public's attention.

'DI Jack Dylan and Detective Sergeant Paul Robinson,' Dylan said to the uniformed officer guarding the scene, when he stopped them in their tracks. The two men flashed their warrant cards at him. He lifted the blue and white tape and allowed them access.

'Sergeant Murphy is expecting you, sir,' he said pointing a gloved hand to the source of the shouting. There was a man-made path that ran beside the river. With a shepherding arm he hurried the detectives towards all the activity.

'The divers are just bringing the body to the water's edge now, sir,' he said.

The three men made their way down a ramp, slipping in the process. 'May be how the deceased lost their footing?' asked Detective Sergeant Robinson. They surveyed the scene. 'That might be badly decomposed, but that's never a woman, sir.'

The underwater search team officers rallied around the corpse. Some were still in the water and debris floated around them. Others were attempting to pull the body to the safety of the banking.

Dylan's heart sank.

'Sorry mate; it looks like you've had a wasted trip,' Sergeant Murphy said. 'We don't know who is he but it definitely isn't your lass from the mortuary.'

'Can I leave it with you, as they say, unless something suspicious is discovered,' Dylan said.

Sergeant Murphy nodded.

Dylan looked at his watch. 'If we're lucky, Paul, I might just make the interview,' he said to his colleague as they turned to leave.

Sitting in his car with a calmness of confident haste, Dylan drove back to the station. Once reinstated behind his desk his thoughts were again full of orderly rapidity that blew steadily across his consciousness, like the clouds moved by the increasing wind that battered his window.

*\*\**

The interview with Jane Simpson hadn't started but the introductions had been made and the questioning he knew would start in earnest. He saw four people sat round the interview table on his monitor. The detectives sat opposite the defendant Jane Simpson and her solicitor.

Dylan took off his jacket and threw it over his desk. He took his pad and pen out of his nearside drawer and considering the detail of the case he began to jot down his thoughts.

'We finished the last interview asking you why you were lying about the death of Billy Simpson in your home,' Vicky said to Jane Simpson. 'You have consulted with your solicitor and you have had time to think about your situation. Is there anything more you want to add to your statement?'

'No.'

'No?'

'Yes.'

Vicky cocked her head but remained silent in anticipation. Her eyebrows were raised in expectation and Detective Constable Andy Wormald's head was bent over paperwork on the desk, his pen poised.

'I just want to say that what I have told you is the truth. I was scared no... I was bloody terrified. I didn't intend to kill anyone and I certainly didn't know that it was my ex-husband until you showed me the photo.'

'Jane, all we need you to do is tell us the truth. We can prove that what you are saying is only part of what really happened that night. What we can't understand is why you are not telling us the rest?' asked Vicky.

'Are you protecting someone?' asked Andy.

'I've told you the truth. How many more times! That's what happened,' she said through gritted teeth.

The detectives continued to ask her questions. They allowed her the opportunity to answer and explain the things that didn't 'add up' to them. But she chose not to answer. 'No reply' became her mantra.

Dylan was on the telephone to the Crown Prosecution Service before the detectives closed the interview.

'You could bail her,' the on-duty CPS officer said.

'And that's not going to happen,' Dylan said, voice raised. 'We've not located the murder weapon yet and a second offender is being sought. She'll be before the Magistrates' Court tomorrow morning for a remand in custody.'

Vicky's chin was resting on her chest as she skulked back into the office dragging her feet on the floor. She threw her paperwork down on her desk and flopped in her chair. Andy brought her a drink from the water dispenser in a plastic cup. She drank the ice cold liquid, savouring the feeling as it hit the back of her throat. In her handbag she found a packet of Asprin and popped two in her hand before throwing them to back of her mouth, she swallowed.

'Get her charged,' Dylan was saying to Andy as he walked out into the CID office. 'Copy of the remand file on my desk for tomorrow morning and do a one liner for the press office news line, Vicky.'

'And say what?'

'Just something brief. A thirty-eight-year-old woman will appear before the Harrowfield Magistrates' tomorrow charged with murder. Send it to HQ press office for Claire Rose's attention. I want you both to keep your eyes peeled in that court room. It will be interesting to see who turns up to watch. Right I have to go see a woman about a dog.'

'Whatever,' said Vicky.

'No, I have really,' said Dylan.

'What about the body in the river?'

'It's looking increasing likely that it's one of their long standing Mispers. A red herring.'

'Herrings in the River Worth? I'll make the press office aware of that too shall I?'

'I do the jokes, Vicky,' he said.

Dylan texted Jen. *I'm on my way home.*

*I'm in shock.*

*Not to worry I'm a trained first aider,* he replied. *Start undoing your tight clothing.*

# Chapter Fifteen

Max bounded down the hallway all dribble and slobber. 'Now that's what I call a welcome home,' Dylan said ruffling his sandy coat.

Maisy stood with the help of the coffee table and Jen clapped her hands excitedly. 'I knew it. I just knew she was going to do that today,' she said, gathering her up in arms and planting a kiss on her cheek.

Her phone bleeped, she picked it out of her bag and threw it back again without answering it.

'Who is it?' asked Dylan.

'Penny. Again,' she said. 'All of a sudden she is taking a very keen interest in the crime, in Harrowfield.'

'That's what the job does to you, doesn't it? It becomes a lifestyle.'

'Well yeah, but I'm not being funny, she's only a cleaner. It's not like she is in the need to know bracket is it?'

'Hey, don't knock it. We need more like her taking an interest. That way we might get more people willing to come forward and give evidence.'

'If I'm not supposed to know about anything Jack, then I'd rather not, so don't tell me. Then if it becomes common knowledge you know it wasn't me who spilt the beans.'

'But, I trust you implicitly and you are involved, like it or not.'

'Not now I'm not. I'm doing personnel, remember? There are enough gossips in a police station without Penny adding to it.'

'Okay, if it makes you feel better I won't tell you anything.'

'It does. Anyway, I've got some news for you,' she said, her eyes bright and shining.

'Go on,' he said.

'Dad's got a girlfriend?'

'He has?'

'Yes, they met through Vince and Jacqui who run Godshill Village Post Office on the Isle of Wight. They won ten thousand pounds last year in a national competition to develop their Post Office as a community hub. Their idea was to try and reduce isolation of older people and offer support to them. Part of that money has been used to give people access to the internet and computer training. Dad, never being backwards in coming forwards to meet people signed up.'

'So he's met this lady online? Your dad's internet dating?'

'No, not quite silly, he met her at the class.'

'And you're not upset?'

'Upset? Why should I be? Dad's on his own, three hundred miles away from us. If she makes him happy I'm pleased for them both.'

'I think someone is feeling neglected,' Dylan said looking at Maisy who was blowing raspberries on Max's tummy.

'Doesn't need much to keep us happy, does it Maisy?' Jen said with a smile.

\*\*\*

It was eight o'clock and Maisy was tucked up in bed and fast asleep. The phone rang.

'Is Mr Dylan there, please?' asked the caller.

'It's for you,' Jen said handing Jack the receiver.

'Control Room, sir. I understand you're the on-call Negotiator?'

Dylan looked about aimlessly. Jen handed him a piece of paper and a pen. 'Go on.'

Dylan scribbled notes. 'I'll be expecting him sooner rather than later then,' he said before putting the phone down. He looked across at Jen and sighed. 'Somebody wanting to jump off the Scarbottom Bridge onto the motorway. They're sending a traffic car for me as they've had to stop the traffic so they want me there as soon as...'

'Possible,' she said.

He got up off the sofa. 'I'll just go throw my jeans and a jumper on. Hopefully I'll be back for breakfast,' he said teasingly. But she knew there was an element of truth in his bravado.

\*\*\*

Blue lights illuminating the dark skies were the first indication that the car was nearing the door. Screeching brakes and skidding tyres the next. 'That should get the neighbours talking,' said Dylan as he briefly kissed Jen. No sooner had he done than he was gone. The lounge felt empty and Jen bereft. She could hear sirens ebbing away in the distance.

'Have we got a name?' Dylan asked Control over the airways.

'A Mr James, sir. John James, a driver working as I understand for Prestigious Funeral Directors in Harrowfield.' Dylan held his stomach as the motion of the speeding car tossed him from side to side. They travelled along dark, narrow roads. 'Thank you,' he said. His voice sounded alien to him.

'Just for your info, he's known to us. It's not the first time he's been up there recently.'

'We'll be there as quick as it is humanly possible, or sooner if my driver has his way.'

Dylan's advanced driver was an experienced traffic officer called Ray Green; nicknamed bullet, because he travelled everywhere at speed. As they moved away from the urban centre of Harrowfield, Ray turned his lights onto full beam. His reactions to other traffic, pedestrians and cyclists were to dip his headlights. This meant his visibility was somewhat reduced and he slightly let up on his speed at that time. Vehicles approached them with their headlights on full beam. Ray cursed. Dylan saw Ray's eyes glance to the nearside of the road instead of into the headlights and as soon as the vehicle had passed he returned to full beam. Bends and dips in the road were cloaked in darkness. Suddenly as they rounded a bend Ray slammed on the brakes. The car skidded dramatically but he managed to stay in control of the car. Dylan lunged forward, his seat belt dug into this shoulder and for a split second he thought he was going through the windscreen.

'Sorry boss, bloody cat. Wife would never forgive me if I'd hit it.'

'I think the idea is that you get me there alive, Ray. Cats have nine lives, haven't they?' he asked, exhaling. 'I've only got one.' His heart was pounding.

'But the wife's a cat lover,' he said, naming his five cats one by one as they weaved in and out of the traffic and cautiously through a red traffic light.'Just round this next corner boss and we'll be at the mouth of the bridge.'

Dylan was grateful. He was not sure if his stomach would have stood much more.

'All units,' came the announcement over the airways. 'We have one fatally injured male on the southbound carriageway of the motorway.'

'Too late boss, Mr James has gone over,' he said turning to Dylan. He slowed the car down and turned off the blue lights and the sirens.

Dylan received confirmation his services were no longer required.

'Back home then, boss?' PC Ray Green said matter of fact.

'Guess so,' Dylan said giving him a spontaneous glance of acute sadness. 'But no rush now, eh?' he asked.

'Point taken. I wonder what troubles a person has that makes them intent on jumping from such a great height?'

'Hopefully we'll never be in such a position to know. If only they knew they might survive but be in a hell of a lot of pain for a long time or disabled for the rest of their life… I wonder if they'd still do it?'

'It's the poor buggers who are travelling below when the jumper gives no warning about their intention that I feel sorry for. Fortunately this time he didn't go over straight away and they managed to stop all the motorway traffic below.'

'One thing for sure he won't be driving funeral cars any more. Carpe diem, Ray.'

'Aye, that's something this job teaches us alright, isn't it boss? To seize the day.'

# Chapter Sixteen

Jane Simpson was due in the Magistrates' Court at two o'clock, when CPS would apply for her to be remanded in custody. Dylan knew from experience, and as a matter of course that the defence would ask that she be bailed. They would tell the magistrates that she was vehemently denying all charges with good cause. Most of the time Dylan could write the script for the defence's approach before he got there.

Jacki Stanley a very experienced Crown Prosecutor had broached Dylan to see if he would give evidence at the remand hearing, which she felt would add weight to the application. He didn't mind, he wanted Jane Simpson where she couldn't obstruct the ongoing investigation.

'It's a difficult one for the Magistrates but if they listen carefully to the evidence they won't let the defence pull the wool over their eyes,' Jacki Stanley said.

\*\*\*

There was a note waiting for him on his desk at the station. A Mr Fisher had telephoned asking if he would call.

'What's this all about?' he asked Lisa.

'Your guess is as good as mine. He insisted on speaking to you. Wouldn't leave a message.'

Although he was still standing Dylan picked up his phone and commenced to dial.

'He's the boss over at the mortuary isn't he?' asked Lisa.

'Yes, Derek Harper's boss.'

'Mr Fisher. Jack Dylan. I'm returning your call.'

Dylan sat. His elbows were on his desk. His chin on his fist as he listened with intensity. 'You mean by "let him go" I take it that you've sacked him?' he asked. Lisa's ears pricked up and she stopped what she was doing.

'Yes, I caught him taking a picture of a deceased lady on his mobile phone today. It appears he has a fascination with tattoos. I ordered him to erase the image immediately. You can be assured you can forget about him. He won't be causing you any more problems. The matter has been dealt with. I wanted you to know.'

'Do you have Harper's home address, just in case we need to speak to him?'

117

'I do but... It's number 5, Hawthorne Terrace but... I don't think...'

'Thank you. I'll get that fed into our system.'

Dylan handed the information to Lisa. 'For the attention of the Incident Room staff, too,' he said.

'Sure,' she said.

In the Incident Room he saw Vicky and Paul Robinson in deep conversation.

'Vicky, Paul, my office please, we need a quick scrum down before court,' he said.

\*\*\*

It was almost time for the court appearance and Dylan picked up his briefcase. DC Andy Wormald was working with PC Tracy Petterson who they had managed to draft in on secondment. The defendant's telephone data had been received but they still needed to firm up on an address for Billy Simpson. 'Before you ask I'm coming to Magistrates Court for the remand of Jane Simpson but I was thinking County Court records might help us get an address, especially if they had filed for divorce,' said Dylan. 'And make sure everything is recorded on action forms, Vicky for the Incident Room, continuity and disclosure and I'll update the policy log.'

\*\*\*

According to Detective Sergeant Paul Robinson who was hard at work on the Kirsty Gallagher enquiry a vast amount of exhibits had been removed from her house. Swabs from the gas pipe had been taken and fingerprints lifted from the empty drawers in her bedroom amongst other places of interest to them.

'We are going through her letters, diaries etcetera to see if we can build up a background picture for her. She certainly liked her foreign holidays to exotic climes, but it appears she kept herself very much to herself.'

'Still interviewing people?'

'Yes. One interesting development is that one of the staff at the funeral directors where she worked for a short time suggested that the photograph from her car we showed him, looked like one of their employees.'

'Ensure the policy log is up to date and everything goes through the relevant Incident Room. There should be no mix ups with names to each of the investigations which are now called

Pullman for the Kirsty Gallagher enquiry and Mallard for the Billy Simpson murder.'

'We sound like a group of chuffin' train spotters. Which weirdo at HQ thinks up these bloody names?'

'Talking of weirdos, after Court I think we need to visit our mortuary attendant Derek Harper. He's been fired.'

'Has he?'

'Yes. I reckon it could be an interesting visit. Let's see what else he will tell us now he's been sacked by Fisher,' said Dylan.

\*\*\*

The Magistrates' Court was full with a relentless, chattering crowd: some of whom Dylan noticed had brought provisions. They were settled for the afternoon it seemed. There was a number of interesting cases listed.

It was raining outside and the courtroom smelt of wet clothes. The windows looked dirty and the room had a green glow about it due to the lighting.

Courts, both Magistrates' and Crown Court used to be imposing places and people had respect for them. In the past visitors wouldn't dare utter a sound or behave improperly within their walls for fear of contempt, thereby receiving the full wrath of Magistrate or Judge presiding. Nowadays it appeared people treated them as nothing more than a place of entertainment. The lead magistrate, one of three, was a large, stocky lady with a square face and a flat forehead: she had a mass of wild, thick grey hair and deep set eyes. Now and again she took a sip of water from a glass on the desk in front of her.

Jane Simpson was brought up from the cells by a police officer and sat in the dock. She looked weary and tired, but steadfast and determined. Simpson's expression suggested to Dylan that she was ill at ease. She sat with her hands clasped tight in her lap until she was asked to stand, by the lead magistrate.

Dylan took the witness stand, when asked to do so. He looked about the public gallery and hoped that there would be someone, a lone male that perhaps appeared to be supporting Jane Simpson. Much to his disappointment there was no one to fit that description. Having given his name and occupation he took the oath and spoke to the Magistrates.

'Your worships, I have attended this afternoon to reinforce the serious nature of the case before you, for which Jane Simpson appears charged with murder. The facts are not as they appear at face value. I confirm we have no evidence of a break in at the defendant's house, one murder weapon is proving to be elusive and the injuries to Mrs Simpson's ex-husband, according to the pathologist, are not consistent with how she states they were caused. Her account of what took place that night is a lie. She would have us believe that she was attacked by a masked intruder and his fatal injuries were caused by her defending herself. At her trial this will be proven to be false. Jane Simpson has no ties to the area and because her story has not been accepted, I believe she may abscond. It may be that there is also an accomplice out there and that she will interfere with the course of justice, thereby obstructing the investigation, if she is released on bail. This murder was premeditated and the aftermath, such as her arrest, was anticipated in my view. I feel that given the opportunity she would not make herself available for a future trial.'

Jane Simpson kept her head bowed. She was very still and silent.

Yvonne Best her solicitor had no questions for Detective Inspector Dylan but told the Court that in her view she thought her client was lucky to be alive after such an attack by an intruder. She stated her client denied knowing him due to the mask he was wearing, until she saw the photo of her dead ex-husband taken at the scene by the police, with the mask removed. 'My client will abide by any restrictions placed upon her, no matter how restrictive,' she said. 'Prison, I'm sure you will agree is no place for her. She is the victim in this case.'

Dylan was impressed with how she pleaded her client's case but hoped the magistrates would remand Jane Simpson nevertheless. He observed the countenance on the faces of the magistrates before they retired to the back room, asking the clerk to join them.

Ten minutes later they returned to inform Ms Simpson that she would be remanded in custody. When Dylan heard the ruling he was conscious of a feeling of great relief.

Jane Simpson didn't flinch when the police officer alongside her touched her arm. She was ushered from the dock and back down the steps, to the cells. Dylan wondered if Jane Simpson had expected the ruling. He knew her solicitors Perfect and Best would be appealing to a Judge in Chambers at the first opportunity and there she may well get bail. Dylan was aware that her solicitors would be considering this, but would make enquiries to see which judge was where before making the appointment. Some Judges were known for being more sympathetic and others were renowned for their hefty sentencing and lack of compassion for the offender. One thing for sure, the legal team would be ensuring all the legal aid forms were completed and signed promptly. A murder enquiry was a good source of income for them.

Dylan left the courtroom with Vicky. The sky had cleared and he was feeling restless.

'Come on, let's go see what Derek Harper has got to say, shall we?'

'Do we have to, he gives me the heebie jeebies?'

'Don't worry, you're probably not his type, Vicky... you've got a pulse and don't have a tattoo,' he said, with a glint in his eye. 'He's been taking pictures of dead bodies and has a fascination with tattoos seemingly. Let's see if we can find out what he's up to.'

'Urgh...' she said, taking the packet of Dylan's mints out of her pocket and handing one to him. 'How do you know I haven't got a tattoo?' she said.

# Chapter Seventeen

On the officers' approach to Derek Harper's house they could see that the downstairs curtains of Number 5, Hawthorne Terrace, Lee Mount were closed. As they got nearer they could see the linings were badly discoloured and haphazardly hung.

'Just so you know if we get offered a drink, I'll be refusing,' said Vicky.

'You're not the only one,' said Dylan.

'Bet his neighbours love him,' Vicky said, easing her scarf from around her neck as they arrived at the gate. She stopped. 'But it's just how I imagined his house would be, horrible and creepy... just like him.'

The gate was rusty and Vicky winced as she cut her finger on the catch. Blood seeped from the wound; her shoe found the gate and she kicked it the rest of the way open. Bouncing to and fro off the wall it broke away from its hinges and crashed to the floor. 'Oops,' she grimaced standing it carefully against the overgrown hedge. Dylan shook his head and sighed.

The two walked up the short path and turned down the ginnel at the side of the house before finding the back door. They were careful as to where they trod. The path was littered with debris held up by clumps of weeds. As Vicky stood under the porch and knocked on the door, Dylan scanned the back yard with his expert eye. They both paused, cocked their heads and listened for a moment. Vicky reached forward and gave the door handle a turn but it was locked. They looked at each other. Vicky shrugged her shoulders and raised her eyebrows at Dylan then turned and followed him around the corner and into the back yard. It was surprisingly empty, quiet and still. There was a brick built shed behind them that might have once been a coal bunker and attached presumably would have been the outside toilet which was standard for the type and age of the terrace house.

'God, it stinks out here.'

'Probably the drains under the yard from the old khazi. Outside toilet to you, Vicky. A bit before your time,' said Dylan.

'My granny had one at the farm and she used to have us cutting newspapers up into squares and threading it on string to put behind the door.'

Most outside toilets had been knocked down long ago and Dylan could understand why when he smelt the aroma which was making Vicky now gag into a tissue. The old soot-blackened brick walls were in shadow, and so too was a tree that pushed its foliage through into the light. The buds of its leaves were making an appearance and old, dark brown, rotting leaves lay beneath it on the flags.

'The mints not working?' asked Dylan.

'No, not this time,' she said. She clenched her teeth, shuddered and showed him the goose bumps that had arisen on her forearm.

Dylan walked across the flagstones and hammered on the door with his fist. To his surprise it was answered immediately. Stood before them in a grubby white vest and Y-fronts was Derek Harper. He had a grey tuft of hair on his chin like a tusk and looked a lot older now than his years.

'What do you want, I'm busy,' he said, clearing his throat and spitting into a filthy rag that he used as a handkerchief.

Dylan re-introduced themselves to him.

'I know who you are. Like I said, what do want? You lot cost me my job, isn't that enough?'

'Aren't you going to invite us in?' Dylan said walking past him into the kitchen.

'And get some clothes on will you. That's not a pleasant sight,' Vicky said, walking in behind Dylan. Her eyes strayed everywhere in the room other than look at his half naked frame. The kitchen had a heavy cooking lardy smell about it. The doors leading off it were firmly closed. Harper muttered something that neither officer could make out, his upper lip appeared to writhe back from his teeth. He turned and reached for a greasy mac that had been strewn over the back of an upright, plastic chair.

'Well? What do you want?' he asked

'Sit down. We'll ask the questions.'

Harper sat.

'Tell me why you were taking pictures of naked dead bodies?' asked Dylan.

Derek Harper's every movement had a deliberate hesitation as if he was used to waiting on an order.

'Well?'

'Fisher told you. I might have known. He said to get rid of it. Come on, it was a joke.'

'And who the hell do you know who would find that sort of thing funny?'

His face was grey and tense. His long neck showed the strain.

Dylan sat down very carefully as though he considered if the seat was fit for purpose. He leaned towards Derek Harper. Derek Harper was hesitant. His lips were pale.

'Some people I know do but I'm not going to name them.'

Dylan raised his eyebrows and tilted his head back slightly as he did so. 'The dead body. It was a female wasn't it?'

'A dead female? Yes. Look it was just a one off.'

'Can we have a look at your mobile, Mr Harper?'

Vicky flinched as if she'd been bitten, and bending down rubbed her leg above her boot with frantic fingers. Derek Harper looked at her for a long moment. 'Why? I told you I erased it,' he said, his purposeful gaze returning to Dylan's face.

'And if we believed everything people told us, Mr Harper, we'd never get anywhere. Mobile phone, please?' he asked, holding out his hand.

'Battery's flat.'

'Mobile!'

Harper hesitated, his eyes grew darker.

'Don't you need a warrant?'

'Do you want me to get one? We...' he said, glancing up at Vicky. 'We were hoping you'd co-operate. Or do you have something to hide?' he asked, staring at Harper with sharp, squinty eyes and a hard mouth drawn in a tight line.

Derek Harper's face twitched, his brows knitted together tightly. Dylan knew he had touched a nerve. Now, which way was Derek Harper going to play it, he wondered.

'It's in my den,' he said getting to his feet. 'If you'll just wait there.' He turned. The officers were right behind him. 'I'll get it. I said wait there,' he said, turning to face them with his hand raised. With a speediness he didn't look capable of he opened the door and slipped inside the adjoining room. He attempted to close the door but Dylan just as rapidly put his foot out to stop it.

'Just making sure you don't try anything,' Dylan said when Derek Harper came nose to nose with him.

Derek Harper took his hand from the door jamb and stepped back into the den. Dylan's foot kicked it wide open.

What the officers saw inside didn't seem to belong to the rest of the house. There were two large computer screens facing them, one with a web cam attached and in front of a big modern desk was two tall, leather executive chairs that Chief Superintendent Hugo-Watkins would have been proud to own.

'Welcome to my little den,' he said, thrusting his hand in the far side desk drawer. His fingers closed on the object he sought and pulling it out he forced himself to put the mobile phone into Dylan's outstretched hand. Turning towards the officer he held out his arms as if to usher them, albeit not touching them, back into the kitchen.

Dylan passed the mobile to Vicky.

Derek Harper closed the den door and stood with his back to it.

'What are you hiding, Derek?' Dylan asked watching intently for any reaction.

'Nothing, I'm not hiding anything. That's mine. It's private. I don't like people messing with my things.'

Vicky addressed Derek Harper. 'It's flat, the battery's flat,' she said, indicating the phone. 'Where's your charger?'

'I'm not sure. I don't know.' He was trembling.

'Convenient. Derek, what's the problem here? If there's nothing on the mobile to incriminate you, why the stalling? We are going to check it either here or down at the station. Your choice.'

Dylan had his back to the kitchen window. He watched Harper go back into his office. Within seconds he returned with a lead. Vicky plugged it into a socket in the kitchen and was soon looking at pictures on its camera. Her breathing was laboured as she stared intently at the images.

'And now we know why you didn't want us to look, don't we?' she said.

'I should have erased them, shouldn't I?' he asked.

'You shouldn't have taken them in the first place. You have no idea of the seriousness of this, do you?' she said, holding the phone out for Dylan to see a selected image.

'What else are we going to find, Mr Harper?' Dylan said.

Derek Harper was physically shaking and he paused before replying.

'I asked you is there anything else?' Dylan said. He swallowed hard.

'Nothing. Now go. Leave me alone.'

Dylan flicked through more images. 'I've seen enough. Get uniform here to transport him to the station, Vicky. I don't want him in my car. Derek Harper, you are under arrest for possession, publishing and distributing obscene images. You haven't just taken pictures of dead people. You have arranged them in poses of a sexual nature. Some of these are of young children. Get hold of the paedophile and high tech crime unit, Vicky. Some of these images I'd say are level five.'

'I think I might need a solicitor,' he said.

Dylan gaze was fixed. 'You will need a solicitor.'

'Can I get dressed?'

'No. I don't think the custody sergeant is going to mind,' said Vicky.

Dylan steered him to the doorway. 'The uniform car won't be long. I don't know about you, Vicky but I could do with some air.'

'Get hold of Sergeant Clegg. We need Operational Support and some detectives over here. I want this place taking apart. I want the obscene publications unit and our computer geeks here, too.'

'I wonder if we'll find images of Kirsty Gallagher?' Vicky asked.

'No doubt. We also need to find out who his friends are...'

# Chapter Eighteen

Derek Harper was marshalled into the car. Vicky eyed the uniform officers putting a hand over his head as he stepped into the vehicle so he didn't hurt himself. 'A bump on his head might do him a bit of good,' she said to Dylan,

'Who's the CSI supervision today? Give them a shout. We need Crime Scene Investigators here to photograph this set up.'

Vicky spoke Dylan's instruction over the radio. Walking to the far side of the back yard Dylan kicked about in the overgrowth. 'Looking for anything particular?' she said. 'You're likely to get something horrible on the end of your shoe doing that.'

'This outhouse.'

'Don't go there. That smell is vile,' she said wrinkling her nose. 'Look here though, a new padlock. Have you got something in the car we can force it with?'

'A jemmy?' he asked.

'That'll do.'

Dylan handed her his keys. Vicky turned on her heels and was back directly, jemmy in hand. Seconds later Dylan was forcing the clasp but the door had seen better days and the screws sprung before the clasp on the padlock broke. 'Stand back,' he said as he grabbed the door with both hands and pulled it off its hinges.

The smell rushed at them with a physical force and they stepped back. 'What the fuck? It's like rotting cabbage.' Vicky gasped. Dylan stepped further back into her path. Her foot slipped on the slimy flagstones and Dylan reached out to catch her from falling.

'Careful,' he said.

He turned his attention back to the building. The smell had taken his breath away. Taking his handkerchief out of his pocket and putting it over his nose and mouth he went back to the doorway to peer inside. Stepping forwards into the dark abyss he could see a pile of flattened, dry boxes. They weren't damp or rusty as the rest of the contents appeared to be. He picked one up carefully by the corner and underneath he saw the dirty, greasy foot of a human corpse and just above the ankle he could see a butterfly tattoo. 'He's got some fucking talking to do,' he said. The head when uncovered was a grinning mass of teeth, nasal bones and skull with shreds of flesh where tongue and pharynx had been and as Vicky looked on a solitary ant crawled out of the yawning mouth.

'Is it Kirsty Gallagher do you think, boss?'

'I don't know...' he said, coughing as though he would be sick. 'But we need to get booted and suited before we touch anything else.' Dylan used his radio to speak to HQ Control. 'We have discovered a rotting body at Number 5, Hawthorne Terrace. I'm treating it as a murder scene and I require uniform presence as soon as possible to keep the scene sterile and to cordon off the area to stop prying eyes. '

Dylan was aware of a sense of horror. All his being seemed to stiffen with a new determination. 'What have we stumbled on?'

'Fuck knows. Let's move down the path a bit away from this stench. Harper's no previous. I ran him through the computer after his comments about Kirsty Gallagher at the mortuary.'

'More to the point, his computers will hopefully tell us more.'

'With some luck we will get a lead that is only possible by the explosion of the social networking sites that people like him subscribe to, via the history on his computer he probably thinks he's deleted.'

'It's going to be an interesting interview that's for sure but before that we need to see exactly what we have and secure evidence. At least then we may have a clue as to what we are dealing with.'

*\*\**

Back-up came round the side of the house in the form of uniform and specialised units. Each, with their own focus to move the investigation forwards with the experience they had in their own field. The area was sealed. PS Clegg had two teams searching to move things along quickly and as one searched the house the other commenced on the outhouse.

'I don't care if you have to pull up all the floorboards, whatever it takes to get me a result,' Dylan said to him. 'Take the bloody lot apart if you have to.'

Crimes Scene Investigation Supervisor, Karen Ebdon was at the scene along with Stuart Viney and Louisa Edwards. Suited and booted they were busy taking the necessary photographs. The cardboard was being bagged up for later examination. The Custody staff at Harrowfield Police Station were informed what

128

was happening. Derek Harper would be arrested on suspicion of murder as soon as Dylan and Vicky returned.

'I want him under constant observation,' Dylan instructed.

***

The smell in the yard was growing ever more overpowering. Dylan saw experienced officers stand back and take a minute to get their breath. Now they had sight of the full decomposing body which was mostly wrapped in polythene sheeting.

'What do you want to do, boss?' asked Simon Clegg pointing to the corpse.'I think the body would be better being removed in that state to secure evidence, don't you? It can be unwrapped at the mortuary.'

'Have you done taking the necessary photographs, Karen?' She nodded. 'I agree Simon, arrange for the body to be taken to the mortuary as it is,' Dylan said.

'It's Kirsty, isn't it boss?' asked Vicky.

'Time will tell but yeah, it's looking that way. He's at the mortuary when she goes missing and we find the body of a female in his outhouse.'

'He's a dirty, evil, bastard.'

'Don't mince your words will you? Although, I have to say you're probably right on this occasion. Believe me I've seen worse and the offenders have laughed in my face in interview. Don't let your feelings get in the way or colour your judgement. He's just a misunderstood individual that needs our help, some would say.'

'Yeah right, we'll help him alright to get him locked away forever.'

'Stay focussed on securing the necessary evidence. It's the key to everything and as much as we can do for the deceased right now. Talking of which we need to find the key to the outhouse to show he was in control of it.'

'He's still a fucking twat,' she said pulling off her protective suit that was no longer required.

Karen overheard her rant and pulling off her face mask Dylan could see her smiling. A light relief perhaps from what she had been photographing. Dylan de-suited. All his garments were bagged and tagged along with Vicky's as an exhibit.

Afterwards he spoke with the search team leader whose team was busily searching the house 'They've discovered a mass of sex toys and lubricants. Not a total surprise,' he said to Vicky as they walked back down the path towards his car. 'Everyday tools of a sex offender.'

*** 

The roads were busy. Dylan and Vicky sat in the traffic.

'So acting Detective Sergeant Hardacre what crime do you think Derek Harper has committed?' Dylan said.

'Well if it is the body of Kirsty Gallagher, then at the very least he's stolen a body?'

'Can you steal a body?'

'Well somebody did.'

'But under the Theft Act is a human body classed as property?'

He threw her a glance and she shrugged her shoulders. 'Ask me one on sport?'

'You need to know these things, Vicky. It doesn't fit the criteria of property under the theft act therefore the offence of theft fails. So it will be obstructing the Coroner and theft of maybe the shroud or sheet it was wrapped in.'

'I think maybe I need a refresher course to brush up on the finer detail of the law.'

'That's not a bad thing especially as, as a supervisor, the troops will expect you to know.'

'I could always tell them to ask you?' she said, a little smile appearing on her face.

'But what else has he been up to do you think? And if it is confirmed to be Kirsty Gallagher's body do you think he may have had something to do with her death too?'

'He doesn't look like the man in the picture that we recovered from her car,' she said thoughtfully.

'And who's to say that's the murderer?' Dylan said as they pulled into the police station car park. 'I need to call Jen, it's not going to be an early finish like I'd hoped.'

'Just had a thought,' said Vicky.

'Now, don't go straining yourself.'

'Very funny. No canteen but the chippy is open across the road. Fancy fish and chips for tea?'

He handed her a ten pound note.

'Vicky?' He shouted as she walked away.

'Yeah.'

'Don't forget lashings of salt and vinegar – and bits,' he said

130

He took the opportunity alone to ring Jen, who at that moment in time was staring down the barrel of a gun.

# Chapter Nineteen

'Is that your phone ringing or mine?' asked Rita, as she tied the exhibit label to the firearm with a piece of string.

'Mine.' Jen put her hand into her pocket but by the time she had got it out the caller had rung off. 'It's Dylan,' she said looking at the image on the screen. 'I should be home by now.'

'Should you go?'

'No, I know Maisy is fine at the childminder's. Chantall will have given her her tea by now. I'll help you get this lot booked in first.'

'You're a star,' Rita said smiling at her friend. 'It's good to have you back. I can't ever imagine Donna getting her hands dirty like this, can you? I won't be a minute. This last load should empty the temporary store. You okay in here while I go get it?'

***

Dylan walked into the station just as Rita was heading back out to the permanent store in the yard, with the property.

'Jen's inside,' she said, nodding her head in the direction of the store in the yard. He followed.

The cache of firearms inside was huge. 'Where did all these come from?' asked Dylan as he squeezed Jen around her waist. 'Hello you,' he said.

'The amnesty. We've had three hundred and seventy three guns and seven thousand rounds of ammunition handed in so far across the area, including a rocket launcher, a gun fashioned from a walking stick and a home-made cannon,' said Rita.

'Unbelievable. But just one of these weapons off the streets,' he said picking up a .357 Magnum revolver and propelling it in his hand, 'is bound to save a life.'

'Oh, that one's not from the amnesty it's from another job.'

Rita picked up the form on which the items were listed. 'A Mr James. Didn't have a current gun licence it appears. But he's dead anyway now.'

'How come?'

'Suicide. The jumper from the other night. Turns out he's was bit of a perv too by all accounts.'

'Yep! We won't be worrying too much about him then will we?'

'Where did you learn that trick?' asked Jen who stood opened mouthed facing Dylan.

Dylan spun the revolver around in his hand again with ease. 'Ah,' he said tapping his nose with his finger. 'I can still surprise you, that's good.' Dylan grinned 'You not clocked off yet, missus?' he asked, putting the gun down and pulling her towards him.

'No, but I won't be long now. You look tired,' she said reaching up to touch his face. 'That belonged to the guy you went out to try and negotiate with the other night?'

'Yes. Hey, have those been checked?' asked Dylan, reaching out quickly towards Rita who had her hand on a trigger of a semi-automatic pistol pointed in their direction. It was his turn to look concerned. He took the gun off her with the confidence of someone trained in the act.

'I guessed so. They were tagged in the temporary store,' Rita said looking a little taken aback.

'I know I go on about never assuming but the exception to that rule is always assume a gun is loaded,' he said, with a furrowed brow.

'How would I check?' asked Rita. 'Go on, give us a quick lesson.'

Dylan obliged by picking up the gun nearest to him. 'Point it in a safe direction. Since the slide lock is closed you'd check that a round isn't still in the chamber. On this particular one by pulling the slide back and raising the slide lock.' He laid the gun down with the muzzle facing in a safe direction even though it was empty.

'And if it was loaded? What would I do then?'

'If there are rounds of ammo in the magazine, press down slightly on the top Round and with your thumb, slide the Round out. You'd have to keep doing that until they'd all been removed. Now, ladies, store them all somewhere safely.'

'What do people do this for?' Rita said, picking up a sawn-off shotgun.

'A modified shotgun is more manoeuvrable and a lot lighter than a full size shotgun, see,' he said handing the gun to Jen, who recoiled from handling the monstrous looking weapon.

Dylan laughed. 'However, remember decreasing the length of the gun will reduce its accuracy and increase the recoil. If the person holding the gun has a hand on top of the barrel...' Dylan indicated this by placing his left hand facing downwards on the shortened barrel, 'they are aware of the recoil, and they would do this to stop it firing upwards.'

Jen screwed up her eyes. 'I can't believe you hadn't told me... Where on earth did you learn that?' she asked.

'I told you, I'm trained,' he said as he turned on his heels. 'Bye love,' he said blowing her a kiss. 'It's looking like a late one so don't wait up,' he called over his shoulder. The property door slammed shut behind him.

***

The guns were safely locked in the secure cabinet. Jen looked down at her dirty hands. 'What's up Jen?' Rita asked as she followed Jen out of the store and locked the door behind them.

'I don't know... Sometimes I just get a glimpse of another side of Jack Dylan and realise how little I know about him.'

'I guess we never know everything about someone, no matter how close we are.'

'I know but you'd think... Oh, don't mind me I'm just being silly.'

***

Dylan was in the custody suite ensuring that Derek Harper had himself a solicitor and was updating the staff on duty. Now they had found a body at Mr Harper's address he was going nowhere. 'CID will be down to arrest him with murder any time now,' he said.

'You may be right there, sir, but he might be going somewhere rather sooner than you thought. We've an ambulance en route.'

'Bloody hell,' Dylan said. 'Not that old nugget?'

The Custody Officer nodded his head. 'I don't think for a minute... but better to be safe than sorry. His solicitor has asked for a call back once we know what's happening with him.'

'Who's he got, Perfect and Best by any chance?'

'No, it's David Scacchetti from over Leeds way. Don't know him.'

Dylan raised his eyebrows. 'Me neither. Let me know when you know what's happening too will you?'

***

Acting Detective Sergeant Vicky Hardacre looked downhearted when she heard the news.

'Look on the positive. It gives us a bit of time whilst his custody clock is stopped,' he said. 'Everything happens for a reason. He won't gain anything.'

'You think it's Kirsty, boss?' asked Paul.

'I think so, yes. The post-mortem is set for half seven tomorrow morning. We'll get the samples checked as soon as possible. The body is in a pretty decomposed state.'

'Is he the killer do you think or just a weirdo?'

'Likely to be the latter, but who knows? We have to keep an open mind and let the facts speak for themselves.'

'I'd planned to see the guy in the photo tomorrow morning. I've been given his duties so I thought I'd drop on him unannounced. See what reaction I get.'

'Good.'

'I've got some good news for you from the Forensic lab,' he said.

'You have? What's that?' Dylan's eyes widened.

'Early indications confirm two different hair samples have been found in the mask Billy Simpson was wearing, and from the house-to-house enquiries it would appear our Jane had a regular male visitor who drove a transit van.'

'When was it last seen?'

'Don't know any more at the moment.'

Dylan's phone rang. 'That sounds interesting, Paul,' he said as he picked it up.

\*\*\*

It was dark outside. Dylan stood at the window. The car park was all but bare, apart from a couple of uniform marked cars. Most of his team were out on enquiries, in the unmarked police vehicles. The search team at Derek Harper's house had finished for the night but he was told they would resume at first light. The technical team had Harper's computers and were about to start to examine the information thereon. Already they knew there was a vast amount of images of a sexual nature stored on various files and each file would be subject to scrutiny.

Harper lived alone so it was likely only he had access to the computer, therefore Dylan hoped he wouldn't have gone to elaborate lengths to conceal things. He reminded uniform of the need for security to be retained overnight at the scene.

Dylan tapped his fingers on the desk awaiting an update on Derek Harper from the hospital. The telephone rang and he picked it up. 'Dylan,' he said.

'Claire Rose, press office. We've got a lot of media attention about an incident at 5, Hawthorne Terrace, today. Is there anything I can tell them?'

'You've drawn the short straw again, Claire?'

'Yeah,' she said. 'I'm working a split shift.'

'Unfortunately not. We need to keep this one under wraps until at least tomorrow. In fact until we know exactly what it is we're dealing with. Sorry, I know it's a pain for you and the press but I'm not doing it to be awkward. You know me, I'd give them a story if I could. I promise I'll update you as soon as I can.'

No sooner had he replaced the receiver than it rang again. 'Patrol's gonna love you, sir,' said the Custody Officer.

'Why's that?'

'Not only have you got their officers guarding the scene at Harper's home address but they're also going to be needed to sit with him at the hospital overnight. Doctor has checked him over, announced he's okay but they want to keep him in for obs as a precaution.'

'Thanks for that.'

Dylan got up from behind his desk and walked into the Incident Room. 'Okay, let's go home. Derek Harper will be in hospital till tomorrow with his alleged chest pains, so that gives us a little breathing space. Go get your heads down and I'll see you bright and early.'

As Dylan walked back to his office he could hear the intermittent mumblings of the team. Oh, for his bed and Jens soft, warm body. He yawned.

*\*\**

All lights were lit in the house when Dylan parked his car in the driveway. The only explanation he could think of was Maisy wouldn't settle. As he put his key in the lock he heard voices.

Penny was slumped on the sofa with an empty wine glass in one hand and a bottle in the other. Jen held a sleeping Maisy over her shoulder.

'Hello, Dylan,' Penny said with a drawl and a glint in her eye. 'I've been waiting for you.'

Jen put her finger to her lips. 'Shh... Penny. You'll wake Maisy.' Jen's eyes went to the ceiling. 'I'll go and put her in her cot.'

Penny winked at Dylan. A slow and very deliberate closing of one eye. She dropped the bottle on the floor. Dylan went to retrieve it and Penny patted the cushion next to her and in doing so Dylan saw the plasters.

'Oops,' she said putting her hand to her mouth.

'Don't worry, it's empty,' he said. 'What've you done there, Penny?' he asked pointing to the marks on her arm. Jen walked into the room and shut the door quietly behind her.

'Just a spot of horse play. Come sit next to me and I'll share the details...' she said. Her voice slurring. She purposefully patted the cushion next to her with more vigour.

He looked at Jen who shrugged her shoulders. 'I'll put the kettle on shall I and make us a nice strong drink of coffee?'

'And I'll let Max out,' Dylan said following her into the kitchen.

'Don't be long, Dylan. I need to get an update before I go...' Penny called after him.

Jen was standing filling the kettle at the kitchen sink.

'When did she get here?'

'She was still here when I got home.'

Dylan looked puzzled.

'She'd been to clean,' she whispered. 'She's not been home. Insisted on seeing you.'

'But it's past midnight,' he said, watching an excited Max who was dancing on his toes at the back door. 'I hope she isn't going to make a habit of it.'

'You and me alike. The bottle of red she brought with her has been empty for an hour and she'd already downed a bottle of ours, but she insisted on waiting till you came home for an update.'

'An update on what?' he asked.

Jen shrugged her shoulders. 'I don't know,' she said.

'What's she saying she's done to her wrists?' He opened the door and Max barked loudly bounding backwards and forwards at the fence perimeter.

'An Indian burn ... something to do with a game her and her new boyfriend play, and no I'm not sharing the details it sounds gross!'

'Max!' Dylan shouted. 'You'll wake the bloody neighbours,' he said, his voice quietening to a whisper. 'That's no burn, it looks more she's been self-harming.'

'What, Penny? No... Max!' Jen called crossly. 'But I think she will do just about anything for him.'

No amount of calling would bring Max in. The security light illuminated the whole garden. Dylan could see Max at the fence and he went and grabbed him by the collar.

'I've got an early start tomorrow. A post-mortem at half seven. It's going to be a long day. I'm not up to idle chat,' he said to Jen through clenched teeth as he led Max into the kitchen.

'No need to worry,' said Jen handing him a cup of coffee. 'Just been in with Penny's coffee and she's spark out.'

'What?'

She put her finger over his lips. 'Let's leave her where she is shall we, she can't drive home in that state? You go up for a shower.'

'Her car wasn't outside,' said Dylan.

'She must have got a lift and expected me to take her home. I'll throw a cover over her.'

'I guess it sounds like a plan,' he said.

# Chapter Twenty

Jen eyes scrunched into a squint as she looked at the clock on her bedside table. She heard the front door close and footsteps on the flagstones under the window, a car door slammed and a car drove off. The clock read half-past five and Dylan was in the bathroom shaving. She struggled to open her eyes, rolled over and rose onto her elbow. He switched off the en-suite light and stumbled into the corner of the dressing table. 'Bloody hell,' he mumbled.

'Put the light on. I'm awake.' Jen groaned as she threw the duvet back.

'Go back to sleep,' Dylan whispered as he reached into his wardrobe for his shirt.

She didn't need telling twice. Jen flopped back down at Dylan's side of the bed. With a little moan she turned and pulled the duvet up over her shoulders and nuzzled her face into his pillow. Dylan picked up his shoes and as quiet as he could he bent over to kiss her. 'Fucking hell,' he said through clenched teeth as he stubbed his toe on the hard piece of wood under the bed. Jen couldn't help but smile. He hobbled away cursing.

'How many times will you do that?' she groaned sleepily. 'Why on earth do you keep that…'

'Just in case,' he said.

'Just in case of what?' she said as he closed the bedroom door quietly behind him. 'Just in case of what?'

'The next thing she knew Maisy was rattling her cot sides. 'Mommy, Daddy,' she shouted.

On entering the lounge with Maisy in her arms she saw it was empty. *I'll see you at work,* said the note from Penny that was left on top of the folded duvet. 'Where's Penny gone?' Jen asked her daughter.

'I kno know,' Maisy said raising her hands palms upwards.

\*\*\*

Dylan arrived at the mortuary. It was seven fifteen. It was dark, cold, damp and felt slightly eerie to be entering at this time of day. Would he get confirmation that the body they had found was that of missing Kirsty Gallagher? If so it was paramount that they ascertained a cause of death.

The pathologist was Daniel Jones. The young, athletic man before him set about preparing for the task in hand swiftly and with little fuss. There was no flamboyant gestures or tall stories, funny or otherwise at Dr Jones's post-mortems, Dylan knew from experience.

'Busy?' Dylan asked, as he hung up his jacket and put on his coveralls.

'Yes. They've got them lined up here for me till six o'clock tonight,' he said as he pulled latex gloves from a box and offered the same to DC Andy Wormald, the exhibits officer who blew into them like a balloon to make it easier to ease over his large hands. Talcum powder puffed out and he coughed.

What a thought, one post-mortem a day was bad enough for him. Dylan grimaced as he popped a couple of extra strong mints in his mouth.

'I couldn't afford to keep myself in these if I did your job,' he said, offering Daniel the packet.

'Your crutch?' he asked.

Dylan nodded.

'We all have a prop,' he said.

***

The team consisting of CSI Supervisor Karen Ebdon, Exhibits Officer DC Andy Wormald and DI Jack Dylan stood above the small skeletal frame. The mortuary assistant was in attendance.

'We have to be particularly careful when performing a post-mortem on badly decomposed bodies because tissues become more delicate as time passes. Don't be surprised if the brain is intact when we remove the calvarium, and then disintegrates completely as a result of the disruption of the arachnoid membrane which supports the liquefying parenchyma, when we attempt to remove it.'

The skin on the palms of the hands and feet of the woman's body had begun to de-glove and was darker in colour. The pathologist offered an explanation.

'This can be due to thermal exposure too – such as fires and immersions.'

'Can we still get fingerprints?' asked Dylan.

'Yes, the epidermis commonly retains enough ridge detail to allow fingerprints to be obtained.'

'Might assist identification boss, shall I take them?' asked Andy.

Dylan nodded.

140

There was a constant clicking of the camera. Karen Ebdon was in full flow.

'The eyes have gone,' said Daniel. 'We can see decomposition is advanced by the green discolouration of the skin and generalised bloating which begins in the abdomen. Although here parts of her skin have a healthier colouring, not the pale blue or grey we would expect. There is a subsequent skin slippage.'

Dylan tried desperately to concentrate his mind on the investigation as the body cavity was opened and the putrid smell became intense. He thrust his hand into his pocket and sought his mints. This was one of the times during a post-mortem he was glad he hadn't eaten breakfast.

'You okay?' he asked Andy and Karen.

The exhibits officer didn't take his eyes off the decomposing organs in the chest cavity but nodded his head. The lungs were deep purple. Karen's eyes found his and she closed them briefly in acknowledgement of his question also nodding her head.

'Congestion,' said Daniel, holding the organ in his hand before weighing it. The mortuary attendant noted the weight.

There was gaseous distension of the intestines. 'The smell is hydrogen sulphide, methane...'

'I think we can assume that wherever this body has been kept there were carnivores such as rodents. Can you see the yellow based defect and scalloped edges? Third metacarpal and proximal phalanx. Fifth metacarpal and proximal phalanx,' he continued.

Eventually it was over.

'There are no obvious signs of injury and further tests will confirm what I think, that carbon monoxide poisoning is the cause of her death.'

'A distinct possibility, considering the evidence that had been ascertained from her house where she was found dead,' said Dylan. 'Have you been to the house, Andy? Did you notice the carbon monoxide detector?'

'Yes sir.'

'We are going to need dental impressions to confirm it is Kirsty, aren't we? Even though we have fingerprints. I'm pretty confident it is. And we are going to have to wait for the test results to confirm the cause of death. If only we had that confirmation at our fingertips because later we'll be going into interview with Derek Harper and we need to be precise.'

Outside, the morning air never felt so good to Dylan. He could only liken it to a cold shower on a sweltering hot day. He filled his lungs repeatedly with the cool fresh air as he walked the short distance to his car. 'Thanks,' he called out to the team. 'See you back at the nick.'

\*\*\*

It was quarter to eleven and he was on his way back to the police station. The roads were heavily congested. His stomach rumbled.

\*\*\*

Jen walked into the office to find the personal files of officers strewn all over her desk. She saw one of the cabinets drawers had been emptied. She lifted her arms in the air. Rita who was sat opposite her shrugged her shoulders. 'Don't look at me, I've only just come up from the stores,' she said. Donna was day off and Margaret was on the telephone. She covered the receiver. 'Avril wants them all updating on the computer system asap,' she said.

'Hence her wanting me in today! Guess that's me tied to the desk for the duration then,' she said to Rita, pulling a face.

'Guess so, kid,' she replied winking at her and making a clicking sound with her tongue.

Jack Dylan's file was in her hands, 'Hey, I might actually enjoy this though,' she said thumbing through the paperwork therein. 'Don't tell, Beaky,' she said.

Rita's phone rang and an animated conversation ensued. 'From Pontefract you say? How about sending me some Pontefract cakes then?'

Jen smiled broadly at her friend, who grinned back. Rita would make a friend in an empty house as her mum would have said.

Settled in the corner of the room with a cup of tea Jen started to read. Inputting the data even for her husband was laborious and she looked on the rest of the pile heaped on her desk ruefully. Page by page she felt as if she was passing through the years with officer Jack Dylan. She was thrilled to read his application that he'd submitted to join up nearly twenty years before and smiled at the picture of him then. Twenty-three years old. She laughed out loud. Rita glanced across the room. 'Sorry,' she said putting a hand to her mouth. 'Oh, bless him, how cute was he with that side parting and slicked back hair... and that moustache!' Jen said holding up the picture for Margaret to see. 'That's when he joined CID.'

'The CID moustache,' said Rita. 'They all had one back in the day.'

Jen touched the image of his face. 'Black and white photographs always make people look very serious, don't they?'

'Sad thing is I remember it well,' said Margaret.

'How long have you been here?'

'Oh, fixtures and fittings me, love... Dylan looked but a boy, I think that moustache was intended to make him look older.'

Dylan's promotion board assessment results were all excellent. She beamed with pride. He'd never shared that information. So many commendations and recommendations for the next rank by his supervisors. He'd not even hinted. He'd only spent two years in uniform. She could recall him telling her about the starched collars and the helmets of the uniform, giving him a red ring around his neck and forehead. No wonder he couldn't wait to get out of it. Burglary squad, Vice Squad, this Operation, that Operation, this Commendation, that Commendation, then a minute sheet that made her jaw drop. He was accepted to the firearms specialist unit. She inputted the date. 10th June 1998.

'That's funny,' Jen said out loud.

'What's funny?' asked Margaret.

'There is a chunk of his personal file missing.'

'Missing?'

'There shouldn't be...' she said with a scowl.

'Dylan went to work in a specialised unit in firearms HQ and then there is nothing... till he comes back here. Not an application to come to division... nothing. Don't you think that's unusual?'

'Ah... that explains how he knew how to handle a gun,' said Rita.

'I think he came back here about four years ago. Not long before you arrived. Ask Beaky she'll tell you,' said Rita. 'His file has probably just never been returned, and most likely if he was on an undercover operation that was a need to know basis he would have only been known by a code name or number.'

'Yeah, that's probably it,' said Jen. 'But he's never mentioned his time in the unit, strange.'

***

Vicky walked into the Incident Room behind Dylan, it was buzzing.

'Shut that bloody door, Hardacre you weren't born in a barn were you?' shouted Ned.

'Take a walk till your hat floats,' said Vicky. Dylan watched her stick one finger up at him.

'Okay you two, it's not a playground,' said Dylan. 'Paul, my office please,' he said. Both Vicky and Ned raised their eyebrows at Dylan.

Dylan closed his office door behind Paul.

'I wonder who knitted his face and dropped a stitch,' said Vicky.

'Don't know,' said Ned. 'Better keep our heads down.'

'We've just come back from a post-mortem,' said Andy, flopping down in his chair.

'I'll go make coffee and toast shall I?' asked Lisa.

'Sounds like a great idea,' said Ned.

Andy shook his head. 'You must have hollow legs,' he said.

***

Paul Robinson was taking notes, Dylan talked and at the same time watched the movements of Paul's pen strokes. So engrossed was Paul in Dylan's update of the post-mortem's findings that when Lisa rapped on the glass, he didn't flinch. Dylan got up and opened the door to allow her to bring the tray in. She placed it directly on the desk. Paul's eyes never left Dylan's face and the DI didn't stop talking.

'Thanks Lisa,' said Dylan offering her a brief smile. Lisa left quickly, closing the door behind her.

'I want you to look at Kirsty's carbon monoxide detector.'

'Why am I looking for?'

'Just make sure it's been fingerprinted. I want to know the batteries have been checked for dabs too. The same with the smoke alarm.'

Dylan offered him the plate of toast, Paul refused.

Vicky stood at the door, tapped twice and walked in.

'Sit down,' said Dylan indicating the chair next to Paul at the other side of his desk. On doing so she passed him a document from Forensic. Dylan proceeded to read it.

'They've found semen stains on the bedding at Jane Simpson's house,' he said picking up another slice of toast. Doubling it in two he took a bite.

'The Praying Mantis,' said Vicky.

'What?' asked Dylan.

'She gets a shag before she kills him too.'

'Vicky, do you have be so...'

'But I guess she's right. Either that or she had shared the bed with someone else lately,' said Paul.

'You wouldn't get me going near any of my exes for a fucking gold clock,' sniffed Vicky.

Dylan's facial expression didn't change. 'What's your thoughts on the acting Detective Sergeant's appraisal of this vital piece of evidence from the murder scene, DS Robinson?'

'Rather crude, sir.'

'Me?' asked Vicky.

'My thoughts exactly.'

'So I suppose neither of you two gentlemen will want any more fucking coffee then?' she said standing up to pour another cup from the pot. 'I'll be mother, shall I?'

'What hope has she got, Paul?' Dylan said shaking his head as he held out his cup. Vicky pulled a face.

'We need to consider our approach to the interview with Harper if he returns...' said Vicky.

'When, he returns this afternoon,' said Dylan.

'Seeing as I'm so crude, I'll play the hard man shall I? You can be his friend this time, boss,' said Vicky wrinkling her nose.

Dylan's phone rang. He picked up and listened. 'Thanks for that,' he said. 'Arrange the solicitor for about an hour, will you,' he said before replacing the receiver. 'Speak of the devil. It's interview time,' said Dylan.

\*\*\*

In Dylan's experience most investigations were never straight forward and none more so than the ones they had running.

In the cell area with Vicky, he saw Derek Harper walking down the corridor to the interview room with his solicitor David Scacchetti. 'Harper looks creepier than ever boss,' said Vicky. 'Like somebody off one of those old horror films coming out of the crypt,' Vicky said, dropping her shoulder forward and dragging the opposite leg.

'Yeah, funny. Know the solicitor?' asked Dylan.

'No, I don't but wouldn't mind, boss, he's a bit of a dish.'

'Talking of your conquests, you seen Eugene Regis lately?'

'Might have but you know me I love 'em and leave 'em wanting more,' she said with a wink.

David Scacchetti was a very smart man in a pinstripe suit. A handkerchief to match his tie sat neatly in the breast pocket of his jacket. He was clean shaven and his hair was combed away from his face. He was what was known to Dylan as a city slicker. Dylan looked forward to seeing how he received them in interview. Dylan however didn't have to wait for a formal introduction as Mr Scacchetti came out to meet them before they began. Dylan outlined the circumstances surrounding his client's arrest and subsequent findings and David Scacchetti told them that his client intended to fully co-operate with them as, to use his own words, 'he says he's done for,' he said with a lift of his chin.

In the interview room the necessary introductions and cautions under PACE (Police And Criminal Evidence Act) were completed. They could now begin to find out perhaps, what made Derek Harper tick.

# Chapter Twenty-One

Dylan opened the interview. 'Mr Harper, we arrested you at your home yesterday for possession, publishing and distribution of obscene material. Do you understand?'

'Yes, I do. But what I don't understand is why? My photographs are a work of art,' he said looking puzzled.

'That's a matter of opinion,' Dylan said.

David Scacchetti gave a little cough.

'You are aware that my officers have been searching your home?'

Derek Harper nodded.

'Please could you say "Yes" instead of nodding your head for the purpose of voice recognition on the tape, Mr Harper,' said Vicky.

'Of course. Yes,' he said.

'Due to the discovery of a body at your address you are also under arrest on suspicion of murder.'

'I haven't murdered anyone. If I am guilty of anything, it's falling in love. Have you never loved anyone Mr Dylan?' Harper said. He was calm and even apathetic. There was no need for the officers to hurry him.

'I'm not sure what you mean, or indeed what you expect us to interpret by that comment. Would you care to explain?' Dylan said.

Vicky remained silent. She was watching Derek Harper with interest. Noting his body language intently, whilst listening to his response to the questions put to him.

Mr Harper sat very still with his hands in his lap. 'It was love at first sight. She was very beautiful,' he said.

'Who are we talking about?'

'Kirsty of course. Don't pretend you didn't notice, Detective Inspector. I know by now you'll have been to her post-mortem and seen her naked body.'

'We have found a body of a female in your outhouse. Are you saying to us now that this is the body of Kirsty Gallagher? If so will you explain how she got there? From the beginning would be helpful.'

Derek Harper took one deep breath and turned to look at his solicitor.

David Scacchetti gave a nod that was hardly noticeable.

'Remember I told you that prior to working in the mortuary I worked in the graveyard?'

Dylan leaned forwarded.

'I've spent most of my life surrounded by dead bodies. We kept Grandma under the window in the front room for a week.' He tutted and stalled.

'Go on...'

'Some friends of mine suggested I photograph some of the bodies at work. Make some money. I knew it was wrong, but what the hell they were dead, so it wasn't going to bother them was it?'

'Just staying with Kirsty for a moment. When did you first see her?' Dylan said.

'When she came into the mortuary... Ah, she was like a breath of fresh air.'

His solicitor's face was a picture of revulsion. He turned his head away from his client and looked towards the door.

'Had you not met her prior to that?'

'No. Oh, sorry I lie. I did see her in the corner shop sometimes in a morning.'

'So you knew her then?'

'Sort of, I guess.'

'Did you know where she lived?'

'Bankfield Terrace.'

'Have you ever been to her address?'

'No, but I pass it regular on the way to my friend's house. Or rather I did.' Derek Harper looked sullen. 'Barrington, Barrington Cook. He died recently,' he said. 'You know I used to worry about things, the why and the how,' he shrugged his shoulders. 'After Barrington died I resigned myself to the fact that if things are going to happen they do. We only live once.'

Vicky looked at Dylan with questioning eyes. *The Barrington Cook that they'd seen fished out of the canal?*

Dylan was focused.

'So you've never been inside her house?' he asked, not taking his eyes of the prisoner.

'Like I said.'

Dylan was puzzled. Derek Harper appeared to be enjoying the interview. He didn't appear at all fazed.

'Did you kill her, Mr Harper?'

Derek Harper cleared his throat and looked offended. 'I told you the only crime I'm guilty of.' His reply was quick and there was no further sign of emotion displayed on his face.

'So, Kirsty was brought into the mortuary. What happened after that?'

'Oh, she's stunning isn't she? I took some photos of her. Just so I could show my friends.'

Dylan and Vicky remained silent to see if he would continue talking. They were right to do so.

Derek Harper seemed to go off into a world of his own. 'Oh, they were so jealous,' he said. 'She was a fit. Lovely tattoos.'

Vicky could feel her stomach flip.

'I didn't want to leave her alone you see. The mortuary wasn't the place for someone like her... You know the rest.'

'But Derek she was dead. The mortuary was the place for her to be. It was your duty of care to treat her body with respect.'

'I know and I did consider leaving her with my friend, Old Alfie but... it just didn't feel right, you know...' he said screwing up his face. 'I know she was dead and what I did was wrong but it was a chance of a lifetime for me and I can't deny falling for her.'

'But she was dead,' Vicky implored.

There was a feeling of animal excitement about Derek Harper. 'Yes I know. I'm not stupid. But you're missing the point. If she had still been alive she wouldn't have come anywhere near me, now would she?' His voice raised slightly. He sat back and folded his arms.

'You said it wasn't the place for her, but surely you will agree that the mortuary is the right and proper place for a corpse? You knew full well that once she was taken out of the specially temperate requirements of the mortuary her body would start to decompose, didn't you?'

'Yes, yes of course I knew that. That's why I put her in the outhouse. Don't you realise I was in-between the devil and the deep blue sea, wasn't I? If I'd left her, I knew the next day she would have been opened up by the pathologist and totally ruined. I know what happens, her insides would've been thrown into a bin liner and dumped back into the chest cavity before they sewed her up, once they'd had their hands all over her. She was far too good for that.'

'But that is the purpose of a post-mortem, to identify the cause of death. You have to all intents and purposes obstructed the Coroner in his duty and let's face it, she ended up in your outhouse rotting. She was in a far worse state when we found her than she would have been if she had been kept at the mortuary, and her body has still had to be subjected to a post-mortem. Your reasoning just doesn't add up.'

His stare remained fixed on Dylan's face for some seconds and then his lip curled. 'Yes,' he said, nodding his head slightly. 'I do tend to act in haste...'

'Did you take a lot of photographs of dead bodies at work, Derek? And before you answer let me tell you we are in the process of looking at all the photographs you have stored on your computer.'

'In that case you'll see for yourself then, won't you. And they are my property so I want them back.'

'Tell me, who are these friends that you show the photographs to?'

'Just friends.'

'We will find out sooner or later through association,' said Dylan.

'Maybe you will but I won't tell you. You may be surprised who is amongst them,' he said cocking an eyebrow.

'Well tell me who they are and then I'll tell you if I am?'

'Sorry,' he said, shaking his head. 'No can do. I've had enough!' he said wiping the palms of his hands on his trousers. He sat up straight. 'Back to my cell please. I'm tired,' he said to his solicitor. David Scacchetti looked across at Dylan. Dylan nodded. It was a good time to break. Dylan terminated the interview.

*\*\**

It was only after Vicky opened the door to the interview room and Dylan felt the rush of cool air that he realised how warm it was within. A welcome gush of fresh air greeted them as they stepped into the corridor.

'Leave the door open Vicky. It might be wise to see if they have some fresh air spray in the cell area,' he said with a nod. Derek Harper and his solicitor were left alone.

'He's as nutty as a bloody fruitcake,' Vicky muttered as they walked back to the Incident Room. 'The psychiatrists are going to have a field day with him, aren't they?'

'He's certainly a weird individual but I don't think he's mad. In my opinion, he knows exactly what he's doing. I'll arrange with the cells to get approval from his solicitor and we'll have him examined to ensure he's fit for interview though. I don't doubt he is. I think he actually enjoys the attention he's getting, but we'll err on the side of caution just in case. We don't want any interviews being disregarded at some future date, do we?'

'Dread to think what his computers will reveal, boss.'

'Time will tell. I'm interested to know who his group of friends are. He's not alone, he's already said as much and we have yet to ask him if anyone helped him remove the body from the mortuary. It's early days Vicky, early days. We know Barrington was his friend so we will have to revisit his past and look at his associates to see what that tells us.'

'Frightening to think you're not even safe when you're dead.'

'Don't worry. You won't know anything about it. I've seen nurses open the windows when a person dies to allow the spirit to leave. I like that thought...'

'That's a bit deep for you, boss?'

'It doesn't do to dwell on things. We'll find out what Harper's game is all in good time and then, if I have my way, he'll go away for a long, long time.'

'Saving grace here, like you said I guess, is that Kirsty Gallagher won't know anything about it,' Vicky looked thoughtful as she slid into her seat opposite Dylan.

'Now who's being deep? Don't get drawn into the emotion or begin to try to understand. I promise you, you never will. I won't let anything happen to you while I'm here, don't worry.'

'Awh... thanks boss, I didn't know you cared?'

'I'm being practical. Who'd make my coffee?' he asked with a grin.

Vicky stuck her tongue out at Dylan.

'Let's see what the computer geeks can tell us about Derek Harper's weird world, shall we, but let's have a drink first and a biscuit wouldn't go a miss.'

'Sexist. You shouldn't assume I should make your coffee, the book says...'

'I'm not sexist. I'm the boss and I'm giving you an order,' he said pan faced and without taking his eyes of his computer screen. 'And then ring Forensics will you and see if they've got an update for me.' A grin spread across his face when she turned her back on him and left the office in silence.

'He'd test the patience of a saint,' said Vicky to Lisa. 'Make a coffee for us both Lisa, will you love,' Dylan heard her say.

'Kettle calling pot black!' he called after her.

# Chapter Twenty-Two

'We've got traces of DNA from the swabs taken from around Jane Simpson's neck,' said DS Robinson.

'So Billy Simpson did try to strangle her?' asked Dylan with a glint of optimism in his eye.

'No, his DNA wasn't a match.'

Dylan looked downcast.

'But, the DNA was an exact match for hair that was found in the face mask along with Billy Simpsons. They're just checking the national database.'

'And if the person who it belongs to has a criminal history we'll have a name,' said Dylan.

Lisa walked into the office with the morning mail.

'Get Vicky for me will you?' Dylan said.

'V I C K Y!' Lisa called, at the top of her voice.

Paul put his hands over his ears. Dylan smiled at Paul Robinson. 'I could have done that.'

'Why didn't you then?' Lisa said shrugging her shoulders.

'What's up with her this morning?' asked Andy.

'I think Ned has been on the cadge again. I'll have to have a word with him.'

Vicky strolled into Dylan's office and sat down next to Paul Robinson. 'Have a word with who?' she said.

'Ned, he's been lifting food out of drawers in the office again.'

'Don't worry, I've got it in hand,' she said with mischief written all over her face.

'Why does that look worry me?'

'Don't ask,' she said.

Dylan's eyes rose to the ceiling. 'Perhaps better I don't know?'

Vicky nodded. 'Absolutely, sir.'

'I'd like you to concentrate on the Billy Simpson murder. I'm going to bring Paul into the Harper investigation. He is after all dealing with the disappearance of Kirsty Gallagher.'

'Can't I do both?' Vicky pleaded.

Dylan cocked his head on one side, lying back in his chair. 'And you know that's not practical. Especially now you're acting up.'

'Okay,' she said. 'It would allow us both to remain focussed, I guess.'

'What no shouting?' he asked.

She grinned. 'No, that makes sense.'

'Paul will you liaise with the computer unit, see what Derek Harper's files are telling us?'

'Will do. By the way, I've revisited Kirsty Gallagher's home and had the smoke alarm and a carbon dioxide alarm dusted and guess what?'

'No batteries?'

'Correct.'

'Somebody wanted to make sure she wasn't warned about the dangers,' said Dylan. 'We thought that person had also taken her body from the mortuary didn't we, but it's looking like that may not be the case as Harper now admits taking it.'

'Ah, but we don't know if he was working alone, do we boss?' asked Vicky.

'No, listen to the copy tape of the first interview will you Paul, before you and I go into question him. It will help you get the feel of what sort of person we are dealing with perhaps.'

Vicky turned her head towards Paul. 'He's an absolute weirdo.'

'But he's no idiot. He knows full well what he's doing. You've got about two hours max Paul, before the next round of interviews. Why are you still sitting here, Sergeant Hardacre, you've lots to do. Find me Jane Simpson's partner in murder,' he said with a growl.

*** 

They both left his office. With a few minutes to spare, he picked his phone up and rang the home number. 'Jen?' he asked. 'Sorry love, it's going to be another late one.'

Jen was in good spirits, Penny had been and cleaned the house from 'top to bottom' as way of an apology she said and she had had a string of emails from her dad, Ralph. The classes were doing him the power of good and so was his new lady friend, so it seemed.

'Jack,' she said with more than a hint of seriousness in her voice.

'Yes,' he said with a frown at her tone.

'Oh, it doesn't matter. I'll speak to you when you get home.'

'No, talk to me now,' he said. 'What's up?'

'Nothing's up, but have you got a minute?'

'Just about,' he said moving the papers around on his desk. He picked up a coin from his desk tidy and rolled it across his knuckles. A trick he had learned as a kid.

'I've been updating the computer system today from your personnel file and I can't find the papers relating to your time in firearms.'

The line went quiet. Now he was between that rock and a hard place... He threw the coin up in the air. Heads or tails? Could he trust such a decision to the spin of a coin?

'You still there, Jack?' she asked.

'Yes, don't worry they'll be at the unit.'

Dylan put down the phone. The urge was to tell her. Would she understand? She was different from other women. In his mind's eye he saw himself sat on the sofa beside her, confessing everything, justifying nothing. He would tell it how it was. 'That's what the job did.' Trouble was, Jen had led a relatively sheltered life growing up. The Isle of Wight, crime-wise was twenty years behind the cities. And the child in her, despite her age was strangely untarnished in spite of the police world she was now part of. She could read, see images, listen to transcripts of victims' horror stories that were shocking enough as they told of man's inhumanity to man but they retained for her their reality, a kind of conventional separateness.

Would she be shocked at his revelation? She worried. It wouldn't be easy to tell her, and as time had passed he had often thought how the edge of that cliff seemed to grow steeper and steeper. His secret was a burden to him and the fact that Avril Summerfield-Preston had told him she knew, was always a worry.

Dylan was mindlessly shoving paperwork from side to side in his trays when he saw the advertisement for Chief Inspector vacancies. Should he throw his cap into the ring? Give Jen something to soften the blow? He had been a Detective Inspector now for a few years, and longer than most in the post, but did he really want to jump through the hoops at the promotion circus? There was nothing stopping him, but to him the whole promotion programme was nothing but that. It had proved to be for him a spectacle that had a variety of juggling acts to be learned, a few electrifying words to recite and a variety of clowns in it that performed in the ring. One positive was an increased pension, but did he want to return to uniform. Some people spent their entire police service doing nothing other than study for promotion boards, involving themselves in the art of assessments, working at police headquarters just so they could achieve the next rank, whilst doing as little actual police work as possible. He'd toyed with the idea, it could be amusing and it would cause some agitation to some of the hierarchy along the way, to think that he was even considering it. There was time before the deadline. He knew some Inspectors would have the application written and already be having their submission vetted by a senior officer so they weren't paper-sifted at the first stage by now. He also knew not everyone who applied would be afforded that scrutiny. The promotion system was a unit that was like a force within a force and a drain on resources, and self-serving for some. He'd only just seen the advertisement and it was already starting to cause him concern. He flung the paper to one side. He had murderers to catch and he needed to speak to the Divisional Chief Superintendent in respect of an extension to detain Derek Harper. The normal twenty-four hours would be insufficient that was now clear. Now, he would request the further twelve hours Hugo-Watkins could give him. If that was still not enough he would have to go before the Magistrates and request permission to detain him for a further thirty-six hours.

# Chapter Twenty-Three

It was Jack Dylan and Detective Sergeant Paul Robinson who sat across the table in the interview room from Derek Harper and his solicitor David Scacchetti. Dylan shuffled in his seat that was secured to the floor. He hated the fact that it wasn't permissible for him to stand in interview as this was deemed as oppressive.

A morbid thought struck him. If he did obtain the next rank he would not be allowed to interview a suspect, no matter how serious the crime. Anyone who reached the rank of Chief Inspector or above under the Police & Criminal Evidence Act deemed someone of such rank would be seen as tyrannical by association of their title.

Derek Harper had been examined both medically and educationally and he was declared fit for interview by the doctor. His solicitor had no comment to make about these findings, he was in agreement. After the usual formalities Dylan opened the questioning.

'Derek, you said you were tired in the last interview and due to that we stopped it for you. Now you have had an opportunity to rest and perhaps also reflect on your situation, do you feel okay to continue?'

'Yes,' he said.

'During the previous interview you stated that you removed the body of Kirsty Gallagher from the mortuary. Is that correct?'

'Yes. I didn't want her spoilt.'

'Spoilt? Can you explain what you mean by that?'

'In the process of the post-mortem they spoil them... I've seen what they do.'

'So, you didn't remove her body to avoid anyone finding out the reason for her death?'

'No. I did not.' His eyes were dark, staring and cold.

'Are you sure about that?'

'Yes. I am very sure,' he said applying a tissue to a rapidly flickering eyelid. 'If she hadn't come into the mortuary, although I'd seen her from a distance, I would have never met her, would I?'

'So the first time you "met her" was at the mortuary?'

Dylan observed Mr Harper.

He spoke with an air of breathlessness. 'Yes, like I told you before. I met her on the Friday.'

Paul wriggled cynical shoulders as he sat at Dylan's side silently.

'I think the alleged breakdown of the fridge, the alarm and the alleged burglary was all instigated by you to cover up what you did, wasn't it Derek?' asked Dylan his eyes narrowing as he looked at him for a reaction.

Derek Harper put a hand to his chin and rubbed it gently: his face was expressionless. David Scacchetti and Derek Harper exchanged glances. All eyes were on Derek Harper now and it seemed that time stood still. There were voices in the corridor outside. It appeared to shift his thoughts. When Derek Harper did speak he spoke directly to Dylan. His eyebrows were raised, his voice clear and strong.

'You believed my story for a while though, didn't you?' he asked with a smirk. 'I managed to have some time with her alone. I laid with her on my bed and held her all night.' It was Derek Harper's turn to look for a reaction. The serious mask of the detectives didn't slip. He paused. His lips curled at the edges. He had expected a response, a consequence for this disclosure but all three professionals present showed none.

'But you abandoned Kirsty's body in the outhouse under a pile of boxes. It was you who left her to decompose and become nothing more than a rotting corpse? A post-mortem, the necessary investigation to find out how she died has now been carried out. You said yesterday that what you felt for Kirsty Gallagher was love. Your actions couldn't actually be described as loving could they? All you've done is cause her body to decompose more rapidly than if she had been kept in the mortuary. I am in no doubt you knew exactly what you were doing and what would happen to her body.'

'And your point is?' asked Derek Harper.

'My point is that you were using her body for self-satisfaction, nothing more, and you've been caught. Just as a matter of interest, what were you planning to do with her body if we hadn't found her? It is very obvious you couldn't leave it where it was much longer because of the smell.'

'Ah, it was always going to be short but sweet, and alas all good things have to come to an end. Better to have loved and lost than never loved at all, so they say. And one thing you can never do Mr Dylan is take away my memories,' Derek Harper put his finger to his lips and licked the end of it.

'We know Kirsty's body isn't the first dead body you've photographed.'

'What's that to do with anything?'

'How do you choose which body to photograph?'

He remained silent. Paul Robinson took over the interview.

'We've got your computer and it'll only be a matter of time before we see the pictures you've taken, in their entirety. Early intelligence suggests to us that there are hundreds. Isn't it about time you were honest with us?'

Derek Harper looked at his solicitor who made no comment but gestured to him with palms upwards.

Dylan and Paul remained silent. It worked.

'Okay, okay! Persistent aren't you? Since I got the job, someone who I won't name, suggested I take pictures of the dead people, post them and call the site "Bare Poster." It seemed harmless. Like I said, they were dead, what harm could it do?'

Dylan wanted to question him regarding his latest revelation but he held back. Derek Harper was talking freely.

'So that's what I did. I fitted out my office. You've seen it. It's my den. I took pictures. One or two to start with and then when they were well received I began to take more. I have a big following.'

'Were these photographs taken at the mortuary?'

'Yes.'

'Are they all of women?'

Derek Harper's brow furrowed. 'No.'

'We will be seeing the pictures you uploaded in due course, but before we do, can you explain how you took them. Did you open the fridge door, or remove the bodies to take them. Tell us, how did you do it?'

'My digital camera's good but it would have been a bit pointless taking a shot of them in the fridge, wouldn't it?' he smirked. 'Of course I had to take them out of the fridges to get the right lighting and position them.'

'Okay, so we've now established that they are all naked?'

Derek Harper nodded.

'For the purpose of the tape Mr Harper is nodding his head. Derek please could I remind you to speak,' said Paul Robinson. 'Are any of the pictures you took in sexually suggestive poses?'

'I did what people asked me to do.'

'So why not do the same with Kirsty Gallagher's body? I don't understand why you needed to remove her from the mortuary.'

'She was unique; in mint condition. I told her...'

Beads of sweat appeared on Derek Harper's forehead and he mopped his brow with his tissue.

'You'd moved on... And what, something more you want to share?'

'Nothing. She looks good on the photos, you'll see. Everyone said they thought they were extremely good...'

'I'm trying to understand. Everyone? Whose everyone?' Dylan said screwing up his eyes.

'Members of Bare Poster.'

'So you are admitting to publishing obscene pictures Mr Harper, is that right?'

'Not everyone can see them. It's a private group.'

'And who is in this group?'

'Ha ha! I knew you'd come around to that. I can't grass, it's secret,' he said. He tapped his nose.

'But how do we know this group exists if you don't tell us?'

'I assure you it does,' he said.

'You sure you're not making it all up? It's not just a fantasy of yours?'

Derek Harper shook his head. 'No, why would I do that?'

'It's not like you haven't lied to us before,' said Dylan.

Derek Harper's head turned on Dylan as if a spring had been released. His eyes grew round and staring.

'You made a comment at the mortuary about the old guy, Alfie, that you'd placed on top of her. Do you recall that conversation?' asked Dylan.

'I do,' he snapped. 'There's nothing wrong with my memory.'

'Was he a member of your group?'

Derek Harper didn't reply.

'So did you find her dead body desirable, sexy even?' asked Paul.

He made no reply.

'Well, did you?'

'I'm not into necrophilia if that's what you're thinking.'

'Well, under the circumstances, if you've slept with a body...' Paul said.

'I know what it looks like but... You think I'd have sex with a dead body?' he asked, pulling a face.

'Really?' Paul asked.

'I knew that's what you'd be thinking.'

'How did you take her home? Was it your vehicle? And before you answer, it is being examined,' said Dylan.

'No.'

'So how then? Why are you keeping things from us?'

Derek Harper sat quietly tearing holes in his tissue, his head was down.

'Are you scared of someone?' Paul said.

He didn't reply.

'Or, is it that there isn't really anyone else involved? You've just been caught and it's a fantasy? You obviously have no respect for the dead or their families. What will they think of you?'

He still didn't respond but his eyes flashed upwards. Dylan knew from his expression that he was listening to what was being said.

'I think you've carried out these crimes for self-gratification,' said Dylan. He leaned back, stretched his legs to the side of the table and crossed them at the ankle.

Derek Harper lifted his head and focussed his eyes on the ceiling.

'If we're wrong, then now is your opportunity to tell us what the reason for your actions is?'

He didn't reply.

'Are you being paid for people to be in this group?'

'Might be.'

'If you want us to believe you were earning money by your little venture tell me how lucrative it was?'

He shrugged his shoulders.

'Was it big money? Was it worth it to do such horrific things if you weren't doing them for your own personal gratification?' Paul was pushing him for a reaction.

'Sergeant please, that's two questions at once,' David Scacchetti said.

161

'Sorry, yes you're right,' Paul said. 'But would you like to answer either or both for me Derek?'

The corners of Derek Harper's mouth rose into a sneer.

Paul leaned across the desk. David Scacchetti sat back.

Dylan terminated the interview before Paul took the bait and reacted. He could feel his inner frustrations. Dylan would speak to the Chief Superintendent and request for extended detention. Twelve hours. Dylan hoped that that would give them sufficient time to gain more intelligence and evidence to put to Harper in the next interview.

The team were working diligently, other specialist teams were involved and they still hadn't set eyes on the photographic data on Harper's computer. Dylan didn't see a problem in the request being approved but he didn't take anything for granted. Sometimes in his experience both Chief Superintendents and Superintendents were over-cautious, especially if it meant they had to sign and record their decision on the detention documents, which they would have to do in this case. It would be recorded on Harper' s custody record. Dylan informed David Scacchetti of their intention but there was no representations.

***

Back in the office Dylan asked Paul for this thoughts.

'Having listened to his first interview and reading the background on Harper my initial thoughts were that he was someone with a low educational ability. However, now I've had chance to sit in on an interview with him I think you're right, that's what he wants us to believe. There is no doubt in my mind he knows exactly what he is doing.'

'I agree totally, he's pausing to think about his answers before he gives them. It's also apparent that he is only telling us part of the truth. Have you noticed how still he is? Body language always gives them away. Not many people can be animated in their gestures and look relaxed whilst telling lies.'

Lisa knocked on the office door. 'The computer suite are into Derek Harper's database sir. They want you to go to their offices to show you what they've found as soon as you're free.'

Paul jumped to his feet.

'Good,' said Dylan. He put his palms down on his desk and lifted himself from his chair. 'Prepare yourself, Paul.'

'If Kirsty Gallagher was a relative of yours, how the hell would you keep your hands off him?' Paul said as he walked up the stairs alongside Dylan.

'I think I'd rip his fucking head off,' he said.

# Chapter Twenty-Four

Vicky could hardly believe her luck. She replaced the telephone on its cradle and smiled. They had a hit on the National DNA Database for the samples taken from Jane Simpson's neck swabs, and the hair found in the mask worn by Billy Simpson.

'Got ya!' she said aloud as she quickly typed the details into the computer.

'Richard Bryant, thirty-two years, his only conviction was one for assault in 2006. Self-employed. Yeah, yeah,' she said tapping her fingers on the desk as she waited for the inputted data to upload. When it did she flicked from screen to screen until she found the information she was looking for. The brief circumstances of the assault which led to his arrest and details being stored on the database were as follows, she read on…

Attack on a male which entailed kicking and punching him to the ground. The motive was unknown.

'It must have been a nasty assault,' she said, 'for Bryant to receive a nine-month prison sentence.' Andy got up from his seat and came to read the screen over her shoulder.

'Suspended for two years too,' he said.

'It's expired.'

'His punishment?'

'To behave for twenty-four months,' she said. 'Or don't get bloody caught. So much for justice for the victim.'

'The guy he assaulted has probably only just recovered from his physical injuries never mind what Bryant did to him mentally,' Andy said returning to his desk.

'Poor bugger. The trauma will stay with him forever, no doubt,' Vicky mumbled as she searched other databases for more information on Bryant. 'What's the link between Jane Simpson and him then?' she muttered. She wanted more about Bryant before she spoke to Dylan. At least to confirm his present address and she wanted to let the fingerprint unit have his details to check against any other marks that had been lifted at Jane Simpson's home.

\*\*\*

In the computer suite, Dylan and Paul sat down either side of Wallace J. Hooper. The first thing you couldn't help but notice was a large brass plaque with his name thereon.

'Let me tell you, Inspector,' he said. 'Harper hadn't tried to hide or encrypt these images. They were easily accessible amongst other meaningless stuff. However, we have found illegal obscene publication sites which he has tried to get rid of and these show the extent of his obsession. These sites are set up and closed down quite frequently,' he said tapping data into his computer and clicking his mouse to enable him to open their links and the Bare Poster site. 'It's not for me to comment on the content of the images, but they're not for the faint-hearted and I've seen some pretty horrific pictures in my time,' he said, as they waited for the images to upload.

'I can guess. I've already seen some on his mobile,' said Dylan. 'Okay, before I start have you any questions?' he asked, looking from side to side at both men.

'How many images are there?' asked Paul.

'So far we have recorded, let's see, some six hundred and thirty-five.'

Dylan cringed. 'I might need you to categorise some for me for easy retrieval,' said Dylan.

'No problem. You tell me which ones you are specifically interested in and I'll create a file for you.'

Dylan and Paul saw very quickly how bad the images were. Most of them depicted naked women. Some bodies he had taken a lot more pictures of than others. One after another the images began to tell the extent of Harper's obsession. The poses he would have the bodies in appeared to be chosen to show a lack of injury or bruising. The cadavers had all been photographed on the trolley. 'And all prior to post-mortem,' said Paul, thoughtfully.

Few were of children. 'God, don't they just tug at the heartstrings?' asked Paul visibly moved.

'Never more so than when you have children of the same age. They're sickening. Place those in a separate file,' said Dylan.

A picture of Kirsty Gallagher appeared before them on the screen. 'We need a separate category for the ones of her,' Dylan said pointing at the image. 'Name the file Operation Pullman, will you?' asked Dylan.

The first ten images of her had been taken at the mortuary, naked and in a variety of carefully constructed poses showing her tattoos. The camera operator had taken close up shots between her legs and of her breasts.

'Stop a minute. Go back,' Dylan said in haste.

Wallace Hooper did as he was told. He glanced at Dylan. Dylan nodded. He clicked the mouse to reveal more.

'Stop! There,' said Dylan pointing to the screen. 'Look to the bottom left hand corner of that picture. I can see someone's trouser leg. I know it's quite dark but do you see it?' The three men leaned in closer. 'Look at his footwear. Whoever it is, is wearing quite distinctive brown, front-laced, heavy duty boots.' He said.

'Obviously they didn't realise they were in view of that shot,' said Wallace.

'Can you enlarge the image? It's the only one that tells us someone else was present so far, isn't it?' Dylan said.

Wallace Hooper nodded his head. 'Separate category for that sir?'

'Definitely. I want work doing on that image to see if it reveals anything else.'

***

The next collection of Kirsty Gallagher was taken at Derek Harper's home address. There were numerous images of Kirsty Gallagher's body laid out on the bed. One image was of her dressed in white lace underwear, the other in a red baby-doll silk pyjama set.

'Look at that image,' Paul said. 'Derek Harper is in the reflection of a mirror taking that... and look there is someone standing behind him.'

'I want that one enhancing, too,' said Dylan.

'The face, it's obscured by Harper's head,' said Wallace.

'Never mind... It might support some other evidence we gain at a later date.'

***

Dylan and Paul walked from the room both quiet, each with their own thoughts.

'In all my years on the force I've never come across anything like it,' said Dylan.

'Me neither,' said Paul.

'No amount of money would make any decent person do that, would it? We need the exhibits officer to go through each one of those images again. I want you to put not one but two officers on it for moral support, if nothing else,' he said.

'Did you notice that at bottom of the screen we have a time and date?' asked Paul.

'Yes, I did. But who's to say that wasn't changed? That won't stand up as evidence in court. Unless we can support it with other evidence. Who's his accomplice in the pictures do you think, Barrington, the man in the canal?'

Paul shook his head. 'No idea,' he said as they turned the corner and headed down the corridor towards the CID office.

*** 

Penny Sanderson was ahead of them wiping the Incident Room door as the two men approached.

'Haven't you got a home to go to?' Dylan said. Hoping it wasn't his house.

'Oh, you can't do enough for a good firm,' she said. 'I asked to work a late shift today as I had a job to do this morning. So, I just thought I'd make sure your Incident Room was spic and span before I left tonight,' she said with a smiling face as she pushed the door open and held it whilst they entered. She walked in behind them. 'Any exciting updates?' she said eagerly.

'Wouldn't you like to know,' said Vicky. She leaned forward and touched the end of her nose. 'Are you sure you're not stalking us?' she asked. 'You've cleaned this office every day this week. You want a drink,' she said turning to Dylan and Paul without waiting for an answer. Penny screwed up her nose.

'Sorry for taking an interest,' she said, flicking her duster around the papers on Vicky's desk. Vicky snatched them out of her view. Penny moved to stand idly looking over Ned's shoulder, at the screen he was working on. He turned and smiled at her. 'Malcolm in the front office has been showing me how to work that system,' she said.

'Well, he shouldn't. You aren't entitled to be privy to that information,' said Vicky.

'Keep your hair on,' said Penny. 'I'm going to apply for a job in admin. The more I know, the more I score for the role profile competence thingy I'll have to fill in.'

'Yeah well, when you're hired you'll get your own numbers to log onto the system with won't you, and someone will train you up properly.'

Penny Sanderson stuck her tongue out behind Vicky's back and Ned Granger turned to her and chuckled. 'You're like a breath of

167

fresh air,' he said. 'You've got balls, hasn't she, Vicky? I like that in a woman.'

'Oh please,' she said to Ned. 'And it's acting Detective Sergeant Hardacre.'

'Yeah, whatever,' he said. It was Penny Sanderson's turn to chuckle at Ned.

***

Vicky walked towards Dylan's office with the drinks in her hands.

'Let me do that for you,' said Penny as she stood in her path and opened his door. She followed her in.

'Is Max okay now?' Penny said to Dylan.

'Yes, thank you but no thanks to the person who put rat poison down,' Dylan said as Vicky handed him his hot beverage.

'Do they really think that's what it was, rat poison?' asked Penny.

'That's what the vet thinks... but I can hell as like think where he got rat poison from.'

'Well, I guess he could have picked it up anywhere... you know what he's like,' she said as she busily polished around Dylan's office furniture. 'Just give it a lick over while I'm here,' she said.

'Let's face it, he's only either out with us and I haven't seen him chase a rodent – or he's in the garden,' Dylan said with a frown.

'Well, no harm done, thank goodness. I'm sorry about the other night. Too much sauce. I must have passed out,' she said with a grimace before leaving.

***

Dylan and Paul sat quietly, mulling over the enquiry.

'Harper's phone will give us clues as to who his contacts are,' said Dylan. He studied the documentation in front of him.

'And his accomplice with any luck,' Paul said absentmindedly as he read through his notes.

'Wallace will give us a list of his contacts on his computer. That information is going to be invaluable to us. Reprobates, the lot of them. That's the only word for them,' Dylan said looking across at his colleague. He brought up his arm, pulled his shirt cuff back and looked at his watch.

'I don't know about you but I think I've had enough for one day. There is nothing truer than the Yorkshire saying, "There's

168

nowt so queer as folk", is there? Our Maisy will have had her bath by now and be fast asleep no doubt.' Dylan sighed.

The door opened. 'Harper's been taken back to hospital in handcuffs,' said Vicky.

'Well, at least his custody clock will stop again. What's up with him now?'

'Ah, same old problem, chest pain but that's probably because he's panicking, if you ask me. He knows he's behind the eight ball.'

'We'll give him another interview tomorrow morning, Paul. If they release him.'

Vicky walked out and Dylan could see her sit back at her desk. 'Fancy a swift pint, across the road before we head home. Wash away some of today's shite?'

'Yeah. I could do with something,' he said.

'I'll just give Jen a quick call to tell her not to wait up.'

'Yeah, I'll ring Olivia too,' Paul said as he reached in his trouser pocket for his phone.

***

Jen, was standing behind the ironing board in the kitchen. She felt warm, tired and her feet ached. The ironing basket contents didn't look to have lessened but the pile that was neatly pressed on the worktop beside her was proof that it had. A bottle of Pinot Grigio looked very inviting stood in the cooler. She reached out and filled a glass, took a gulp and sighed heavily. 'Enough,' she said to Max who lay watching her from the door to the hallway. She turned at a noise and peered out of the window. It was pitch black. She reached up to pull down the blind. Max rose. He growled a disgruntled sound. 'In a minute,' she said. But he had bounded to the door barking uncontrollably. Jen followed him and unlocked the door quickly to allow him to go out. 'You'll wake Maisy,' she hissed after him. She shut the door on the cold night air. In the distance she could hear him still barking. She put the ironing board back in the utility room and emptied the iron of the distilled water then went back to the door. She turned the outside light on but Max was still nowhere to be seen.

Jen had questions to ask Dylan to help her solve the mystery of the missing paperwork in his personal file. She took another gulp of wine and picked up the neat pile of pressed clothes. Maybe a drink would loosen his tongue, she thought as she started to climb the stairs. No, she smiled to herself, she knew him better than that.

Dylan was different from any man she had ever known she considered, as she hung his shirts in his wardrobe. He was honest, loving and kind. He had told her about his early life. His brothers, his sisters and they had laughed together when he had told her how as a boy he'd been the receiver of hand-me-downs from his two elder brothers. He always said he was thankful his sisters had been born after him. He often reminisced about his love of telling stories to his siblings over a packet of ice cream wafers they saved up to buy from the ice-cream van. He had, had a happy childhood surrounded by a mother's love and steam engines. What boy wouldn't want to live in a railway house? Joe, Jack's dad had worked on the railway. He was an investigative inspector in his own right into the causation of rail accidents. Although Jack had looked up to his dad he had always remained somewhat a little mysterious to him, he said. Joe was guarded about sharing his war stories from Burma, Jack told her and he never did know the truth of how he'd earned his oak leaf that was pinned to the ribbon of one of his war medals. He had been mentioned in dispatches at Dunkirk. She looked up at the picture of his mum and dad who had died long before she met Jack and felt a moment's sadness. Maybe Dylan's dad, Joe, had tried to protect the ones he loved by remaining tight-lipped about what he had witnessed at war and perhaps Dylan shared some of his dad's reticence in talking about his work, she pondered. There was a thud and Max barked at the back door. She ran down the stairs and opened the door. 'Oh, no,' she said as her heart sank to see he had been sick again. Max appeared to be unperturbed and instead of appearing unwell he wagged his tail as he carried in a bone. 'Where on earth have you got that from?' she said taking it from him and throwing it in the bin. Max was not amused.

\*\*\*

Dylan and Paul were standing at the bar of the King's Head, it was relatively empty but for a group of women that stood nearby singing and swaying to the music from the juke box. Seeing all the empty lager bottles on the bar, and that their eyes were significantly wide, it suggested they had been there for some time. Dylan ordered a pint of lager for himself and one for Paul and headed for a seat in the alcove by the stained glass window.

'Cheers, mate,' Dylan said, lifting the cold, wet glass to his lips.

'Cheers, boss,' Paul said with a wan smile. He looked as tired as Dylan felt.

Dylan had barely put his glass on the table when his mobile phone rang.

'Vicky,' he said and looked at Paul, his eyebrows furrowed. 'Hello,' he said, walking away with one ear pressed to his mobile phone and a finger in the other ear in an attempt to hear what she said. He stepped out of the bar and into the cold but quieter porch. A woman walked out with a string of balloons in her wake and two ladies followed letting the swing door bang nosily behind them.

'Where the hell are you? I need to speak to you. We've got a breakthrough on the Billy Simpson murder.' Vicky sounded excited.

'You still at the nick?' Dylan said.

'Yeah, looking everywhere for you,' she said breathlessly. 'I thought you might be with Chief Superintendent Hugo-Watkins but the top corridor is in darkness.' Dylan could now hear the pitter patter her shoes made on the steps.

'Well, it is after five. Me and Paul, we've just popped into the King's Head.'

'Mine's a pint. I'll be with you in two shakes of a lamb's tail,' she said hanging up on him abruptly.

'Another pint,' he said to the barman. Paul looked at him quizzically. 'Vicky, she's got news,' Dylan said. He could hear car horns blaring over the music.

'Vicky, crossing the road,' he said to Paul and sure enough the King's Head door swung open and Vicky breezed in panting as if she had run a marathon. 'Oh, my God,' she said.

'Slow down and get your breath back,' Dylan said nodding in the direction of her drink. 'And then you can tell us your news on Mallard.'

# Chapter Twenty-Five

The clock struck half past nine. It was late. Too late to start asking questions of Dylan when he came home. Jen laid newspaper at the back door, 'just in case Max, right?' she said stroking the soft fur at the top of his head, as he lay quietly in his bed. His big brown eyes looked up at her pensively. 'Hope you feel better in the morning, if not I'm calling the vet,' she said softly.

Treading the staircase to bed in her stockinged feet Jen could hear noises from the nursery. Maisy was awake, melodiously chattering. Jen stifled a giggle as she stood in the shadows and observed her daughter for a moment or two. Maisy lay on her back in her cot quite oblivious of her mother's nearness. For a split second Jen was tempted to sing along with her but the thought was a fleeting one. Instead, she went in to the nursery, gently put her hand to her daughter's brow and slowly bent down to kissed her. Maisy turned her head with an angular rigidity at the touch, half-smiled, closed her eyes and bottom up nuzzled back into her slumber.

The phone rang. Closing the door behind her, Jen hot-footed it into the bedroom and sliding to a halt at Jack's side of the bed she reached out, stubbing her toe. 'Fucking hell!' she said under her breath.

'Jen,' said a slightly inebriated woman's voice, questioningly.

'Yes,' she snapped. Sitting down on the bed she rubbed her toe vigorously.

'You okay?'

'Yes,' she said biting her bottom lip.

'Just wondered if...could I come round tomorrow?'

'Penny?' Jen said.

'Yes,' she giggled, 'who else did you expect at this time of night?'

'I thought it might be Jack actually. He isn't home yet.'

'Oh, has something happened? He seemed preoccupied when I was in the office.'

'You were working today?'

'Overtime. Can't do enough for a good firm.'

'I can see they've got you brainwashed already. I don't know Penny, I really don't know. I'll see you Monday at work, yeah?' she said.

She took a length of wood from under the bed and stuffed it in the bathroom bin.

\*\*\*

The pub was filling up. Vicky spoke excitedly.

'Two different hair samples found in the face mask worn by our deceased Billy Simpson. One is his,' said Vicky, 'And one is from a guy whose DNA is on the National Database.'

'You lucky old thing,' Paul said. 'I think some people think everyone in the country is on the database, but in my experience when I'm looking for someone, they're almost never there.'

Dylan raised his eyebrows. 'And?' he asked, looking intently at Vicky.

'He's got previous for assault which got him prison for nine months, but the judge suspended the sentence for two years. Before you ask. It's spent,' Vicky said.

'What else do we know about him?'

'He's called Richard Bryant. Have you heard of him?'

The two men shook their heads.

'He's thirty-two years old and we have contact details for him – although I don't know how up-to-date they are.'

'So, the next question is, what are you going to do with this intelligence, acting Detective Sergeant Hardacre?' Dylan said leaning forward and picking up his drink from the table. He sat with it in his hand and waited for her response.

'Well, tempting as it might be, I haven't gone and kicked his door in, yet,' she grinned sheepishly.

Dylan took a sip of his drink and put his glass back on the table. 'It's a start. Why not?'

'The main reason is I'm still in the process of confirming his current address.' Vicky half-smiled awkwardly. 'I'm also waiting for CSI to get back to me. I want to know if his DNA has turned up anywhere else in Jane Simpson's house. I would ultimately like to show him being there if I can, before we interview him.'

'Good, and?' he asked, cocking his head to one side.

Vicky was thoughtful. 'I've arranged for Jane Simpson's telephone data to be checked to see what contact, if any, there has been between the two. If so I'm thinking, are they in a relationship?'

'Do we know what vehicle he's driving?'

'Well like everything else, that could be out of date... but the vehicle registration is for a van. There isn't any very recent intel on him.'

'Check out and confirm the information we have. Tomorrow hopefully, we'll progress. Then we can plan together our approach to lock him up. If Billy Simpson doesn't live at Jane Simpson's any more, we need to try find out what the real reason for his visit was. And we need to ascertain what the motive to kill him is. Food for thought, but that's great news in the right direction. Right,' he said putting his hands on his knees. 'My bed is calling me. I don't know about yours. I'll see you guys tomorrow.' Dylan stood and put his arm in his jacket sleeve.

'Another one for the road, Paul?' asked Vicky, picking up their empty glasses from the table.

'Why not,' said Paul, 'just the one.'

# Chapter Twenty-Six

Dylan woke to the sound of rain battering the window pane. It was dark, he was cosy but the space next to him in bed was empty. He could hear Jen cajoling Maisy into eating her breakfast downstairs. Dylan lay quietly for a moment or two thinking. His first priority today would be Derek Harper. He would instigate one last interview with him, then they needed to get him charged and before the next available court to get him remanded in custody. The last thing he wanted was Harper warning the others in his little gang. That would spoil the surprise when he and the team arrived ultimately at the respective homes of his associates. Afterwards it would be time to focus on Richard Bryant, before trying to catch up on the rest of the paperwork and the monthly returns needed his attention. Dylan got up and dressed. He frowned at the wood in the bin, took it out and returned it to its rightful place – his weapon should they ever have an intruder and much more subtle than the pickaxe handle he kept under the bed when he lived alone.

At ten o'clock they were in the interview room with Derek Harper. The usually preliminaries were carried out and Dylan was straight into the questioning.

'Feeling better this morning, Mr Harper.' said Dylan.

'Yes.'

'Good. We have now had the opportunity to see the images stored on your computer. It appears that they are of dead people of various ages, mainly of women positioned in such a way that tattoos and their genitalia are exposed; all taken at the mortuary. With the exception of some you took of Kirsty,' he said.

'Why have you really taken them? Your bank account shows no regular payments, so it's not for the money is it? Unless they paid you cash? Is it a fetish of yours?'

Harper remained silent.

'We also know from the images that someone else was present when you took some of the photographs of Kirsty. One particular image shows someone's reflection, in the mirror in your bedroom. Can you tell me who that person is?'

Derek Harper's eyes were staring.

'Why the silent treatment, Derek? Be assured we will find out who it is. You have this opportunity to explain yourself, before we do.'

'I don't have to explain to you or anyone else. It's my life and I'll do what I want with it, and as for another person being present, that's ridiculous.' Derek Harper appeared angry, or was he frightened?

'Yes, you're right you don't have to explain anything to us, that's your prerogative. However this is an opportunity, if you so wish to explain why you did it. Let's face it, it must be very difficult trying to explain why you would photograph and interfere with dead bodies.'

His silence continued.

'You have shown no dignity or respect whatsoever in your dealings with the bodies in the photographs. You have also interfered with a burial, and obstructed the Coroner in his duty and that's apart from your depraved attempt at photography.'

Paul remained quiet. The detectives watched and waited to see if a response from the prisoner was forthcoming. His solicitor David Scacchetti sat perfectly still.

More questions were put to Derek Harper by Dylan and DS Paul Robinson but he chose not to respond to any of them. A wall of silence now faced them and Dylan took the decision to end the interview.

What Derek Harper had done was immoral, indecent and illegal and they all knew it.

'DS Robinson, please could you charge Derek Harper with the necessary offences,' Dylan said before turning to David Scacchetti. 'Your client will be put before the next available Magistrates' Court, which will be tomorrow morning,' he said glancing at his watch, 'where we will seek to remand him in custody. And of course technically he'll be bailed in respect of his arrest for murder, those enquires will of course continue.' The detectives left Derek Harper with his solicitor.

\*\*\*

'He'll no doubt apply for bail,' said Dylan to Paul as they left the interview room. 'But you and I both know the magistrates won't grant it. We've got a lot of work to do to identify the others involved.'

Paul disappeared to compile the list of charges.

'Vicky,' Dylan shouted.

'In the kitchen, boss,' said Lisa. 'Ned's nicked her sandwiches again...' she grimaced.

Dylan found Vicky eating a bag of chips. 'Time to eat, have you?' Dylan said.

'Don't go there. First thing I've had today. That bastard's eaten my snap again and this time it's one too many,' she said, vengeance written all over her face.

'I told you, I don't want to know,' Dylan said, as he filled the kettle. 'Coffee, tea?'

'Tea.'

'Richard Bryant?'

'Lives in Midgely Court, Tandem Bridge, you know the place where Barrington Cook lived? He's self-employed so he must be doing okay to afford one of those apartments. I've just been speaking to Sergeant Wilson in Traffic and funnily enough he stopped him while he was driving his work's van a couple of weeks ago – so we know we've got the correct vehicle registration number for him – hence how I got his address.'

'You two are speaking again are you?'

'If I didn't speak to my exes I'd never speak to anyone,' she said with a half-hearted laugh.

'So, what do you think our next move should be?' Dylan said.

'Time to take the bull by the horns?'

'I agree,' Dylan said. 'When?'

'Thinking about seven in the morning?'

'I'd do it at six. He might have an early start too. After you've eaten we'll get a team sorted. If we brief them this afternoon we can come in and be straight on our way tomorrow morning.' He smiled.

'What you smiling at?' she said.

'I remember back in the day when detectives called eleven in the morning a dawn raid. Does he live on his own this Bryant?'

'It shows he does on the checks I did with local authority, but who knows until we get there? Did he know Barrington Cook do you think?'

'Maybe so, acting Detective Sergeant. Are we taking his door off the hinges?'

'Well, he's a suspect for joint murder. I'd like to but I think we should start with a loud knock don't you?'

'You're in charge. Do we know if there is any CCTV at this complex? May be relevant if we need to dispute whether he is in or out at certain times of the day or night?'

'There was on the landing where Barrington Cook lived.'

'Promising then. By the way. I'm told that the applications for the role of Sergeant are out with a month's window to get the applications in. Have you seen the advert?'

'Well that's bloody great isn't it? I'm investigating a murder, how the hell am I supposed to do that justice?'

'Don't worry you will. We'll discuss it later. There is plenty of time and I want to see your application before you submit it.'

'But...'

'No buts... if you want something bad enough you'll find time. The applications for Chief Inspector are advertised too. I might even throw my hat in. Might be fun.'

'You have a peculiar take on what's fun,' Vicky said.

'I'll come with you in the morning,' said Dylan.

'No pressure then.'

'No pressure at all, unless you have the wrong address. It wouldn't be the first time that's happened either will it?'

Vicky made a mental note to double-check all basic details. Now to get to the supermarket. There were things she needed if she was going to get her own back on the inerrant Detective Constable Ned Granger.

*** 

Dylan shuffled through his internal mail. Searching somewhat haphazardly for anything that might be urgent or interesting. A number of Home Office circulars with a signature sheet attached, for all officers to sign when read.

He noticed that the first signature after the Divisional Commanders was that of Inspector Justin Gaskin. He put the circulars to one side, if he got a chance he would read them. He'd make sure that Vicky did too.

Paul returned from the cell area having charged Derek Harper. His face a blaze of colour. 'Do you know what that tosser said when I charged him?'

Dylan shook his head. 'Surprise me.'

'I don't know what all the fuss is about?'

'I bet the custody staff love him.'

178

'Yeah, the door to his cell was shut so quickly behind him that it nearly took his hand off.'

'He could save us a lot of time though Paul, if only he'd tell us who else is involved,' Dylan said with a grimace.

'He's not going to do that though is he? He doesn't think he's done anything wrong.'

'I hope they come back to haunt the bastard. I'm doing the raid at six in the morning with Vicky to lock up Richard Bryant so will you look on at Court for Harper's remand if I'm not back? I'll leave a message for Claire Rose at the press office to just basically say that a man will appear before Harrowfield Magistrates tomorrow charged in connection with the disappearance of a body from the local mortuary.'

'I'm sure the press will still want to speak to us.'

'You'll cope, Paul. Just choose your words carefully and have respect for the dead.'

\*\*\*

Penny hadn't turned up at Jen and Dylan's as threatened. Perhaps she had succumbed to another afternoon of 'delight' with her new man. With any luck tonight, Jen would get time alone with Jack and get some answers to her burning questions. Maisy was in her pyjamas and demanding supper. 'How can you eat supper when you've only just had your tea,' Jen said. Maisy presented a bowl to Jen. 'Do it!' she said. Jen's heart melted, Dylan was missing out on so much. She put Weetabix and milk in the microwave and Maisy happily sat in front of the fire on her little chair being spoon fed. It was the only meal she would let Jen feed her now. Once eaten she picked up her favourite soft toy, 'Bedtime,' Jen said and Maisy gave a sleepy yawn and put her arms out. 'Let's go and get a book shall we? Which one would you like to read tonight?'

'The Gruffalo,' she said sleepily.

\*\*\*

The front door closed. Jen walked onto the landing and the top of the stairs. She put a finger to her lips. Dylan walked towards her up the stairs and she beckoned him to the nursery. It was warm and cosy. The light show from the baby monitor was effective in the darkened room. The colours and shapes fading as they spanned the ceiling. Dylan put his arms around Jen's shoulders and kissed her cheek.

'Bless her,' he said softly.

Jen grabbed his hand, squeezed it tight and led him out of the bedroom into theirs. 'Dinner will be ready in half an hour if you want to jump in the bath?'

'Great. I might just do that,' he said. Dylan started to undress and Jen nipped into the en-suite and started to run the bath water for him.

'I'll see you downstairs,' she said standing on her tiptoes to kiss him.

'Everything okay?' he asked.

'Well, Max was sick again but he doesn't seem to have had any after effects this time. He brought in a bone from the garden.'

'Where did he find a bone in the garden?'

'I don't know. Maybe kids threw it over. But it might have been that that made him sick. I never give him cooked bones they're too brittle. I threw it straight in the bin,' she said. 'Apart from that everything is fine. I am intrigued though,' she said.

'Intrigued about what?' asked Dylan.

'Intrigued to know more about you... about the missing paperwork from your file,' she said. The lighting was dim and the temporary shadow he cast on her passed as she moved away from him, leaving his eyes and face softly luminous.

'Okay, but you will have to be patient with me.'

Jen reached out to his bare chest. 'Why?'

'I don't know if you will understand,' he said taking the words from her lips.

'Of course I will. Don't be silly,' she said but her smile was gone.

'I should have told you from the start.'

'Now you're frightening me. Told me what?'

He couldn't see her face for shadow as he stood over her but her face was hazed over with expectancy. Her eyes were half-closed, lips slightly trembling. She stood very still.

'Let me have a bath and we will sit down and I promise I'll tell you everything.'

'Everything?'

'Yes,' he said turning away from her. 'No more secrets,' Dylan said as he went in the bathroom and closed the door behind him.

\*\*\*

Dylan and Jen sat opposite each other at the dining table. She had laid the table specially and lit candles. Dylan picked up the wine glass, as if he wanted something to hold. He drank the contents straight down and poured himself another.

'Jack?'

'I meant to tell you a long time ago... but it's serious. What I am going to tell you might upset you. That's the tragedy of this whole business, someone always gets hurt... I can't justify anything. I'm not even going to try but please just hear me out.'

Jen put her hand over his.

'No don't,' he said pulling his hand away. 'And don't look at me like that,' Dylan's eyes were glazed.

'You could never hurt me unless you're going to tell me you don't love me any more or you've found someone else?' she said.

'Oh God, it's nothing like that. I love you more than anything. Do you honestly think I have the time for someone else?' he asked forcefully.

'Well then...' She smiled. 'Everything will be okay,' she said gently.

Dylan sat rigidly. His voice when he began to speak had a harshness about it. It was as though the revelation was like picturing the awful scene. She watched and listened as his eyes appeared to grow large and bewildered. What was he talking about?

'What I'm talking about, Jen, is an incident, some time ago now, when I was on the firearms unit. We had a response call to an armed robbery taking place, at a local Lloyds Bank. A gunman had walked in, waving a firearm around and demanding cash. When he walked outside we were on site. Cars were broadsided, and we challenged him. He raised the handgun that he held in his right hand and pointed it in our direction. He wasn't for surrendering.' Dylan paused for a moment. 'Three firearms officers, including myself shot him. He died instantly. We had to do it, before he shot one of us.'

Jen was conscious of feeling shocked, dismayed. He hurried on with intensity.

'The shooting. It was all over in a moment. If we had waited any longer... But we didn't wait. Either one of us, or all of us killed him.'

For the first time he looked at her. His face cracked into a shaky smile that grew tragically kind. 'I'm sorry.' Dylan could see her bemusement, her shock. She was far less strong than he thought. He spoke very gently. 'Now I've explained it you might just begin to understand.'

Jen's hands went up to her face. He took one hand in his and he could feel her shaking as he had felt others shake in moments of terrible anxiety and fear. Dylan wanted to hold her, but feared rejection himself. 'I haven't told you before because I knew how much it would upset you.' Her hand fell from her face and he could feel her shudder. She rose from the chair and stood with her back to him. The blind was still open and she saw a light whip across the lawn. She pulled on the cord and the blind dropped heavily. For a while she stood still. Eventually she turned. Dylan hadn't moved. His eyes found hers.

'Doing the job you were doing I guess it was something that might happen,' she said.

'It happened so quickly and not as I expected it would,' he said. 'I saw the sudden terror on the man's face, an open mouth, eyes wide. The letter box on the blue door of the bank and the scarlet creeper up the wall became visible. A limp hand let the gun fall as if in slow motion to the floor. There was glass spraying everywhere. The shouting had stopped. A flicker of leaves sifted through an oblique ray of sunlight. The officer stood next to me had highly polished toes on his boots... he trod silently for two steps towards the gunman before he went to his knees.' Dylan's voice cracked.

'But there was a threat to life?' Jen said.

'Yes.'

'The gunman. He was given time to surrender?'

'Yes, but we could have still been charged for murder. We were all decorated firearms officers, we all knew the killing was lawful. The man was an armed robber in a team who had been under surveillance by air and on the ground for months. The intel was that they were all wearing body armour and armed. We had no choice but to shoot at his head. He was a high-risk suspect. He was holding one gun and another loaded revolver was found in his pocket. One bullet went in his shoulder, one in his ear, the other in his head.'

'You could justify the shot?'

'Yes, we all could. I could be a killer, Jen. 'Forensically it's known which weapon each bullet came from, and at the post-mortem they would know which bullet caused his death. That to me only means that one of us is a better shot than the other two firearms officers. We were all responsible for his death. Even if the court, which they did, deemed it was a lawful killing.'

'But you're not a murderer, Jack. You did what you had to do, like the others. You had to kill him or risk being killed.'

'It was still taking someone's life, or being party to it.'

'Lawful though, a lawful execution.'

'Words. That doesn't make it feel any better.'

'Maybe not, but when it came down to it, you did the job that you were trained to do.'

Dylan was silent, his head bowed.

'And that's why the details are not on your file,' Jen said.

'There should be no details on mine or any of the other's personal files. The identity of those involved remains anonymous except for the hierarchy who needed to know for obvious reasons, and the Independent Police Complaints Commission, the IPCC investigated it fully. It was a massive enquiry.'

A lone tear escaped from Jen's eye and ran down her face.

'You're crying,' said Dylan reaching out to wipe it from her cheek.

'Not for him. For you. Is that why you came out of the unit?' she said with a sob.

'Yes, I don't know if I could react the same again.'

'He was evil.'

'He was a bastard. His family talk about him as if he was a bloody angel too. In their eyes we murdered their son, brother, uncle, cousin...'

'So there is no mystery?'

'No, no mystery,' he said with a weak smile.

'Just a piece of you I didn't know about?'

'And Avril knows. Well, she knows something. She hints at it often. Some paperwork I understand initially came through under confidential cover. Hugo-Watkins took it off her, sent it back to HQ and created hell. It was sent in error apparently.'

'It just hurts that she knew something about you that you didn't feel you could share with me. Her of all people.'

'It's past, Jen and that's where it has to remain, buried.'

She looked away from him. Maisy's red coat, hat and gloves were hanging on the peg. She shuddered at the redness... What shocked her was her reaction to it. 'It could have been you that had died, couldn't it?' Suddenly something broke in her and she burst into tears. 'We might never have met... we wouldn't have Maisy.'

Dylan found Jen sitting at the pillow end of the bed sometime later. She looked dishevelled. Her cheeks were red and tear stained. He was hesitant but lay on the bed next to her and she turned into his arms. As Jen slept he lay on his back and looked up at the ceiling, barely visible in the darkness of the room. He was sweating. Telling Jen about the incident had opened up old wounds and in his mind he relived the events of that fateful day. Sleep eluded him for a long time. He had survived but it could have turned out so different.

# Chapter Twenty-Seven

The team were all present at Harrowfield Police Station as instructed. They stood in the basement of the police station, a large expanse of space known as the Void, waiting for last minute instructions. Glancing around, a few of those present looked as if they hadn't been to bed, Dylan felt the same, but hoped his restless night didn't show. Dylan expected his team to be able to work hard and play hard and he expected nothing less of himself. Work was their priority. The role of a police officer demanded one hundred per cent commitment. The job description didn't allow for shirkers. There was no room for laziness and no ability to carry such on a homicide investigation. Carelessness cost lives and evidence. Of course mistakes were made but if they were done through conscious neglect, Dylan would deal with it quickly and effectively. He wouldn't allow anyone to intentionally or otherwise bring disrepute to the investigation. His officers knew where they stood with him, and were aware that should they overstep the line they would be ousted from the team.

Acting Detective Sergeant Vicky Hardacre was 'on her toes,' checking the uniform units were ready, then the two cars set off in the semi-darkness from the police station yard. Daylight hadn't quite arrived in Harrowfield. The air conditioning in Dylan's car was activated to maximum ensuring the windows were clear of condensation. It was drizzling and the windscreen wipers rocked to and fro intermittently. Once they left Harrowfield town centre behind, the road lighting along the country lanes became intermittent. High hawthorn hedges made the single track roads appear much darker. The lead car's main beam illuminated the way forward and the other found it easier to ride on its tail lights.

At their destination of Midgley Court the officers re-grouped in the car park.

'Looks like he's here, boss,' Vicky said pointing to his transit van in the designated parking bay.

Swiftly they made their way to the suspect's door. The loud knocks with a baton handle, echoed along the corridor. A light could be seen from within and was accompanied by angered shouting. 'Alright. Alright.'

'And I was hoping to use the door ram,' Vicky said to Dylan quietly as they heard the locks being retracted.

'Hopefully with more effect than they portray the act on TV,' he said.

'I've been on the course,' she said as the door swung open. The occupier stood in nothing more than a pair of black boxer shorts. He was a tanned, middle-aged man with a six-pack. 'What the fuck do you lot want?' he asked, screwing his eyes up at the light outside his door. The odour from the flat was of spent whisky.

'Richard Bryant?' Vicky said.

'Who's asking?'

'Acting Detective Sergeant Hardacre, Harrowfield CID. Can we come in?'

His fists that were by his side clenched, Bryant stuck out his chest and his nostrils flared. The non-verbal signs to the officers that suggested he was going to kick off.

'You are being arrested on suspicion of the murder of Billy Simpson,' Vicky said.

'Who the fuck are you?' he asked as he stepped forward towards Dylan.

'Detective Inspector Dylan,' he said, flashing his warrant card. Dylan didn't back away. 'And you'd better get some clothes on or you'll be coming with us like that.'

Seeing the back-up that uniform supplied he wisely backed down and the two detectives followed him into the bedroom. He pulled on tracksuit bottoms and a cut away T-shirt. Sitting on the bed he looked up at Dylan with cold blue eyes as if contemplating something but Dylan couldn't tell what. Whatever it was he decided against it. Standing up he put his arms out at Vicky's request and was handcuffed without any problems, before being led out to the police car by uniform. The search could now begin in earnest on his flat for evidence that would connect him to the murder of Billy Simpson.

'Good job he didn't kick off, he looks a strong lad,' Dylan said.

'Yeah, he's fit,' Vicky said with a quick raising of an eyebrow.

Dylan looked at her and shook his head.

'What I mean is he keeps himself fit,' she said rolling her eyes. 'Do you ever get the feeling when you're speaking to someone that the wheel's turning but the hamster's not present?'

'Yeah, know what you mean,' he said with a snigger. 'I don't want to burst the bubble but the muscle's more than likely steroid

186

enhanced looking at all the tablets and containers of protein powders in his kitchen. Did you see his thick yellow toenails?'

'No, but then I wasn't looking at his feet,' she said.

'Calm yourself. He could be a bloody murderer,' said Dylan. 'I'm off back for breakfast. Find me some evidence and then be ready to interview your would-be Adonis. Don't forget to have his van searched and examined by CSI.'

'Yes, boss,' she said.

*** 

Jen woke with a cracking headache. She was on the verge of nausea. She held two painkillers in the hollow of her hot hand, and filled a small glass of water from the sink. Maisy was still asleep. Opening the door to the kitchen she felt the full force of last night's declaration again as she faced the dinner plates that sat, food mostly untouched, on the kitchen table. She opened the window. The coffee she poured smelt strong to her sensitive nose. Her heart felt heavy. An optimistic sparrow hopped onto the window ledge, it's eye on her, hoping for a scrap or two. Its feathers all fluffed up. She shut the window quickly. The sparrow flew away. 'Wild birds in the house are unlucky,' Jen could hear her mum say.

Maisy woke and Jen found comfort in her smile and playfulness. As she threw back the curtains of the nursery, with Maisy in her arms she discovered the sun and the fresh day seemed to touch the wound of what had happened last night. The room was peaceful in colour and scent. Jen would check on Dylan today at work to see if he was okay. They could face anything together, she knew that deep down. The coffee and drugs seemed to soothe her headache. Maisy played happily with her toys and Jen lay curled up on the sofa ignoring the room's unusual state of untidiness. Poor Jack, she felt she had somehow let him down by making him relive the events of the fatal shooting. She caught a tear as it spilled onto her cheek and Maisy looking up at her held out her hand with gentleness. She held her daughter's hand for a brief moment and smiled at her. At least Max appeared to be alright, that had to be a positive.

*** 

In the CID office, Paul was diligently going through the enquiries into Operation Pullman. He had news for Dylan when he

187

returned. He believed now that Richard Bryant was the plumber that had been in attendance at Kirsty Gallagher's home.

'That's interesting,' said Dylan. 'Fancy the same name coming into both enquiries. What are we missing?'

'I don't know. What could the connection be? Women? Sex?' Paul wondered aloud.

'We'll see what his reaction is to the questions we put to him about Billy Simpson's murder first. Then we'll drop it on his toes about his link with Kirsty Gallagher.'

\*\*\*

The detectives were ready to go into interview. The local solicitors from the old Co-op buildings had been contacted on the suspect's behalf by the custody officer. Lin Perfect was on her way, Dylan had been informed. 'Those two must be making a packet,' thought Dylan, with the frequent requests they got for their services at Harrowfield Police Station alone. Having said that he couldn't complain, they were straight and attended in person rather than sent 'runners' – untrained staff to attend at the police station. If a 'runner' was sent to the station to speak to a client on behalf of a solicitor they would write down the details and tell the suspect not to reply to any questions until they had reported back to the office. That didn't help the suspect or the police on many occasions in Dylan's experience. A simple explanation could mean an early release for their client, which should in fact be the solicitor's priority although that was not always the case.

As Dylan waited for Richard Bryant and Lin Perfect in the interview room he sat wondering how Bryant would react. Some prisoners wanted to fight. No doubt these were the ones that were annoyed with themselves for being caught for the crime they had committed. Some prisoners were talkers and would try to dominate the interview. Others remained silent throughout and avoided eye contact with the interviewer by looking at the floor or the ceiling, whichever took their fancy. There was nothing on display or of interest in an interview room. Intentionally it was left with bare walls so that suspects had nothing to focus on other than those speaking. It would only be a matter of minutes before Dylan's question were put to this prisoner.

It would be boring if all interviews were the same. Each held a new challenge for Dylan in his search of the truth. The importance for Dylan was to take control in interview and remain in control throughout, using his body language to get a reaction even when there was silence.

Lin Perfect he knew, would be pleasant as always but when the case got to court there was always a show for the gallery from her and her partner Mrs Best.

Dylan heard the heavy fire doors on the corridor open and close, and getting up to stand at the entrance to the interview room, he could see Richard Bryant strutting down the corridor from his cell. He gave Dylan the evil eye as he passed. Dylan stepped out into the corridor. The door closed behind him and Lin Perfect.

Twenty minutes later, after private consultation with his solicitor, Dylan and Vicky went in to the interview room and took their seats across the table from the two. Silently Mr Bryant shook his head from side to side suggesting to Dylan that he felt aggrieved to be there. He ground his teeth annoyingly, tutted and sighed.

Dylan was going to enjoy the next forty-five minutes.

# Chapter Twenty-Eight

Dylan leaned forward towards Richard Bryant and he reacted by lounging back in his chair just as Dylan expected. 'You understand why you have been arrested?' he asked.

'Yeah,' he said. He tapped his fingers under the table, his eyes downcast.

'Would you explain to us what your relationship is with Jane Simpson?'

Bryant shuffled in his seat. He raised his head and his eyes met Dylan's. 'That's her in the papers, that topped her old man, isn't it?'

'What is or what was your relationship with her?' Dylan wasn't going to be distracted that easy.

'I know now that she's got a gob on her like the Mersey Tunnel.'

'Why?' asked Dylan.

Bryant seemed to ponder over the question.

Dylan and Vicky remained silent expecting him to continue. He did.

'Okay, look I'll be straight with you. I met Jane at this fancy dress party. And I've spent the odd night at hers, but she told me her and her hubby had split.' Bryant sat up straight and leaned in towards Dylan. 'She did all the running. She said it turned her on, me wearing the mask.'

'So, what happened?'

'The usual. She got clingy. Wanted me to get serious. Look, it was a bit of fun while it lasted. I'm not going to go bragging about it, especially now she's locked up, am I? It's not good for my reputation, know what I mean? That's me, I can't tell you anything else,' he said holding his hands up before resting them palms down on the table. 'Why didn't I come forward? Because I didn't think me spending a few nights with her was relevant.' His head lowered and his voice with it. 'The rumour that's going around is her ex broke in and attacked her. Is that right?'

'How old are you, Richard?' Dylan asked ignoring his question.

'Thirty-two,' he said. He gave a sudden jerk of his head.

'Do you go for the older woman?'

'I didn't know how old she was and she didn't know how old I was under that mask, did she? Know what I mean?'

'When did you last see her?' Dylan continued well aware Bryant had mentioned the mask twice.

'Not sure,' he said.'

'About?'

'A month or two, I guess.'

'Lucky you weren't staying over that night, wasn't it?'

'Well yeah, but if I had I might have been able to stop her getting hurt.'

'We'll be checking your mobile and home phone numbers to check your contact with her. What are we likely to find?' Vicky was very matter of fact. Her manner was composed, her facial expression impassive.

Bryant looked sideways at his solicitor.

Vicky glanced at Dylan. His scrutiny of the prisoner was almost tangible. He wasn't happy with Bryant and she knew why, he was far too confident and he appeared to have all the answers at his fingertips – was it all rehearsed?

'Oh yeah, yeah she was always ringing me, asking me to go round, missing me like you know what. You know what women are like.'

Vicky looked at him half-questioningly, as though she might have misheard. Bryant's mouth formed a perfect 'O', 'I mean...'

'I know what you mean. When did you last speak to her?' asked Vicky.

'Not sure. She carried on sending me messages and ringing me long after... Wouldn't take the hint.'

'You seem to remember a lot of things about your relationship with Jane Simpson, Richard, why not when you last spoke? '

'Hey, I don't remember exactly what was said on what date for every phone call, do you?'

Vicky looked at his greasy, alcoholic face and his messy hair.

'Where's the mask now?'

Bryant shook his head. 'I don't know. What would I want it for? She kept it on the coat hooks at the bottom of the stairs; said it would scare people off...' He stopped. Jerked his head, that looked like it had been hung out to dry on a stalk. 'Ah,' he said. 'I know what this is all about. It said in the papers something about the dead man wearing a mask. THE mask, was it? You don't think she thought it was me do you?' Richard Bryant's eyes grew wide and round.

'Your DNA was found inside the mask along with Billy Simpson's. And according to her recollection of the event she never said she gave it a thought that it could have been you wearing it. Strange that, don't you think?' asked Dylan.

'And that's why you think I'm involved because of the mask. No way,' he said jumping up. 'You're trying to set me up? I want out of here,' he said looking towards Lin Perfect.

'Sit down, Mr Bryant,' said Dylan. 'Did you know Billy Simpson?'

Bryant hesitated then sat down. 'Did I know Billy Simpson?' he asked.

Dylan remained quiet. Bryant appeared to be considering his response to the question.

'Small town, you know what I mean.' Bryant shrugged his shoulders. 'Probably,' he said with a nod of his head.

'You were knocking his wife off and staying in his house. I'd have thought you'd have wanted to know what he looked like?'

'I can look after myself,' he said with a swagger of the shoulders.

'Yeah, we know that from your previous, but you didn't answer my question. Did you know Billy Simpson?'

'Someone pointed him out to me in the boozer.'

'Who?'

'I don't remember who,' he said.

'Well, why should someone who you don't remember point him out to you. Had you told them you were seeing his wife? If so, surely it is someone you know?'

I can't remember.'

'Which pub?'

'I don't remember.'

'So you don't know who it was or where it was?'

'I don't know. It was a while ago. I didn't put the date in my diary.' Richard Bryant looked more composed.

'Jane Simpson didn't kill her husband by herself, somebody helped her. Was it you?' Dylan asked.

'No. No way are you pinning that on me. I've told you what I know. I want a private word with my brief.'

192

It seemed like a reasonable time to have a break so the first interview was concluded. Tapes of the interview were taken from the machine and sealed before being signed by all present.

*** 

DC Ned Granger was hopping around the Incident Room in an excited fashion. 'What the bloody hell have you put in 'em,' he yelled to Vicky as she walked through the door. Waving the sandwich in the air he looked to her as if he was about to combust.

'V i c k y...' growled Dylan, showing her the whites of his eyes.

'My office now,' he said striding out in front of her.

Vicky took a small detour past the water dispenser where Ned was guzzling water as quickly as he could extract it.

'Serves you right,' said Andy.

'You won't do it again, will you?' Vicky bristled as she grabbed his ears and pulled his red, dribbling bulbous face towards her. She kissed his forehead. 'Truth is you didn't notice you'd been eating cat food for most of last week so I decided I'd spice it up a bit for you,' she said. She bit her bottom lip to stop herself laughing. She let him go and with that she picked up her pad and pen from her desk and self-satisfied she ordered two coffees. 'And we'll have biscuits please, Lisa,' she said. Dylan's office door was shut behind her, she sat opposite him, jigging a black pump off the end of her bare foot.

Dylan was running his fingers over a folded piece of paper. He placed it in an envelope and cleared his throat. 'I should be angry,' he said.

'But?' she said raising her eyebrows. 'But, you know he deserved it.'

'But, I can't very well preach...' His lips turned up at the corners.

'No... You didn't? Spill the beans?'

'Well not exactly, but let's say our rota had once to take the shift Sergeant home after his pipe, that he had kept filling up from the other's tobacco pouches, had been mysteriously filled with cannabis.'

'No way?' Vicky's smile reached from ear to ear and she leaned in closer for more.

'But if he makes a formal complaint...' Dylan said.

'I know I'm up the river without a paddle for the Sergeant's boards.'

'Yeah, well it's not the best stunt to pull right now.'

Vicky gave a little twitch of her shoulder and rose as Lisa brought in the coffee on a tray. She wiped away a tear.

'You okay,' said Vicky.

'I'm crying with laughter.'

'Is he okay?' asked Vicky tossing her head in the Incident Room's direction.

'His pride's taken a knock. He'll be fine.'

'Cost me nearly twelve quid for that Ass Blaster Sauce from Amazon. Worth it though for that reaction,' she said with a chuckle.

Lisa held the drinks tray flat to her body, still tittering into her tissue, she turned to leave.

'Send Andy in, will you?' Dylan asked, before she shut the door behind her.

'Well, what do you think of Bryant?' asked Dylan biting into a Digestive biscuit.

'He had all the answers. Didn't attempt to cover up. Plausible story about how they met and the mask... Think maybe he could be telling the truth, in part anyhow,' she said dunking her biscuit. 'I've seen Inspector Farren from the Safeguarding Unit do this and she's a pro,' she said peering down into her cup.

'But, he's also lying through his back teeth. He's only telling us what he knows we'll prove easy,' said Dylan staring over her shoulder into the Incident Room as if he was in a daze.

Vicky took her eye off her biscuit to look at him and when she did half of it disappeared. 'Bloody hell,' she said pulling a face at Dylan. 'I will master it one day.'

'Watch his eye movements in the next interview. Listen to the way he repeats the questions we put to him. Note how still he is when answering... My money is that he's involved. We need to find out if he is involved in the murder and also why.'

'Well if you're going to lie, what do they say? Stick as near to the truth as possible.'

'Trouble is he's had plenty of time to prepare.'

\*\*\*

Detective Constable Andy Wormald knocked on the door and walked in. He had been heading the initial search on Richard

Bryant's property and while the pair had been interviewing he had seized some items of interest. A black expanding toolbox found inside Bryant's van had a number of items that were in the process of being preserved for examination, inside they had found a stiletto knife.

'Get it off to Forensic. I also want Bryant's footwear. Seize anything else, you know like a watch or jewellery, anything that might retain a microscopic piece of material or blood.'

'Sir.'

Paul Robinson walked in the office as Andy walked out. 'I've got Fingerprints checking Richard Bryant against the marks lifted from Kirsty Gallagher's house.'

'It would be good if we could put him there.'

'Let's hope the specialists come back with something positive that we can use in the next interview. I'd love to watch the cocky bastard squirm,' said Dylan.

'You sound like a man on a mission,' said Paul.

'He's got his back to the wall, and in the next interview I want him to realise he's going nowhere.'

# Chapter Twenty-Nine

Richard Bryant slouched in his chair but this time as Dylan and Vicky entered the interview room, he was rocking noticeably from side-to-side. The sterile room had an unusual chill about it. Yvonne Best sat alongside her client. There was only one door in an interview room and as Dylan entered he shut it firmly behind him. Silently Dylan and Vicky sat at the opposite side of the table from the pair. Vicky placed the exhibit she had brought with them out of sight, on the floor by her chair. Richard Bryant didn't look at them but Yvonne Best gave them both a weak smile. It had already been decided that Vicky would open the questioning, introduce the knife and ask about the whereabouts of Bryant's mobile phone. Dylan would watch Bryant's every move, intentional or otherwise. He would soak up his body language. Dylan was ready to play at cat and mouse if that's what Bryant wanted.

The atmosphere in the room was tense before they started the questioning.

Preliminaries over, Vicky produced the stiletto knife in the transparent circular exhibit tube referring to it by its unique identifying number it had been given as an exhibit. Bryant sat forward. 'Is that mine?' he asked, referring to the item put before him. Then he looked up at Vicky. 'What are you doing with that?'

'So, you can confirm that is this your knife?' she said.

'Stupid not to.'

'It was seized from your toolbox so it can be forensically examined. Did you know it was a prohibited weapon – length of the blade?'

'You what? Don't be so fucking stupid,' he said pulling a face at Vicky. 'I cut plasterboard with it.' Bryant was looking agitated.

'Well if that's all you've done with it, then you have nothing to worry about, do you?' she asked, with a forced smile. 'You wouldn't expect us to be anything but thorough in a murder investigation would you? You see this knife is very similar in shape and size to the knife that caused the fatal wound in Billy Simpson's chest.'

'There must be loads of bloody knives that fit the bill. You're just trying to fit me up.'

'Well, we'll leave that to the experts to decide shall we. Your van. That will be having the once over. Are we going to find anything?'

'Why would you?' Bryant asked.

'We leave nothing to chance. Like I said. If you've nothing to hide...'

'What a waste of bloody time. I'm self-employed, don't you realise my time is money and that van you've seized is my living?' his hands rested on the table.

'And I've told you we are just being thorough.'

'Pathetic,' he said, shaking his head.

'Can't you see that it looks mighty suspicious that on your own admission you were in a relationship with Jane Simpson, her ex-husband is stabbed to death wearing a mask that used to be yours and a knife that could have caused the fatal wound in that enquiry is not at the house where the murder took place, but you have a similar knife in your toolbox? Worth checking out for us isn't it?'

'It's not me. I keep telling you. It's nothing to do with me.' Bryant was breathing like a creature in distress. He moved to the edge of his seat.

'You have had plenty of time to think about what you were going to say to us. To try explain away your involvement, haven't you?' Vicky pushed him.

'I didn't need time because it's the bloody truth!' he said through his bared, gritted teeth. He sat back, his head in his hands.

Dylan took over the questioning.

'We all have to face up to things we don't want to from time to time, and it's now time for you to face up to this. I don't believe you are telling us the truth. Have you spoken to Jane or her solicitor since her arrest?'

'What?' Bryant looked bewildered.

'You heard me. It's a simple question. Have you spoken to Jane Simpson or her solicitor since her arrest?' Dylan said.

'Err... I don't think I should comment.' Richard Bryant said as he turned towards his solicitor.

'So I can take it that you have. You see you can't even be honest about that. A yes or no would suffice. What is it you're not telling us Mr Bryant?' Dylan asked, leaning closer to him across the table.

'There's nothing to tell. It's you two that's got it all wrong,' he said. He was wringing his hands.

'It appears that Jane Simpson had been separated from her husband for some considerable time. What reasons would he have for suddenly turning up at her house do you think?' Dylan asked. His eyes grew more intense.

'How the bloody hell would I know?' he asked.

'Because, you were there. You helped her attack her husband and then one of you put the mask on him. Between you, you even tried to make it look like he had broken into the house,' Dylan was going out on a limb and Vicky knew it. If he was wrong, Dylan knew from experience that Richard Bryant would sit quiet, confident in the knowledge Dylan was fishing.

Bryant slammed his fists on the desk. 'Like I said before this is a fucking set up,' he shouted.

Neither Vicky or Dylan flinched. His solicitor jumped, turned and stared at her client.

'Calm down, please,' she said.

'I'm not saying anything else. I can't believe you'd think... Why don't you say something?' he asked his solicitor.

'We can't understand either. That's what we need to find out and prove. And be assured, Mr Bryant, we will,' Dylan said.

'I want out of here now!' he said standing up.

'You're forgetting a minor detail, Mr Bryant. I'm in charge in here,' said Dylan. 'We don't do what you want, we do what I want,' he said looking up at him. 'Sit.'

'Would it be possible to have a break, Inspector?' asked Mrs Best,

Dylan considered the request.

'Yes, perhaps it will give your client chance to reflect,' he said.

'I'm innocent,' Bryant said loudly. 'How many more times.'

Dylan could see his hand tremor.

'Then how about you start telling us the truth. Interview terminated,' Dylan said calmly.

\*\*\*

Dylan was pacing outside the double fire doors of the Incident Room with his hands in his pockets. Jen walked towards him. The back yard was almost empty bar a couple of marked police cars. She smiled. He stopped on seeing her and walked towards her. He stopped in front of her and sighed. She smiled and reached out to touch his face.

'You can have one of mine,' she said pursing her lips.

'What?'

'Smiles, if you can't find one of your own.'

His lips curled up at the corners. He looked grey. 'I know this isn't the place but I'm glad I told you. Sometimes circumstances... Then we're caught up in a moment of overwhelming emotion, and we are spun over the edge. It's the very strength of that feeling that hurries it along. I spoke to the other firearms officers afterwards. No one plans to shoot. No matter how highly trained... What some people don't seem to realise is that like them we are human too. I understand that we push the rules to the limit but like the others I didn't feel we had any choice but to do what we did in the situation we were in.'

'Shhh... you don't need to explain. The enquiry didn't condemn you for your action so why do you condemn yourself?'

'I don't know. I guess I could have understood a need for reprisal, expected it even, but there wasn't any. I still expect it. At the time I felt I needed to feel some suffering for inflicting such pain on another human being. Do some sort of a penance. Although others might not have seen it as such, I did. I might have taken a life, Jen,' he said looking deep into her eyes. 'I had to make sure that that could never happen again – justified or not.'

'So you left the unit?'

'Yes – never to return.'

'And the piece of wood under your side of the bed that you put back the other day when I'd put it in the bin?'

Dylan laughed a little. 'Pathetic isn't it? The weapon used to be meaner when I lived alone.'

'A gun?'

'No, not a gun. Never again. I haven't held a gun since... until the other day in the property store,' he said. 'I felt as if life would ever be the same again. I had this dreadful feeling of loneliness. I hated myself.'

Jen wanted to take him in her arms. She looked to the grey flecking at the sides of his dark hair. She felt so confused and inarticulate. 'You're right this is definitely not the right time or place.'

Dylan reached out, grabbed hold of her hand and held it lightly in his, then he squeezed it as if he would never let it go. He turned his head at the banging of the door and the appearance of Vicky.

'Get a room you two,' she shouted as she ran towards them. 'You ready to go for another interview, boss,' she said. 'Okay, Jen?' she asked, giving her friend a fleeting hug.

Dylan and Jen's eyes met over her shoulder. Jen saw his lips move and briefly closed her eyes tight.

***

Back once more in the interview room. It was Yvonne Best representing Bryant. Yvonne had told Dylan with regards to issues surrounding representing both clients it was for them to consider if there was any conflict, they would be doing that. Procedural issues and caution were administered as Dylan sat alongside Vicky as she opened up the questioning.

'Like we said earlier, Mr Bryant we are thorough, which is what you would expect from a murder investigation. Now, we don't appear to be able to locate your mobile phone for some reason. Can you help us with that?'

His forearms were rested on the table and he sat forward. His head bent. Eyes to the table. Vicky also leaned forward.

'Lost it... It might have been stolen,' he said. 'I don't know which.' Dylan noticed Vicky's hands had a waxy whiteness as they lay before her on the table, whereas Bryant's opposite were big brown paws. It was the contrast in their hands that made him look at their faces. Vicky's eyes were large and alive as she scrutinised Richard Bryant intently.

'Since you spoke to Jane Simpson?'

He didn't respond verbally but his body language suggested it was.

'Convenient,' she said. 'What's the number?'

'Number?'

'Of your mobile.'

His lips drained of colour. 'I can't remember.' He tapped on the back of his brown hand.

'Don't worry,' said Vicky. 'By the way we've got your laptop.'

'What? What's that got to do with anything? I use that for work. All my contacts, accounts... everything is on there.'

'We will be as quick as we can, be assured of that,' Vicky told him. 'And no doubt we'll find something with your mobile number on it. Do you have a business card?'

Dylan looked at Yvonne Best who had slitted eyes – she was watching him.

'This is getting stupid. Look, I've done nothing wrong. Jane fought with a burglar. She was in fear of losing her life – stabbed the intruder, end of.'

Although Vicky was asking the questions Richard Bryant kept looking at Dylan as if waiting for him to comment. Dylan remained quiet.

'That's what she wants the world to believe. There was a poor attempt at trying to make it look like a burglar had entered through the kitchen window, but it hardly seems likely that he would then head into the hallway, chance upon the mask and put it on before going back into the kitchen to lie in wait for her, does it? Did you know he didn't have a weapon?'

'Maybe he thought he didn't need one because he knew there was only Jane at the house?'

'Maybe. But he might have also gone to her house because he had been invited and had been let in through the door,' said Vicky.

'How would I know?'

Dylan cleared his throat. 'We think different, hence your arrest. You don't remember the man who pointed out Billy to you. You don't remember when or where. You've lost your phone but don't know when and you can't remember your phone number. How convenient.'

There was a knock at the interview room door. The fact was verbalised for the tape and Vicky also said that Detective Inspector Dylan had left the room. On his return, he apologised for the interruption. Vicky knew it must be of major importance for no one would dare interrupt an interview and especially one DI Jack Dylan was in on, if it wasn't.

Once again the officers went over old ground in the interview, until Yvonne Best raised the issue that her client had already answered the questions being put to him more than once. 'If there are no more questions to ask Mr Bryant then please could he be charged or released?'

Richard Bryant looked smug.

Dylan terminated the interview.

***

Vicky and Dylan collected their paperwork from the table and left the room but Dylan asked to speak to Yvonne Best out of earshot of her client.

'We are going to bail Mr Bryant in connection with the Billy Simpson murder.' She looked taken aback.

'You are?'

'Yes, but we are going to arrest him in connection with the murder of Kirsty Gallagher. The interruption...' said Dylan, Yvonne Best nodded, 'was confirmation of evidence connecting him to that murder, which will be disclosed shortly.'

Yvonne Best looked bemused. 'Another murder?' she said her eyes widening. 'He's going to blow his top!'

'He's not going anywhere now,' said Dylan.

'Once you've told him, I will need some consultation time.'

Dylan nodded. 'Yes, no problem.'

'I'm going to have to get Lin Perfect over as I've got other appointments today that I need to keep.'

'That's okay. You must be very busy. You'll be expanding again over there before you know it.'

***

Yvonne Best went back into the interview room.

Minutes later Dylan was joined by DS Paul Robinson. Inside the interview room, Richard Bryant was told that he would be technically bailed in connection with the Billy Simpson murder as he was being arrested for another murder, that of a female by the name of Kirsty Gallagher.

'Can they fucking do this?' he yelled at his solicitor. 'Are you going to let them keep arresting me on the off chance I might admit to one of their fucking murders? Fucking ridiculous! This is madness... madness,' he called out as he was frogmarched back to his cell protesting his innocence and yelling obscenities at the top of his voice.

'That is one angry man, Inspector,' said Yvonne Best. 'I'll get my colleague over here as soon as possible. Will you be doing an interview this evening?'

Dylan explained the quality of the evidence behind his arrest. 'Yes, I think once he knows the reasons for his arrest he may quieten down, but that's up to him. The cells are built for purpose

202

and the staff are used to dealing with angry men, sober or otherwise,' he said with a wry smile.

As they went back to the Incident Room Dylan was pleased they had rattled his cage. He knew he was involved in both murders but what was frustrating him was what was the motive?

# Chapter Thirty

One of the hardest decisions for an investigator in an enquiry is to 'best guess' after liaison with the crime scene manager, those exhibits likely to yield evidence and therefore prioritise the submissions to be forwarded for forensic examination. Each exhibit submitted, whether it is a left sock or a right sock it carries an individual price that is charged to the budget; and murder investigations do not, contrary to belief, have a bottomless pit of cash. All monies spent must be accounted for by the Senior Investigating Officer and best value had to be sought in this case by Dylan.

The Forensic service would be receiving a vast amount of exhibits from the incidents Pullman and Mallard over the next twenty-four hours and prioritisation was essential. Dylan's staff would be reminded in the briefings that although the incidents had not been officially linked, one suspect, now known to be Richard Bryant, was connected to both. It was of paramount importance that the samples and exhibits were kept in sterile conditions, so that there could be no suggestion by the defence at some future date of contamination at any point of collection, retention or storage.

Dylan telephoned the fingerprint department and thanked them personally for their work in identifying Richard Bryant's marks at Kirsty Gallagher's home – it was a breakthrough for them.

'I understand the marks were lifted from the smoke detector and also the carbon monoxide alarm by Karen. Neither contained the required batteries, I understand,' said CSI Sarah Jarvis. 'Good of you to ring, Dylan. It's nice to be appreciated and Karen will be thrilled to hear her diligence paid off.'

Next he made a quick call to Jen intending to update her but she wasn't at her desk so he left her a message with Rita.

A sandwich was brought into the office for their refreshments then it was time once again to speak to Richard Bryant. This time however Dylan would hold the interview with Detective Sergeant Paul Robinson. There would be just the one interview to let Bryant know the evidence against him then they would let him rest overnight and reflect on his position. Dylan was informed that Lin Perfect from Perfect & Best solicitors would be at the station within the hour.

The hour passed quickly as the forthcoming interview strategy was discussed between the two detectives and it wasn't long before once more Dylan was sat facing Richard Bryant in the same interview room.

After the necessary introductions and cautions Dylan opened the questioning.

'How well did you know Kirsty Gallagher?' he asked.

One of Bryan's eyes was closed as if he was trying unconsciously to avoid looking at something unpleasant. He didn't reply.

'You do know who I'm speaking about?'

Bryant gave Dylan a guarded look.

'Let me refresh your memory. Fourteen Bankfield Terrace ring any bells? We both know you've been there so let's not beat about the bush, eh?'

The prisoner gave Dylan a wary little nod.

'Would you like to tell us about your relationship with her?'

'Are you going to try accusing me of the murder of everyone I've worked for now?' he sighed.

'When did you last see her?' Dylan asked, eager to move on.

'Way before she died and was taken from the mortuary.'

'So you know about that?'

'I just said so, didn't I? I'm not deaf and blind.'

'So we have established you did some work for her. Was she your girlfriend?'

'For a bit.'

'What work did you do at her address?'

'I fitted a boiler and a fire.'

'Do you check your work?'

'I'm a professional plumber,' he said with a frown. 'Do you want to see my certificates?'

'You see our understanding is that Kirsty Gallagher died from carbon monoxide poisoning, which wasn't accidental.'

'And you're trying to blame me for that? Easy target. Nice one.'

'The gas pipe had been tampered with.'

'Tampered with?' he asked, leaning towards Dylan. 'I don't tamper... I'm qualified. It's what I do for a living.'

'Weren't you concerned that she'd been found dead?'

'Course, she was young.'

'Why didn't you come forward?'

'Why should I? I had nothing to do with it, did I?'

'I don't know, you tell me?'

Bryant didn't speak.

'It's quite feasible that you were seeing Jane Simpson at the same time as you were seeing Kirsty Gallagher, is it?'

'What?' he asked, raising his voice.

'Is it possible you were seeing Jane Simpson at the same time as you were seeing Kirsty Gallagher?'

'I don't remember.'

'You see, we know someone tried to clean up Kirsty Gallagher's home after she died. They removed the bed sheets but stupidly they forgot the toothbrush that we can get DNA from. Was that you?'

'No.'

'Are you sure? The exhibits have gone for examination and we'll soon know one way or another.'

Bryant hesitated. 'I might have used the toothbrush at some time.'

'What do you know about the bed sheet?'

'I don't know nothing about the bed sheet,' he said shaking his head with little jerky movements.

'Apart from the gas fire and the boiler, did you do any other work at 14, Bankfield Terrace?'

'Don't know what you mean?'

'Well, she had a smoke alarm and a carbon monoxide detector but both were devoid of batteries, suggesting to me that someone didn't want her to be alerted to the danger she was in.'

'They were?' he asked. His eyes shot open wide.

'And it's odd that your fingerprints are on both alarm casings.'

He paused. His body was still. His eyes were the only thing that moved to look from Dylan to Paul and back to Dylan. 'Yes, well they would have, because I check them as a matter of routine when I do work at houses,' he said.

His body language told Dylan he was relieved. What was he relieved about?

'So you remember checking that there were batteries in them?'

'I don't remember but I would have.'

'Okay, so you'll have some sort of worksheet?'

'Somewhere.'

Richard Bryant looked thoughtful. Dylan felt a little tremor of anticipation.

'Good, we'll look out for it. Just to confirm, are you telling us that all the facts we have put to you in this interview so far are nothing more than coincidence?'

'Guess so.'

Dylan threw his head back and closed his eyes briefly. He inhaled deeply and then looked back at Bryant. Paul glanced at his boss. 'I don't believe for a minute that what you are telling us is the truth,' he said shaking his head slowly.

'Look,' Richard Bryant said. He leaned forward and put his hands together. 'For some reason you are intent on getting me banged up for something. But, you can't because you have no evidence to prove I've done anything wrong – because I haven't! I've done nothing. What I am, is sick of being here,' he said. Bryant used his arms and the table to help him get to his feet. He walked towards the door. 'Let me out,' he said banging on the closed door.

'Sit down.' Dylan stood. Bryant's boots squeaked on the flooring as he turned. Paul felt the pressure of Dylan's hand on his shoulder. 'Hold on,' he said pointing to Bryant's footwear. Bryant stopped. Dylan walked around the table towards him. Bryant's boots were devoid of laces which Dylan knew would have been extracted as a matter of health and safety procedure when he was taken into the cell. 'We need to examine them,' he said looking across the table at Paul. 'We'll end this interview now, so you can calm down and I'll speak to you later,' he said looking coldly at Bryant.

'I've done fuck all wrong!' he shouted his arms flaying. 'Charge me or for God's sake let me go.'

Dylan and Paul left the interview room and headed back to the office.

'Get the laces that were in the boots when he was brought in. Those boots are dead ringers for the ones worn by the person on Derek Harper's photo. I want them examined as soon possible.'

Paul struggled to keep up with Dylan, who took giant strides as he headed back to his office.

'What we're putting to him is getting under his skin. I can feel it. We just need him to carry on digging a hole so bloody big that he can't climb out.'

'Then we'll either get the truth out of him or he'll go on the back foot and no reply,' said Paul.

'Exactly,' said Dylan.

*\*\**

It was time for home, Bryant could have another night in the cells. Work would be done on the knife and the boots as a matter of urgency. Dylan was more than aware of Richard Bryant's custody clock but he needed some time away. He needed to clear the fog in his head. He knew the work would be done diligently without him being physically in the office. Something he had learned with age and experience. His priority in the morning however, would be to check it had all been done.

By the time Dylan arrived home Jen was in bed. He found his dinner that she had left for him, along with a note. *'Five minutes in the microwave should do it. Enjoy! Jen x'*

He saw the kitchen clock had stopped at half past nine – three hours ago. The heating was still on. A forgotten tray with a feeding cup upon it and Maisy's baby pink dressing gown hung over the back of a chair, Jen's dog-eared slipper boots sat under it. On the hallway table lay a couple of opened letters. He noticed Max was absent from his usual spot at the foot of the stairs. Knowing him he would have snuck onto the foot of their bed in Dylan's absence. Jen had left the occasional lamp on. He moved on careful feet back into the kitchen conscious not to wake his wife and Maisy. He made himself a drink and sat on the chair with the pink dressing gown hanging over it, to eat his meal. A sense of utter solitude came over him. He covered his eyes for a moment with his hand and let the silence of the room sink in. There was a sound, a movement in the living room. Dylan stopped and cocked his head. 'Max,' he said as he opened the adjoining door to let the dog out. 'What on earth are you doing in there?' Max came hurrying out his tail swishing excitedly. He buried his nose in Dylan's outstretched hand. 'Jen shut you in, mate?' he asked, taken aback to see someone lying on the sofa. He strained his eyes to see who it was. Penny Sanderson grunted, turned and now open mouthed snored loudly.

'Not again,' he said. 'We might as well have a bloody lodger.'

# Chapter Thirty-One

Dylan woke feeling surprisingly refreshed. Jen's head that was on her pillow turned towards him. She relayed to him Chantall, Maisy's childminders concerns about a little boy who had been diagnosed with Scarlet Fever.

'Goodness knows what we would do if Maisy got it now,' she said.

'We'd cope.'

'How?'

'One of us would have to take leave.'

'Yes, and I know which one,' she said. 'And Avril would love that.'

'Jen, stop worrying. Maisy hasn't got Scarlet Fever.' Her talk turned to Penny. His mind wandered.

'Have you listened to anything I've said, Jack?' Jen asked as he slipped out of bed a few minutes later.

'What?' he asked, his eyes wrinkled at the corners. 'What is she doing here again?' he asked through gritted teeth.

'He's gone walkabouts. Her fella. He's not answering her calls. It's almost as if he's vanished off the face of the earth. Poor love. She thought it was the real-deal this time. Give her a break.'

Dylan looked at his wife with scorn. 'We're not a women's refuge, Jen.'

'I'll sort it,' she said. She pulled the duvet up over the bed and straightened the pillows.

'You'd better,' he said gruffly. 'If she's got a drink problem I've a number for a clinic.'

Jen looked at him crossly.

'Sorry. This Bryant bloke is doing my head in.'

'Jack, its work, that's what you tell me. Stand on the outside, look in, you tell me. Don't be drawn, you tell me but that's exactly what you're doing.'

'I know. I know, I'm trying not to, but this one is getting personal.'

'They all get personal Jack, you just don't admit it.'

'You know what Maisy is going to say when she's asked to write a diary at school don't you?'

'Enlighten me...'

'My daddy doesn't come home till I'm in bed.'

'That's not true,' he beseeched.

'No it isn't, it's until Mommy and me are in bed.'

'You mean Mommy and I?'

Jen tutted.

'Okay... I hear you... but she could say a lot worse.'

'Such as?'

'My dad's in prison.'

'Don't you dare trivialise it, Jack. By the way the promotion board applications are out for Chief Inspector did you see the advert?'

'Yes.'

'Are you thinking about going for it?'

'Maybe, if it makes you happy. I might... If I get time. The Sergeant's board are out too. Vicky's applying.'

'Make time.'

'I'll think about it.'

'By the way I've booked us a table at Prego tonight. Penny said she'd babysit – least she could do after last night.'

'What time?'

'Eight o'clock.'

'I'll have to see you there after debrief.'

'I'll get a taxi,' she said gathering the dirty washing from the laundry basket in her arms and leaving him to get dressed. 'And then we can travel home together. It'll be like a proper date.'

***

Jen's words about the promotion boards felt like a challenge but Dylan's first priority was to find out if there were any updates on Richard Bryant. He would be interviewing in an hour. For once Dylan was in luck. The night crew Crime Scene Investigators had examined Bryant's van and they had found traces of blood on the rear of the van's floor. They had also lifted some fingerprints that they had proved to be belonging to Derek Harper. It had been confirmed that in the shaft of the stiletto knife there were traces of blood. Things were looking up, but he needed to know whose blood it was before he got too excited.

Another piece of interesting information that had come in overnight was Bryant's telephone link with Derek Harper and how they had increased around Kirsty Gallagher's death. The billing had also shown up links with Barrington Cook prior to his drowning in the canal. Dylan was pleased to have something new to put to Bryant in respect of Kirsty Gallagher although in respect of the bloods he would have to wait for Forensic confirmation. The evidence against Bryant was building nicely.

It was time for the interview. Just before they left the office Dylan was passed a piece of paper. An update from Detective Andy Wormald who was at Bryant's flat.

The news he hadn't been expecting was that in Richard Bryant's address book were Dylan and Jen's details and also folded inside were printed documents from the police computer systems. There was a handgun under his pillow.

\*\*\*

Dylan felt like a coiled spring as he opened the interview room door. 'What the hell was this bastard up to?'

'This is getting fucking ridiculous,' Richard Bryant said as he stood and approached Dylan nose to nose the moment he and Paul entered the room. 'I've answered all your bloody questions,' he said pointing his finger at Dylan.

'Sit down, Mr Bryant,' said Dylan with a voice of authority.

Paul did the caution and opened up the questioning.

'You can't keep me locked up just in the hope I'll admit to something that I didn't do,' said Bryant.

'No, you're right that would be totally wrong if you were innocent, but you're not are you? Your vehicle has been examined and traces of blood have been found on the floor in the rear. Are we going to find that is Kirsty's blood?'

Bryant's eyes were big and round but he didn't speak.

Paul cautioned him. 'I also have to tell you, you are also under arrest for unlawful possession of a firearm that was recovered from beneath your pillow when we searched your home. Do you want to tell us what you are doing with it?'

'I know nothing about a firearm. Perhaps the tooth fairy left it there?'

'How well do you know Derek Harper?'

He sat perfectly still. He didn't respond.

'You know, Derek Harper, the mortuary man who is presently charged in relation to taking Kirsty Gallagher's body from the mortuary. Did you use your van to help him take Kirsty Gallagher's body to his house from the mortuary?'

'Why?'

'I'm just asking you. How well do you know him?'

'I've known Derek Harper for years.'

'How do you account for the increased number of telephone calls made between you two recently?'

'Did you find my phone?'

'No, we found your business card with your phone number on.'

'But how can you get information if you haven't a phone?'

'We just have. Tell me, was murder the ultimate challenge for you?'

Bryant's eyes bulged. His face looked hot. His fists clenched in his lap.

Dylan took over. 'So, Derek Harper... Can we now establish that he is a good friend of yours?' he asked.

'I know him.'

'Did you know a Barrington Cook who lived in the same apartment block as you?'

'Don't know anyone there by that name.'

'Lying isn't easy is it Richard. You've got to have a good memory. Trouble is once you start the web you weave gets bigger and bigger, doesn't it? Have you ever been to Mr Harper's house?'

'Yes.'

'Kirsty's body was there did you know? She was photographed naked in some obscene positions and more to the point Harper wasn't the only person present at the time. In fact someone wearing boots just like yours, was also there.'

'And I suppose I'm the only person who wears boots now am I? You're clutching at straws aren't you? How many more times do I have to tell you? I'm not involved.' Richard Bryant's voice rose to a crescendo.

The detectives ignored his outburst.

'We also have fingerprint evidence that shows Derek Harper has been in your van. How do you explain that, Richard?'

Richard Bryant shook his head in short jerky movements. 'I'm not denying he has, probably at one time or another.'

'We now have the phone activity, the blood staining in your van, fingerprints, evidence linking you to Kirsty Gallagher's home... I wouldn't call that clutching at straws would you? Not only are you involved but you're one of the main players in this crime aren't you? So why not save us all time and try being honest about it. Why did Kirsty Gallagher have to die?'

'Just fucking charge me if you've got so much on me.'

'Why are you angry? Are you angry with yourself because you thought you'd covered your tracks?'

'I'm not involved. How many more times do I have to tell you? I'm not answering any more questions.' Bryant crossed his arms across his stomach and sat back in his chair letting his head fall to his chest. He closed his eyes.

'Was killing someone and getting away with it the ultimate challenge for you? But now you've been caught,' said Dylan. 'Why do you have my name and my wife's name in your address book?'

He made no response.

The interview was terminated.

***

Dylan was satisfied, they had enough to charge him in connection with Kirsty Gallagher's murder and the subsequent involvement of removing her body from the mortuary. Paul did the necessary. He informed Lin Perfect, Bryant's solicitor that depending what came back from the lab Dylan was hoping that he would be able to charge him with the joint murder of Billy Simpson. Now Dylan needed to catch up with Vicky to see how things were progressing.

There was a lot of issues bugging Dylan about Richard Bryant and the two enquiries. Maybe the team and their partners would enlighten him further in the next briefing.

Back in his office he shoved his paperwork to the side. Urgent or not, he wasn't in the mood for mundane routine. He saw Vicky in the Incident Room and shouted her name.

'You called?' she asked as she stood leaning against his door frame.

'You penned anything for that promotion application of yours yet?'

'I have actually,' she said. 'I don't know how good it is though.'

'Fetch it me. I want to look, if you've got a minute?'

'Have I?' Vicky said as she scurried away. Minutes later she was back with her document. 'I'll get the coffee whilst you're casting an eye, shall I?'

He picked up the red biro. 'No, not the red pen boss, please not the red pen,' she cried theatrically. Laughing she closed the door and left him alone. There was an art to writing a promotion application and experience was essential. The specific role profile for the job needed to be covered in the applicant's document otherwise it wouldn't achieve the paper sift stage.

Dylan was quite relaxed when it came to writing applications. He smiled to himself as he thought of the time when he was interviewing for a surveillance motorcyclist to work with the crime squad. Undercover work, but the ability to ride at excessive speed on occasions meant it was a dangerous job and needed officers with specific skills and experience. People in interviews, he found would say things that they thought you wanted to hear, as in this specific case. 'If you told me to go through a red light boss, I would,' said one interviewee. Totally the wrong thing he wanted to hear. Safety was always paramount.

Many applicants owned their own motorbikes and knew everything there was to know, including being able to strip them down and put it back together wearing a blindfold – he never failed to be impressed with their expertise. Experienced riders all of them on this occasion though except one, who for some unknown reason hadn't been. This officer confessed that having worked in the cell area for a number of years, he fancied a change of scenery. The candidate once owned a Honda 50 motorcycle when he was sixteen years old but never ridden since, he said on his application. Dylan had checked the date on the form wondering if it might be April Fool's day or a wind up? It wasn't. The officer was genuine and would, "agree to take lessons". Feeling as though he would probably need to brush up on his skills.' Dylan had let him down gently on that particular occasion.

By the time Vicky had walked back in with the coffee Dylan was two thirds of the way through her application.

'Bloody hell, boss, I thought you'd cut your hand,' she said lifting his hand from the paperwork.

'It's not as bad as it looks. I've just reworded it. You need to write it from a sergeant's perspective,' he said inviting her to sit opposite him. He passed the papers over the desk. 'Now, you have a read of that and let me know what you think. Don't just agree with my alterations. It's your application remember not mine.'

Vicky studied the suggested amendments carefully. She could see that where she had put things like 'I was involved' he had changed the wording to read, 'I took charge.' Which was true. 'It's good,' she said. 'Let them try to paper sift that. Thanks, boss,' she said with a smile. She started to rise from her chair.

'I want to see it again when it's typed up,' Dylan said. 'And check it. You would be surprised how many people don't check their application for typing errors or spelling mistakes. Remember typists are human too,' he said.

'Will do.'

'Jump one hurdle at a time. Get through the paper sift then it's onto the role playing and interviews. You can do it, so get positive.'

'Give us a shout if you want any help with yours, boss,' she said.

His look gave her his answer.

There was a knock on the door.

'Sir,' said Paul. 'I think there is something that you should know.'

'Go on,' said Dylan. Paul's serious tone cast a dark shadow over his face.

'You're not going to believe this but we've found a photo of Penny Sanderson, the cleaner, with Richard Bryant at his home address... And there's more, he has Warfarin, rat poison amongst his drugs next to a bag of knuckle bones.'

Dylan stopped what he was doing. 'He doesn't have a bloody dog... but I do. My God, that might explain a few things. Are you absolutely sure?'

'I'm sure, sir. Do you think the cleaner's involved?'

'I'd have said I'd bare my arse on the Town Hall steps if Penny was involved in anything sinister but...'

'Oh my God,' said Vicky. 'She needs to be spoken to as a matter of urgency.'

'Uniform are at her home but she's not answering,' said Andy.

Dylan rolled his sleeves back. 'No, that's because she's probably already at our house by now. I'm supposed to be at Prego...' he looked at his watch. 'She's babysitting Maisy.'

Both Paul and Vicky looked to Dylan for direction. He picked up his mobile phone.

\*\*\*

Jen meanwhile was standing talking to Vittorio at the bar. Her phone vibrated. She picked it up and read the message before tossing it in her bag.

'Delayed?' asked Vittorio, who was in his shirt sleeves drying glasses. 'That man of yours, he works too hard, *amica*. Like him,' he said casting his eye in the direction of a man sitting at the table in the corner who was working on his laptop.

'So tell me something I didn't know,' said Jen. Vittorio the manager shrugged his shoulders. 'Never mind we will look after you until he gets here won't we, Lidia?' he asked, flicking his head in the direction of the owner who was making her way from the restaurant. Lidia had the biggest, friendliest smile on her face. She reached out to hug Jen.

'Oh no,' she said sharing glances with Vittorio over Jen's shoulder. 'Prosecco is called for here I think Vitto, to cheer our friend up,' she said.

'Sounds like a plan,' said Jen with a smile.

'*Salute*!' the ladies said in unison as they raised their glasses.

# Chapter Thirty-Two

Dylan was in his car driving with the speed and experience of someone who had been making instant response calls to police related incidents for a number of years. The unmarked CID car with Vicky and Paul in it followed his vehicle also at speed. They rode as close as safety allowed on his tail lights. Dylan sped down the country lanes of the Sibden Valley under the darkness of the cloudy sky. The heater was blowing warm air to clear the windscreen. Dylan's eyes felt dry and burned as unblinking he concentrated hard on the twists and turns of the long, dark country road ahead.

It was nearly half past eight when Dylan's car reached the driveway of the house. His heart that under extraordinary police related circumstances stayed calm started to beat erratically in his chest. The lights in the house were on and everything appeared as normal. As Dylan got out of his car the CID car pulled in behind him. Dylan looked back at his colleagues as he walked down the pathway. As he put his key in the door he felt a tremor inside. Maisy could be heard sobbing. He felt a moment of relief. Max raced down the stairs to greet him. Instinct told Dylan that Maisy and Penny were upstairs. He grabbed hold of the handrail and raced up the stairs two at a time. Vicky and Paul with a well-practiced search sweep checked all the rooms downstairs. Dylan pushed open the door to the nursery and found Penny sitting with Maisy on her knee, reading a book. His daughter's sobbing ceased. Relief overwhelmed him but the mask of the detective served him well. Maisy had her dummy in her mouth. At first she blinked her eyes unbelievingly at seeing her daddy standing before her. Her lashes were wet. Then a big grin spread across her face. She spit the dummy out and sat upright on Penny's knee. She reached up to him.

'Jack,' Penny said, her pale white face looked startled. 'What are you doing here? Jen's waiting for you at Prego.'

'Shall I take her?' he asked quietly, reaching out for Maisy.

'No, I can manage. I was just going to get her teething gel. She will be fine once I've found...' she said as she struggled to get to her feet from the low seat with Maisy in her arms. Dylan put his hands swiftly out for Maisy and pulled her to him before Penny could protest further.

'When I find the gel,' she said, opening the top drawer of the dresser and fumbling around frantically. Shuffling footsteps could be heard climbing the stairs and Penny looked over Dylan's shoulder. She saw Vicky at the doorway and Paul behind her.

'What's happening?' she said.

'I want you to come with us,' said Vicky stepping inside the nursery. 'We need to ask you some questions Penny about a serious matter. Probably down at the station would be best.'

'What questions?' she said looking bewildered. 'Can't we do it tomorrow? I'm looking after Maisy. Can't you see that?' she said looking backwards and forwards to her, then Dylan.

'It's quite urgent, Penny,' said Vicky. 'And if you're wondering where your boyfriend Richard Bryant is, he's locked up for murder.'

'I'll look after Maisy. Penny you go with them,' Dylan said holding his daughter close.

'Richard? But he wouldn't hurt a fly. What's all this about, Jack? Am I being arrested?'

'No, not at this moment in time, but I think it's best we talk at the station,' said Vicky.

Penny willingly went with the officers.

'I don't see how I can help you,' he heard her say as they went down the stairs.

*** 

Dylan found Jen in the lounge area of Prego. She was sitting laughing surrounded by Vittorio, Lidia, Kelly, Sarah and Eugene Regis.

'Dylan! They all know Eugene and he knows you and Maisy? Maisy? What are you doing here?' she said jumping off her stool. A little unsteadily she walked towards Dylan and held her arms out for her daughter.

'Eugene,' Dylan said with a nod of his head.

'He's been telling me all about him and Vicky...' she said with a puzzled look on her face. 'She's a dark horse. She never said she was going out with him. Where's Penny?' she said looking over his shoulder towards the door. 'Is everything alright?' she whispered.

Dylan reached for Jen's hand and when he found it he squeezed it tightly. His face was serious.

'I'll get you a drink, *amico*,' said Vitto. 'You look as if you could do with one.'

'Let me take the little one,' said Lidia. Used to Lidia, Maisy was happy to be carried off to the foyer of the Waterfront Hotel anticipating with excitement the attention she knew she would get there from the staff.

'Jen, we need to talk,' said Dylan. 'Excuse us Eugene, Vittorio.'

'Of course.'

'If you need me?' Eugene said to Dylan.

'Thank you,' he said.

'If you would like to come this way, sir. Your table is ready for you, Mr Regis,' Vittorio said.

\*\*\*

Jen looked flushed. Her chin quivered; her knees shook. 'Could I have a drink of cold water, please?' she said as Kelly who was behind the bar brought a glass of Jack Daniel's and Coke and placed it on the table in front of Dylan. Dylan gently withdrew his hand from Jen's and placed two hands upon either side of her face. He gathered her towards him and held her close. 'I think you'd better sit down,' he said gently. 'I have something to tell you.' The couple sat facing each other. Dylan now held both Jen's hands in his.

As if in slow motion, on hearing what he was telling her, Jen closed her eyes and breathed in deeply. She was quite clearly not able to comprehend what he told her. He could only watch her chest rise and fall quickly as her face gave away nothing. Dylan talked on. He leaned towards her seeing her distress and eventually held her tightly when he'd finished. Her head fell on his shoulder. He saw her open her eyes wide and look up into his face. The light threw a faint shadow, so that her forehead and eyes seemed more dim and elusive than her mouth. Jen said nothing but she didn't take her eyes off him. Neither of them saw the waitress approach them with the glass of cold water. Jen was paralysed and voiceless. Her lashes wet.

Dylan took the glass from Kelly's outstretched hand and held it to Jen's lips. Some of the water ran down her chin onto her neck. Jen put her hand up to catch it and Dylan offered her his handkerchief.

'She okay? Can I get you anything else,' said Kelly.

'She'll be fine, thanks. We'll be fine,' said Dylan.

It was all beginning to make sense to Jen. All the attention Penny had been showing in Dylan's work. But she could never forgive her for the danger she had put them in.

Dylan's phone bleeped. 'Jane Simpson's fingerprints have been identified from marks lifted from the mirror in a jewellery box at Kirsty Gallagher's house,' he read.

'What is it?' Jen asked. 'Do you need to go?' her eyes were suddenly full of anxiety.

'No, no it's not important,' he said. 'You are. Are you okay?'

'I'm just glad I know you're not going anywhere tonight.' she said.

# Chapter Thirty-Three

It had been established that Jane Simpson had been at Kirsty Gallagher's home. How did she know her? Would this turn out to be another case of joint enterprise? Who else was involved? Dylan's head was spinning as he sat at the breakfast table.

'What's going on in that head of yours?' Jen said.

'Just trying to understand who murdered who and why?'

'Jack, I've been thinking. Penny can't be involved with these people. Maybe the new love of her life wasn't all she thought but... I can't believe she doesn't care about us. Me and Penny... we've been through too much together. There has to be a reason.'

'We'll it's eluding me. After they've interviewed her I hope I'll have some sort of explanation for you.'

Jen's face took on a look of torment. 'At this moment in time I want to rip her head off her shoulders. She was supposed to be my friend. I've been used, haven't I?'

'It's looking that way.'

'How can you be so calm about it? Do you think Richard Bryant has been to our house when we were at work.'

Jen sat down next to him and he held her hand.

'Try not to think about it.'

'No, I can't believe that she would do it... not knowingly. He's basically a stranger to her and we are, were, her friends.'

'She thinks the sun shines out of his backside. Remember, he is probably just using her to find out what we, the police know about him and his so-called friends. When she finds out about the other women in his life her world is going to implode. I guess that's when it'll sink in just what she's done.'

'Will she go to prison? Her kids Carly and Toby what will happen to them?

'Assisting offenders? Maybe. I don't know.'

'She had better stay away from me.'

'I'm sure she won't come anywhere near. We can't change anything about what's happened but it does show how vulnerable you, we can all be. Let's not let it fester. I'll keep you updated.'

'You look very smart,' she said as she held onto his suit jacket lapels, before kissing him goodbye. 'Definitely Chief Inspector material,' she said. Her face was puffy, her eyes looked red and sore.

'Not very subtle,' he said, touching her face. He kissed her nose. 'Vicky's done with her application and I'll get round to mine before the due date.'

Jen looked at him with suspicion in her eyes.

'I promise.'

'Good. Tell me something. Be honest. Do you think I am naive?' Jen's lips turned down at the corners.

'Sometimes,' he said quietly.

Jen held onto him a little longer than usual. 'I'll try and get some answers for you, Jen.' He said.

\*\*\*

Nothing could be as clear and as tranquil as the morning drive into work. There had been a heavy dew, and the grass in the Sibden Valley sparkled with it.

There was an old wives' tale that a corpse would bleed when the murderer was brought into its presence... how he wished that superstition was true; it would certainly make his job a lot easier.

The police station yard was full of cars and he was thankful for his allocated parking spot. It seemed everyone was in early with as much desire to get the job in the bag as he was.

'What came out of the chat with Penny last night?' Dylan asked as soon as he saw Vicky.

'Well she's obviously besotted by Richard Bryant. In her own words she said, "I've never loved anyone like..." and you can guess the rest. We locked her up on suspicion of theft of documents from the police station, which she was well pissed off at. Her house is about to be searched shortly,' Vicky said. 'Oh, she knew about the gun. She was told it was an imitation, she says. How's Jen taking it?'

'Not good. Apart from blaming herself one minute, she wants to kill Penny the next.'

\*\*\*

At the morning briefing Dylan shared with the team the fingerprint information and asked, 'Do we have any other connections that we know about, between this group?'

There was nothing forthcoming. The room was silent but the atmosphere was brimming with expectation. They awaited updates from Forensic with anticipation.

'I want an Anacapa Chart creating showing the links we have established between Derek Harper, Jane Simpson, Richard

Bryant, Barrington Cook and now Penny Sanderson, the two deceased Kirsty Gallagher and Billy Simpson and also include anyone else who is linked by telephones, vehicles or premises. It may just show us the relationship between these people and others we don't know about yet,' he told Ruth who was the person doing the Crime Pattern Analysis. 'At least then we will have a visual check that is readily available for all, as new evidence and data unfolds.'

Dylan was satisfied he had the people responsible in custody, what he now needed for the Courts was the true interpretation of what had happened and why. He always got impatient, when things were going well. He wanted to sprint to the end, but he knew 'it would all come out in the wash.' Jane Simpson would have to be produced from prison and arrested and interviewed in respect of the Kirsty Gallagher murder. Arrangements would have to be made with the Courts and the Prison authorities for her to be remanded to police cells for questioning. This wasn't simply a couple of telephone calls. It would require written reports incorporating specific details of her detention arrangements. Dylan set Vicky and Paul on with it. 'Good experience, lots of red tape,' he told them with a glint in his eye.

That delegation allowed him to look at the advertisement for Chief Inspector and he set about typing up his own application. Using operational incidents he had commanded to emphasise his personal skills and necessary requirements of the next rank. To his amazement on completion, he was quite pleased with it. He didn't have the luxury of some time to spend re-writing it. However, he was satisfied the content supported his application. But before being sent off to HQ it would have to go to the Divisional Commander for his support and comments. Dylan addressed the envelope that he'd marked Personal and Private to Chief Superintendent Walter Hugo-Watkins' secretary, Janet. This way at least he knew it would be recorded and be dealt with in accordance with force procedural time constraints. He wished he could see the look on Hugo-Watkins face when he read it. One of shock, perhaps? Hugo-Watkins would already be nurturing his favourite applicants for the next rank. Dylan was already questioning the integrity of the system and he had only completed the first stage of the procedure. But the deed was done as he'd promised Jen it would be. It was double space typed and sent as officially directed. He would pop it to Janet tonight before he left. Back to reality he told himself as he looked at the brown A4 envelope. Who was he kidding, really? Detective Chief Inspector Jack Dylan?

The Incident Room outside his office continued to be industrious.

'Boss, update from Forensic. We have confirmation that it is human blood in the handle of Bryant's stiletto knife and not only that they are confident of getting a profile,' Detective Sergeant Paul Robinson said.

'Good.'

'I can go one better, boss, Forensic have put Kirsty Gallagher in Bryant's van by way of her blood.' Vicky smiled sweetly at Paul.

'That's great news. I knew it. I wonder? What if we produce Harper and Bryant at the same time as Jane Simpson is in? We could cell them up so they could talk to each other, having made sure they know the others are in the cells, of course.'

'That's devious, boss,' Vicky said. 'So I'm guessing we would listen in and record their conversation? They'll have to be produced from prison to the cells because of the new evidence, to give them an opportunity to make comment if they wish, won't they?'

'CPS won't like it. Will they accept it as evidence if it's not under caution?' asked Paul.

'Probably not,' said Dylan. 'But we might glean something from their conversation that we can put to them in interview. They wouldn't feel so restricted during the night in the police cell would they and they might just try to make contact as they do by shouting to each other.'

Dylan knew that any conversation the prisoners had would be unsolicited so it would be a decision for the trial Judge as to its admissibility in court. It was worth the risk and an opportunity he couldn't miss. He would write up his decision in his policy book. He took out his pen and opened the policy book at a new page.

*'The suspects charged in connection with the murders of Billy Simpson and Kirsty Gallagher need to be produced from their respective prisons to police cells so that they can be afforded the opportunity to make comment, should they wish to do so, on new evidence in connection with the offence charged and also the one*

*that they are still suspected of. Derek Harper will also require producing from prison to police cells to afford him the opportunity also to comment on new evidence in connection with the offences he is charged with. Whilst it is necessary to question them about the new evidence, out of their presence in one police cell area arises an opportunity to take note of any unsolicited conversations that may arise by the defendants shouting to each other and whilst being unaware of police presence in the cell area corridor.'*

Vicky Hardacre rang Dylan from Penny Sanderson's home. 'Ned is nearly having a coronary at the sex aids that he is having to seize as exhibits.'

Dylan smiled. 'Anything else of note?'

'We have more police documents marked confidential, print outs from our computers, it seems she's been helping herself.'

'So we basically have theft of paper to charge her with?'

'Yes. She's mortified at being here but I don't honestly think she knows a lot more than she has already told us according to DC Wormald who has just interviewed her.'

\*\*\*

'I'm going to shoot off and see how Jen's doing,' Dylan said. He was on his feet when his telephone rang. He hesitated. In his head he could hear Jen's voice telling him to 'leave it.'

He strode out of the door. He had his promotion application in his hand and passing Janet's office he popped it in her in tray. Janet acknowledged Dylan but kept on typing.

Rita was heading towards him down the corridor.

'And before you say anything, this thing that Ned Granger decided to put in my temporary store, fully blown up I might add,' she said. 'This should come with a government warning, not an instruction manual.' Rita stood a full sized blow-up doll in a full set of lacy white underwear in front of him, from where it had been tucked under her arm. The blonde Marilyn Monroe lookalike appeared nothing like the picture on the booklet. Rita grinned and her smile made her look younger than her fifty years of age. 'How does that?' she said pointing to the plastic effigy, 'look remotely like that?' she said moving her pointed finger to the image on the manual that was tied to the doll's wrist by a plastic handcuff. The doll's short, blonde, curly, nylon wig looked like something only a granny would wear and her puckered red lips that were formed in a perfect 'O' were indented with a two inch wide hole. But her eyes that were blue like it said, it was true, were the funniest of all as they stared back at her, cross eyed.

'Knowing Ned he will have put it there to shock you.'

'Shock me? He should know I'm too long in the tooth to be shocked by anything I find in my property store, Dylan,' she said matter-of-factly. Then her face softened. 'Is Jen okay? What a blow for her, if it's true what Penny has done.'

'She'll be alright. I think the most frightening thing for her is that she trusted Penny to look after the most precious things in her life and although she didn't hurt Maisy I think she might have indirectly nearly killed Max.'

'But why would she do such a thing?'

'I don't know the full details yet, but the only thing I can think is that she was so infatuated with Richard Bryant that she did everything she could to please him. Including the sex toys and getting information from our works computers for him.'

'Why did he want that sort of information?'

'I don't know. I think we are only just seeing the tip of the iceberg with this gang, Rita and we're just scratching the surface of that. Goodness knows how big the distribution network is. By the way, that inflatable isn't that bad looking. Not when you've seen what I've seen lurking in dark corners in nightclubs around here, believe me,' he laughed.

# Chapter Thirty-Four

Penny had been bailed for six weeks. In interview she admitted taking documents from the police station for Richard Bryant who she said was curious about what the police had on him, and some of his friends. It was, she thought a way of her finding out more about the new man in her life and, 'The bottom line, boss,' Vicky said 'is that she would do just about anything for him.'

HQ had immediately suspended her and she would receive written notice terminating her employment.

Dylan was livid. Penny had been conned by a charmer maybe, but that was no excuse in his book for betraying a friend. He was glad she was away from the cells when Jane Simpson arrived. Although, a confrontation between the two women may have proved interesting.

The timing and production of the three prisoners had to be right. Their respective names and cell numbers, along with time and date would be charted on an A1 size board immediately behind the custody desk so that on their arrival, albeit at different times, they would see that their associates were also present in the cell block. In large letters written in red ink he had instructed it to also read, 'NO CONTACT' – that should grab their attention. Jane Simpson would be obviously detained in the female block that ran parallel with the male cells separated by a secure door. Cell area staff would be briefed in detail about further planned interviews and what else was to take place on the relevant date, which would be as early as physically possible.

Paperwork, continuous telephone calls, meetings and the seeking of relevant authorisation meant the Incident Room remained a hive of industry twenty-four/seven. The week passed quickly and at last the day arrived for the operation to take place. The Forensic laboratory and Fingerprints updated the Incident Room as to the position of outstanding exhibits and marks. Dylan wanted to have up-to-date information available and ready to use at the tips of his fingers.

'Vicky, Paul, are you sure we have the latest from the lab, fingerprints, phones, computers etcetera?' he asked on entering the office that morning.

'Yes, boss.'

'Everybody knows what they are doing?'

'Yes, boss.'

*\*\**

Dylan was doing a lot of pacing around his office, the investigation was gathering momentum. He wanted to know more about this group, if they were part of a larger network, or simply local reprobates and like-minded people seeking each other out?

His telephone rang, 'DI Dylan,' he said.

'It's Janet the Chief Superintendent's secretary. He's asked me to see if you are attending the meeting that is about to start in his office, regarding the scrum down for sergeants who have applied for promotion this time around?'

'It's now is it, Janet? I'll have to get myself a secretary.' Janet could hear his smile in his voice.

'Yes, it's now, Dylan. I did send out a message earlier, after it was decided at the morning meeting.'

'Tell him I've been delayed momentarily due to operational work and I'm hot-footing it up to the top floor right now.' Of all the bloody days to have this meeting. Why Hugo-Watkins had chosen today, God only knew.

He let the Incident Room staff know where he was going should there be anything urgent needing his attention before taking the stairs to the upper floor. He strode out along the corridor and turned into the door marked: Chief Superintendent Hugo-Watkins.

'They're all inside, Inspector, waiting for you,' Janet said. Dylan pulled a face at her.

'And, Jack,' she said 'something to look forward to. There are some of your favourite chocolate cookies inside, on a plate for you,' she said with a little smile.

'You're an angel,' Dylan said with a wink as he opened the door and walked in the Chief Superintendent's office.

'Ah, he's here,' said Hugo-Watkins. 'Morning, Dylan, I know you're busy, we all are, but it's essential we put the right candidates forward. We have four applicants but HQ have asked each Division to limit their support of nominations to their top two, hence this urgent meeting.

Inspector Justin Gaskin was present and Dylan noticed he couldn't have been more laid-back in his chair if he had been on a sun lounger. A whole chocolate cookie was going in his mouth and he had another in his hand. Dylan snarled. The plate was

228

empty, albeit for a couple of custard creams. Dylan knew Gaskin wouldn't be doing Vicky any favours after she stopped him entering the Simpson murder scene. Human Resources were represented by Officer Hilary Carter. Hilary was prim and proper with what Dylan called a basin haircut. An attractive slim woman in her fifties she had eventually found her police vocation in her present role. Front line policing was not the strongest part of her skill-base, but nevertheless she was straight talking and he liked her. Inspector Carter saw some good in everyone and he knew she would ensure there was fairness within this procedure as with anything else she was involved in. So this was where the paper sift would start? Dylan had hardly had time to sit down before Justin Gaskin spoke out in his booming loud voice. 'This shouldn't take long,' he said, pulling himself into an upright position and picking up his cup of coffee from the table. 'There is only one candidate for me and that's Graham Thornton. Eddie Thornton's lad. He's a graduate entry, big lad, he'll be an Acting Chief Constable one day, just like his father, mark my words.'

'Let's not be too hasty, Justin, we are here to consider all four candidates with an open mind. Perhaps I should read out their applications,' said Hugo-Watkins. Hugo played with the handle of his best china cup.

'That would be most helpful, sir, as I perhaps am the only one among us, who is aware of only one of the applicants,' said Dylan.

'My apologies, Jack. They are Graham Thornton, uniform patrol on Justin's shift. Victoria Hardacre, your acting sergeant,' said Hugo-Watkins. He took a moment to look over his half-rimmed glasses at Dylan, Dylan nodded. 'David Baxter, uniform patrol who's represented by Hilary as his shift Inspector is on nights. She has already liaised with his Inspector Mark Baggs. Last, but not least is Kay Smart, who is currently working with HQ Community Liaison on attachment. I've personally spoken to her immediate supervisor.'

Hugo-Watkins commenced reading the applications out one by one. The office was warm and although they had been provided with refreshments before Dylan had arrived Dylan could hear Justin Gaskins fat stomach rumbling. Once or twice Dylan saw the Inspector's eyes close and his head fell but on reaching the conclusion, Inspector Gaskin couldn't contain himself. He sat upright and leaned towards the table with a loud belch. 'I told you. Thornton's the man for the job and I give my other vote to that smarty pants from HQ. Easy as that,' he said clapping his hands together.

Chief Superintendent Hugo-Watkins' response was a quietly spoken one in comparison and his feedback on each one was laboured and typically non-committal. He stroked his dyed moustache that was groomed to perfection as always. Dylan concentrated on the walnut panels on the walls in Hugo-Watkins' office and his expensive looking paintings. He poured himself a glass of water from the jug that was stood on the coffee table in-between the two leather sofas and waited patiently for his views to be sought. 'Inspector Gaskin, having given careful consideration to all four candidates I do see that Graham Thornton's application reads well,' he said running his fingers through his short dark Grecian 2000 dyed hair, 'but so does Vicky Hardacre's.'

Dylan was intentionally remaining quiet. He wanted to hear what Hilary had to say.

'I think we should look beneath the applications, we are not stupid. No doubt all candidates will have had some assistance in penning them,' she said. 'And that might not be what we can call equal opps.' She put her cup she had been nursing on her lap down on the coffee table. 'Who is more suited to the role, and perhaps more to the point, who will make the best supervisor?'

Before she finished Justin jumped back in. 'I've just told you,' he said grabbing the last of the biscuits. At least if his mouth was full it would keep him quiet, thought Dylan.

'If you let me finish. David Baxter and Victoria Hardacre have both been selected to act in the role of Sergeant already. David some months ago for a short time, and Victoria I understand is acting up at this moment isn't she, Dylan?' Dylan nodded. 'I have heard nothing but glowing reports about how these two officers have embraced the supervisory roles and in Vicky Hardacre's case she definitely seems to be blossoming into her new position according to what you were telling me earlier Mr Hugo-Watkins.' She went on to read out comments from other supervisors about the candidates she had mentioned. It was more than obvious that Hilary had done her homework.

'That's a very good point about the officers who are 'acting up',' Hugo-Watkins said. Dylan smiled inwardly, he was having to do very little for his officer.

'Yeah, but Graham Thornton would do us a sterling job. He just hasn't had a chance to prove himself yet.' Justin was once more beating his own officer's drum, very loudly. Dylan leaned forward and topped up everyone's coffee cups.

'Whose fault is that, Justin? Maybe if you'd have let him act up?' Hugo-Watkins said wagging a finger in the air. 'Jack, you haven't made a comment yet. Not like you to not voice your opinion,' said Hugo- Watkins. 'What do you think?'

'I was just listening to everyone else make comment. The successful candidate will be initially at least, a front line patrol supervisor and that may not be at our Division, but they will be representatives of Harrowfield wherever they are.'

'Yeah, big strong lads is what we need like Thorny,' Inspector Gaskin said baring a fist and speaking in a deep gruff voice.

'I'll ignore that sexist remark this once.' Hilary turned and rounded on him. Justin Gaskin screwed up his nose.

Dylan continued. 'Whilst we perhaps have our own personal favourites, having closely worked alongside them. I feel that experience is absolutely essential to a supervisory role and we have two officers who have proven their ability. Although they have both only worked a short time in the role I think it says a lot to say we selected them and headquarters have approved it. I, like Hilary have heard nothing but positive feedback about the two officers she talks about from their supervisors and work colleagues. Therefore I am inclined to agree with Hilary, for me David Baxter and Victoria Hardacre are our strongest candidates, based on operational experience. Good leadership skills are essential to take on this supervisory role.' Hugo-Watkins' body language especially his head movement told Dylan he was agreeing with his comments.

'So, what you're saying is that because Graham Thornton hasn't acted up yet he doesn't get our support?'

'Justin, that's not what I'm saying. The two officers we are speaking about like I said have been selected at Divisional level to work in a supervisory role already. I am sure they were chosen because of their ability and experience and the decision to allow

231

them to be acting Sergeants has been endorsed fully by HQ in letting them act up. We cannot simply ignore that.'

'Thornton is a far better officer than that woman detective of yours will ever be, in my opinion,' he said.

Dylan smiled inwardly. 'Is that so.' Gaskin was showing his true colours. Hilary gave him a warning glance before focusing her stare at Hugo-Watkins.

'Do you not like her because she's a woman or because she stood her ground when you tried to bully your way into the Simpson murder crime scene she was protecting for me. I believe she refused you entry, didn't she?' Dylan said.

'Huh... I was the duty Inspector on that shift and I needed to see what we were dealing with.'

'Really? We all know it's both fundamental and imperative to keep a scene sterile, so she was doing a job as a supervisor and doing it well in my view to stop someone as bullish as you from contaminating that scene,' Dylan said.

'Well, it looks like you've already made up your minds,' Gaskin said slapping his thighs.

'Yes, it appears we have,' said Hugo-Watkins. 'Thank you all for your time. It is my decision that we support Police Constable David Baxter and Detective Constable Victoria Hardacre as our candidates for the next round of the Sergeant's boards.'

Dylan and Hilary nodded. Justin Gaskin shrugged his shoulders. 'Waste of time,' he muttered as he walked out of the office throwing his hands in the air at a startled Janet.

'Dylan, could you just give me a moment please?' asked Chief Superintendent Hugo-Watkins.

Hilary shook the men's hands and left.

'Sit down, Jack. I know now is not perhaps the right time to discuss your promotion application, as I know how busy you are today but will you give Janet some dates when you can make yourself available to me. You are serious about this, aren't you?' he asked, looking straight into Dylan's clear blue eyes.

'Never more so. Like I have just been saying I believe that operational experience is essential for taking charge of, and dealing with current issues. I believe I am more than ready to meet the challenges of the next rank.'

'Err... quite. Yes. Right, well let's have a chat sooner rather than later then, please.'

Dylan smiled to himself. Hugo-Watkins really didn't know what to make of Dylan and Dylan wanted to keep it that way.

'Oh, should I tell Victoria Hardacre about your decision or shall I tell her to nip in to your office? She is working.'

'Would you ask her to pop along? I'd like to inform her in person. Thank you, Jack for your contribution this morning. I found it most helpful.'

'You're welcome, sir.'

Dylan shut his office door quietly. Janet smiled. 'Did you enjoy the cookies, Dylan?'

'I didn't get a chance. Gaskin had them in his mouth before I got a look in,' he said, his lips turned downward.

Janet opened her drawer and took out a packet. 'Thought he might. Here, don't tell anyone,' she said handing him a packet containing the last two.

\*\*\*

The more time Dylan spent with Hugo-Watkins behind closed doors the more they seemed to get on. The man was growing on Dylan, even if his choice of women, in Dylan's opinion, left a lot to be desired. God knew what he saw in Avril Summerfield-Preston? Dylan made his way to the Incident Room with a promise to ring Janet with times he was available.

As he strode back through the Incident Room he wore a very serious face. He headed for his office without speaking to anyone. At his office door he turned and stood quiet. In a serious and loud voice he called out. 'Victoria, my office now, please.'

The office went quiet. You could hear a pin drop as all eyes were upon Vicky as she walked into his office. Dylan told her to close the door.

'The Chief Superintendent wants to see you immediately,' he said. His head was down and he was reading a report he had picked up from his desk.

'Why?'

'It's about your application so look sharp,' he said. 'When you go in don't sit down until you're asked. Sit up straight and don't fidget. Be polite and most of all don't keep crossing and uncrossing your legs, which you do when you're nervous by the way.'

'I do?'

'Yes, you do.'

233

She laughed nervously.

'Smile. I'm sure it will be good news,' he said. His mouth twitched upwards at the corners. 'Then get back here we have a lot of bloody work to do.' Dylan smiled. 'Practice that dead pan serious face when you walk out of here and don't say anything in the office yet.'

Vicky gritted her teeth in a fake smile. 'Eek...'

'Go on then, what're you waiting for?' he asked with a wave of his hand.

***

It was thirty minutes before she returned carrying some documents under her arm.

'You knew all the time didn't you?' she asked. Her face was flushed. She looked happy.

'Of course, but I had to stop your mate Inspector Gaskin blackballing you for his favourite, a PC Graham Thornton. Piece of advice, he's going to like you even less now. We need to talk about the next stage of the promotion process, you're not home and dry yet, but it'll have to wait till we have sorted these murderers. The last thing I want is bloody promotion boards getting in the way.'

'On a serious note, thanks boss, if it wasn't for you pushing me I know I wouldn't have even applied.'

'Just shows, we all need someone to kick us up the backside every now and then. He's obviously given you a lot of reading material,' he said nodding towards the paperwork she carried over her arm. 'So make sure you do read it.'

'But..'

'No excuses. Find the time.'

'He says he will speak to me again before the boards.'

'Good. So you know you have our support. All you need to do now is get your mind set.'

# Chapter Thirty-Five

Dylan's day had been somewhat derailed but he was glad he had been to the meeting. If only to stop Inspector Gaskin.

Detective Sergeant Robinson walked into his office his face full of optimism. 'We have good news about the trace of blood on the shaft of Bryant's knife. Vicky's just getting coffee. I'll let her tell you the rest... '

'Promising?' Dylan asked.

'All good sir, all good.'

\*\*\*

Jen sat at her desk. She had been happier than she had been in a long while. Her home life settled, the love of Jack Dylan and the birth of their daughter Maisy had all helped her move on from the death of her mum in a road traffic accident.

Her dad Ralph was enjoying a new found freedom with the use of the Internet and his new love interest. Jen had felt at peace with the world lately – until now. Now the sun had gone out of her sky and her stomach felt heavy with foreboding. She put her head down on her hands, and tried to think. Think! What was there to think about? Nothing. Now she was finding it hard to begin to know how to deal with the fact that someone she had considered her friend, her only friend for a while when she had relocated, had not only used her, and to what extent she was unsure, but to think that Penny could have potentially put her life and the lives of those she loved whether intentional or through naivety at risk was hard to bear. What she did know was that she would never speak to Penny again. It astonished her how deeply she felt the disloyalty. Dylan could never begin to understand how good Penny had been to her in the early days when she had felt dreadfully alone and isolated, three hundred miles away from her family, with only Max for company. They had been through a lot together had Penny and her in the last few years. She had once potentially saved Dylan's life when she had found him collapsed due to exhaustion when Jen was at her dying mother's bedside... now she had to accept that their friendship had come to an end.

'I hear Penny Sanderson was putting it away at the King's Head last night,' said Rita breaking her
reverie.

Jen sat up. She put her elbow on the desk and cupped her chin in her hand. 'I feel sorry for her in a

way... but more so for her kids.'

Rita's face was like stone. Her eyes were as cold as those of a seagull. She had always given Jen the impression that she had become hardened by her life experiences, learned to live with the unpleasant things she dealt with in her work, that her sullen eyes looked upon the whole world as tainted. Albeit Jen had also seen the softer side of her at times. Rita set her eyes on Jen. 'Don't you dare go losing any sleep over her,' she said crossly. 'You hear?' she said rising from her chair at the desk opposite. Jen nodded her head but her eyes swam with unshed tears. Rita walked past and stopping behind her chair she put a loving arm around her shoulders and gave her a squeeze. Nothing more was said.

\*\*\*

Dylan's head turned to door at the sound of Vicky's rat-a-tat-tat. Paul stood to let her in.

'We've hit the jackpot... it's Billy Simpson's blood,' she said glancing up from the drinks tray to Dylan. She put the tray down on his desk and handed a cup to Dylan and Paul before taking her own. She sat cradling it smugly in her lap, before reaching out to take a biscuit from the plate.

'So the bastard was there, and it was him that more than likely inflicted the fatal stab wound. But why?' asked Dylan. 'Why did he want to kill him and Kirsty Gallagher? Had he wanted to kill and got the taste for it. Maybe it excited him?'

Vicky took a noisy slurp of her coffee.

'I'm really hoping by listening in on the cell corridor that we can glean something else to put to them in interview. Let's have another interview with Bryant before we put our plan in action. I want to drop this on his toes and we'll have to re-arrest him for Billy Simpson's murder now we have this new evidence.'

\*\*\*

Dylan was informed that two of the prisoners were already in the cells and the anticipated third was en route. It was game on. He was looking forward to seeing Bryant's reaction when they put to him the new evidence and he wouldn't have long to wait. Dylan's mind was set on the forthcoming interview and Lisa's news that Yvonne Best had arrived was another step closer. He could feel his heart quickening. He needed to speak to her and disclose the fact that her client Richard Bryant would be re-arrested due to new evidence in the Billy Simpson murder case and there would be further disclosure in connection with the offence of murder for which he was already charged.

Thirty minutes later and he was sitting in the interview room with Richard Bryant, his solicitor Yvonne Best and acting Detective Sergeant Vicky Hardacre. The relevant caution was read.

'You are being arrested for the murder of Billy Simpson,' Dylan said. He looked directly at Bryant.

Richard Bryant grunted. He appeared as if he had been struck dumb. Dylan eyed him narrowly for a moment or two.

'So what's new? It's bollocks.' He leaned back in his chair and appeared to reflect.

'The double edged stiletto knife, the one you identified as yours from your toolbox. You said you used it for cutting plasterboard. We've found blood on it.'

'Yeah, and no doubt mine. I've cut my hand on that bugger a time or two.' He wiped a hand over his face.

'It's Billy Simpson's blood.'

'No fucking way,' he said his eyes widening to the size of a golf ball. 'Jane admitted that to you, did she?'

'But what you need to explain to us is why a knife in your toolbox has got blood from the deceased on?'

'How the fuck would I know. You tell me,' he said turning to Yvonne Best. Yvonne didn't take her eyes off Dylan.

'The pathologist tells us that it was a double edged knife that was thrust into Billy Simpson's chest. And this was the killer wound,' Dylan said.

'I didn't do it. Ask Jane she'll tell you I wasn't involved.' Richard Bryant remained calm.

'God knows why but the sad thing is Jane would probably do anything for you wouldn't she, and you'd let her,' Vicky said.

'I can't help it if women find me irresistible.'

'Why do you think women are so besotted by you?' asked Vicky.

Richard Bryant shrugged his shoulders. 'You tell me?' he smirked. 'How the hell would I know? As far as I'm concerned it was all just a bit of fun. Look, for fuck's sake, the fact is Jane's ex has broken into her house, she has to fight for her life and then she ends up killing him. You two might not like it, but that's what happened.'

'That's what you would like everyone to think happened, but the facts speak for themselves,' said Vicky. 'There was no break in. Oh yeah, there was a poor attempt to make it look like there was. Was that your idea?'

He made no reply.

'Billy Simpson was stabbed whilst wearing a mask, your mask that he just happened to come across in the hallway you would have us believe, wouldn't you?'

He made no reply.

'Billy Simpson was stabbed three times, once in the chest and twice in the back. The latter we know was inflicted when he was already down on the floor. It has been shown that these two subsequent wounds were caused by a different knife to the one used to strike him in his chest; your knife, from your toolbox, which we can now prove has got Billy Simpson's blood on it. This knife is the right length, thickness and it has a double edged blade. A dead ringer for the murder weapon,' Dylan said. 'Isn't it about time you starting telling us the truth?'

He made no reply.

'Well?' Vicky said after a moment or two.

'She must have taken it. Put me back in the cell. I'd rather be in there than listen to this load of shite.'

'If that's true, Richard,' Dylan said. 'She must have also managed to get it out of the house after the incident and back into your toolbox without your knowledge. Can you tell us how you think she could do that?'

He made no comment.

'Your present girlfriend we understand is a Penny Sanderson. She has admitted to printing off information from police computers she says was for you. Is that right?'

'Might be.'

'We have also found other such material at your home address. Did you encourage her to do that for you?'

'Might have.'

'Why do you think anyone would risk the chance of being sacked from her job and face prison for the likes of you?'

'I didn't make her do it. She said she could and she did.' Richard Bryant shrugged his shoulders.

'You don't care how many lives you wreck with your deviant lifestyle do you? Or maybe you do and you enjoy the power you seem to have over others? The truth I suspect is that you killed once and enjoyed the thrill.'

Richard Bryant didn't answer but turned his head away.

'Is there anything further you wish to say to us?' asked Vicky.

He made no reply. The interview was terminated.

The prisoner was escorted back to the charge desk where in the presence of his solicitor he was charged with the joint murder of Billy Simpson. He was then brought back to the interview room. 'What the hell's going on now?' he asked. 'You've charged me.'

His outburst was ignored as they all took their seats and invited him to take his. He sat down reluctantly. Vicky made the relevant caution.

'We wish to inform you that in respect of the Kirsty Gallagher murder we now have further evidence that we feel you should know. The blood found in the rear of your van has been forensically examined and it has been identified as belonging to Kirsty Gallagher. How do you wish to explain that?'

'It's not, not, not, not. Lies, lies, lies, lies,' Bryant chanted over and over again.

'That depends on which side of the table you're sitting at,' Dylan said. Richard Bryant raised an eyebrow at Dylan.

\*\*\*

Richard Bryant was taken back to his cell. Dylan could hear him dragging his feet on the corridor. The smirk had been well and truly wiped off his face and Dylan hoped he would think about what had been said in the interview and offer some explanation to his solicitor. Dylan gave the nod for the next interview with Jane Simpson to commence. Again the interview procedure was instigated in the same interview room. She was told of the developments in connection with the offence for which she was charged which was the murder of her ex-husband Billy Simpson and the fact that Richard Bryant had also been charged jointly with his murder. She remained silent.

'I also wish to inform you that you are being arrested in connection with the murder of Kirsty Gallagher,' said Paul who further cautioned her. Her expression changed to one of utter disbelief as she turned her head sideways to glance at Lin Perfect, her solicitor.

'Can they do this?' she said.

'Have you ever been to 14, Bankfield Terrace, Harrowfield.'

'I don't…' she said hesitantly touching her nose. Dylan saw the slight tremor of her bottom lip.

'Your fingerprints had been found at that address.'

'They have?' she said.

'Yes.'

'I remember Richard, Bryant, was doing some work up Bankfield Terrace.' Jane Simpson's face was flushed. Her mouth opened and shut without her speaking. The hands she clasped on her lap began to fumble with the hem of her cardigan.

'Is there anything else you want to tell us?'

'We, well we... we .... Richard was working on his own there.'

'Go on...'

'We had sex there.'

'Where?'

'In the bed.'

'Were you aware that Richard Bryant was having a relationship with the owner of the house, a Kirsty Gallagher?'

'No, no I didn't,' she said. Jane Simpson looked as if the wind had been taken out of her sails.

\*\*\*

The interview over, Dylan opened the door for Vicky to go before him. There were certain times in an investigative officer's life that were more exciting than others and that was no more so than when updates of proven facts and evidence on an enquiry were coming in thick and fast from all different departments and partners. Dylan, Paul and Vicky worked through the paperwork and took the phone calls.

'Fingerprints have almost concluded the examination and identification of all marks but for one fingerprint that had been lifted from the rear door of Richard Bryant's van. It's important as it has traces of Kirsty Gallagher's blood in it and it doesn't belong to Simpson, Harper or Bryant,' Paul said.

'No chance it is Penny Sanderson's?' asked Dylan.

'No, sir. I think to all intents and purposes her involvement appears to be on the periphery to the murder investigations.'

'So we've got potentially another party involved?' Dylan said.

'The telephone links show activity between Harper, Bryant, Simpson and Gallagher and Barrington Cook when they were alive. It's all becoming clear on the charts.' Vicky said. 'But we have a lot of other links especially via telephone data to enter.'

'How soon will the Anacapa Chart be ready?'

'When it is, I guess.'

'See if Ruth will work some overtime. We need the crime pattern analysis working flat out on this right now. What about the computer team? Is the historical data flagging anything up? How are we doing at proving the links there?'

'They need time,' Paul said.

'Don't we all. Forensic update?' asked Dylan.

'There's nothing new. Although they are checking footprints found at the murder scene with shoes taken from the suspects' addresses. You wouldn't believe how many men are a size ten shoe size and women a size six. That's not likely to prove today,' said Paul.

'So it's back to basics. We'll have another interview with Jane Simpson again Vicky, about Kirsty Gallagher's murder to see if she can or will tell us anything more. Then you and I, Paul, will drop it on Harper's toes about what we know about his network, and see if that gets a response. I'm hoping something comes out of the cell corridors tonight. Quick sandwich?' he asked.

Acting Detective Sergeant Vicky Hardacre sat eating her sandwich at her desk and was in conversation with DC Andrew Wormald and DC Ned Granger. Pen in one hand, she briefly picked up her cup in the other, and alternated it with holding her sandwich to take a mouthful. Eagerly she wrote notes. On the other side of the office, DS Paul Robinson mirrored her image concentrating instead on writing down points as he conversed with Ruth who was working on the Anacapa Chart. Dylan was impressed how the team was working together. Lisa on the other hand, who sat directly outside Dylan's office looked across at Dylan who was watching them intently.

Before he knew it he was once again back in the confined space of the interview room. 'Jane you admitted in the last interview, you had been to Kirsty Gallagher's house?' Vicky said.

'I told you I went there to see Rich.'

'Yes, do you remember the date, or was there more than one occasion when this happened?'

'What?'

241

'What was the date, or the dates that you visited Richard Bryant at 14, Bankfield Terrace?'

Dylan remained silent as he let Vicky talk to Jane Simpson, woman to woman.

'I didn't say that I'd been there more than once,' she said looking somewhat confused.

'No, I'm asking you, did you?'

'Well yes… Rich wanted me to meet her. He wanted me to… you know… try it on with her. I thought she was pretty but she said it was a non-starter.'

'Well, for whatever reason he killed her. Were you party to that?'

'No. I know nothing about it.'

'Do you know a Derek Harper?' Dylan said.

'Yes, he's a bit strange. Rich calls him G.D.'

'G.D?'

'Grave Digger. He told me he'd known him for years. One of those people you call uncle because he was his dad's friend, but he's not related really. Well at least I don't think he is…'

'Has he introduced you to any more of his friends?'

'No.'

Dylan was pleased. She was opening up and in his estimations she appeared to be being quite genuine.

'Has Richard or Derek Harper ever taken a photograph of you in the nude,' Vicky said.

'You're a bit nosey, aren't you? Yes, but we used a webcam more. He liked me to send him pictures of myself to him from my mobile a lot.'

'Do you know if he showed the pictures to anyone?'

'Probably. I don't mind if it turns him on. If you've got it flaunt it, that's what I say.'

'Did you know he took pictures of Kirsty too?'

'I guess he would've.'

'Did you see any?'

'Of me? Yeah.'

'No, of Kirsty,' Dylan said.

'No.'

'Have you ever talked to him about how she died?'

'No.'

'Do you know a Penny Sanderson?'

She shook her head. 'No, I've never heard that name.'

The interview didn't feel to be going anywhere and didn't reveal any more. As they strolled back to the Incident Room, Vicky was morose.

'We'll get there,' Dylan said. 'Don't look so down. 'Paul and I will go straight into the interview with Derek Harper, if his brief David Scacchetti has arrived. Let's see what he will say to us now we can put more to him.'

# Chapter Thirty-Six

Derek Harper had lost weight on remand, in prison. The former gravedigger looked grey and gaunt. His nose marked out by a little red triangle with its congested tip and a network of minute blood vessels.

Looking a picture of health in contrast, Leeds based solicitor David Scacchetti sat next to him. Dylan explained to Harper why they had him brought to the police cells.

'It's a waste of everybody's time,' he said. 'I'm not saying anything.' Harper constantly laboured his reply to all questions put to him when he bothered to answer at all.

'Your production from prison is to tell you of the evidence against you we have now secured since your arrest and affording you an opportunity to comment if you so wish.'

'I've enjoyed pissing on a few graves in the past, who knows who's I'll piss on in the future. Yours maybe?' said with a cold, defiant stare.

With that inference, and his negative response to answer any further questions put to him, Dylan ended the interview and Harper was returned to his cell.

All three prisoners were in their relevant cells. Their location manufactured to enable them to communicate with each other – albeit by shouting through the small observation hatch in the cell door. The opportunity to be a fly on the wall for the team was too good to miss. Dylan hoped the prisoners would speak freely, especially during the night when there would be limited movement in the corridors. This intelligence seek he hoped would glean something that the team didn't already know.

'Nothing ventured, nothing gained,' he said to Vicky as they prepared to leave DC Granger whose job it was to sit on the bleak cell corridor till his shift ended in the early hours. Only tomorrow morning, when Dylan and Vicky returned would they know if the exercise had been worthwhile.

'I know you're here G.D. You dirty old git can you hear me?' shouted Richard Bryant. There was no reply.

'Rich, I'm here. I wish you were in 'ere with me.' Jane shouted at the top of her voice.

Just at that moment the whole cells erupted with a couple of drunk and disorderly prisoners who had been brought into police custody.

'Damn,' said Dylan. He and Vicky looked on as they watched the prisoners shouting and lashing out at everyone in their path. Their voices, along with the officers trying to restrain them echoed around the holding area with its shiny, white tiled walls.

Drink and drugs were a massive catalyst. It was no excuse for people's behaviour and never would be, but defence solicitors would plead their client's case and tell the judge and jury that the causation of their downfall was the cocktail of drink and drugs. The solicitors should tell it as it was, in Dylan's view, that the obnoxious twats that stood before them were violent, aggressive individuals who upset and sometimes destroyed the lives of thousands of peace abiding citizens with or without any kind of intoxication. Now that would be a breath of fresh air. He knew that would never happen.

The staff in the cell area showed great restraint. The prisoners spat and kicked out but all was under control. Hopefully, and in Dylan's experience, once in their cell the prisoners would sleep it off and not ruin the possibility of his officers listening to the rants of their reprobates, who were strategically housed for best interaction.

\*\*\*

Back in his office, Dylan picked up his phone to speak to personnel at the Imaging Department. 'Any news for me on that request to enhance the computer image showing the boot on the Harper pictures from the Pullman enquiry,' he said.

The guy on the other end of the phone was upbeat and positive. 'I'm working on it now, sir,' he said. 'We've enhanced the stills from the computer images and photographed Bryant's boots for comparison purposes. I am pleased with the similarities thanks to the specific wearing to the heel of the boot that can be clearly seen. Mr Bryant has a unique gait to his walk it seems. The cuts and stains to the leather uppers are also providing especially encouraging results, even at this early stage. I will have a report supported with appendices of photographs outlining the similarities for you within the next few hours,' he said.

Still with the boots, he wondered if Forensics had identified any blood splattering. If so identifying who that belonged to was of paramount importance. Dylan wanted, no he needed, as many nails as possible in Bryant's coffin. He picked up his ringing phone.

'Yes,' was the first word he heard. 'Yes! DI Dylan we have found a minute trace of blood on Bryant's left boot and on checking it on the database it had been positively identified as Kirsty Gallagher's.'

Things were coming together. The evidence trail was building nicely but Dylan wouldn't become complacent. He was feeling tired and it was time for home.

'I'll be at the end of the phone, Andy, if you need me,' he said to Detective Constable Wormald, who was to take the reins as the night detective.

Dylan drove towards Harrowfield. The market square spread out in front of him. A big open space into which the more dark shadowy High Street flowed. Beyond, as he sat in traffic, he could see Stan Bridge where he had spent many an hour as a force negotiator for suicide intervention. Dylan's car came to a standstill beside one of the two semi-elliptical arch ribs that supported the Yorkshire stone piers. He marvelled at the architecture. Not a bad place to be stuck to feel that life was less of a hectic scramble. A policeman came towards him in the middle of the road. Dylan wound down his window. 'Don't tell me, I'm required,' he said with a low groan.

'No sir,' he said jerking a thumb in the opposite direction. 'A minor accident, no one injured. It'll be clear before you know it.'

The time out gave him time to ponder. Although the evidence against the three prisoners was excellent and continued to increase in value to him, he still didn't have a motive? He couldn't see why for the life of him anyone would go to the extent of murdering two people. Little did he know that the vacuum of silence he was experiencing alone in his car was in vivid contrast to the noise that the detectives were experiencing in the cell corridor.

\*\*\*

Detective Constable Andy Wormald and Detective Constable Ned Granger were on two hourly shifts in the cell area. They were to all intents and purposes spending the night in the cells, like a prisoner. As the night rolled into the early hours the silence became deafening. Had they missed their chance?

Suddenly a male voice pierced the silence. Ned's pen jolted ready to take down the talk that ensued, verbatim. The noise echoed around the tiled walls.

'G.D. Talk to me before they come round to check on us. Have you grassed?'

'No.'

'Well, remember to keep it that way, otherwise you'll be digging your own grave, old man,' he said. Richard Bryant laughed like a hyena.

'Rich?' asked Jane Simpson.

'What?' Bryant said.

'Will I see you in court?'

'Looks like it. Every time the bastards speak to me they charge me with something else. Just remember it was self-defence and we'll be alright.'

'Shh... Someone's coming.'

The gaoler was on his rounds. The sound of his keys rattling gave him away. Ned screwed his face up tight. 'Hell fire,' he whispered. What a conversation stopper. The night returned to a dark silence and that's how it continued. It was a long night for which the officers didn't have anything that could be used as evidence or actioned further. The next morning after breakfast, arrangements would be made for the prisoners to be returned to prison.

***

Dylan was disappointed. He had high hopes of bringing them together. It would have proved more fruitful had he been able to instigate them meeting face to face but he knew that was not possible. His phone rang, 'It's Janet, Dylan. Chief Superintendent Hugo-Watkins is asking if you are available to talk to him this morning in relation to your promotion board?'

Dylan was waiting updates from his team. It seemed like he was always waiting for something. He agreed to see the Chief Superintendent and made his way slowly up to his office.

The leather sofa in Hugo-Watkins' office, where Dylan was directed to sit, was made of a soft natural leather that smelt like a saddle. The Chief Superintendent rose from behind his desk and came to sit opposite Dylan. A coffee table separated the two with a percolator full of fresh ground coffee that was brewing, and two china cups upon it. Dylan smiled to himself, Hugo-Watkins was very obviously practising his informal approach.

'Jack, I wanted to strike whilst the iron is hot as they say, help yourself.'

Dylan didn't need asking twice.

'Firstly, I have liaised with the Assistant Chief Constable, Edward Thornton, as all Divisional Commanders have been asked to do in respect of our candidates who are putting themselves forward for selection. The reason being of course is that you are not simply being considered for the rank of Chief Inspector but we need to be sure that if we invest in you, you are future Force Superintendent material.'

'You mean Eddie Thornton? I knew Eddie Thornton long before he changed his name on achieving the rank of Superintendent,' Dylan said looking over the rim of his cup at Hugo-Watkins. He sipped his hot drink slowly.

'Quite. I have to be honest with you,' he said. 'Headquarters are suggesting to me that I should be supporting Inspector Martin Telford, a graduate entry and someone who has been chosen to be the Chief's staff officer shortly.'

Dylan sat perfectly still. His eyes never left Chief Superintendent Hugo-Watkins face. Dylan had a blank look on his face.

Hugo-Watkins coughed into his fist. 'You can see their reasoning, can't you?'

Dylan realised that Hugo-Watkins was firmly closing the door on him. He continued. 'Truth be told I have been asked to limit my support to one candidate. Hell, Dylan I know how busy you are. Their directive doesn't leave me with much room for manoeuvre.'

Dylan considered what he was really telling him in his roundabout way.

'Well, if you have nothing to say, can you excuse me?' Hugo-Watkins said hurriedly. He attempted to get up from the sofa with his china cup and saucer in his hand but fell back on the soft cushion. His coffee splashed all down the front of his pristine white shirt. Dylan had to suppress a laugh.

'Tell me, does my application address all the relevant issues? And in your opinion under normal circumstances, if it was being vetted independently would I be paper sifted at this stage?' Dylan asked.

'Your application is excellent and shows a vast amount of experience. It wouldn't be paper sifted, but you can see what a difficult situation they have put me in?'

'Yes, and whilst I appreciate your position you must also appreciate mine. In line with equal opportunities I will be insisting that it goes forward with a similar endorsement from you, to which you have just stated.'

Hugo-Watkins stood up and walked to sit back behind his desk. 'Jack, I know exactly where you're coming from. I'm just thinking of the rocky road ahead and the disappointment your quest will be to you if the powers that be are not backing you.'

'I understand. But I am asking you to allow me to deal with that if and when it arises. I'm in this race to win, not to come second and I certainly won't be ruled out of entering just because of someone else's prejudices. Believe you and me, I won't accept it lying down if you don't support me.'

Chief Superintendent Hugo-Watkins raised his hand. 'I get the message loud and clear, Jack.'

'I'm glad. Tell Eddie from me, this detective isn't for giving up that easy.'

'That's... very positive and the promotion assessments has to be fair.'

'And transparent.'

'Yes. Quite. Leave things with me, Jack. I'm pleased that you're not approaching your promotion boards light-heartedly.'

'I'm not trying to create problems for you by being awkward. It just makes my blood boil when from the outset such comments are made. It's a total breach of equal opportunities and shows me what we all know by the way, that they only playing lip service to the promotion system. It so obvious. Look what happened in our meeting for the Sergeant's boards? Justin Gaskin is a prime example of the "transparent" system they supposedly have set in place to stop things like that happening behind closed doors. We are aware they already have people they want for certain posts circled to get through. A round peg for a round hole as they see it. How they insult our intelligence when they think we don't all know it. I'll take my chance in the ring, but one thing I won't be, and that's stopped from entering without good reason at the first hurdle.'

'I will do my best. And, Jack. I'm pleased you're so passionate about this promotion. At first I must admit I thought you may be just testing the water, but now I realise how much it means to you.'

# Chapter Thirty-Seven

Dylan's first feeling was one of anger against the hierarchy but before he had reached the admin office where Jen was sat, he had realised the absurdity and misuse of his brawn.

Jen smiled as he relayed the conversation. Out of every negative comes a positive, she thought. Dylan might not have been too keen on trying for the next rank to start with, but now she knew from his tone he was certainly determined to see it through.

'Well, Eddie Thornton should have known not to throw down the gauntlet,' he said.

It was Jen who felt the nausea of the obvious discouragement. She knew only too well that if an officer was prompted to go for the next rank it was highly likely it would be achieved. If they were discouraged at the first hurdle it was often a telling sign they didn't feature in the contest. And Dylan thought she was naive?

'Well I've got to go, I'll see you tonight,' he said.

Jen's eyes were very solemn. 'I guess we will just have to see what happens, won't we?' she said to Rita who had heard the conversation.

'You know as well as me what the outcome will be. I wouldn't hold your hopes up if I were you,' she said.

\*\*\*

Vicky and Paul walked down the central reservation of desks in the Incident Room, towards Dylan's office. They had news he could tell by the look on their faces and the determination of their walk. He felt like a gust of air had blown in when they entered. Vicky's face suggested some inward excitement.

'Remember the un-identified fingerprint in the rear of Richard Bryant's van?' Paul said.

'The one in Kirsty's blood?' asked Vicky.

'Well, it's no longer unidentified. We have a positive ID... and wait for this, it belongs to none other than Brian Fisher.'

'Harper's boss at the mortuary,' said Dylan.

'They had his fingerprints for elimination purposes because of the alleged burglary, but Karen Ebdon who took the fingerprints remembered a specific marking and checking it out, she was spot on for us.'

'I didn't expect that,' Dylan said.

'Never assume anything's what you tell me, boss, and if it doesn't make any sense it's probably either something totally weird or some sexual perversion.'

'So… the plot thickens,' Dylan mused as he stood with his back to the charts on his wall.

'And there's more,' Vicky said sitting down and indicating to Paul to sit next to her. 'The telephone intelligence show links between Fisher, Bryant, Harper, Simpson and Gallagher. There are clusters of calls around relevant dates. They also show calls too, wait for this one, to Barrington Cook, the man we pulled dead out of the canal and there are others who we will make inroads to seek out. It's all being charted up for simplicity. Ruth says she will have the updated analysis charts on this, ready for you for tomorrow morning's briefing. Also the computer geeks have retrieved some sort of distribution network from the computers we have seized. It could prove to be a worldwide network they are warning us. The staff in the office are coming over in the morning to go over their findings with us.'

'That's great news. We will need to do a vast amount of research on them before we consider our approach to this obviously ever increasing group. I don't suppose they suggested how many we are talking about by any chance?'

'No.' She gave Dylan a comprehending look.

'Don't worry. It's all coming together nicely. It will be good to know who their other links are. I've a feeling we've only got the worker bees in the net so far.'

Brian Fisher was the man in charge of the mortuary and had worked in that post for a number of years. He had no police record. They would have to wait to find out more about him and who his partners in this network were. Dylan liaised with the Obscene Publications Unit. Perhaps they could take this side of the enquiry forward in unison with his team who could then keep focused on the double homicide investigations. This way any relevant information would be shared. Ultimately the outcome would be available for disclosure purposes prior to any court case.

Dylan picked up the telephone and spoke directly with the supervisor asking him to pass on his personal gratitude for the excellent work in identifying marks found at the variety of scenes. The personnel in the department worked hard behind closed doors. It was a highly skilful job, done with enthusiasm and determination. A lot of their work went unnoticed, but not by Dylan. They were a very important cog in the investigative unit's wheel and like the rest of his team they were industrious in their approach. On numerous occasions by identifying marks left at a scene it gave the detectives, not only evidence but a name which resulted subsequently in a person standing before the Court.

Dylan's head was bent over his work. It would be an embarrassment for the Coroner's Office once news broke of Fisher's involvement, he thought. He would speak to the Coroner, in confidence, prior to the media being given the information. He sat reflecting on who else would be on the list, and from what walks of life would they would come? He was never shocked by what people did any more, although he found it bizarre on occasions, but that didn't stop him from feeling repulsed. Never more so than when the perpetrators were revealed to be in positions of trust and should be an example to others as pillars of the community. There would be a lot of red faces in the coming weeks and the usual comments would follow. 'We will look closely at what lessons need to be learned,' was always a good one that they put out.

Dylan pondered on the saying, 'the quiet ones are always the worse,' and he wondered where the saying originated and how it stood the test of time, for he was sure he'd heard his parents say the same kind of things. He had heard the saying used many times at a road traffic accident or a major crime scene when as a first aider you were always told to deal with the casualty that was the quietest, as the ones 'making the noise' were the ones still breathing – hence the quiet ones are the worst. One thing for sure, he wouldn't be quiet about it once he knew who was involved. The public needed to know, although they would be disgusted and repulsed to find out that even in death people were not safe, they would gain some satisfaction from those responsible being brought to justice.

Tomorrow would move this enquiry forward and bring it out of the dark shadows. It concerned him that he was unintentionally being side-tracked by promotion issues. His main focus was the murders and the only motive so far being that the perpetrators were sexually driven, the climax being murder.

'Vicky, will you let Paul know about tomorrow's meeting?' asked Dylan.

'Yeah, I'll send him a message subject heading Bare Poster.'

'*Bare Poster*? Ah, the name Harper gave it,' said Dylan.

'It's also an anagram of reprobates,' she said. 'Uncanny that isn't it?'

# Chapter Thirty-Eight

Dylan was the first in the office after a restless night. It was quarter to seven and he was sat at his desk eager to start the day. Now he had to wait for the others.

He looked at his computer to see what had occurred in the last twenty-four hours that was serious enough to be sent for the Chief Constable's information, known as the Chief's Log. He shuffled his papers in his in tray, took out anything marked urgent and put it back a few moments later. He plucked a folder from the shelf next to him marked 'Of Interest for Promotion'. The contents had grown considerably since its creation. A few minutes later he tossed it to one side. He needed to make some important decisions today and at the moment his mind was in turmoil, a frenzy of his own caged energy. Was the real struggle about promotion with himself he wondered, and not the hierarchy? But they indeed played their part. He had learned through experience that transparency didn't mean the same to them as it did him and others like him.

The first to arrive in the office was Paul Robinson and Vicky followed. There was no disguising the arrival of Detective Sergeant George Buck, the head of Obscene Publications. He was an ex-sergeant major who always brought about a cyclone effect wherever he went. He shook Dylan's hand, clicked the heels of his brown boots and gave a guardsman's salute, his big hand quivered. Dylan had come across George some years ago when he had done some undercover work for the Obscene Publications Office. George hadn't changed in his manner, he was a big, raw-faced creature, all belly, voice and a blonde moustache. He cast off his long raincoat.

'Come to report, sir,' he said. His face was like undercooked beef with two blue round pebbles for eyes.

'Long time no see, George. How's things?' asked Dylan, standing to shake his hand.

'It's quite like old times... except you're the boss now. Office bound mostly these days apart from targeted arrests, hence the weight,' he said. George Buck moved his fat hands to grab his wholesome belly.

'What happened to the mop of hair, George?' asked Dylan with a laugh.

'It will come to you, Dylan. It's called old age. I decided to shave off what remained a while ago. Still got the old raincoat.'

'Ah, a stark reminder of the good old days?'

'If I remember rightly, you had far too much fun when you worked undercover. Didn't your team hold the record, twenty-four visits to a brothel before there's "sufficient to raid it, sir?"'

'I was a young back then. "Martine's!" my God, it was a classy joint even by today's standards and I was getting paid to go there.'

'A classy brothel? Surely not, sir,' Vicky said as she entered.

'Don't get him started, Vicky, some of his stories will even make you blush.'

Wallace J. Hooper from the computer suite joined them, briefcase in hand. 'Anywhere I can set up the presentation?' he asked Vicky.

Vicky took him into the Incident Room and George Buck took control. He made no bones about who was the boss and who was his junior. He outlined the decoding and subsequent download from the systems recovered from Derek Harper's computer. 'Bare Poster' created some seven hundred images which were classed as indecent. The three main categories for convenience were named men, women and children.

'This team are relatively newbies. The earliest date of publication being just over a year ago,' said George. 'However, we must be aware we have intelligence only from Harper's computer at this time. There are ten identified main players on our patch who feature and who visit and download from this particular site on a regular basis. As you are aware we are in possession of some of their computers and work is ongoing.' Wallace held up a chart showing the links between the individuals. Their plotted activity resembled a spiders web. Those present didn't utter a sound but listened intently to what they were being told.

'These ten people, through the web have been identified as the following individuals. Derek Harper, Richard Bryant, Brian Fisher.' Dylan nodded his head in acknowledgement. 'Jerry Noble, Mark Stringwood, Lance Tenby, Nigel Smith, Jason Coombe, Barrington Cook, the recently deceased John James. We have prepared schedules for each showing their individual activity and downloads from the Bare Poster site.'

'John James, he worked at the funeral directors. I was on-call negotiator when he jumped to his death,' said Dylan

'How awful for you,' said Wallace Hooper.

'I didn't actually get to speak to him. He went over just as we arrived.'

'Just on him, boss. John James has been identified as the guy in the photo in Kirsty's car.'

'Well he's one less to worry about. Maybe he knew we were getting near to finding out about his association. What we need to know now,' said George, 'is where the other people are. Then we can decide if our office can pick them up.'

'As you are aware Harper and Bryant are in custody. Our team are heavily involved with them at present. It's what we can find out about the others that's important to us now. Jerry Noble... that name ring a bell.'

'It's best to pick up the outstanding six in simultaneous raids in my experience, Dylan, to ensure they don't get a chance to destroy any evidence if they so much as get a whiff of what's going down.'

'Whilst we know the names of those involved I want to know more about these depraved people and what they have in common in their lifestyles,' said Dylan. 'I want you out and about on your urgent enquiries today. The raids need carrying out as soon as possible in case any information is forthcoming in relation to the ongoing murder enquiries.'

\*\*\*

A defence statement from Perfect & Best Solicitors was waiting for Dylan on his desk, along with a covering letter in respect of their client Richard Bryant. Bryant had entered not guilty pleas in respect of both murders for which he had been charged and they were demanding separate trials. If the prosecution couldn't link them it was likely he would get his wish.

'Doing a spot of reading?' asked George as he stood before him. Dylan hadn't heard him enter the office. The big man could be very quiet on his feet. He wore his coat and was ready to leave.

'The brief outline for Bryant's defence statement to the charge of murdering Kirsty Gallagher is...' he looked at him.

'Not guilty.'

He nodded his head. 'He's admitting to obstructing the Coroner and disposal of the body through "sheer panic" would you believe,' he said. 'He's yet to put forward a defence statement in respect of Billy Simpson,' Dylan said waving the piece of paper in his hand. 'He will have to come up with a good one to convince a jury with the evidence we have.' Dylan was more than confident a jury would see through his lies after he had been in interview with him.

'They're not stupid,' said George.

Dylan threw the piece of paper down. 'What links do the Bare Poster lot have, George, apart from their perverted intent?'

'Probably nothing. Some will know each other through social networks. People tend to seek like-minded people out.'

'And the murderers?'

'Taking it to the ultimate level to get their kicks. But as long as we can link them conspiring together for a conviction are we really bothered how they met?'

'No, you're right, and we won't ever know how far the chain goes, will we? I still feel as though we are only scratching the surface.'

'Time will tell,' said George.

\*\*\*

The day had passed quickly and Dylan wanted some home time and that was where he was heading. A copy of the Anacapa Charts in his briefcase. A determined look was in Dylan's eyes. He knew these charts showed the extent of the communication and liaison between the perpetrators and the increase in their activity at relevant times and dates, and he would not hesitate to seize the opportunity of casting another eye over them.

'*I'm on my way home*,' he texted Jen.

# Chapter Thirty-Nine

Vicky had spent time with Chief Superintendent Hugo-Watkins going over what he thought she might come up against at the future promotion boards. Dylan insisted she kept the appointments no matter what was happening on the enquiries.

He also took time to talk to her about promotion boards from his own experience. 'Don't think like a detective Vicky, that'll get you nowhere. You need to think like a uniform supervisor. Don't forget to include health and safety and other relevant issues that might present themselves, and be sure to leave nothing to the imagination. Presume the evaluators know nothing in the scenarios they set, sometimes in my experience they don't,' he chuckled. 'Above all be confident and on no account use one of your casual, throw away comments. Do you hear me?'

She was ready for the next rank, that he was sure. He also knew she would do her best and that was all anyone could ask of her. Soon it would be over and within a matter of days she would know the outcome.

\*\*\*

Dylan scanned the charts on the walls in his office. He loved detail. His fingers traced a line. His mother had often said his fingers, long and straight, the ungula phalanges bent slightly back, were the fingers of someone with a passion for exactness and she hadn't been wrong. He looked about his office. His lever arch files and boxes were as neat as his fingernails. He continued to follow the map around the room and he eventually reached the window. White clouds moved in a blue sky. 'I am a Detective Inspector,' he said as he stared out of the window. He was proud of the rank he had reached and only he knew how hard he had had to work for his position and keep it. Fragments of his dad's philosophy drifted through his head. 'It is not so much the rank achieved, son, but the way you do the job that matters,' he said.

Lisa bustled in, some papers in hand.

'Operation Mallard, Billy Simpson. Some telephone contact results and text messages from his mobile. I'll get you some coffee. It makes good reading.' There was a smile at the back of Lisa's eyes. 'I think you're going to be pleased.'

He took the papers from her silently and sat down at his desk to study them.

There was a knock at his office door. Hugo-Watkins entered. Dylan held the documents in his hand, he was in his shirt sleeves. He pushed his chair back and casually rose.

'You look very pleased with yourself,' Hugo-Watkins said.

'I am sir, yes,' he said.

'Vicky around?' he asked.

'She should be,' Dylan said pointing to her desk in the Incident Room.

Hugo-Watkins strolled down the office. There was a first for everything, Dylan thought, a Chief Superintendent walking into a working Incident Room.'

Dylan smacked his desk with a paper truncheon he'd made. 'Brilliant, just bloody brilliant,' he said as Lisa walked in.

'Knew you'd be pleased,' she said.

'Pleased? I can't stop smiling,' he said flourishing the baton made out of the paper.

'The telephone data not only shows the recent links between Billy and Jane Simpson it also shows us the link to Billy Simpson and Richard Bryant. The essence of which Richard Bryant is telling them both to stay away from Kirsty Gallagher. "I told you stay away from her,"' he said reading from the paper. 'The very last one on the eve of Billy Simpson's death asks, "Are you both in? I'm coming round. I want to know what happened. It's all your fault Kirsty died. You continue to ruin my life." That's damning.'

Whilst Dylan was over the moon with the content of the data he wanted to know why they hadn't found this connection before with the information they had on Jane Simpson or Richard Bryant's telephone data? And also why they hadn't known before that Billy Simpson knew Kirsty Gallagher? Dylan now had a motive, once disclosed to the defence which it had to be, Perfect and Best would perhaps rethink their client's approach at Court. Dylan made some telephone calls to try to find some answers for the delay. He would have loved to have had this valuable information prior to the interviews when they had all been produced from prison. But it wasn't to be. Dylan got a mixed response from the intelligence unit supervisor.

'There's so much going on in the force at the moment,' he said.

Dylan turned his chair to see the green mould on the bricks on the yard wall. 'Sickness has played a part and the service providers were hit and miss with their returns, but we get there in the end.' Dylan struggled with a flare of rage and a fog of acceptance. He wanted to tear a strip off the silly little desk bound Inspector but he knew it wouldn't change anything. The serious side of this was that it could have meant the difference between charging or releasing the offenders. He drafted a quick report to the ACC Operations outlining the circumstances and the need for the Force to review their approach and staffing levels as a matter of urgency. 'It may be the difference between life and death if the person reoffended due to incompetence by the force in retrieving intelligence data,' he said.

The team was eating lunch sat at their desks when Dylan broke the news. He would review the urgently marked enquiries carried out by the investigative teams, in follow up to those enquiries marked as 'Priority' like this one had been, so it doesn't happen again. Mountains could be moved without slamming doors, swearing and throwing things about. Was he mellowing in his old age? The younger Dylan would have been looking for someone's blood for letting the team down. He now realised that ultimately he was in charge and the responsibility was his for everything that happened or didn't as the case maybe.

DS George Buck and his team with assistance from PS Simon Clegg and PS Carey Megnicks at Operation Support unit would pick up five known offenders leaving Dylan and his team to concentrate on Brian Fisher.

The date set was for Wednesday, the date of Vicky's promotion board.

'Sorry, Vicky, but it's how it is. I want you to take some time off. Paul and myself will deal with Fisher.'

*** 

The smell from the kitchen was delightful as Dylan opened the front door.

'Starving?' asked Jen as Dylan put his briefcase down on the kitchen floor and leaned forward to kiss his wife. Maisy stood at the kitchen chair her face all pink and shiny from her bath.

'Starving?' Dylan pondered. 'There are several varieties of starvation,' he said. He looked fixedly down at Maisy. His hands formed a bear's claw and he swept her up in his arms. 'I could eat you all up,' he said blowing raspberries on Maisy's tummy.

'Everything okay?' Jen said.

'I'm fine love, why?' he laughed.

'We'll you're not usually home at this time for one...'

'I'd had enough for today.'

Jen raised her eyebrows.

# Chapter Forty

Wednesday arrived. Dylan picked up his mobile phone and texted Vicky. '*Good luck for today, not tha you'll need it,*' he said.

Her reply was instant. '*I'd rather be coming with you.*'

'*Just enjoy it. You can do the job so show 'em how.*'

'*I'll see you back at the nick later.*'

'*Remember, don't speak to anyone when you're finished. There will be some candidates still to go in.*'

'*Give Fisher what for.*'

'*No worries on that score,*' he said.

***

Albert Promenade looked dreary when Dylan and his team emerged from Manor Heath on their way to Furze Cottage. The open landscape was wet, bleary grey with rain driving before a vicious, westerly wind. The cream, rough cast walls of the cottage were discoloured with damp and the laurel bushes that formed a southerly edge to the garden shook in a succession of waves.

Dylan was tempted to have the door taken off its hinges but it seemed a shame to ruin it. He wondered what the mood of Brian Fisher would be as he stood waiting on the doorstep for the door to be answered. When Brian Fisher's middle-aged wife answered in her curlers, he asked for her husband. Mrs Fisher took off her Marigold gloves and adjusted her apron. She had an air of kindly austerity that would have made some people take her for an old maid.

'Wretched weather,' she said. Her voice was quiet, level and unhurried. She touched her headscarf that kept the hairpins in place. 'Come in. Brian is in the dining room having breakfast.'

Mr Fisher stood and wiped his mouth with a napkin when he saw Dylan and Paul entering the room. He swallowed something quickly and coughed heartily. His wife went to him and patted him on the back.

'Don't fuss, woman,' he said.

'Mr Fisher, Detective Inspector Dylan.'

Brian Fisher nodded his head in short jerky movements.

'I'm here this morning to arrest you in connection with the removal and disposal of Kirsty Gallagher's body thereby obstructing the Coroner and also for distributing indecent material,' he said.

Brian Fisher's face drained to the colour of the cottage's white walls. His wife's chin wobbled. She gasped and went limp. Paul caught her fall and taking her by the arm he guided her to a sofa. Her brown eyes were turned towards her husband who had gained his composure.

'Tracy, a cold cloth please?' Dylan said.

Mary Fisher held out her arm and whimpered. 'Brian, how could you?'

Fisher fleetingly glanced at his wife. 'It's nonsense. This is absolute nonsense, Mary. I'm calling my solicitor and the Chief, he's a personal friend you know. Oh, you'll see you're making one hell of a bad judgement call here, Inspector.'

'Take him away,' Dylan said to the uniformed officers who were stood in the doorway.

PC Tracy Petterson and PC Fearne Robinson took an arm each and frogmarched him to the car. He protested vehemently. 'Mary, ring Jerry quickly,' he said. His voice trailed off as they watched PC Petterson put her hand on the top of his head and urge him into the back of the police car. Mrs Fisher's eyes met her husband's and then fell away, but Dylan caught the distant, critical look in them before Brian Fisher was promptly driven away.

***

Mary Fisher stood leaning on the oak door jamb. Her primness swept away as Dylan explained who he was and why they were there. He explained to her that they had a warrant to search the premises. She walked unsteadily into the lounge, sat down on a chair with a thud and flopped backwards, her breathing coming and going in great heaves. 'A warrant? That can't be right. Brian's a pillar of the community.' She sat up suddenly, listening. The house was silent all but for the hourly chime of the grandfather clock in the hallway.

'Can we look in Mr Fisher's office?' asked Dylan. He always found it was better to do things with consent. Easing herself out of the chair Mary Fisher stood silently, steadied herself and slowly made her way into the lobby before them. She appeared to have developed a stoop. The detectives followed her stilted movements down the passageway. At one time she stopped and reached out to steady herself by way of the brass standard lamp with a pink shade that matched the wallpaper patterned with rosebuds. Rose coloured scatter cushions lay upon a window seat under an ornate leaded window. The decor was all very gentile. She stopped, looked over her shoulder at the men and eventually turned into the far room on the left. Inside was a large oak writing desk. Against one wall was a three-seater Chesterfield sofa which was opposite a floor to ceiling bookcase. Straight in front of them was a desk on which sat two computers, a desktop and a laptop. Directly above it was a large, signed oil painting, depicting naked well-fed children at their mother's breast. Dylan couldn't help noticing in Mrs Fisher's eyes something that was very like hatred of the modern technology. 'We will have to take things away, Mrs Fisher. But we will ensure you have receipts for everything we do.'

'Alright,' she said with trepidation. 'I'll have to ring Mr Noble, our solicitor, like he asked.'

Dylan realised at that moment that Mary Fisher was just about waking up to what was happening. Her hospitality would no doubt elude her once she had made that call. The last thing he wanted was to have an irate woman to deal with. He smiled knowing full well that she would find out soon enough that her husband's friend, Jerry Noble was one of the people on the hit list and at that time also being arrested. He was also only a civil lawyer and would have been no help at all in the criminal case.

Mary Fisher was joined by a neighbour as the team commenced the search and began seizing items. There was no need for Dylan to remain at the house. Reinforcements had arrived to expedite the search in the form of DC Wormald and DC Granger and they were more than capable to do the necessary, which meant that Dylan could return to base and oversee the other enquiries.

He nodded at Karen Ebdon and Stuart Viney who were just arriving in their CSI van as he was leaving.

\*\*\*

Dylan was pleased to find on his return they had five out of the six prisoners in the net. Fortunately, John James deceased hadn't destroyed his computers prior to taking his own life by leaping off the motorway bridge. These had been recovered from his house. Dylan spoke to DC Buck, 'Went like clockwork,' he said.

'And I would have expected nothing less than military precision,' Dylan replied. Buck grinned from ear to ear of his red bulbous face.

'You'll like this one, Jack, Lance Tenby has just been accepted by us to become a Community bobby and Nigel Smith a Special Constable.'

'Why aren't I surprised, George, when you look at who does the interviews these days and you can't always blame them, its often the training they get.'

'I'll update you later, Jack,' he said.

'Look forward to it.' Dylan knew that they would be bailed until such time as they had been able to decipher and download the data on each individual computer. 'Talking of interviews,' he said to Lisa. 'We need to arrange one with Brian Fisher. I wonder how Vicky is doing?'

'Janet tells me the Chief Superintendent is there watching via the video link,' she said. His eyes met hers.

'Don't look so surprised,' she said with a smile. 'He does occasionally.'

'I'm pleased to know he's taking an interest. She must be in with a shot.'

\*\*\*

The interview with Brian Fisher was an important one. If they could get him to talk they both knew he would save them a lot of time. Dylan caught Paul's eye before they entered the room. 'You ready?' he asked.

Paul nodded.

Lin Perfect sat with a stiffness of her neck next to her client in the interview room. To Dylan and Paul's utter amazement he was frank about his involvement.

'I've been stupid,' he said. 'But I became addicted. What else do you want me to say?' he asked with eyes full of alarm. 'They threatened to expose me if I didn't help them with the removal of Kirsty Gallagher's body.'

'And that is why you were reluctant to sack Derek Harper?'

'Yes initially, but then to put you off the scent I sacked him thinking everything would quieten down. I'm not the only casualty of this whole sorry mess. Penny Sanderson was totally besotted by Richard Bryant and would have done anything for him. She was easily led. I can only apologise for my behaviour

266

and accept what punishment is forthcoming, Inspector. You understand I cannot comment on the others, I have family to think of.'

'You know Penny Sanderson,' said Dylan.

'Bryant introduced her to me recently. I wondered if she'd be the next target. I have a daughter at university. He knows that. I couldn't take any chances with them, they were becoming obsessed with killing. No longer were they satisfied with looking at the indecent images.'

He was bailed pending further enquiries.

'Well, I didn't expect that,' Paul said as they watched Brian Fisher shuffle from the room in his coverall.

'No, I didn't expect him of all people to fall on his sword, but it does make our life easier. Just think if everyone rolled over so easily?'

'I think he is the only one so far who has actually got the intelligence to see that the evidence we will get from the computer will damn them all. Like he said, he was addicted but once he became involved, the others had him over a barrel.'

*** 

It had reached five fifteen and Dylan noticed that Vicky had not yet returned from the promotion assessments being held at HQ. There were no messages left for him from her. He hoped everything had gone well. When she did return she looked exhausted from the day's events.

'Well, did you give it your best shot?'

'Yes, and as far as I could tell there were no low ballers. Nothing I couldn't deal with. But who knows if it was good enough?'

'I hear Hugo-Watkins was watching.'

'He was?'

'Yes,' he said with a glimmer in his eye that Vicky saw was respect. 'Fisher fell on his sword and admitted his involvement and meeting Penny Sanderson.'

'He did? And he was supposed to be in charge of our local mortuary. It beggars belief.'

'He's out on bail.'

'None of them should have their freedom after what they've done.'

267

'He says the others threatened to expose him for downloading indecent images. His excuse – he was addicted.'

'Gross. I wish I'd been there.'

'You missed nothing. It was a short confessional.'

'Is he married?'

Dylan nodded. 'And a daughter at uni.'

Vicky turned.

'Where you going?'

'I'm off for a pint,' she said. 'You coming?'

'Can't at the moment, and don't you go getting drunk either. You've got to lead by example from now on.'

'Yeah, yeah,' she said waving her hand to him over her shoulder. 'I'll get the train home, don't worry. See you tomorrow.'

\*\*\*

Dylan walked to his car with two things on his mind. A bottle of wine and a bunch of flowers for Jen. He was pleased with how the day had gone and tomorrow he planned a proper debrief with the team.

As he sat in the car with his mobile in his hand ready to text Jen, he saw Hugo-Watkin's car out of the corner of his eye, pulling into the yard. He parked next to Dylan in his own parking bay and got out of his car with the nimbleness of youth.

'Been at HQ all day, Jack, watching the candidates for Detective Sergeant. We chose well, in confidence mind,' he said tapping the side of his nose with his finger tip. 'Commendable performance by our Vicky Hardacre. I'm glad I put her through. Mum's the word, Jack, though. Mum's the word. It's your promotion assessment in a couple of weeks, Jack, isn't it? Better get studying. Can't let the side down,' he said before walking off whistling.

Dylan shook his head.

\*\*\*

'What are we celebrating?' Jen asked, when Dylan produced the flowers and wine.

'Us,' Dylan said. He reached for her hand and put it to his lips, and then with sudden tenderness he cupped her face in his hands and kissed her lips.

# Chapter Forty-One

'Now everything is coming together and the files are being prepared I've decided to take a week off before the promotion boards. I want to read up on the Forces Strategic aim and a few Home Office policies,' he said as they lay next to each other in bed.

'Good, I'm glad you're taking it seriously. I shall see if I can take the week off, too.'

'Why wouldn't I?' he asked. 'Fail to plan, plan to fail as they say.' Dylan turned to Jen.

'You show 'em, Jack,' she said with a contented smile on her face as she snuggled her head into his bare chest.

'I don't know about that but I'll not be caught out on something that I could have read up on, especially with the chips against me.'

Jen looked up at him. 'You think so?'

'I'm not daft Jen. I know so,' he said.

'A week of you, at home. How will I be able to control myself?' Jen giggled. Maisy called. Jen raised her eyes to the ceiling.

Dylan chuckled.

\*\*\*

Was the rebel Jack Dylan becoming a conformist in the desire to achieve the next rank? During the week he sat for hours reading Home Office Circulars and preparing notes.

Jen kept Maisy as quiet as she could. They went on long walks with Max and played in her room. Jen's admiration for his commitment was expressed when she spoke, over the phone to her colleagues at work.

'I have never seen him so determined.'

Dylan would gaze at his wife and daughter from the dining room table as he worked. The weather was kind enough to allow Jen to take a deckchair and a blanket to the bottom of the garden and under the shade of the old oak tree he could see her blonde head moving to and fro as she chased after their lively little girl. Her face could be serene, puzzled and troubled in the space of just a few minutes. An anxious motherliness watching their daughter on the edge of experiences that could be joyous one minute and potentially harmful the next.

Jen sat quietly reading her book after dinner on the last day of their leave. The house was quite. Jack worked on raising his head for no more than to eat his meals or sometimes watch the news.

On the morning of the assessment board Dylan and Jen were sat eating breakfast when the postman knocked at the door. 'Letter to sign for,' the postman said. He heard Jen shut the door and saw her throw the letter he had delivered down on the breakfast table. Dylan juggled with a slice of toast and his pen. She picked up her the cup and studied the handwriting on the envelope.

'I think it's from Penny,' she said pushing it towards Dylan.

'Are you going to open it?'

'What can it say that I don't already know?' she said. They exchanged a glance and his face lost its patient look.

'For goodness sake, open it.'

Jen stood and picked up the envelope and putting her foot on the dustbin peddle she stuffed it in the bin.

'It could contain evidence.'

'Take it out then and read it if you want. Penny betrayed me. I could never, ever, forgive her.'

'I think she knows that and you've made it quite clear,' he said retrieving the letter from the bin and ripping it open.

'Sorry,' he read. 'I hope we can still be friends. I got things wrong. I didn't know he would try and silence Max so he could get to you.'

'She... he poisoned Max?' Jen said in a whisper.

'He told me the gun was fake,' Dylan continued.

Jen's eyes opened wide. 'He had a gun?' she asked.

Dylan grabbed her by the shoulders and held her still. She grabbed the letter and tore it into tiny little pieces. 'The bitch! She won't get the chance to get anything wrong again.'

Dylan's phone rang and he reached for it.

'I P A S S E D,' Vicky screamed. Dylan held the phone away from his ear. His smile spread from ear to ear.

'Drinks are on me.' Vicky's excitement was infectious and Jen hearing her delight couldn't help but smile through her tears.

'Not until I've sat mine,' he said.

'Good luck, boss. Although nobody wants you to get through because you would have to leave us,' she said.

\*\*\*

Dylan was dressed in his best suit, shirt and tie. 'I'm heading off early, so I don't get stuck in traffic,' he said. Nothing stopped Dylan's appetite and over lunch in Headquarters canteen he chatted with a few other hopeful candidates. They all had something in common, a time full of scenarios, mock incidents, paperwork and in amongst that an interview with two Acting Chief Constables, Edward Thornton and Miles Carter. Dylan was in no doubt ACC Thornton would be aware of Dylan's involvement in the scrum down meeting for his son's promotion board from Inspector Gaskin.

At the close of the day he enquired how many candidates still had to be interviewed.

'The results will be out in the post next week under confidential cover,' he was told.

***

For now it was back to normal. Dylan had had the debrief and charges had been laid. Ahead of him lay meetings with prosecuting barristers and then a trial would eventually commence but that could be a year away. He felt for the jury if they were to be subjected to the photographic evidence. But, he hoped the perpetrators would plead guilty and limit the damage to more poor souls. He had to be realistic, these reprobates were the lowest of the low, who thought only of themselves and self-gratification. If they thought there was the slightest chance that they would get off they'd plead not guilty, that he was sure. A plea of not guilty would also mean that they could re-live the whole sordid episode again in court and in front of an audience. DI Dylan shuddered at the thought. The Bare Poster site would have worldwide implications. Thankfully that would be taken on by a national unit which would would have the necessary time, budget, expertise and resources allocated to deal with those involved. He wondered if his friends Phil and Yin Johnson, renowned International Private Investigators had come across the Bare Poster site as they daily tracked and investigated people on the worldwide web?

Jen started watching for the postman in the week ahead. Much to Dylan's amusement.

'It won't be here till Thursday,' Dylan said.

On the Thursday morning the postman arrived with an official marked private and confidential envelope for Dylan

'Open it,' he said.

'No, I couldn't, you,' she said offering it to him with trembling hands. Her heart raced as he pulled her to his side and ripped open the envelope...